Derek Hansen is a novelist who loves writing short
His books have attracted a following in Great Britain an
Europe as well as Australasia. *Psycho Cat* follows on from
Dead Fishy, his first collection of stories which sold out on
publication. Derek lives on Sydney's northern beaches, is
married with two children, an idiot of a dog, and an eight-
year-old lilac Burmese cat with attitude.

PSYCHO CAT

DEREK HANSEN

HarperCollins*Publishers*

HarperCollins*Publishers*

First published in Australia in 1996
Reprinted in 1997, 1998
by HarperCollins*Publishers* Pty Limited
ACN 009 913 517
A member of the HarperCollins*Publishers* (Australia) Pty Limited Group
http://www.harpercollins.com.au

Copyright © Derek Hansen 1996

HarperCollins*Publishers*
25 Ryde Road, Pymble, Sydney, NSW 2073, Australia
31 View Road, Glenfield, Auckland 10, New Zealand
77-85 Fulham Palace Road, London W6 8JB, United Kingdom
Hazelton Lanes, 55 Avenue Road, Suite 2900, Toronto, Ontario M5R 3L2
and 1995 Markham Road, Scarborough, Ontario M1B 5M8, Canada
10 East 53rd Street, New York NY 10032, USA

National Library of Australia Cataloguing-in-Publication data:

Hansen, Derek, 1944–   .
Psycho cat.
ISBN 0 7322 5746 8.
1. Cats–Fiction. I. Title.
A823.3

Printed in Australia by Griffin Press Pty Ltd on 79gsm Bulky Paperback

10 9 8 7 6 5 4 3   98 99 00 01

To the memory of the countless skipjack tuna, bonito, mackerel and pilchards that gave their lives so that the family moggy could sleep twenty-three and a half hours a day.

Contents

Acknowledgments

None of the stories in this book is true, though many are based on actual events and real cats. For instance, Reg the psycho cat, after whom the book is named, was very real and every bit as wicked as I've painted him. My wife will testify to that, although I've assigned the story to two fictitious characters. We were victims again in Sri Lanka, and almost gave up chicken curry for life. Other people inspired other stories, and their contributions should be acknowledged: Margaret Gee for 'Cat Sausages' and 'Must Like Cats', Suzie, Frank and Mary for 'The Battle of the Bonsai Cat', Morris and Fiona for 'Psychic Cat is Never Wrong'. Others also contributed but rightly insist on anonymity. Who could blame them?

The Quiet Man

Milton de Crespigny had been searching for the quiet man for more than ten years, without ever knowing exactly who it was he was searching for. All he had to go on were the regrets of antique dealers from Adelaide to Brisbane who, without exception, told stories of selling Clarice Cliff lotus vases and teasets for a song minutes before the Clarice Cliff revival began. They spoke of unique pieces with rare patterns in mint condition that were now worth fortunes. They spoke of Susie Cooper Mountains and Moon plates and vases that had slipped away through their doors before they'd learned their true value. But what interested Milton was the beneficiary of their ignorance. They all spoke of the quiet man who was always one step ahead of them, who ghosted in, waltzed off with their treasures and, apart from a post office box number, left nothing of himself for them to remember him by.

Some dealers insisted that he had to be a buyer for overseas collectors, and Milton was happy to let them think that. 'How else could he know?' they demanded. 'How else could he know what was about to take off?' But that argument cut no ice with Milton. While it was true that prices in Australia lagged behind those fetched in Great Britain and America, they didn't lag two and three years behind, and sometimes that was the sort of jump the quiet man had on the market. Besides, every now and then top quality pieces would appear in auctions and all the dealers would run around like headless chooks, desperate to discover the source. Everyone believed the collector was fabulously wealthy, almost certainly a celebrity, and were anxious to get their hooks into him or her. Milton believed otherwise. He'd tried bribing clerks at Sotheby's and Christie's to be indiscreet – in a jokey sort of way, of course – but had met with flat refusals. For the sake of his good name, he didn't dare raise the matter again.

Milton did have a good name. De Crespigny was a far better name for an antique dealer than Cross, which was the name his plumber father had passed on to him. To a conman and thief, a good name and reputation are everything. Reputation buys credibility, trust and a theatre in which to ply the craft. Milton had been extremely successful plying his particular craft, because he was extremely careful where his name and reputation were concerned. He was a very discerning thief. He didn't steal from just any collector and he didn't steal very often. He was only interested in theft on a grand scale. Entire collections made up of the rarest pieces, which he bubble-wrapped, crated and dispatched to a dealer in England who had a similar deficiency in scruples.

The beauty of his scheme, as far as Milton was concerned, was that he didn't have to go looking for victims. Sooner or later they came to him. He was respected for his knowledge – his articles in the antique dealer magazines were always among the best read – and he was often asked to open antique fairs. He was also known for his generosity, which is not a trait normally associated with thieves. Milton guarded and nurtured his reputation, and his reputation brought him his victims as surely as a flame draws moths.

His reputation brought him Lady Hilda Gold, pillar of Melbourne society, patron of the arts, and proud owner of an art deco collection any museum director would kill for. She was a widow and she was lonely. She was also frighteningly rich, courtesy of a husband who'd built up a construction empire. Her husband had a weakness for good food, fine things, and faux blondes with big boobs, one of whom was to prove his undoing on the plush carpet of his office. With straight faces his fellow directors were able to inform his widow that he'd died on the job. Lady Hilda Gold innocently assumed he'd died from overwork and bore her loss stoically. She had no idea she was about to suffer another which would upset her even more.

She approached Milton because his reputation identified him as the one person who might be able to fill some glaring omissions in her Lalique collection. In passing she asked him if he could keep an eye out for a Royal Doulton pansy teapot. Her maid had inadvertently stepped back upon her Persian cat as she was lifting the teapot down from a shelf to dust. The cat had survived but the teapot had not. Milton found the blue budgie vase and fish bowl Lady Hilda had requested. When she came to collect them, Milton made sure his Joseff of Hollywood zodiac brooches were on the counter where they were certain to catch her eye. It was all so predictable. She couldn't resist buying her own sign, and from there it was the easiest thing in the world to discover her birthday. He wrote down Lady Hilda's address in his police book as the law required, a piece of bureaucracy Milton warmly applauded.

Two months later on the anniversary of her birth, Milton took the bold step of calling upon her unannounced at her home. If Lady Hilda had thought him rather presumptuous, everything was forgiven when he handed her a birthday card and a beautifully wrapped box containing a Royal Doulton pansy teapot in mint condition. What else could she do but invite him in for a cup of tea, a leisurely stocktake, and a close scrutiny of her security systems?

Milton followed up with earrings that matched the Joseff of Hollywood brooch, and he became her dear friend, bid for her at auctions, and used his contacts abroad to find her the very special pieces that made her collection world class. When she went off to France for her holiday, he silenced her alarm system, broke in and stole the lot including the Royal Doulton pansy teapot.

Of course, Lady Hilda was devastated. She returned home from Paris the instant the theft was reported to her. Somewhere over the Indian Ocean she probably passed her collection heading the other way. She was distraught, she was vulnerable and she was insured.

'Don't worry,' said Milton, with a consoling arm around her and a fierce determination in his voice. 'I'll scour the earth to replace the pieces you've lost. Your collection will be better than ever, even if it takes me all my time for the next ten years. Leave it to me.' It only took Milton two years to spend all of Lady Hilda's insurance money, retaining a hefty commission along the way for himself. That, combined with the proceeds of the robbery, helped finance Milton's move to Sydney, his new premises and his new home overlooking Double Bay. Lady Hilda's gratitude for his kindness and consideration in the aftermath of the robbery greatly enhanced his reputation.

Milton changed cities because of his natural caution. He was a great believer in lightning not striking the same place twice – well not in sequence at any rate – and he couldn't see the point in dealing honestly when the real money was in dealing dishonestly. Besides, he had his sights set on his next target, his next victim, the quiet man whoever and wherever he may be. Lady Hilda had been a major coup, stinging her coming and going and endlessly thereafter, but her collection had shown a major weakness. It was the product of a collector gifted with cash rather than exquisite taste. Milton knew that when he located the quiet man's collection it would consist entirely of the most immaculate, the most perfect, and the most rare examples. Lady Hilda's collection had been replaceable, that was its weakness. The quiet man's collection would be one that could never be replaced. That was its strength, its great attraction and the reason for Milton's obsession. He waited patiently for the quiet man to find him.

It's a funny thing but when the quiet man first walked into Milton's new premises, he was gone before Milton even knew he'd been. He visited Milton's shop three times before he bought, and even then left before it dawned on Milton that he might be the man he was looking for. The quiet man had walked away with a rare lightning pattern vase that Milton had been unsure how to price. Well, he knew now, didn't he? Obviously taking the lesser option had been a mistake. But the vase had been indelicate, thick-walled, almost amateurish and even the Clarice Cliff signature had seemed hand-drawn. His jaw dropped at his own stupidity the instant he connected all the oddities. The vase was obviously a prototype, hand-made and hand-painted by the great lady herself. And he'd sold it for a song. He racked his brains to try to remember what the customer had looked like but couldn't pin down an image. Hell! He hadn't just been quiet, he'd also been nondescript to the point of total anonymity. The address he'd given for the police book, a box number, was also consistent in its anonymity. But Milton's shadowy customer had known exactly what the vase was and had zeroed in on it. That was when Milton really began to believe that he'd found his man. That was when he began to think seriously about setting a trap.

As soon as he got home he stood before his private collection and searched for a sacrificial offering. He knew it would have to be good and he also knew it would have to be one of the best pieces he possessed. His hand reached up and touched his precious Luxor wall plaque, believed to be the only one of its kind. Lady Hilda had cost him – temporarily at least – a thousand dollar teapot. The Luxor plaque was worth ten times that. But one had to speculate to accumulate, didn't one?

Cyril Wardrop didn't know he was the quiet man. He was an upper-middle level public servant in the Department of Immigration. At the age of fifty-two he had clocked up thirty-four years with the department. By rights he should have been a very senior public servant because he was very good at his job, knew everything there was to know about immigration, and was too conscientious to ever take a sickie. The problem was he didn't understand the fundamental truth of how to succeed in the public service – or any large private corporation for that matter – and demonstrated his ignorance daily. He failed to understand that in order to succeed, he had first to fail.

Right from his school days, Cyril had set his sights on becoming a public servant. There was nothing particularly altruistic about this. He wanted to become a public servant because of job security, and the prospect of a substantial superannuation payout to retire on. His father had been a systems analyst who consulted to businesses that wanted to improve their efficiency. He was a time and motion man who spent half his time out of a job going through the motions of looking for another. His father's quest for work had taken him all over Australia, so Cyril had been brought up almost single-handedly by his mother who also went off to work every day. Cyril had been mother and father to his four younger sisters, more mother than father because in those days fathers weren't expected to help out in the kitchen. By the age of fifteen Cyril could cook, clean and sew as well as any girl his age. Sometimes when no one else was home he dressed up like one, too.

Given his line of business, Cyril's father should at least have taken the time to explain to the young boy the basic facts of life. He should have explained to him what is perfectly obvious to anyone who has ever analysed business. He should have explained that it is dumb to be smart and smart to be dumb. Work is inevitably attracted to smart people because it gets done. Dumb people who can't do the work get assistants to help them. If the assistants are carefully chosen and also dumb, they get even dumber assistants to help them. This is how empires are built, and the really successful ones are the ones with the most incompetent people. The original dummy sits at the top of the heap, does nothing except receive a large salary commensurate with the size of the empire controlled, and travels the country speaking at seminars on how to succeed in business, dispensing second-hand platitudes and being warmly applauded for doing so.

Cyril's father should have told him this. Instead, Cyril became the busy man and, as everyone knows, if you want something done in a hurry you give it to the busy man to do. Cyril always had a heap of work on his desk, often work that other people in other departments should have done. But it landed on Cyril's desk because Cyril always saved the day. He was a nit-picker, a detail man, accurate to the point of pedantry, but he was also smart. His superiors, who had risen to the top on the basis of their incompetence, didn't say as much out loud but they all knew: Cyril was far too useful to ever risk promoting.

Cyril never married. He liked to say he had no need for a wife, being well versed in every aspect of home management. The office girls used to ask his advice on which iron to buy, which washing machine, which brand of soap powder, and the best ways of removing unwanted stains. Cyril often gave up his lunchtime to go shopping with them. He particularly liked Lucinda. Lucinda was his special friend and had the sort of looks and figure Cyril would have liked to have had if only he'd been born a girl. He loved it when Lucinda took him with her when she was buying new clothes. Cyril had impeccable taste and knew instantly what went with what and what looked best on Lucinda. He liked to imagine it was him buying the dresses and blouses, the naughty bras and lacy knickers, and secretly wondered how he would look in them.

But Cyril's taste went far beyond the clothes he helped to choose and never dared wear, at least not in public. He had an eye for the decorative arts that ran years ahead of the market and mass popularity. He was into Moorcroft china when prized pieces could be picked up for forty or fifty dollars in antique shops and for a song in the markets, pieces that three years later fetched upwards of a thousand dollars. He was into Chiparis bronzes before they became worth more than precious metal. He was into Clarice Cliff before the Brighton retrospective exhibition which relaunched her Bizarre pottery onto a whole new, extravagantly appreciative generation. Sotheby's had valued a Lucerne teaset he'd bought years earlier at around ten thousand dollars. Cyril had paid thirty shillings for it. As a public servant Cyril had never earned a lot, but what he had earned his canny eye had converted into serious money.

But like his taste for black, tight-fitting, mid-thigh, off-the-shoulder numbers, he kept the fact that he was a collector a tightly guarded secret. When people asked him how he could afford to buy a house one back from the water but still with a sweeping view over the Pittwater estuary, he simply smiled and said, 'I chose my aunties carefully.' Everybody assumed he'd scored a sizeable bequest and was happy for him.

Cyril loved his home and all its precious contents, but sometimes he felt very lonely in it. One night as he sat out on his balcony staring up at the canopy of stars, trying to calculate the Southern Celestial pole by extending the long axis of the Southern Cross and the point where it intersected with an imaginary line drawn from the mid-point between Alpha and Beta Centauri, he was overwhelmed by a profound sense of aloneness that made him cry out in despair. The vastness of space, the emptiness of the void, the thought of suns like our sun blazing away in the vacuum of space bringing warmth to no one, gladdening no one's heart, causing no bulbs to grow, no flowers to bloom, no birds to sing or bees to collect honey, filled him with a sorrow of cosmic proportions. He identified with those suns. He realised he was no different from Alpha Centauri, utterly alone, unreachable, and untouchable. He brought warmth to no one and nothing. He was all alone in a universe of his own making. He had neighbours, nice people who he'd failed to reach out to and touch, and who had failed to touch him. His hellos and nice days had no more impact on their lives than the passing of Halley's comet. For days he contemplated suicide.

Sometimes he went out with Lucinda and the girls from work, but they had boyfriends, husbands and their own lives to live. Lucinda was always kind to him but kindness is a far cry from affection. He set out to make friends among his own kind, to involve other lives with his. A young man whose family had come from Corinth moved in with him, and for a while their lives became happily entwined. But the young man's orbit also touched others, and when Cyril challenged him for his lack of fidelity, they'd had the sort of row that degenerates into a competition to see who could say the most hurtful things. Perhaps the relationship may yet have survived if the young man hadn't thrown a Clarice Cliff muffineer at Cyril. Showing an agility he had no idea he possessed, Cyril had caught the muffineer and saved it from destruction. But the young man had highlighted the vulnerability of his prized collection in their volatile relationship. From that point on, nothing could save it.

Again Cyril contemplated suicide but bought a cat instead. It was female and Cyril called her Cosmos. Gradually Cyril made more friends but none moved in with him, and none claimed more of his affection than Cosmos. Cosmos was always there waiting to make a fuss of him when he came home from work, snuggled up to him on cold nights, and took to lying on his shoulders and across the back of his neck as he cooked and vacuumed. It was impossible to feel lonely with Cosmos around. She filled the void in Cyril's life.

Cosmos repaid Cyril for his friendship by bringing home dead rats with their heads chewed off, and leaving them where Cyril couldn't help but see and appreciate the gift. Appreciation was never the emotion that flashed across Cyril's brain. Revulsion came closer. But Cyril never scolded Cosmos. Cyril liked to be tolerant. In his thirty-four years in the Immigration Department, the faces he saw every day had changed considerably. Where once they'd all been Anglo-Saxon or Irish, they were now Italian, Greek, Chinese, Malay, Indian, Turkish, Egyptian, Maori, Chilean, Baltic, and even Russian. Cyril treated them all equally and fairly, was tolerant of their idiosyncrasies, and they in turn were tolerant of his. Cyril accepted that Cosmos was a cat and that cats killed rats. But then Cosmos also started bringing home lorikeets with their heads chewed off, and defenceless, decapitated little bandicoots. Cyril tried hard to be tolerant but in the end bought a collar with a bell on it. Cosmos hated the collar and cut Cyril cold whenever she was forced to wear it.

About this time Cyril saw Milton's ad for the Luxor wall plaque, knew that four thousand dollars was an extraordinary bargain, and walked blithely into Milton's trap. He wasn't interested in keeping the plaque for himself. He already had one that was even larger, which he'd bought at a country town auction in 1970. He decided to buy and on-sell the plaque to supplement his income. He often supplemented his income in this manner.

Cyril went to Milton's shop looking for a bargain not a friend, but came away with both. Milton was not gay but moved easily and comfortably in gay circles. He was as tolerant of gays as Cyril was of his associates at work. Over the next few months, Cyril would drop by and they'd talk endlessly about their common interest in art deco. Cyril believed a genuine friendship was blossoming, a friendship that was honest and open and without romantic or sexual attachments. He believed Milton liked him for himself, no more, no less, just as he had grown to like Milton.

On Cyril's fifty-third birthday Milton made his move. He took Cyril to dinner at Tetsuya's to celebrate. Milton brought the wines, a splendid Pouilly Fumé, a ten-year-old Petrus, and a '67 Chateau d'Yquem, a lavish selection that had set Milton's cellar back more than six hundred dollars. He also paid for the meal.

Cyril had never had a friend like Milton before, whose generosity knew no bounds, who hung on his every word, and who asked for nothing in return. Cyril repaid his gift by breaching his self-imposed confidence. He told Milton something he'd never told anyone before. He made him a gift of his trust. He told Milton all about the collection he'd painstakingly built up over the years. He even offered to show it to Milton one day. But if love is blind, so is true friendship to the lonely. Milton was no different from Cosmos in that he also had his faults.

Cosmos was a killer. Milton was a thief.

When Cyril invited Milton to lunch to view his collection, Milton arrived bearing gifts. A tiny tin of *pâté de foie gras* which had set him back one hundred and thirty dollars, some chevre from Sancerre, some brie and an extravagant bunch of poppies. In the right Clarice Cliff vase, poppies could look absolutely brilliant. No thief ever showed more thoughtfulness nor consideration when arriving to case a joint. Milton thought he'd come prepared but nothing could prepare him for what Cyril had to show. The enormous Honolulu snake tree umbrella stand with its almost Japanese dried arrangement should have given him some inkling.

'My God!' he blustered. 'Oh my God.' The search was over, the quiet man had revealed himself in all his glory. Cyril's house wasn't so much a house as an art deco shrine. Most walls had glass-encased shelves housing the finest examples of English pottery from the twenties and thirties that he had ever seen. The ones that didn't wore Tamara de Limpicka paintings. He stumbled open-mouthed and speechless from display to display, barely aware of the Bauhaus and Biedermeir furniture he was forced to negotiate.

'How long have you been collecting?' he gasped finally.

'Since I was fourteen,' Cyril said proudly. 'Since I used to help the church ladies look after the old-age pensioners in our parish. My first pieces were given or left to me by old ladies I'd cared for. Dear things! All they'd wanted was company.'

Forty years! He'd been collecting for almost forty years, picking up glorious pieces at a time when people would have paid somebody to take them away.

'How did you know?'

'Know what?'

'That these pieces would become so valuable.'

'Oh I didn't! I only began to collect things because I liked them. I keep my glass in here.' Cyril led Milton into his dining room where museum quality Lalique, Daum and Tiffany glowed on underlit shelves.

'Oh my God!' said Milton repetitiously. But what else could he say before what was to him a divine revelation?

On the last Sunday of every month thereafter, Milton visited Cyril for lunch. Cyril enjoyed Milton's friendship and Milton enjoyed just sitting and absorbing Cyril's wonderful collection. Whenever they lunched out on the terrace he always positioned himself so that he could at least see the glorious Honolulu snake tree umbrella stand, with its arrangement of stark white twigs and dried bottlebrushes. Milton was in no hurry to steal it. It was already as good as his anyway. And Milton knew that once he'd made his move the collection would be lost from his sight forever. So once a month for almost a year, he sat and enjoyed its completeness, its perfection and the fact that he, alone among all the dealers, had believed in and tracked down the quiet man.

'I can't understand why you don't have a security system,' said Milton.

'Why should I protect what nobody knows I have?' replied Cyril.

'I can't believe it's not insured,' said Milton.

'Insurance would cost more than I earn,' replied Cyril. 'Besides, who'd steal it? What thief knows about Clarice Cliff and Susie Cooper, Daum and Lalique? Where would they sell it?' Cyril didn't see any need to tell Milton that he'd photographed every piece, marked their bases with a code number visible only under ultra-violet light, and registered them with the local police.

'All the same,' said Milton. 'A wise man would insure as much as he could.' It worried Milton that Cyril wasn't insured. Normally his victims were rich and insurance wasn't a problem. Cyril would have to bear the loss himself and there'd be no money for Milton to help find replacements. 'Oh well,' Milton said to himself on his way back home to Double Bay, 'I did my best to warn him.'

Milton worried about Cyril's lack of insurance when he should have been worrying about Cosmos, Cyril's cat. Cosmos was worried about Cyril's lack of attention and affection, and knew who to blame. Cosmos did not like Milton. In fact, she was jealous of Milton. Cosmos liked having Cyril all to herself, to tickle her tummy and talk to her. It worried her that the more Cyril talked to Milton the less he felt the need to talk to her. So Cosmos set out to win Cyril's undivided attention and affection all over again. Obviously headless rats, decapitated lorikeets and bandicoot torsos failed to achieve the desired result, so Cosmos upped the ante.

One day Cyril woke up to find a gift of a headless possum on the door mat. On another, the headless corpse of a blue-tongue lizard. Cosmos watched proudly as Cyril wrapped the fresh kills up in newspaper and dug a hole in the garden to bury them. That was all right with her. She just thought that was where Cyril kept his treats to chew upon later. Like stupid dogs digging holes and burying perfectly good bones. Cyril would pick Cosmos up and lecture her on the need for the protection and management of indigenous fauna. Cosmos didn't understand a word he said, but understood all the attention she was getting and purred with pleasure. She didn't understand why Cyril always responded to her purring by making her wear the stupid collar with the annoying bell. How was she supposed to catch anything wearing that? And if she didn't catch anything, how was she going to get Cyril to talk to her?

Cyril didn't know what to do about Cosmos. He stopped leaving pieces of apple out for the possums that stalked his balcony by night, and sunflower seeds for the lorikeets, galahs and corellas that stalked his balcony by day. He started pushing Cosmos away when she tried to lick his hand, or his ear while he was cooking, or his cheek while he was lying down. The thought of the headless lizards and possums and where Cosmos' tongue had been and what else it might have been doing, made him feel positively squeamish. Cosmos didn't take at all well to this shunning of her affection. She didn't understand why Cyril had changed, or why her little displays of affection were now unwanted. Perhaps Cyril preferred his treats live. Cosmos certainly did, so it seemed logical that Cyril would as well.

One evening Cosmos burst through the cat-flap with a slightly damaged but still highly mobile mouse, and she and Cyril had endless fun chasing it around and around the Biedermier cocktail cabinet, until Cyril had tired of the game and nailed the mouse with the electric iron. Cyril had been ironing at the time and the singed fur had made a really neat smell. Cyril had collapsed onto the floor, legs apart, back resting against the wall with Cosmos clutched tightly to his chest. Cosmos had never heard Cyril whimper before. She thought that must be the sound he made when he was having a real fun time. She liked being clutched tightly to Cyril's chest as well. She liked the rapid, arhythmic flutter that came from within. Obviously, the move to live treats had been exactly the right thing to do. Cosmos purred her heart out.

It took Cyril's nerves days to settle down. He told Lucinda and the girls at his office, and they squealed in horror. They were all terrified of mice and even more terrified of ones that ran on three legs and a bleeding stump. He was almost back to normal when Cosmos chose to bring him a present of a live swamp snake at three in the morning. Perhaps if Cyril hadn't got up to go to the toilet, Cosmos might have got bored waiting for the alarm clock to ring and chewed the snake's head off. But Cyril answered nature's call and stepped out of bed, vulnerable in his bare feet and nightie. If anyone had bothered to ask, Cyril would have told them he slept in a nightshirt, but he didn't. What he wore to bed was a very tasteful silver and black silk nightie he'd pretended he was buying for his mum. He'd taken three steps before the sound of Cosmos leaping around caused him to pause. He felt movement around his ankles and jumped nervously. His hand brushed the light switch and turned on the light. He peered down to see his feet straddling what looked like a snake, hissed like a snake and was clearly very angry.

Cyril made no effort to identify the species, whether it was venomous, non-venomous, venomous but unlikely to strike, or venomous and certain to strike. He simply jumped, though to describe a standing jump that exceeded both Olympic high and long jump records simultaneously as simple hardly does the leap justice. Cosmos was in raptures. She'd thought Cyril had enjoyed the game with the mouse, but the snake had elevated the fun to a whole new level. She seized the snake and chased after Cyril, tossing the unfortunate serpent high into the air in an attempt to emulate Cyril's fantastic leap. Cyril ended the game with the Chinese chopper he used for cutting up vegetables for stir-fries and pumpkins for soup. He slumped to the floor, back propped against a glass cabinet filled with the best of Susie Cooper's art deco designs, mouth open, gasping for breath.

He clutched Cosmos so tightly to his chest she could feel the blood rush through his over-worked ventrical chamber. Cosmos purred and padded like a cat possessed. She reached up and licked the tiny streams that ran from Cyril's eyes. They tasted deliciously salty, a fitting reward for her little gift.

Swamp snakes are not bad as far as snakes go, unless you happen to be a lizard, frog or smaller snake, in which case a swamp snake is likely to be both the most frightening and the last thing you'll ever see. They rarely exceed nine hundred millimetres and only come out at night when the weather is warm. Although venomous, they're also very timid and not considered dangerous to humans. Cyril discovered all this when he showed the salami-sliced remains of the snake to the pest control man, who counted the mid-body, ventral and sub-caudal scales and made his identification. But the news did little to calm Cyril.

Milton was very sympathetic.

'You need a holiday,' he said. 'Somewhere where there are no snakes and no cats with a warped sense of humour.'

'I don't know,' said Cyril doubtfully.

'Well I do,' said Milton. He'd enjoyed Cyril's magnificent collection enormously, and he knew he'd miss it when it was gone. But he couldn't live on admiration. Admiration did not fund his lifestyle or his ambition, or fuel his ego. It was time. Time to don the cloak of the thief. Time Cyril went on holiday and his collection shortly after. 'Tell me, have you ever been to Staffordshire?' he asked.

'Staffordshire?'

'Tunstall, Cyril.'

'Tunstall?' said Cyril, the idea slowly budding.

'The six pottery towns where all your precious Clarice Cliff, Susie Cooper, Charlotte Rhead, and your Mabel Lucie Attwell came from.'

'My goodness,' said Cyril, the idea bursting from bud to blossom to bush in full bloom.

'Keith Murray. Wedgwood. Royal Doulton. Isn't it time you actually went there? Visited the potteries?'

'Oh my,' said Cyril.

'I know someone who has an open invitation to all the potteries and museums. My colleague in London. He can be your guide.'

'I don't normally go on holidays,' said Cyril.

'Think of it as a pilgrimage. With art deco's answer to Moses leading you through the Holy Land.'

Cyril did. He thought about nothing else for two weeks. The quiet man became even quieter than usual. The girls at work wondered what had got into him. They thought he'd at last found Mr Right. At home, Cosmos was going bananas trying to get Cyril to talk to her. She'd even shredded Cyril's favourite nightie, the sheer, black Italian number he was only ever game to wear when he'd drunk too much crème de menthe. All to no avail. Cyril was distracted and nothing Cosmos did could get him back on the rails. Then Cyril took the plunge.

'I've already taken the liberty of informing my man of your imminent arrival,' said Milton. 'He suggests you come next month, before all the tourists. I've rung the travel agents and Qantas have the best deal, provided you pay thirty days in advance and stay a minimum of three weeks. It's like an auction, Cyril. If you want something you have to go for it. No second chances. Do you want it? If so, put your hand up now.'

Cyril did, more like a schoolboy eager to answer teacher's question than a serious bidder.

'Well done!' said Milton. 'I can't tell you how much my colleague is looking forward to meeting you.' Milton loved his little ironies as well.

Cyril's bosses weren't happy, but what could they do? Nothing, of course, until he got back because their empires were built on people who were expert only at doing nothing, and incapable of doing anything. However Cyril, who was the one man in the department who not only knew what he was doing but also what everyone else should be doing, was already owed more than eleven years' holiday entitlement, and to deny him three weeks seemed a touch extreme.

Cyril was in a state of panic. His life revolved around routine, and a minor interruption to his routine represented a major disruption to his life. But he hadn't felt so excited since he'd spotted the snake tree umbrella stand in the parlour of a country pub out near Gilgandra. Sometimes he grabbed hold of Cosmos and cuddled her and ruffled her so that she could share in his excitement. Other times he forgot all about her as he wrestled with what to pack. Could he go three weeks without his little, black, off-the-shoulder numbers, or his tricksy high-heels he'd had specially made for him by a leather artiste in Oxford Street? And what about his precious Italian nighties? What if his case was opened by Customs? It took him a week to work out that London might be the perfect place to supplement his wardrobe. He could always pretend he was bringing his purchases home as gifts.

Cosmos was confused. For some reason, which she couldn't begin to understand, Cyril had made her wear the loathsome bell non-stop for five weeks. Sometimes Cyril played with her, other times the only contact they had was when he accidentally tripped over her. One day he brought home a female of his species who made an enormous fuss of her. She cuddled Cosmos tightly to her chest like Cyril did, only it was even better when she did it. Her chest was padded. The female also had a magical scent that made Cosmos want to rush out and proposition every tomcat from Manly to Palm Beach.

When Cyril called into the shop to say goodbye to Milton and thank him for organising his guide, he told him about Lucinda. Milton was dumbstruck. It had never occurred to him that Cyril would arrange for anyone to live in and look after his house while he was away. That hadn't been part of the plan. It had never occurred to him that Cyril had any close friends other than himself. Then Cyril mentioned Cosmos and Milton understood. Someone had to look after the cat. The trouble was, Milton had planned to rob Cyril's home over two or three days so that all the precious pieces could be properly packed for shipment on site, placed inside removalist's cartons and stacked gently into his van. Now he had to contend with Lucinda. It wasn't a total disaster because she would be out all day at work, but it did mean he'd have to do everything in a single day. That meant bubble-wrap sleeves, corrugated-card petitions, inevitable scraping and possibly even breakages. But it couldn't be helped. It also meant repacking for shipping to England, and Milton was never happy having stolen goods in his possession. Generously, he put aside his disappointment and wished Cyril the holiday of a lifetime.

Cyril had everything packed before dinner on the eve of his departure. He called Cosmos so that she could wrap herself around his neck while he cooked their dinner. Both were very fond of lightly grilled whiting fillets. But Cosmos ignored him entirely. She deliberately walked away from him with her tail held high so that Cyril could see her least attractive part. Cyril got the message and undid the collar with the hateful bell. It was a decision that would have a profound effect on Cyril's future, both immediate and long term. Cosmos greeted this act of conciliation by leaping onto Cyril's shoulders and licking his ears.

Cyril didn't get much sleep that night, partly because of excitement but mostly because Cosmos decided to reward him for removing the bell. She brought him a whole new live snake to play with. Once more Cyril discovered the new toy en route to the toilet, but, warned by Cosmos' bumping and leaping in the dark, had the foresight to switch on the light. What he saw nearly caused him to jump out of his nightie. He didn't realise that this snake was any different from the previous snake. He was in no mood to count mid-body, ventral and sub-caudal scales. He only noted the presence of a snake, one that was larger than its predecessor, considerably angrier and doing its very best to nail Cosmos with explosively fast strikes. Even Cosmos seemed to be treating it with healthy respect, as it finally dawned on her that she might have bitten into a bit more than she could chew the head off of.

Cyril screamed, he tap-danced, he pranced and he leaped. None of this helped. Cyril remembered what the pest controller had said about swamp snakes not being considered a danger to man, but the pest controller had obviously never encountered a swamp snake like this. It set its beady eyes on Cyril and struck. Cyril cleared the Biedermier cocktail cabinet in a single leap. Cosmos joined him. The trouble was, both lost sight of the snake, and by the time they'd plucked up enough courage to peep around the sides of the cabinet it was nowhere to be seen.

Perversely, if there's one thing worse than seeing a snake in your lounge room, it's not seeing a snake in your lounge room. Cosmos made a few tentative sniffs to determine which direction the snake had gone but lost interest in the game. It wasn't fun anymore. She let Cyril pick her up and make a hasty retreat to his bedroom where he slammed the door, and stuffed a blanket under it to keep the snake out. They needn't have bothered. The snake didn't care much for the game, either. It had recently swallowed a bandicoot which needed a quiet week's digesting. So it looked for a hiding place and found one beneath the dried bottlebrushes and stark white twigs, in a dark, dry hole with just a single narrow entrance. The tiger snake probably thought it was quite fortunate finding somewhere so safe and easy to defend in which to hole up. The fact that its hiding place had a beautiful green snake tree pattern on it was entirely irrelevant.

Even though tiger snakes belong to the same family *Elapidae* as swamp snakes, anyone with a mild interest in snakes would have no trouble telling them apart. Tiger snakes have more robust bodies, and heads that are quite distinct from their necks. Their aggression and neurotoxin venom make them one of the most dangerous snakes in the world. You don't have to count their scales to know you have a tiger snake on your hands. Their strike stance is quite unambiguous. Tiger snakes are snakes with attitude and they make no attempt to conceal it.

Cyril still assumed his intruder was a swamp snake, but it could just as soon have been a taipan crossed with a black mamba as far as he was concerned. It was a snake, it was poisonous and it was in his house. Somewhere. He rang

Lucinda. There was no possible way that he could allow her to stay in his home. She agreed with disconcerting speed, but did offer to look after Cosmos in her tiny apartment, with its even tinier balcony and minuscule planter box. He arranged to call in at the Department of Immigration on the way to the airport so he could hand Cosmos over.

'You're going on a holiday, too,' he told her. But Cosmos took one look at the cat box and assumed she was going to the vet's. Cyril only just beat her to the cat-flap. While he waited for his taxi to arrive, Cyril sat perched on his kitchen bench, his feet safely off the ground. He rang Milton for a last goodbye and told him about his adventure with the snake.

'Another swamp snake?' said Milton, desperate to conceal his glee. It was hard to cluck sympathetically when he wanted to leap for joy. He urged Cyril to go to the airport early, settle himself down with a stiff, double Tia Maria, hung up, punched his fist into the palm of his hand, and blessed the swamp snake's little reptilian heart. What had Cyril told him about swamp snakes? Small. Timid. No danger to man. He rang the zoo to check.

'Big ones might bite if provoked,' the zoo lady said, 'but they're only mildly venomous. Can be painful though,' she cautioned. Milton decided he could live with that.

Milton waited three days, during which time he rang Cyril's office twice during each day and his home at night. The office said he was on leave and his home phone went unanswered. Milton always liked to be sure. Late on the evening of the third day he received a fax from his colleague in crime. 'The sparrow has landed,' it said.

On the fourth day, Milton drove his van up the peninsula to Cyril's home. He knew Cyril's neighbours all worked, and checked to see that there were no cars still in driveways. There weren't. He backed his van up Cyril's driveway until it was hidden behind a screen of gums and bottlebrushes. Then he calmly jemmied open Cyril's terrace doors. He put the kettle on and made himself a coffee so he could sit, sip and admire Cyril's wonderful collection one final time. However, all good things must come to an end and he set about the process of packing up Cyril's collection. He moved his roll of bubble wrap into the lounge and his pile of flat-folded cartons. He put a new blade in his Stanley knife and opened a new roll of brown tape. He began with the Clarice Cliff which was his target for the day. His work was unhurried and meticulous. There was no way his London connection would be able to claim that pieces had broken in transit and sell them privately on the side.

The next day he took the Susie Cooper, Charlotte Rhead, Shelley, Royal Doulton and Keith Murray Wedgwood. On the third day he took the glass. He was tempted to steal some of the Biedermier furniture and Temara De Limpicka paintings, but he had his back to think of. As he took one final look around, a last check of the scene of the crime, he realised his oversight. It amazed him how some things can become so familiar that the eye accepts but fails to register them. How, he wondered, had he come so close to missing the magnificent, unique Honolulu snake tree umbrella stand?

Milton didn't bother wrapping the umbrella stand. He just tossed out the dried arrangement, slipped it into a bubble-wrap sleeve and wedged it between four cartons in the back of his van. He slammed the rear door shut, walked around to the front, hopped in and started the engine. At that moment Milton didn't have a worry in the world.

Behind him in the umbrella stand the tiger snake coiled and uncoiled nervously. It had never been for a ride in a van before and didn't like it one bit. Its tongue flicked in and out, feeling for vibrations, trying to gain some understanding of what was happening. It put up with things for some time before the erratic movement began to upset its equilibrium. It's a little known fact that motion sickness can upset snakes as well as people. It began to consider what was happening to it as an act of extreme provocation, and tiger snakes can become very aggressive when provoked. It raised its neck from the umbrella stand and took a peep at its surroundings. Slowly it eased its way out and among the cartons. The van hit a pothole and it immediately adopted its strike position. As a courtesy to its intended victims or to over-ambitious predators, tiger snakes usually emit a hiss before they strike. The tiger snake hissed.

'Damn,' said Milton. He stopped the van, got out and checked the tyres. If he had a flat tyre he wanted to know before he drove onto the Harbour Bridge and attracted unwanted attention. His tyres seemed fine. He climbed back into the van and slammed the door just as the tiger snake was considering a bolt for freedom. Naturally, it regarded this as another deliberate act of provocation. How much was a tiger snake supposed to put up with? It slithered along the top of the cartons towards the animate thing that bobbed and bounced and had caused all the aggravation. The snake set itself, hissed and struck.

'Aghhhh . . .' screamed Milton. He grabbed at the back of his neck with his right hand. The snake didn't like the sudden movement at all. That smacked of retaliation. It struck again on the back of Milton's hand.

'Aghhhhh!' screamed Milton again. He caught a glimpse of the retreating reptile in his rear-vision mirror just as it ducked between two cartons. He wanted to stop, get out and find something to kill it with before it did any more damage. But people don't normally park vans on the Harbour Bridge, besides which there was nowhere to park and no likelihood of finding anything with which to kill the snake. So he drove on, heading for the Macquarie Street exit. What had the zoo lady said about swamp snakes? Mildly venomous but with a painful bite? Well she was certainly right about the latter and he sincerely hoped about the former as well.

There was nowhere to stop in Macquarie Street so he drove on until he could turn left into the Domain. He stopped by the art gallery. He didn't feel at all well. Disoriented. Heavy limbed. Cold and sweaty. And the pain was becoming almost unbearable. He pushed open the driver's door and waved to attract attention. There was a group of young ladies nearby, but they knew better than to respond to strange men in vans, especially ones who were so drunk they could hardly sit up. They watched him slump forward against the steering wheel and they snorted disdainfully.

When Cyril returned from his holiday he was devastated to discover all his treasures missing. He wanted to commit suicide once more but rang the police instead. Of course, he refused point blank to believe that his dear friend Milton had been a thief. As he told the police, given the choice he would rather have his friend back and alive than recover his collection. No, Cyril maintained, there was a much simpler explanation. His friend had always expressed concern about his lack of security and insurance. Milton had simply taken the collection away for safekeeping until his return.

Cyril retired from the Department of Immigration, took his superannuation, long-service leave and outstanding holiday pay, and bought Milton's business. He was sure that this was what his friend would have wanted. He also made Cosmos wear her bell permanently.

Cat Sausages

'Where is he? Where is the bastard!'

No one ever said Moira Monaghan had the voice of an angel, nor was she ever asked to join the Sunset Downs town choir. She once auditioned though, and no one was game enough to tell her that she'd failed to make the grade. Instead, they passed the bad news on the way everyone passed on bad news to Moira. They told her husband. Doubtless he'd chosen his moment well before gleefully informing her that her diamond-cutting voice was surplus to requirements. Doubtless she'd flown into a rage and, equally beyond doubt, would have been made to pay for her tantrum.

Her voice wasn't a total loss though. She'd won the Sunset Downs coo-ee contest for nineteen consecutive years, and her voice was still improving. They say the whole of Collarenebri heard her last winning coo-ee, and Collarenebri was over eighty kilometres away. The pilot of a Qantas jet reckoned he heard it as well, and he was flying thirteen thousand metres overhead. So when Moira barged into the pub and hollered, all seven occupants listened. They had no choice.

'Where is he? I know he's here!'

The pub interior would never win any awards for artistic lighting. The fluoros were off because one had a dicky starter and the flickering caused Barry the day barman to fit. Nobody minded that Barry was epileptic except when he fitted and they couldn't buy a drink. So they sat in the gloom by choice, windows shaded by the overhang of the tin verandah roof and closed to keep out the heat. Apart from the dodgy starter the pub was in pretty good nick, which was more than could be said for most of the other buildings that lined Sunset Downs' main street. Half were unoccupied and falling apart. The remaining half had seen better days.

Sunset Downs was given its name by an English gentleman banished to Australia because of his part in a scandal involving the daughter of one of Dorset's largest landowners. He stumbled upon Sunset Downs after five consecutive years of good rains, and thought it reminded him of the lush rolling downs of his county. Perhaps it did, but that was the last time Sunset Downs ever had five consecutive years of rain, and now had about as much in common with Dorset as the Gobi Desert.

'Where's Heinz? Where is the bastard!'

'No need to shout, love, I'm here.'

All eyes turned to the doorway that led to the lounge bar. Beer was dearer in the lounge bar because it had a television, even though a watchable picture was never much more than a fifty–fifty proposition. Heinz was in the process – at least appeared to be in the process – of restoring the television to working order. He filled the doorway, screwdriver in hand, black suit rumpled, a picture of tolerance and patience.

'You murdering bastard!' Moira flew at him. She stood just on five foot tall by the old measure, one hundred and fifty centimetres by the new, but she was broad across the beam and big of breast and belly. She would never be invited to do a testimonial for Jenny Craig. Heinz liked to say she was five foot tall whichever way you looked at her. Standing up, lying down, on her back, on her side. He reckoned he had to wait until she ate something before he knew which way up she was. But the speed with which she flew across the bar room, her fists clenched, teeth bared, left him in no doubt as to which part pointed skywards. She was amazingly fast for her size, a ball of spitting fury.

'Bastard!' she spat.

'That's enough, love,' said Heinz calmly as he grabbed her fists and held them prisoner. Heinz was two metres tall and solid with it. He could have killed them at football if God hadn't made him unswervingly affable, bone lazy and given him a taste for drink. 'Let's not be unseemly in public,' he said gently. 'There's no call for that sort of language.'

His implacable calm infuriated her more, and she raged and ranted until she'd spent all her energy battling the strength of his grip. She began to sob.

'Not Smokey,' she sobbed. 'Why did you have to do that to Smokey? And Snuffy! Poor Snuffy!' She burst into tears. Heinz let go of her hands and she waddled into the far corner of the bar where the light was dimmest and nobody could see her tears. Barry the barman brought her a middy of brandy, as was her fancy, so she could drown her sorrows. Round One was over but it was still early.

Young Stan, the stockman with the leg in plaster, went back to drinking his way through his workers compensation, helped by his three mates who'd already drunk their unemployment benefit, and a travelling salesman who sold irrigation tubing. Young Stan thought that was a hoot, him selling irrigation tubing. The whole country for hundreds of kilometres around was in drought and needed irrigation, but nobody had the water to pump through the pipes and no money to buy them anyway.

'What was all that about?' asked the salesman as Heinz disappeared back into the lounge bar to continue his assault on the TV aerial.

'Cats,' said Young Stan with a smirk. 'He's her husband. He hates cats, she has a house full of them. Dozens of the bloody things. Every time she gives him the shits over something he gets even by chucking a couple into the freezer.'

'You're kidding!'

'Nuh. Takes her a day or two to notice they're missing.'

Round One was usually followed by Round Two, which was the kiss and make up phase. Nobody took much notice of Round Two because it was always followed by Round Three. For the duration of Round Two Heinz and Moira would exchange apologies, buy each other drinks and be briefly nice to each other. Then the alcohol would kick in and Round Three would begin. Moira would lift her head and look around at the dismal, depressing surroundings and be reminded once more of the hopelessness of her situation, the mess of her marriage, the futureless town, her cat piss sodden home, and the wreckage of her life. She'd once had a future, had hopes, had optimism, had believed that things had to change for the better, that something would happen to take her away from Sunset Downs and give her the life she'd missed out on. Naturally, she blamed Heinz for her lost opportunities.

She'd look around and realise that nothing would ever change and all she had to look forward to was another middy of brandy, and that the only love she'd ever receive would come courtesy of her cats. Then she'd be reminded of the frozen statues, awful parodies of creatures she'd cherished, loved and clutched to her heaving bosom while the winds of loneliness howled around her door. Her eyes would fix upon Heinz, the source of all her woes and misery, and Round Three would begin. Heinz was always slow on picking up on the transition and his black suit would wear the consequences. It didn't matter. In the fourteen years he'd owned it, his suit had never once seen the inside of a dry cleaner's nor felt the slippery touch of soap. And nobody could remember seeing him in anything else.

If the customers in the bar were waiting for Round Three to begin to break the monotony and ease the grim process of nursing a beer past its use-by date, they were due for a disappointment. The television burst into life with a half-decent picture, provided nobody sat or stood to the right of the screen. Heinz had hardly begun Round Two when little Maggie Gee rode up to the pub on her giant of a horse. Her news was grim. Cockatoos had bent and snapped off elements from their aerial and eaten half the ribbon. Heinz had another job.

The disappointment in the pub was palpable as Heinz pulled his pushbike beneath him and set off pedalling the seventeen dusty kilometres to the Gees. Maggie walked her brute of a horse alongside and slightly ahead of him so that she was up wind. You didn't want to be down wind from Heinz. He washed his body as rarely as he cleaned his suit. And it didn't rain often enough to catch him unawares. Maggie rode with him, not just because it was the polite thing to do since she'd dragged him away from the pub, but because Heinz was a born storyteller. Nobody knew where he got his stories from but he always had a new one to add to the old ones. He told them all anyway. She rode her horse and waited for the stories to flow.

He always told his favourite which described his unique parentage. His mother was German and his father Irish. He reckoned that made him ruthlessly inefficient. He told that story often enough for the townsfolk to decide to make it his epitaph when he finally fell off the perch. *Heinz Monaghan 1945–19 . . . He Was Ruthlessly Inefficient. Sadly Missed by All of Us with Dicky Teevees.*

Most of the stories he told were about Moira, and he was merciless in ridiculing her. Of course many were apocryphal, but there were the others that weren't, and the difficulty came in sorting which from what. There was the time Heinz had decided to farm worms to sell to fishermen who came after the cod and yellow bellies in the Barwon River. It looked like he was on a winner until the rains went elsewhere and the Barwon slowed to a trickle. On the other hand, Heinz's worms decided they liked whatever he was doing to them to make them grow, and bred like rabbits. They overran the breeding trays, oozed out of every crack and crevice in the breeding shed. Moira kept telling him to do something about them, and in the absence of any action did something about them herself.

Heinz reckoned the spaghetti bolognaise was the best she'd ever made, helped himself to seconds and thirds before she told him about the wonder ingredient. He turned as pale as a dead gum tree, as pale as the boiled and bloodless worms he'd just eaten, and dashed off to the outhouse. She turned bright scarlet with laughter and damn near choked in her glee. She had her hour of triumph and he had his shortly afterwards when a couple of her cats went missing. That was the first time Heinz dabbled in pussy cryogenics, and Moira spent a week searching for the lost members of her family before she had cause to open the freezer.

Her turn to fade to white.

From that day on, Heinz knew he was on a winner. He never abused Moira in public and never laid a finger on her. He never lost his temper, not that anyone could remember at any rate. He liked to administer punishment in a way that not only hit the mark, but gave everyone a bit of a laugh at the same time. Cat freezing seemed to be the perfect way to keep Moira in check. For a while it worked until she gradually overcame each of her losses. If anything, the freezings made her more vindictive and more determined to hurt him. To hurt and humiliate him as deeply as he hurt her.

She did little things like sneak out at night and let down the rear tyre of his bike – not right down so that Heinz would guess what she'd done, but just enough so that it needed pumping. Heinz's pump was in sore need of a new washer and had been for a year or more. She'd do the same night after night until Heinz was convinced he had a slow leak. She'd watch from door and window as he'd submerge the tube in a tub of water looking for telltale bubbles, and became frustrated when there were none. She'd watch him change the valve rubbers only to change them again the following day. When he switched tubes from back to front wheels, she began letting down the front tyre. Heinz was thoroughly perplexed. He couldn't go about his job, and if he couldn't do that he couldn't tell stories because there was no one to tell them to. Heinz wasn't the sort of man who could keep things bottled up. He was a storyteller. He needed his audience as much as he needed his booze. Laughter was his lifeblood and he believed making people laugh was more his real job than fixing aerials. Anyone could fix aerials, not everyone could make people laugh. His frustration grew. Moira kept up the torment for a month before telling him in front of his mates in the pub what she'd done. She thought she had him. Shown him up to be the fool he was. She expected his mates to piss themselves laughing and they did. But she didn't expect Heinz to join in.

'Good one, love,' he'd said and meant it. Maybe it appealed to the Irish in him. Maybe he immediately added it to his repertoire of stories. Whatever, his unswerving affability was unshaken and no little crosses were added to the tomato patch.

That was another thing. Whenever one of her cats met a frosty end, Moira always buried them and erected a little wooden cross over the grave. Heinz would then add insult to injury by planting a tomato plant on the grave, using the cross as a stake.

'Shame to waste all that good fertiliser,' he'd say. And, 'It's what pussy would have wanted,' which was patently untrue. All the cats hated Heinz as passionately as he hated them. The survivors made a point of pissing and spraying on his plants.

On the way out to the farm, Heinz told Maggie Gee about Moira's latest transgression. Every morning Heinz moved into the outhouse like an army of occupation into a conquered country. He didn't just go for a visit but for a stay bordering on permanence.

'Some things can't be hurried, love,' he'd say, and he could not be moved despite Moira's needs and discomforts until nature had run its course. He'd take a cup of tea in with him, a piece of toast and marmalade, the morning paper or his book of great sausage recipes. His occupation of the outhouse was the greatest cause of anguish and dispute within their unhappy home, but Heinz could not be moved.

So Moira decided that if Heinz wanted to stay on the unkingly throne forever, she'd help him in his ambition. She ducked out before him and put gobs of glue on the toilet seat, little blobs that looked no different to the splash-back droplets which dotted the seat every time one of them pulled the chain.

'There I was, trousers around my ankles, stuck fast to the dunny,' Heinz told Maggie. Maggie shook with laughter. Nobody talked about toilets in her family and the story was not only funny but deliciously naughty. She jiggled about in the saddle so much her poor horse thought she wanted to go six different ways at once.

'What did you do?' demanded Maggie.

'What could I do, love? She wasn't going to help me and I couldn't very well go marching down the main street of Some Sit Downs with a toilet seat stuck to my bum, could I?'

Maggie chortled. Nobody said bum in her family, either. 'So what did you do?'

'I took my courage in both hands by planting them firmly either side of the seat and stood up, all sudden like.'

'Ouch!' shrieked Maggie.

'Yep!' said Heinz proudly. 'Moira had to use the blow torch to remove the patches of my bum still stuck to the seat. Couldn't ride my bike for a week. Even now I've had to borrow Mrs Monaghan's doilies out of the front room and stick them down my trousers for padding.'

Maggie looked at how he was pedalling and saw how gingerly he perched on the saddle. Just like he had a boil on his bum. She began to giggle helplessly, gave up on the reins and held fast to the horn of her saddle so she wouldn't fall off.

'Cost her two cats,' said Heinz. 'Two of her favourites. Still, we can always do with the tomatoes.'

Heinz fixed the aerial in two hours and told tales for another three. The Gee family sat and listened transfixed, albeit at a distance. Cleanliness was next to Godliness in their household and they all said their prayers. They listened in awe, horror and fascination and laughed till the tears flowed. Heinz downed half a dozen beers to keep his larynx lubricated before setting off home in the fading light.

Riding a bike in bull dust in pitch darkness was not a new experience for Heinz, but on every previous occasion he'd had the weight of his massive cheeks overhanging the sides of his saddle to stabilise him. Denied this facility by recent injury, the ride home turned into a slip-sliding, tumbling nightmare. He lost count of the times he ploughed the dust with his face. By the time he reached home his temper was as filthy as his suit, his bum was on fire and bleeding again, and he just knew there'd be no dinner worth eating awaiting him.

At least his dinner was hot. Moira had left it in the oven and kept the oven hot. The mashed potato had formed a dry and barren crust, the tinned peas had blackened, and the sausages had shrunk to a shadow of their former selves.

'These sausages bought?' Heinz asked suspiciously. It must have been the German in Heinz because he had a passion for sausages. Some said that snags were the true love of his life.

'Does it matter?' Moira replied sweetly. She was stroking her newly installed favourite, a ginger tom called Mogs which purred contentedly in her lap. It had the most disconcerting yellow eyes.

'Yes it does, love. Are they bought?'

Moira looked at him and kept smiling. 'That's for me to know and you to find out.' Her voice slurred from an afternoon spent nursing brandies but she hadn't altogether lost her wits.

Heinz was hungry, desperately hungry, but not so hungry that he was keen to bite into her mystery bags without first determining what was in them. Not after the episode with the spaghetti. If she could fool him with spaghetti, what could she do with sausages? Her smile worried him. He sniffed the snags. They smelled wonderful as all sausages do when they're cooked, even the really cheap ones. But that brought him no closer to a solution. He could usually tell when sausages were home-made or shop bought, but not when they were so shrivelled up.

'What kind are they?'

'Why would you care? You put on so much tomato sauce. They could be dead cat for all you'd know.' She smiled archly. Ginger Mogs blinked smugly.

'You wouldn't do that to me would you, love? Not after a hard day's work?'

'Nah . . . not seeing as how you hate frozen sausages.'

Heinz winced. Her smile was as frosty as her late cats.

'C'mon, tell us,' he whined. Heinz hated it when he whined, hated being at her mercy for anything, but his cavernous belly had set to rumbling and wasn't to be denied.

'Store bought,' she said abruptly. 'Steve claims they're chicken. You'd never know.'

'Store bought,' repeated Heinz nervously. She'd given in too easily. She usually liked to see him suffer. She held all the cards so why had she thrown them away? 'Store bought,' he muttered again, desperately trying to add credibility to the claim. He gave up and plunged his fork into a snag and bit it in two. He examined the remaining half as he chewed, saw plenty of bread and gristle and an unhealthy ooze of fat, the kind of stuff Steve the butcher added to make the meat go further. He began to relax. For bangers that were nigh cremated they weren't half bad, particularly when dipped in a puddle of Big Red, and followed by scorched mashed potato impregnated with pea buckshot. He was almost begining to enjoy himself when he noticed Moira watching every bite.

'Home-made,' she said, triumphantly. There was no mistaking the glee and malice in her voice. 'Just like Steve's. Plenty of fat to hide the taste. Ya shouldn't have done it Heinz, not to Smokey, not to Snuffy.' She turned away leaving Heinz wondering just what the hell he was eating.

He looked around helplessly and saw more pairs of yellow eyes glaring malevolently back. A piece of sausage stuck in his throat. What did they know that he didn't?

'Ever heard of cat sausages?' asked Moira vindictively, and began cackling like a witch.

Heinz had a terrible night. He couldn't believe that Moira would feed one of her dearest departed moggies through his sausage mincer, but his head had trouble convincing his stomach of the fact. Then there was the other disconcerting thought that if she hadn't made the sausages out of dead cat, what had she made them out of? Maybe Smokey and/or Snuffy were the better option. All the same, he could see the funny side of it. It would make a hell of a story. All night long his stomach churned and his bum burned so bad it made lying on his back impossible.

He finally fell asleep just before the sun dragged itself over the horizon for another wearying day of relentless heat. Moira woke him at seven but he couldn't get out of bed. His limbs felt leaden, his sight uncertain. Just trying to get up made him feel dizzy and sweat oozed pungently from his skin.

'I'm not well, love,' he said. 'Reckon it was the sausages.'

'Serves you right,' said Moira and disappeared to make a cup of tea. She brought him a cup and began to take things seriously when Heinz couldn't sit up to drink it.

'If it ain't enough that you try to poison me,' he said. 'Now me bum's giving me gip as well.'

'And whose fault is that?' she said. But Moira was worried. She knew the sausages weren't to blame because Heinz had made them himself when they'd slaughtered a couple of chooks a week earlier. All she'd done was discover them hidden behind jam pots in the fridge, given them a cursory and precautionary sniff, and cooked them. At worst they were only a tiny bit off. But she wasn't about to tell Heinz that. True suffering, she knew, was mostly in the mind. Let him think he'd eaten Snuffy.

'Better call a doctor.'

'You kidding? You reckon a doctor's gunna come all the way out here just 'cause you're running a temperature? They don't come till you're dying and don't get here till you're dead. Far as I can see, you're neither.'

'Feel real crook, love.'

'Tough.'

Moira left him and went to tidy up and start making lunch and dinner. She'd discovered years ago that a little early preparation went a long way after an afternoon in the pub. It was no good trying to do things once the brandy had taken hold as it had a habit of doing, usually about the time the sun sank into the bull dust. She liked to arrange things so that all she had to do was put a few pans on the cooker and hope to take them off before they'd boiled dry. Mostly she got her timing right, but the black bottoms of her saucepans bore mute testimony to the times she hadn't. She decided to make Heinz veal schnitzel for lunch to cheer him up. The only problem was, she wasn't sure if she had any veal. The kitchen freezer was full of frozen bread, lamb chops and pieces of steak, a can of beer that Heinz had forgotten to take out and which had popped, but no schnitzel. Her only chance lay with the big walk-in commercial freezer, the little kitty Auschwitz and relic from pastoral days. The freezer was in the shed where Heinz lovingly made his sausages, and they used it to store the sides of lamb, beef and pork, and the slabs of chuck steak for the cats, all of which they bought direct from the abattoir. A couple of cats followed her as she walked reluctantly across the yard to the freezer shed. She didn't like going inside the freezer because the inside door release had long since given up the ghost. She was afraid the door would slam behind her and trap her inside.

Typically, Heinz had a Heath Robinson system of preventing such a thing occurring, something that did the job but never entirely satisfactorily. Moira eyed with trepidation the stake he used to prop the door open, and cautiously stepped inside. Heinz always labelled and dated everything he put in the freezer, her unfortunate cats being the one notable exception. But they weren't meant to be eaten, not even in sausages. Moira read the labels on the little freezer packages impatiently and was about to give up when she finally found what she was looking for. 'Snizzles,' said the label, which she reckoned was near enough. She stepped gingerly over the stake, kicked it down and locked the freezer behind her.

The morning heat hit her like a blast from a large explosive. She was already sweating from tension and effort and was lathered by the time she reached the sanctuary of her kitchen. She poured herself a little fortifier, a cup of brandy to steady her nerves. It helped her handle the shock when midday rolled along and she took the schnitzel in to Heinz, generously crumbed and fried golden. He knocked it back. Didn't want to eat it. Didn't want to eat anything. Didn't even want a beer. Didn't want a beer? Moira couldn't remember a single occasion when Heinz had said no to a schnitzel, let alone said no to a beer.

'You must be sick,' she said, flopping onto his bedside chair.

'What I've been telling you, love,' he croaked.

'Reckon you're dying?'

'Might be, love. Just might be. Don't know for sure because I've never died before.' He lay sweating and helpless on his massive stomach, gasping like a beached pilot whale in faded pyjama bottoms.

'Turn over,' said Moira, 'so I can feel your forehead.'

'Can't, love,' mumbled Heinz. 'Bum's too sore.'

Moira put her hand on his shoulder and pulled it away sharply. 'You're roastin'! You're burnin' up. Coulda cooked the veal on your back! Reckon you're sick enough to call the doctor.'

'What I've been saying.'

'Yeah, but you look more like dying now than you did this morning.' She thoughtlessly put her hand on his bum to help herself get up out of the bedside chair.

'Yeeooowwwwww!' said Heinz.

'Sorry!' Moira snatched her hand away. It was something she always did, used him as leverage whenever she was getting to her feet, and she'd done it without thinking. 'Sorry, love, sorry!'

'Yeeoowwww . . .' moaned Heinz.

Moira struggled to cope, what with the heat, the effects of the brandy and Heinz knocking back his lunch. Now this. She'd never heard him carry on like it before. Heinz never seemed to feel pain, he was just too big and strong and affable. She thought pain had given up on him. His writhing and squirming staggered her.

'Let me have a look,' she said, and gently eased his pyjamas over his twin hummocks. 'Oh love a duck!' she said. 'Oh bloomin' heck. Oh Jeez, love.' She'd expected to see little raw patches where he'd parted company with bits of his epidermis, but found instead angry, swollen, pus-filled, suppurating craters. She hadn't poisoned him with the sausages but poison had found him anyway. 'Oh deary, deary me!' she said.

Moira rang the doctor in Collarenebri, but he was down in Sydney cooling off. She rang the hospital at Narrabri, but could only get through to a nurse who sounded about fifteen years old. The nurse suggested she ring Dubbo or the hospital at Tamworth. Moira poured herself another cup of fortifier to steady her nerves. It wasn't supposed to be like this. Heinz never got sick. She got sick but Heinz, never. She'd never had to call a doctor for him before, not even when he recklessly caught the tip of his wozzer in his zip. You could still see the scar, like lizard tracks. She got through to a doctor in Dubbo who sounded suitably concerned. He told her to keep Heinz cool with damp towels and a fan, and to try to bring his temperature down. He asked if she had antibiotics. She didn't. He asked if she could get some. She couldn't. The Sunset Downs pharmacy went belly up before the stock and station shop, and that had folded ten years earlier. He said he'd arrange for a doctor or a flying ambulance, and to ring him every hour.

Flying ambulance! Moira sat stunned in her kitchen chair, immobile but for the steady movement of cup to lip, staggered by the sudden turn of events. It all seemed like a bad dream. It couldn't be happening to Heinz! What would she do without him? What would happen to her? She sipped harder and harder on her comforter as one dire consequence after another scrolled past her eyes. Finally she remembered the doctor's instructions and soaked some towels.

By the time she'd set about reducing his temperature Heinz had become incoherent, slipping in and out of consciousness. Moira was frightened. Sure their marriage wasn't everything it ought to be, but they were all either of them had. Sure they fought and tormented each other, but how would they fill their days if they didn't? Their lives revolved around each other. Moira set up the fan so that it blew a steady stream of air across Heinz's bottom. As an afterthought, she took his temperature the way she'd seen nurses do in smutty English comedies. The thermometer sat up proudly from his awful orifice like the flag atop Iwo Jima. But not even her shaking hands or the fine print could deny the evidence. Forty-point-five! She rang the doctor.

'More wet towels,' he said. 'Make ice packs. Try to keep his temperature down.' A plane was on the way to Collarenebri he assured her, and an ambulance on the way from there.

Moira thought of hopping on her bike and riding the six kilometres into town to get help. But who would she get?

Who'd still be sober? And besides, she didn't want to leave Heinz just in case. Just in case what? She thought about the question but didn't dare answer it. She stole into the bedroom and once more planted the thermometer in the spot between Heinz's cheeks. Forty-one. Forty-one! She wrung her hands. What could she do? She knew the system. They didn't send a doctor out unless someone was dying, and he never got to Sunset Downs before they'd died.

Died. Dead. Gone.

Tears actually flowed from Moira's eyes as she confronted the prospect. What could she do? How could she get his temperature down? She just knew it was going to keep climbing until his poor heart burst. She absently picked up the plate of cold schnitzel to give to her cats when she remembered where she'd got it from, and slammed headlong into the obvious solution. Both she and Heinz had matching steel frame beds but with one significant difference. Moira had taken the castors off hers so she didn't have to climb up so far to go to bed. Heinz had left his on so he didn't have so far to fall when he was drunk. Given their difference in height, it was a fair arrangement.

A comet tail of curious cats led by Ginger Mogs gathered behind her as she began the tricky job of man-oeuvring Heinz's bed through the house and out onto the verandah. Heinz moaned every time she collided with a door frame or side-swiped a table, but she finally succeeded. She needed a brandy desperately but the circumstances demanded sacrifice. The steps down to the yard posed a bit of a problem but Heinz always left bits of wood lying around. She found a couple of palings roughly even in length and a broken piece of fibro to lay over them. Even to her inexpert eye the make-shift ramp looked dodgy, but what choice did she have? She lined Heinz's bed up and, watched by her faithful followers, threw her weight behind it. It teetered briefly on the brink before gravity took hold. Everything went well until the front castors hit the soft bull dust and dug in. The bed stopped dead, catapulting Heinz forward. If his head hadn't hit the bed end quite so hard the castors would probably have stayed stuck there, leaving Heinz exposed to the full blast of the sun. Instead, the bed bucked under the impact and jumped a giant step into the yard. The ramp collapsed beneath the rear castors, but by then she only had two steps left to negotiate.

'Uuurrghh!' said Heinz.

'Ahhhhhh!' said Heinz.

'Ooohh!' said Heinz.

But the first hurdle had been successfully negotiated and the bed sat squarely on the ground. Moira heard a high-pitched squeak from Ginger Mogs, turned and saw him watching with the strangest look on his face. All the other cats were following suit. She couldn't be sure but it crossed her mind that this was the cat version of laughter.

'You cut that out,' she scolded, but to no effect.

They followed her as she put her shoulder to the bed and heaved and shoved it across the yard and into the freezer shed. Sweat poured off her in streams large enough to fish in. Her dress clung to her like a wetsuit. She collapsed, moaning, onto her knees. Her cats gathered around her. Perhaps they would have liked to show concern but they still couldn't wipe the silly looks off their faces. Nothing like this had ever happened before.

Moira crawled on her hands and knees around the bed, staggered to her feet and opened the freezer door. Problem. How could she prop the door open while she pushed the bed in? More importantly, how could she make sure it didn't close behind her? She realised she'd have to hold the door open with her bottom while she pulled the bed partly inside, then use the bed to keep the door open while she crawled under it to get back out. The cats watched in fascination.

To Moira's credit, her plan worked to perfection. She managed to push the bed the final half a metre into the freezer using her leg to keep the door open. She backed slowly out, the cold air slowing the flow of her sweat. She picked up the stake and jammed it to keep the door partially open. After all, she didn't want to risk freezing Heinz to death as he'd frozen her cats. Satisfied that she'd done all she could for him, she staggered back to the kitchen to do what she could for herself. It had been years since she'd exerted herself so much. Her heart pounded, her breath rasped, and her hands trembled like a stray cat in a dog pound as she poured herself another cup of brandy.

'Cheers,' she said automatically then let the fiery liquid work its spell. Lord, she was buggered. She gulped when she should have sipped and let her head loll heavily upon her heaving breast.

Meanwhile, the cats had been seized by that sometimes fatal affliction called curiosity. Ginger Mogs led the way, taking the first tentative steps into the unknown. It smelled meaty and interesting and like no place they'd ever been before. Temporarily at least, it also afforded a blessed relief from the heat. Other cats followed, noses flexing inquisitively, brows furrowed in concentration. They stood on hind legs to sniff frozen carcasses. Ginger Mogs stopped rigid when he encountered a frozen stream of cat piss, the legacy of the recently deceased Snuffy. It spooked him. Ginger Mogs didn't know the first thing about freezing but he knew Snuffy was dead. He also knew dead cats don't piss. If Heinz's hand hadn't slipped off the bed at that critical instant and cuffed Ginger Mogs about the ear, there'd have been no cause for the cats to panic. Ginger Mogs shrieked and spun in mid-air, his claws fought desperately for traction on the icy floor, finally bit and propelled him back out through the door like a steel ball bearing from a slingshot. The other cats hadn't waited for their leader. They'd fled at first cry. God only knows which one of them had sent the stake flying, but Ginger Mogs was lucky to scrape past the door before it slammed shut behind him.

The cats bolted back to the kitchen to tell Moira what they'd done, but she was long past being told anything. She'd surrendered to the heat, the tension, the exertions and her little cup of medicinal. If the wind had been blowing from the west, her snores would have been heard in the pub.

The ambulance arrived guided by Barry the barman and followed by everyone who happened to be in town at the time. They found Moira in the kitchen and didn't wait for her to wake up and tell them where Heinz was. You didn't need a black tracker to spot the trail leading to the freezer shed and work out his probable whereabouts. The paramedic had come expecting to treat toxaemia and a raging temperature, and instead found himself dealing with advanced hypothermia. He didn't know whether to leave Heinz out in the sun to thaw or rug him up in the back of the ambulance. In the end they rugged him up and arranged for the plane to meet them at a bush airstrip belonging to a local wool grower.

The doctors were unsure just how Heinz managed to beat the system and survive. Some reckoned hypothermia shut down his vital systems before the poison in his blood-stream could, and that had saved him. Others claimed that freezing slowed down his metabolism just enough to buy them the time they needed to treat him. The more reasonable among the fraternity reckoned it was just one of those things that happen from time to time. But Heinz never entertained the slightest doubt about what had saved his life. Not what so much as who. Moira had saved him. He owed his life to her and her quick thinking, and his belief increasingly assumed the substance of fact the more he told his tale.

Moira never understood why the freezer door had closed after she'd been so careful to prop it open, but kept her concerns to herself. Everything had turned out for the best and, besides, Heinz made her out to be a heroine. She saw no reason to confuse the issue. It would be nice to think they got on like love birds from that day on, having realised their dependence upon each other and the consequences of the loss of either, but of course they didn't. They still belittled, humiliated and sabotaged each other every chance they got. But Heinz was never again as hurtful in gaining his revenge, and the tomato patch gained no more little crosses.

Psycho Cat

I don't like cats. I've never had a cat. So for most of my life my dislike of cats has been irrelevent, a matter of no significance whatsoever. Then Reg came along. Apparently it's not unknown for cats to suffer from mental disorders like schizophrenia and paranoia. When I tell this story a lot of people automatically assume Reg was in the grip of some kind of psychosis and feel sorry for him. If you're tempted to join these bleeding hearts, take my advice – don't! There was nothing wrong with Reg that drowning couldn't fix and, believe me, that's what the little bugger needed far more than your pity. Reg wasn't mentally disturbed, he was simply deliberately malicious. Vindictive is another word that springs to mind. Reg never did anything without weighing up the consequences. He liked to maximise pain, disruption and destruction. Yes, I know what you're going to say. Cats' brains aren't capable of complex thought, of planning things like revenge; that cats lack the ability to reason. But you're wrong. Wrong, wrong, wrong. Reg proved that.

Never look after anyone else's pet, particularly if that pet is a cat, and more particularly if it means admitting it into your home. Especially if home is on the second floor of a

51

three-storey apartment block. It doesn't matter how well you know the cat's owners or how much you like them. Just tell them no. No! You can attach any excuse you think they might swallow. Cry asthma. Plead allergies. But say no.

I wish we'd said no to Yvonne and Alan. Perhaps they'd still be our friends. Perhaps my nice raw silk shirt would still have long sleeves. When Yvonne and Alan announced they were going to Lord Howe Island for two weeks, I don't think my wife, Mish, raced to volunteer to look after Reg. Mish is not a cat person. The only tummy she rubs is mine and even then nowhere near as often as I'd like. We'd met Reg before, when we'd had dinner at Yvonne and Alan's, and he seemed a perfectly ordinary cat. Slept most of the time. But Mish didn't cry asthma and she didn't plead allergies, and Yvonne did pour a bucket of wine into her. So we wound up with Reg.

It wasn't the first time Yvonne and Alan had gone away and dumped Reg on unsuspecting friends. We should have been suspicious when none of their other friends volunteered to take him on. Suddenly they were all going away, or looking after other people's dogs, or pleading asthma, allergies, anything that would disqualify them. That really should have warned us.

My memory of Reg was that he was mostly white with two ginger patches, a small one over his left eye and a larger one like a saddle on his back. It wasn't until they'd dropped him off and I'd had a chance to look at him that I noticed that Reg had another side to him. He had a black patch, like a pirate's, over his right eye and cheek. I had to check with Mish that we'd got the right cat and they hadn't pulled a switch on us. He didn't look like the same cat. He didn't look anywhere near as friendly or as sleepy. That should have warned us as well.

I've heard of cats sleeping on the warm clothes in driers and being inadvertently sent for a terminal spin. Well, who's to know whether it was inadvertent or not? If only Reg had chosen to sleep in the drier. It would have saved us a lot of aggravation. Would have been the perfect crime as far as I'm concerned.

Reg arrived in a nineteenth-century French wicker cat basket which probably cost as much as a small car. It was a cunning arrangement with two side flaps meeting at the top so that the precious beast couldn't do a runner. Funnily enough, I think Mish was quite looking forward to playing with Reg and having him sit purring on her lap. A substitute for the child we had no intention of having. She couldn't wait for Reg to get out of his little basket. She talked to him and coaxed him and generally made a complete babbling idiot of herself, but do you think that stroppy cat would budge? No way.

He yowled through the seven o'clock news. Cried pitifully through the 'Seven-Thirty Report'. I figured he was just tuning up so that it could be a cop car siren when 'NYPD Blue' came on.

'You'll have to do something,' said Mish.

Me? Do something? When did Reg become my problem? I could have sworn Yvonne asked Mish to look after the bloody thing. I don't recall her asking me. And I'm damn sure Yvonne didn't pour a bucket of wine down my throat. But Mish was writing a creative strategy for the relaunch of a detergent. Clearly she could not be interrupted by something as trifling as a cat when someone as trifling as her husband was alongside, doing nothing but keeping the telly company. I was wearing my nice raw silk shirt, a legacy from the days when I also worked in an advertising agency as a copywriter.

I'd just put the gun to the creative director's head for a massive salary hike when the recession hit and the business contracted. I was out faster than a bad curry. Now I sell used cars while I try to find a way back in. My wife, who now earns almost five times more than me, is very sympathetic. That's why I had to get up and do something about Reg, not her.

In hindsight I should have just tipped the basket upside down and given it a good shake. Where was the cat going to go? What was he going to do? He couldn't have held on forever. Instead, I reached into the basket. It may have been an antique cat basket but it felt more like a high-tech shredder.

'Yeeooowwww!' Reg screamed.

'Yeeooowwww!' I screamed. You wouldn't believe that one cat could do so much damage so quickly.

'What are you doing to him?' screamed Mish.

What was *I* doing to *him*? I offered the olive branch, he drew the sword. Twenty of them to be precise, five per paw, all needle sharp and all strategically employed. The sleeves of my nice raw silk shirt never stood a chance. Reg turned them into spaghetti. Then he tried to turn my arms into bolognaise. I lifted them free of the basket but the problem was Reg was still attached. The next mistake I made was in trying to shake him free. Have you ever seen a possum sliding down a tree trunk? Now imagine the trunk is your arm.

'Yeeooowwww!' I said.

'Yeeooowwww!' Reg said.

'*What the hell are you doing to him!*' screamed Mish. She raced over and snatched Reg from me. Reg let her. Reg lay on his back in her arms and gazed soulfully into her eyes.

Reg let her tickle his tummy and cuddle him. Reg became her Reggie-weggie pussy-wussy. He gave her what I like to call his brown eye, though it was really ginger.

'What did he do to you?' said Mish. She cooed and soothed and oohed and ahhhed.

'Stuff him!' I said. 'Look what he's done to me. Look what he's done to my nice raw silk shirt. Stick his front legs in the blender so he'll learn.' I showed her my ripped and shredded shirt. I showed her the scratches all over my arms, parallel and intersecting, like a miniature railway shunting yard. I showed her the blue–black and bleeding puncture marks where Reg had sunk his teeth.

'You must have done something to him,' she said. Then, 'Don't drip blood on the carpet.'

Reg sat on her lap and purred while she wrote her creative strategy and pointedly failed to ask my advice. I was once a copywriter. She'll only ever be a suit. What would she know about creative strategies? I painted my wounds with antiseptic and brooded over the destruction of my shirt. Did I tell you it cost me one hundred and fifty dollars? Not much for an advertising man but a fortune for a used car salesman. Even so, I was still prepared to give Reg the benefit of the doubt. Perhaps he was just nervous being in strange surrounds and I'd frightened him. How I flattered myself.

I was the one who spread newspapers on the floor, filled a large plastic laundry bowl with Kitty Litter, and set it in the kitchen with a saucer of milk in case the little darling needed to replenish any fluids during the night. I padded out his little basket with a bath towel so he'd have a nice, cosy little nest to sleep in. Job done, we went to bed.

Our apartment block was built on three sides around a triangular courtyard and garden. This was so that on hot nights none of the inward facing apartments would get any breeze, no matter how wide we opened the windows. It also guaranteed a lack of privacy. So on hot nights we'd temporarily draw the curtains until we'd finished reading, turn off the lights then throw back the curtains and pray that a breeze would somehow find our window. Our first night with Reg was a hot night. We lay on top of the bed in the darkness without a stitch on, looking out and into the windows of the apartments opposite that still had their lights on, wishing they'd turn them off. Mish's hand began to tickle my tummy. This can be interpreted as a good sign and so it proved to be. Until Reg decided we should go public.

Mish said he was just bored. She said he must have seen the shadow on the door surrounds and thought it was a lizard or some other small creature. So he attacked it. I've always believed that cats could see in the dark. If so, I don't know how Reg could possibly mistake the light switch for a lizard. But apparently he did. Suddenly the cat leaped up, hit the switch and put us in the spotlight, providing AO entertainment for the entire apartment block. And didn't they clap and cheer! Mish dived under the covers but I had to face the additional humiliation of jumping off the bed to turn out the light. More laughter. And ironic jeers directed, I suspect, at my fading glory.

I didn't get much sleep that night and no more of what I had been getting before Reg pulled his stunt. Mish said he'd settle down and I believed her. But oh, no. I made the discovery when I came back from my run. I undressed and stepped blithely into the shower. There was something in there that had never been there before. A horror beyond imagining, squelching through my toes, assaulting the olfactories. I've heard of cats peeing in baths and basins before but Reg had surpassed himself.

He'd left a pussy pudding on the plughole.

Reg had walked past his Kitty Litter to do what he did in the shower. It was a deliberate act of intimidation so that he could gauge the extent of our tolerance, or the force of our retaliation. Did we retaliate? Of course not! Mish wouldn't allow it. Neither would she allow any size ten boot up the tail shaft when Reg walked back past his Kitty Litter to pee on the carpet. He learned that he could pee with impunity, so he did.

What do they put in cat's pee that makes it impervious to all known stain removers? Before long, our lovely white carpet which had been bought on a copywriter's salary had become patterned with yellowing maps of Australia. Three thousand dollars' worth of pure wool carpet destroyed in three days of deliberate provocation by that cat and his Made-in-Taiwan bladder. The trouble was, with both of us working and no one home to supervise, Reg the deliberately incontinent had gone about his business wherever the fancy had taken him.

I caught him at it one night. I'd always believed that cats like to pee in private. They're not like dogs. Dogs are very social piddlers and do it wherever they can whenever they can and preferably with an audience. Like Frenchmen on holiday. Every lamp post, tree, fence, car tyre is fair game. But you rarely catch cats doing it. I caught Reg doing it alongside the telly while we were watching 'Cracker'. I went ballistic.

'Bloody cat!' I screamed, and leaped up to convert him into a Davy Crockett hat.

'Don't hurt him!' yelled Mish.

Hurt him? I wanted to *kill* him. But you can't kill what you can't catch and I couldn't catch Reg. He was off, literally, like a scalded cat. Under tables, under sofas, under beds. I admit I overreacted. I admitted as much to Mish. But she ignored me, turned her back on me. Honestly, you'd think I'd deliberately knocked her Clarice Cliff vase over. Personally, I think if someone special like your grandmother leaves you a four thousand dollar vase, you should keep it somewhere safe. Not leave it on the table with a whacking great bunch of flowers in it so that it can easily overbalance. I blamed Reg, she blamed me. After she'd mopped up the water and picked up the broken pieces of vase, she took off to our bedroom to sulk. Reg lay under the sofa and gloated.

I thought my luck had changed at the yard next day when a bloke and his wife came back for a third test drive of a Mazda 626. It sounded to me like he was selling her so I just let him get on with it, agreeing with him whenever I thought it appropriate.

'Corners well,' he said.

'Yeah,' I agreed. 'Like a scared cat on carpet.'

'Goes,' he said.

'Like custard out of a cat,' I said.

'Quiet,' he said.

'Like a cat under water.'

'That's enough,' his wife said.

I thought she was sold but when we got back to the yard she showed no interest in the car at all. Couldn't get away fast enough. How about some people! They jerk you around for days, waste your time, cost you money, then just take off. How am I supposed to make a living with people like that around? How am I going to get four thousand dollars to buy Mish a new vase?

Things went from bad to worse. A lady came in who'd had her eye on a little Barina. The price was right but more importantly, the *colour* was right. Forget the sticky valves and dodgy shocks. The *colour* was *her colour*. You dream about customers like this. In the trade they're known as wood ducks. So we went for a little drive. She was a bit nervous so we gave the main road a miss and trundled around the narrow back streets. Now, I ask you, what harm can you come to trundling around narrow back streets? Well, you see, there were these two cats, a black one and a big tabby. I don't know whether they were having a blue or having it away, but the tabby made a bolt for it just as we drew near. Why did it have to run out onto the street? Why did the black one have to chase? My dream customer panicked, swerved and nearly drove up a lamp post before bringing the car to a stop. Perhaps if she'd only run over one of the cats I might still have made the sale. Perhaps congratulating her on her aim wasn't the smartest thing I've done, either.

The boss called me into his office and put me on notice. Shift cars or shove off was his basic drift. You can imagine how I was feeling when I got home. Reg didn't make me feel any better. He'd amused himself by climbing up the curtains and sliding back down. Our lace curtains must have had just enough resistance to ensure a pleasant trip. They hung in strips. If you've ever torn up an old sheet for bandages you'll appreciate how they looked. When I saw them I should have stopped and taken in the damage. But I was dumbstruck. Italian lace turned into tagliatelli. I walked up towards them wanting to feel and touch, unwilling to believe that what my eyes were telling me was true. If I'd been able to drag my peepers away I might have noticed the little booby trap Reg had left in the middle of the hall, but I didn't, and trampled it all through the lounge. Pussy pudding in the velvet plush.

I'd had a hand in the demise of two cats that day and was hustling Reg towards the spin drier when Mish walked in.

'Look what you've done!' she cried.

Look what *I've* done? Reg came out from under the sofa and rubbed up against her legs.

'Look what Reggie-weggie has done to our curtains,' I said.

'My God,' she said.

'And guess what?' I said. 'It wasn't me but nice little pussy-wussy who did nasty little poo-poos on the carpet.'

'Oh my God,' she said.

'You hold him down,' I said. 'You don't have to kill him. I'll do that. I think I'll enjoy it.'

She looked down at Reg. Reg looked up at her. Then calmly stepped into his Kitty Litter and christened it. How can you beat a cat for doing what it's supposed to do?

'Good cat,' said Mish. She looked at me uncertainly. 'I think he's got the message,' she said.

That night we shared a bottle or two of commiserating wine and discussed what we were going to do about Reg. Mish had spoken to a carpet cleaning outfit that assured her they could restore our carpet to its former glory. The local dry cleaner's sewing service assured her my nice raw silk shirt would still be nice with short sleeves. That just left fourteen hundred dollars worth of lace curtains and the four thousand dollar Clarice Cliff vase unaccounted for. I suggested we hand Yvonne and Alan a bill for damages, but Mish wouldn't hear of it. So we sat and tried to figure out how we could possibly survive the remaining ten days without going bankrupt in the process.

We decided that Reg was anxious because he missed his owners, and bored because he was locked in all day. The more wine we drank the more we convinced ourselves that this would explain Reg's aberrant behaviour. Apparently he was well-behaved at home. There were no torn curtains or tie-dyed carpet at Yvonne and Alan's. No nasty little surprises in the shower. When Yvonne and Alan fobbed Reg off onto us they told us he was a little angel, always used his Kitty Litter and liked nothing more than to snuggle up close and deafen them with his purring. Yes, this was the same cat they were talking about.

We decided the cat should be let out for a wander every morning and evening. Let him have a bit of a sniff and a play, and let him brown innocent little patches of grass. He would be safe enough in the triangular garden below. We thought that after so much unrelieved excitement all he'd do all day was sleep. We went to bed, smug and secure in the knowledge that we'd solved all our problems. We turned the light out, pulled back the curtains and Mish began to tickle my stomach. A gentle breeze somehow found its way to our window. God was in his heaven and Reg was in his basket. So we thought. Mish had forgotten to close the bedroom door so Reg attacked the lizard on the door frame. Once more we went public.

I start work before Mish but for some reason it also became my job to take Reg outside for his morning prowl. Mish said something about not being able to face the neighbours. I could, I suppose, because I sell cars for a living and therefore have a hide thicker than a rhino's. I put Reg down in the middle of the triangle of grass.

'Have a good sniff, mate,' I said. 'Then do what a cat's got to do.'

Reg hesitated, looked around, weighed up his options, and bolted. He took off. Across the lawn and out through the arch that was the only exit onto the street. Where was the lady in the Barina when I needed her? I raced after Reg but by the time I reached the pavement there was no sign of him anywhere. There weren't that many places to hide. A row of letterboxes, a waist-high brick wall, a patch of grass, a strip of flowers and two struggling gums which were the developer's nod to landscaping. For once there were no parked cars outside. So where was Reg? My watch was unequivocal. It was time for me to go to work. Mish was also unequivocal. There was no way I was going to work until Reg was found.

I promised and I lied. As soon as her car was out of sight, I took off as well. Losing a cat was one thing. Losing my job was another.

Am I wrong to ascribe malice to a cat? Is it possible for a cat to be evil? If you believe the boffins, cats' brains aren't big enough or sufficiently developed for them to be troubled by such trifling matters as morality or philosophy. Cats don't ask who am I, where did I come from, where am I going? There have been no great cat philosophers, not even in the Pharaohs' time when cats were regarded as gods.

No, according to the experts, cats know exactly what they are. They're cats. They know exactly where they came from, which is where they've just been. And they know exactly where they're going, which is the direction they're facing. That's it as far as morality and philosophy are concerned if you're a cat. They might think, but they don't reason. But none of the experts have met Reg, and if they had, they might revise their opinions, rewrite their textbooks, perhaps even rejig the evolutionary tree.

Reg reasoned. Reg had worked out exactly what he had to do to upset us most. We'd taken to speaking in whispers in case he was listening, trying to ferret out another weak spot, another point to attack. Reg was evil, knew he was evil, enjoyed being evil.

When he ran away from me in the garden he'd had no doubts about the consequences, the chaos and distress he'd cause. It was quite a masterstroke, when you think about it. If I stayed home to look for him I'd lose my job. Reg had overheard us talking about that. If I went to work – that is, if Mish found out I'd gone to work – I'd lose all marital privileges until the year twenty-fifty, or the death of Prince Charles' heirs and successors, whichever occurred last. Don't tell me Reg didn't know what he was doing.

I went to work and got bawled out for being late. Ditto when I left early. Well I had to get home before Mish so I could at least pretend that I'd spent the day looking for Reg. I must admit that when I finally began looking in earnest I did hope to find a Reg-coloured road rug, a moggy mat, a flat cat whose use-by date had come, preferably under the twenty-six wheels of a Mack truck.

No such luck. He wasn't up the tree or in the yards of any of the houses nearby. Mish arrived home and together we knocked on doors. Nobody had Reg and nobody had even seen him. Mish started to fret and panic.

'You'll have to do something,' she kept saying.

I was doing something. I was trying not to smile. I was trying not to laugh. I was trying to think of the name of the little restaurant someone had just recommended, where I could take Mish for dinner to celebrate Reg's disappearance and assumed demise without making it seem like a celebration. Honestly, it was the best I'd felt in a week.

We didn't change or phone to book a table. We just turned up and were shown a table for two in a quiet corner. Maybe the waiter took a look at Mish's face and realised we'd suffered a recent bereavement. We had an excellent meal, an excellent wine, and tried to work out what we'd say to Yvonne and Alan. By the end of the night Mish seemed to have got over the loss and didn't entirely dismiss my suggestion that a bit of tummy tickling might be in order. I'd just put the car in the carport when Mish remembered that we hadn't collected our mail.

'You get it,' she said. I wonder what would have happened if she'd got it instead. I flicked up the little metal door and stuck my hand in the letterbox. It's one of those long thin jobs that require you to stick half your arm in to reach the letters at the front. I'd done it a hundred times before and I did it without thinking. How did Reg know which box was ours? How did he know that I'd get the mail, not Mish? How long had he lain there, waiting, anticipating? You must have seen those machines councils have that munch up tree branches. One minute you have a tree branch, next minute you have sawdust. Reg must have seen one too because he gave a damn good impression of one.

'Yeeooowwww!' said Reg.

'Yeeooowwww!' I screamed.

'You found him!' squealed Mish. She dragged Reg out, she cuddled him, she fussed over him and he gave her his sweet-as-pie brown eye. He purred and padded his paws against her hand-knitted top. Even by the carport light I could see his claws pulling out tufts of wool so that Mish could never wear that top again. I said nothing. Let Mish suffer loss as well. My right hand and wrist were scratched and stinging. Blood soaked into the linen cuff of my nice linen shirt. It didn't matter. The sleeve was shredded and facing amputation. How many times can a man lose his arms, I ask you? How many short-sleeved shirts is enough?

I gathered the tattered remnants of what had been our mail. There was one Telstra envelope that would never be re-used, and inside it a bill which would never be paid. How can you pay a bill you can't read? ASIO's shredder couldn't have done a better job. There was a card from Yvo . . . and . . . lan showing . . . d's Bea . . . Yvonne and Alan showing Ned's Beach. I could work that out. But I couldn't work out the letter from the advertising agency, J. Walter Thompson. Reg had saved his best work for that. I could read my name on the envelope so I knew it was a reply to my job application, but I couldn't make out much else. I knew the creative director and I know I should have rung. But I'd have to ring from the car yard and leave the yard's number. I couldn't see my boss copping that for an instant.

Reg had actually eaten the important bits of the letter. Everything beyond the 'Mate! Great to hear from you!' bit. I suppose I could get Mish to ring and ask for his secretary. She could explain what happened and ask them to send another copy. Mish could make a joke of it. Even so, what kind of a joke would I look?

I didn't get my tummy tickled that night. Mish thought it was important that she stayed up, talked to Reg and calmed him down. She tickled his tummy instead. But it wasn't Reg who needed calming down, it was me. That damn cat had destroyed two shirts, our carpet, our curtains, a Clarice Cliff vase and now his ambition had extended to my career. He wanted to destroy me! Make no mistake. Cold-bloodedly, with premeditation and pure malice, he wanted to destroy me.

Mish took my linen shirt to the dry cleaner to be modified like my raw silk shirt, and rang J. Walter Thompson. They arranged an interview. There was light at the end of the tunnel. Mish told me some of the lines she'd used to make fun of the disaster. 'Carson would have rung himself,' she said laughingly, 'only the cat got his tongue as well.' Apparently the creative director's secretary thought that was wildly funny. She probably told her boss, who told his mates, who told their mates, who laughed like drains. Good old Mish.

Over the next few days, Reg discovered new ways to irritate me. Sharpening his claws on the furniture was a neat trick. Mish said she had enough material left to repair the arms of the sofa. No amount of material, however, could repair the centre pedestal of our round, Victorian, walnut dining table.

'Don't make such a fuss,' Mish said. 'Nobody can see it.' I could.

It was about this time I discovered that Reg also liked to join me in a beer. I didn't know cats liked beer. Perhaps they don't. Reg, not being an ordinary cat, did. I can't believe it had taken me so long to catch on. I just thought I'd copped a ropey batch. You see, I enjoy a glass of beer when I watch TV. I don't guzzle but sip quietly and patiently. I put my glass down on the floor by the side of the sofa where it can't be knocked over when the football gets exciting. When you drink like I drink, you don't keep a watch on the level. Even so I seemed to be drinking more and liking it less. One night before I'd even taken a sip, the level had dropped by a quarter. I took a sip anyway and put my glass back down on the floor. I was puzzled and my curiosity got the better of me. I dragged my eyes away from the Sunday movie to find Reg's head in my glass and his tongue working overtime. Tuna breath had been hopping out from under the sofa and helping himself.

Was I angry? Do mozzies suck blood? We'd been sharing a beer night after night and I hadn't known. I nearly threw up. I nearly threw Reg out of the window. I nearly threw a terminal wobbly. But Mish just laughed. Thought it was hysterical. That, of course, was why Reg was always peeing. It's one of the effects beer has. That was the night I realised I had to do something. That I had to make a stand and exact revenge, not just on Reg, but on the callous, thoughtless, witless wonders who had dumped the little bugger onto us.

The cat had to be re-trained, re-programmed if you like. Before I went to bed, I half filled his bowl with beer and left it by his Kitty Litter bowl, having first topped it up with fresh Kitty Litter. I guess Reg saw this as a kind of capitulation because he came up and rubbed against my leg. I bent to stroke him and gave him a clout that shocked the daylights out of him.

'Yeeooowwww!' said Reg.

'What are you doing to him?' said Mish.

What indeed.

Mish had a breakfast meeting with a client and had to leave early. Have you heard of anything more ridiculous than breakfast meetings? Is nothing sacred? I mean, how important do some people need to feel? What the heck, let the egos rage. It suited my purposes.

Reg had responded to the bowl of beer by saturating his Kitty Litter. He'd also left his trademark pussy pudding on the plughole. I enticed him out from under the sofa with little gifts of mince to help him over his hang-over, picked him up and carried him into the shower to confront him with his indiscretion.

'Good pussy,' I said. He looked up at me suspiciously. 'No really,' I said. 'Nice pussy.' I stroked him and Reg was confused enough to let me. I gave him some more little mince balls. Well, you have to reward a cat when he does the right thing, don't you?

I set about booby trapping his Kitty Litter box while he savaged my favourite socks, the ones with the fish on them. I'd put them out on the bed along with my best trousers, best surviving shirt, and tie with matching fish. It's always a good thing to look your best when you have an interview, particularly one upon which your salvation, your sanity and the rest of your life hinges. I suppose I should be glad Reg only savaged my socks. I stripped a couple of wires and ran them around the bottom of the Kitty Litter box and connected them up to my spare car battery. I covered them with a thin layer of Kitty Litter. It didn't matter where Reg chose to go, there was no way that his little cat pee wouldn't make contact with the exposed wires and complete the circuit. I didn't think he'd want to use his Kitty Litter again for a while after that. By the time I'd finished, Reg had pulled so many threads in my socks he'd turned them into pompoms.

'Good pussy,' I said. Reg thought I'd finally lost it. Do cats smile? This one did. A Cheshire smile of triumph. I rewarded him with more little mince balls for destroying my socks. Another smile. It took him a moment to realise the last mince ball contained a chopped up dried red chilli. Well if he wasn't such a greedy guts he would have noticed and left it. He backed away, mouth gaping, looking at me incredulously. This was a cat unused to people fighting back. He really did not know what was happening. He rushed over to his saucer of milk, which I'd replaced with a bowl of beer, and drank it dry. I refilled it, just to show what a kind, thoughtful, considerate person I am. Sooner or later he was going to have the pee of his life. My only regret was that I wouldn't be there to see it.

I was late to work again, a fact that the boss wasted no time in pointing out.

'Give me one reason for not firing you now,' he said.

'I'm the son you never had,' I said.

'What do you mean?' he said. 'I got four sons.'

'You were meant to have five,' I said and walked off. He was still thinking about that when a couple of customers came in, tyre-kickers if you've ever seen them. The boss duck-shoved them onto me as punishment. I sold them the Holden Vacationer we couldn't even off-load onto other dealers, and sold it at sticker price. The boss was chuffed. A kid came in with his older brother moments later to look at the cat-killing Barina.

'Does she go?' he asked.

'Like a cat with diarrhoea,' I said.

They both laughed, thought I was a great guy. His brother talked a big act but failed to pick the sticky valves or the dodgy shocks and only screwed me down two hundred dollars on the ticket. The boss was doubly chuffed. I hoped his state of chuffedness would stand me in good stead when I came back late from lunch. Advertising interviews can drag on. And an interview is no guarantee of a job.

I made myself a coffee, sat back and put my feet up on my desk. 'How're you guys doing?' I asked the other two salesmen. They looked like they'd just swallowed a mince ball loaded with chilli. Life was definitely looking up. Would you believe I sold another car before lunch? Yep. That's how things go in the car biz. You sell nothing for days then you get mobbed. My two comrades in con grabbed the next two customers through the door. I took the third. Only the third bought. He was a young Frenchman who made straight for the Peugeot diesel wagon. There was nothing he didn't know about Peugeots and he knew enough to know that this was a good one. Hadn't been in a prang or anything. I just held his dark glasses for him then took his deposit.

'*Merci*,' I said. '*Vous avez un bon jour.*'

'My boy!' said the boss.

'Told you,' I said and held up five fingers representing the five sons he should have had. He liked that. There was no doubt about it, my luck had definitely changed and I was convinced it had changed because of the stand I'd taken with Reg. When Reg crossed my path he'd brought bad luck. When I crossed his, the bad luck rebounded onto him. I wondered how he'd coped with the little surprise in his Kitty Litter, whether the chilli had passed through him yet with its little after-burn surprise, and I wondered how he was coping with his hang-over. Two cans of full strength beer are a lot for a cat. Even for Reg.

My interview went well. The creative director took me to meet the managing director, which is always a good sign. They liked my work, but best of all they loved my cat stories. Reg had misjudged in spades. They broke up when I repeated the story about the letter, near wet themselves when I told them about my newly cropped short-sleeved shirts, and darn near bust their guts when I told them how Reg had turned the light on while Mish and I were at it. They thought I was a genius when I told them about the wired-up Kitty Litter and the chilli surprises. It's a funny thing, but for Reg's deliberate acts of sabotage I don't think the interview would have gone nearly as well. Or lasted as long.

I was an hour and a half late back from lunch. The boss just smiled and my comrades just scowled. I let them grab the next customers into the yard. It didn't matter. I knew that whoever I saw that day would buy, and that's how it turned out. I got rid of the Statesman that had got caught in the floods out west. The boss gave me a cheery wave when I left work early.

Reg was asleep when I got home, absolutely out to it. It took no time at all to move my big Bose speakers to either side of his cute little head, inches from his cute little ears, crank up the amp and let it rip. There's one thing that can be said for the 'Immigrant Song', Led Zeppelin wastes no time getting into it. Honestly, I've never seen a cat move so fast. You'd never have suspected that it was hung-over. You can forget your Ferraris and your turbo Porsches. We're talking traction here. We're talking lone cat on a greyhound track. Never mind that Russian dog they sent out into space, Reg went higher and faster.

The bowl of beer was bone dry. Yes! The Kitty Litter box had flipped over and scattered its contents all over the kitchen. Yes! Yes! And there was a trail of pussy pudding from the kitchen to the shower. Yes! Yes! Yes! I got rid of the battery, cleaned up the kitchen and washed the floor, having first confronted Reg with his indiscretion and given him a chilli-free reward. He didn't know whether he was coming or going. He didn't know what to think. Can cats look confused? Reg could and did. Then we both sat down and had a sociable beer together while we waited for Mish to come home. I played with Reg and entertained him. I dangled pieces of wool in front of the arms of the sofa so that he could rip the upholstery to shreds while he played. I laughed in triumph when he lay on his back and sank his claws into the sofa's underside to drag himself along. I was so pleased I topped his beer up again and gave him more mince.

Of course, the beer took effect before long but there was no way known that he'd go near his Kitty Litter. I'd refilled the bowl to give him the choice but he didn't want a bar of it. Instead he peed on the sofa.

'Good pussy,' I said. 'Good pussy.' And topped up his beer again. Reg purred. I do believe he was anxious to please me.

Throughout Reg's stay with us, Mish had steadfastly refused to accept my contention that he was deliberately destructive. She thought he was just upset because Yvonne and Alan were away, and he was among strangers in a strange home. After all, she kept reminding me, Reg behaved himself at home, didn't he? Mish's attitude implied that somehow we were at fault, that we were doing something wrong. She accused me of paranoia. She said I should see a shrink. She just could not accept that Reg was a full-blown, eleven to the dozen, paranoid-schizoid psychopath. But towards the end of our torment, she began to get little intimations that I might be right. She was making a cup of tea for herself at work when a junior account executive and the studio head sidled up to her.

'How are you coping with Reg?' asked the account executive cautiously.

'What do you mean?' replied Mish.

'How's the carpet bearing up?' asked the studio head.

'And your curtains?' added the account executive.

'Oh no,' said Mish.

'Oh yes,' they said. 'We've looked after Reg, too.'

'But Yvonne and Alan's place is always so immaculate,' Mish protested.

'Perhaps they refurnish weekly,' said the studio manager.

'No, Reg just behaves at home,' said the account executive. 'He saves his mischief for when he goes visiting.'

'We couldn't say anything to Yvonne and Alan,' said the studio manager, 'because they'd never believe us. I'm sure that's what Reg counts on. We didn't say anything even after Reg did his messes in the clothes drier.'

'What?' said Mish.

'My wife was in a hurry and just threw the clothes in on top. We never suspected a thing until the cycle had finished. You can't get that cooked cat poo smell out, you know.'

Mish told me all this on Friday evening, the evening before Yvonne and Alan came home. We'd gone to a little restaurant to escape the smell of Reg's bodily functions. A little wine loosened her up and made her want to confess that perhaps, maybe just perhaps, I might have been right about Reg, and that he really did have the devil's birthmark lurking somewhere beneath the thatch of his fur. When she told me about the drier I had to admire the nerve of the little blighter. In the drier of all places. In the rotor of death. What nerve, what audacity, what arrogance! When Reg decides to take it to you he never does things by half. Then again, neither do I.

Despite our earlier conversations, Mish still felt the need to reach down and pat the little vandal when we got home.

She tried to give him a goodnight pat. She didn't try to pat him again, I can assure you. Reg struck and Mish almost shattered glass with her scream. My re-training programme had concluded without Mish ever being aware that it had taken place. But Yvonne and Alan would know soon enough. They'd discover a side to their precious little moggy only their ex-friends and exploited work mates knew about, a side which they'd chosen to ignore despite the evidence they must have seen.

More previous Reg minders had come forward, all with the same horror story. Yet Yvonne and Alan had never once asked about the torn curtains which they couldn't help seeing, or the urine stained carpet beneath their feet. What did they think when they collected their fiendish, furry little bundle? Did they think everybody in the world had torn curtains? And torn sofas? That they tore them into shreds for the fun of it? Did they think people peed on their own carpets? Because, if not them, then who or what had done the dirty deeds? Did they ask themselves these questions? Did they reach the inescapable conclusion? That their placid pussy was, in fact, the feline equivalent of Charles Manson? Of course they did! Yet deliberately and callously they chose to ignore it. They willingly traded friendships for two weeks of cat minding. That was the value they put on friendship. I wanted to give Yvonne and Alan a spin in the drier along with Reg.

As I bathed and bandaged Mish's hand and arm, we took stock of the havoc he'd wreaked upon things that had once been precious to us. Perhaps Reg had had a bad day or simply saved his worst for last. Maybe he'd woken with a blinder of a headache and taken it out on the sofa and chairs. Their covers hung in tatters. The pattern had once been floral but it looked as though someone had got at it with a whipper-snipper. Reg hadn't just attacked the furniture, he'd savaged it. The Mongolian hordes could not have done a better job. I looked upon the destruction as an investment. If Reg hadn't been so completely in the doghouse I would have given him some mince balls for encouragement.

It was no accident that Reg had savaged Mish's hand but an outcome of my re-training. I'd begun by reaching down and stroking him. Just when he was certain that reaching down meant that I was going to stroke him, I'd pluck out a bit of fur. Not a handful or anything. Just enough to sting. He'd arch his head up to meet my hand and in return I'd pluck a whisker from his cheek, a hair from his ear, or pluck his coat. Reg didn't like that at all. First came the reaction, then retaliation, then pre-emptive first strike capability. Of course, in the process of encouraging retaliation I'd copped a few wounds, but by then I'd learned to override my basic instincts and not try to pull my hand away. That lessens the damage, it really does. This was something Mish had yet to learn.

I watched Reg pee on the carpet then head for the shower to complete his daily double while I got undressed for bed. His Kitty Litter was still in pristine condition. It would still be in pristine condition in the morning. Nothing in this world could make Reg use his Kitty Litter. If you wanted to see a cat go completely feral, all you had to do was pick him up and threaten to drop him in it.

As Mish and I lay in bed, I told her how I'd quit my job in the car yard. She was aghast. Hell, I said, I'd sold eight cars that week. What better time to quit than when you're on top? She thought of all the redecorating we had to do and began to panic. Redecorating takes more money than the CES provides. Then I told her how J. Walter Thompson had offered me a job. As Group Head. At twenty grand more than I was asking for when I got fired. The advertising business is a funny business, it truly is.

Yvonne and Alan called around and picked up Reg on Saturday afternoon. I'd made a point of going to the football so that I wouldn't be there. Apparently they had the devil's own job of getting Reg into his antique French cat basket. Ripped one of the wicker hinges clean off. Ripped one of Alan's shirt sleeves clean off. Yvonne and Alan had studiously ignored the torn curtains, ripped upholstery, piss-soaked carpets and the all-pervasive cat smell. Mish couldn't help noticing the weeping, red lines on Alan's arms as he carried the bucking cat basket to their car.

'Like a peppermint stick,' she said.

On Monday morning, Yvonne charged into Mish's office waving her bandaged arms about and demanded to know what we'd done to their Reg. Turned him into a monster, she said, a screaming banshee – not that Yvonne had the slightest idea what a banshee was. She accused Mish of deliberately tormenting her dear little pussycat, of turning him into a defiler of carpets, a shredder of curtains, a destroyer of furniture, and a biter of the hands that stroked it. She screamed and raged at Mish, carried on like a mad woman. Well it didn't take long for the cavalry to arrive and set Yvonne right about her dear little Reggie-weggie. It seemed as though everyone who'd ever harboured the little wretch and given him food, comfort and shelter had just been waiting for the chance to unload. They ganged up on Yvonne and told her in no uncertain terms what she could do with her cat in future. Yvonne left Mish's office in tears. Mish became something of a hero.

As for Reg, I hear he settled down again after a while and became his old brown-eye self. Yvonne and Alan had to refurnish their apartment and so couldn't afford a holiday the following year. They wouldn't have gone anyway, as I hear it. They're too worried about leaving Reg with friends.

The Battle of the Bonsai Cat

I caught sight of Mrs Beaulieu out of the corner of my eye and ignored her. She stood by the side of the road with her back to me, and stared fixedly down the hill as if she could conjure up a Jaguar or Rover by the sheer force of her willpower. I must admit, I was always slightly in awe of Mrs Beaulieu – pronounced Bewly according to the *grande dame* herself – and I was one of the few people who seemed to get along with her. Among ourselves we called her Grace, but only Suzie, our neighbour, and my wife Mary ever dared call her that to her face. I guessed Grace was going down to Avalon village to do her shopping, but couldn't bring myself to offer her a lift. It would have been an easy enough thing to do, but things never went easily with Grace. Even when you submitted to her every whim, became her chauffeur, carried her shopping and waited patiently as she put shop assistants and bank clerks through the mill, she had a way of making you feel incompetent, insignificant and angrier than a guard dog on a chain. She was ninety-two years old, bright as a button and smart as a whip. She used her age as a weapon and created an illusion of dottiness to get her own way. She was eccentric, there was no escaping that, but I doubt that there had been a single moment in her life when she hadn't known exactly what she was doing or been in absolute control. That was one of the reasons I admired her. But there was no way I wanted to offer her a lift. Another day, maybe, but on that day I couldn't marshal the will to face her. Not with all the business going on about the cat.

I glanced guiltily into the mirror to see if I'd escaped unnoticed and saw Grace stride out into the middle of the road, right in front of a Jaguar. I had to smile. She disappeared from sight as I turned right but I had no need to see more. I knew exactly what would happen. As soon as the car stopped, Grace would hop into the passenger seat and tell the driver where she wanted to go. The amazing thing was, no one ever refused to take her. But, inevitably, they all wished they had. Grace was never happy just to impose herself upon the hapless drivers, she'd then tell them in clear and unequivocal terms how she expected to be driven. She was the worst backseat driver in the world, and the worst thing you could do was answer back. There was a lovely story doing the rounds in the cafes about a driver who dared to take her on. Grace insisted he pull over to the side of the road and then ordered him out of his own car. Apparently the driver obeyed! A lot of people think this story is apocryphal but I'm not so sure. I've felt the edge of her tongue and, believe me, it cuts to the bone. She would flirt shamelessly with a male driver if there was another woman in the car. Even at ninety-plus she was sassy and provocative, and transmitted sexual signals as blatantly as Eva Gabor. She liked the company of men and had a man's attitude to other women. She saw them more as an inconvenience than competition, certainly inconsequential. She was sufficiently notorious for some motorists to detour around by Pittwater rather than risk being accosted driving by her front door.

Grace hadn't always imposed on other drivers. She drove a monstrous black Packard with whitewall tyres up until she turned eighty-two when, as a kindness to other road users, the police relieved her of her licence. If she ever passed you by you'd swear there was no one at the wheel. God only knows how she saw over the bonnet. It was amazing how such an enormous will could be compacted into such a tiny body, and how such a tiny body could handle such a large car. There was no doubt that the police had acted wisely, and the Packard sat silent and unused in her garage. I must admit to a sense of sadness that I no longer see her reversing it up her steep, winding driveway, hear the whine of its massive diff and the warning blast from her horn as she neared the top, knowing darn well that all Grace could see through her rear window was blue sky. Who would dare stand in her way?

Her driveway ran down the hill between our house and Suzie's, and Grace lived in a nice little cottage at the foot of it. The cottage had commanding views north over Whale Beach and the ocean, and was surrounded by an immaculately kept English garden which, along with the pets that came and went, were the remaining loves of her life. Her husband had been her principal love, and was a member of the family that originally owned one of the major grocery distributing companies in the United Kingdom. He died suddenly in his early fifties, but had the courtesy to leave Grace his wealth, most of which was tied up in an extensive share portfolio. I'm not aware of Grace ever spending up big, but she didn't want for anything either.

Over the years her cottage had fallen into disrepair. She didn't see the flaking paint, the peeling wallpaper or the cracked timbers. Occasionally I'd be summoned to change a light bulb or mend a fuse, or, if the job proved beyond my limited capability, call the plumber or electrician. She always gave me something in return for my service. She wasn't the sort of person who would allow herself to be beholden to anyone. Over the years she gave me lipstick – for my wife, of course – to replace the lipstick Mary normally wore. Grace disapproved of the colour, thought it 'unsuitable for her complexion and lacking in style'. Grace always wore traffic-stopping red lipstick that might have been a sensation in the forties, but looked somewhat out of place in the nineties. Perhaps Grace still saw herself as she was when she was young and beautiful and broke men's hearts with casual disdain. Whatever, the colour never varied, only its placement. Sometimes she missed rather badly when she was applying her lipstick, and her mouth would slide a few centimetres away to one side. Or she'd slip with the eye make-up and it would flood upwards beyond her eyebrows. She was generous with make-up and never allowed herself to be seen without it. Somehow she even managed to carry off the imperfections with elan.

Sometimes she'd give me a jar of handcream long past its use-by date, or a packet of frozen peas. I don't know what it was about peas, but Suzie had a freezer stuffed full of them as well. Doubtless Grace kept buying them because she kept giving them away. And she kept on giving them away because we kept on accepting them. Perhaps she kept on giving us peas just to see how long it would take before one of us spoke up about them. I certainly wouldn't put it past her. As I say, she was nowhere near as dotty as she made herself out to be. But the point is, Grace did not like being helped, did not like anything that in any way compromised her sense of independence or community standing. She was a local personality, Queen of the Street and a Beaulieu, and we were never allowed to forget it. She came from a family that dispensed largesse and was not conditioned to accept it from others. She either rebuffed kindness or immediately repaid it with a gift. But mostly, it must be said, she rebuffed kindness. Only Suzie could sneak under her guard and even then only occasionally.

One time after Suzie had found Grace in Avalon and helped her home with her groceries, she'd asked her if she was ever lonely.

'You're a beautiful woman,' she'd said. 'Why didn't you ever re-marry?'

'Suzannah,' she'd replied haughtily, 'if I want sex I can always buy it.'

Suzie had wandered into our place laughing hysterically and clutching a packet of frozen peas. There's no doubt that Suzie liked Grace and was fascinated by her. Although Suzie was more than forty years her junior, the two of them had a lot in common, not that we were ever foolish enough to say so in front of either of them. But they were both striking women, both intelligent, both eccentric in their own way and both of them lived alone. They shared the same wicked sense of humour, and neither of them was ever wrong about anything. There was a time when they'd drink tea together in the garden, and their gales of naughty laughter would waft up to our place. It made us smile just listening to them. But for the battle for custody of Suzie's cat, I think they could have become close friends.

Suzie fell out of a marriage shortly after her only child was born, and had subsequently survived a number of long-term relationships that should have gone somewhere but ultimately didn't. She was kind, witty, big-hearted and generous, but like a lot of people who live alone she could also be very self-centred, paranoiac and often sorely depressed. She was mercurial, up one minute and down the next. Fortunately, she was more often up than down.

Like Grace, she had her own peculiar view of the world and would become passionate about it, yet her fundamental insecurity would demand second party endorsement of its rightness. People didn't always agree with her but that never deterred Suzie. She'd keep ringing around until she found somebody who did, and that would be all she'd need to take on the local council, or local butcher, telephone company, or water board. Suzie was always pushing one barrow or another, or righting some perceived wrong. Nobody ever emerged from an encounter with Suzie unscarred, and along the way she acquired the sobriquet 'Mad Suzie'.

I was around at her place one day when the Sheriff called by. Suzie was on the losing end of another court case and had refused to settle as the Court had demanded, or even pay costs. In her mind at least, the battle was not yet over.

'I'd advise you to comply,' said the Sheriff, 'otherwise the other party may be obliged to liquidate you.'

Suzie leaped to her feet. 'I take exception to that,' she shouted. 'I find your choice of words offensive.' She looked at me for inspiration. 'I'm Jewish,' she snapped. 'Enough of us were liquidated by the Nazis. We don't do that any more.'

I burst out laughing. Only Suzie could drag two such disparate thoughts together and hurl them with such conviction. To his credit, the Sheriff also doubled over with laughter. Suzie just stood there defiantly with her fists clenched until the penny dropped for her. She joined in. By the time we'd all had a coffee, Suzie and the Sheriff were the best of friends and he was giving her priceless inside advice on how she should proceed. That was Suzie. The mouth and the brain were both quick, but frequently the mouth was quicker. Her apparent thoughtlessness got her into all sorts of situations.

One night we dined at a local restaurant with Suzie and the then current man in her life. Suzie dominated conversation with a passionate dissertation on the inadequacies of a local alderman over an issue that only she found at all significant. Between diatribes she ordered brains for her entree, which raised eyebrows, goose for her main meal and finished off with goat's cheese.

'Brains, goose, goat,' observed her partner wearily. 'How apt.'

I suppose in the end all her relationships broke up for the same reason. She was just too exuberant, too full on, and ultimately too demanding. We'd be there to help her through the inevitable bottomless depressions that followed. She was a victim of a mind that refused to accept conventional wisdoms, that could make gigantic leaps of perception which left others floundering in her wake, but one that was also often sadly and obviously blinkered. She was a victim in the same way that Grace was a victim. They were both victims of their eccentricity.

There were three emotional anchors in Suzie's life. One was her grown-up son who wasn't always in the country or on hand when needed. Her friends, whom she used ruthlessly but who also had their own lives to live, were another. By far the most constant, the most stable and the most loving was her tiny Burmese cat, Tush. Even by Burmese standards, Tush was tiny. She never grew much larger than a kitten and every time she had a decent meal her belly would swell so that she looked full-term pregnant. The other neighbours and ourselves often referred to Tush as the Bonsai Cat.

Suzie was devoted to Tush and Tush to Suzie. When Suzie was lying down, Tush would lie on her chest with her front paws either side of Suzie's neck, like a small child hugging its mother. Tush slept with Suzie when no one else would, sat with her through the long nights spent sewing or packing, was always there to welcome her home in the evening and see her off in the morning. That was the problem. When Suzie was out selling, Tush was left at home alone.

Sometimes Tush would wander into our home and honour us with her company. She was always welcome. Other neighbours felt the same way and opened their doors and their hearts to the tiny bonsai cat. At that time, our section of the street had formed its own little community. We didn't crowd each other, but we all knew one another well enough to stop and chat or share the odd cup of coffee. We accepted Tush as our joint daytime responsibility, partly out of consideration for Suzie whom we all adored, but also because of the nature of the cat. We always felt privileged when Tush chose to visit us over the other neighbours, and when I mentioned this one day I discovered that everyone felt the same way. You could do anything with Tush. She trusted absolutely. If you picked her up she would just lie there in the position you put her. On her back, upside down, it didn't matter. Mary used to say you could throw her on the barbie and she'd stay there. She was that kind of cat. I'm sure Tush drew great satisfaction from the fact that she was welcomed into so many homes. I suppose it was inevitable that one day she would decide to expand her territory and wander blithely into Grace's clutches.

One of the great sorrows of growing old, one that I also face, is the loss of friends. There is no glue that can stop people from falling off the perch. It's the way of things. Unfortunately, the longer you live the more sorrows you face, and the lonelier you become. It must have saddened Grace immeasurably to lose all her friends, and I think that is one reason why she hesitated to make more. There is no doubt that she was once one of the most popular women on the peninsula. She was a great beauty and a great character, and she had the front and the intelligence to exploit both to the full. Her days and nights were richly peopled, and often peopled by the very rich. She was legendary even then for her outrageous behaviour, her outspokenness, and for the casual flaunting of her extravagant jewellery. She dripped diamonds and rubies. Sadly, somewhere along the way much of her jewellery had been misplaced. However, she still wore diamond stud earrings, each the size of my small fingernail, and jewelled rings as heavy as knuckle-dusters. And in her bright, diamond-hard eyes, the grandeur of former days remained.

As her friends disappeared, Grace transferred her affections to her pets. She had a magnificent, regal Dalmatian and a pair of Australian terriers. She also had a series of Burmese cats. Grace didn't trust vets but trusted her own remedies. Unfortunately it doesn't matter how much you love and cherish your pets – and Grace certainly loved and cherished hers – boiled herbs are no defence against paralysis ticks. One by one her pets died, and Grace had the sad task of disposing of their remains. I was often the means of disposal, summoned to dig a hole or to cart a corpse off to the vet's. I must say it upset me when I was called upon to perform these duties, and I'd take her to task. But she'd dismiss me with disdain, ridicule my advice, humiliate and savage me with her tongue. She really could be cruel, though in hindsight I think this may have been a way of concealing her grief. Apart from the business with Tush, these were the only occasions when we really fell out. But it never stopped her giving me a packet of peas for my trouble.

When Tush wandered into her lonely world, Suzie, Mary and I were probably as close as anyone to Grace, and she kept us at a distance. Tush wandered into her life and was immediately swept up into her arms and cradled like a baby. The cat wasn't so much adopted as possessed. Tush would not have objected to any of this. She loved attention and affection and would have purred and padded her little heart out. Who wouldn't have found Tush irresistible? What little old lady wouldn't have found her the answer to her lonely prayers? But Grace knew Tush belonged to Suzie, knew beyond doubt. She simply chose not to believe it.

Suzie arrived home tired and worn out just as night was about to wash over the last lingerings of day. She'd stopped at the deli for some smoked salmon for her dinner and as a special treat for Tush. She called but didn't panic when Tush failed to appear. No, Suzie saved the hysterics for us, as together we knocked on doors and finally tried to console her and allay her fears over a cup of coffee. It only occurred to me as Suzie was leaving that the little runaway might be with Grace. I didn't say anything but let Suzie slip off home. Grace had killed all of her own pets with kindness, what would she do to Tush?

I knocked on Grace's door and called out so that she'd know it was me and not a stranger who might mean her harm. She opened the door and stood there with Tush snuggled in her arms.

'I see you've got Tush,' I said. 'Thank heavens. Suzie is worried out of her mind.' I thought that by positioning her as a saviour rather than a cat napper she might be gracious enough to hand Tush over without a fuss. But then I consistently misjudged her, underestimated the strength of her will and her bloody-mindedness.

'Suzie?' she said.

'Yes Suzie.' I could feel things slipping away and decided to be blunt.

'Suzie? I don't know any Suzies.' She drew herself up to her full height and glared at me defiantly. 'Do you mean Mrs Thing up top?'

Grace always referred to people she didn't know, or whose names she couldn't remember or didn't care to remember, as Mrs Thing. It was a bad sign.

'Mrs Beaulieu,' I said, sounding more patient than I felt, 'you know Suzie very well. She brings your shopping in for you. I hear you laughing together in your garden. You know Suzie very well, and you know very well that Tush is her cat.'

'Oh you mean Suzannah,' she said haughtily. 'The only Suzies I've ever known were maids. Suzie is a maid's name. If you mean Suzannah, call her Suzannah. Call her by her proper name.'

'I mean Suzannah and that is Suzannah's cat.'

'No it isn't. Suzannah's cat has a white belly button. This cat does not have a white belly button. See?' She held Tush by her front legs so that I could examine the entire underneath of the cat. I didn't need to. I knew Tush didn't have a white belly button.

'Mrs Beaulieu –' I started to say but she interrupted.

'See? No white belly button! Ha!' She grinned in fiendish triumph and closed the door on me. She refused to answer my knocks. I climbed back up her steep, twisting driveway, full of foreboding. Two strong minded, unyielding people were about to clash head on. Countries have gone to war for less. I knew both would overreact and both would dig in.

I suggested to Mary that no harm would come to Tush in the course of a single night, and that perhaps things might best be left until the following day. But Mary knew and I guess I did as well, that Suzie wouldn't sleep a wink while Tush was missing. Reluctantly I wandered next door. She waved me in. She was busy on the phone organising a search party with torches to scour the bush. She was convinced that Tush was lying paralysed somewhere, victim to a tick. The rims of her eyes were red and shiny.

'Suzie,' I whispered urgently, 'it's okay. Everything is all right. I know where Tush is. She's safe.'

'Thank God!' she said and abruptly got rid of whoever had been on the line. 'Thank God!' she repeated.

So far so good.

Suzie was so relieved to hear that Tush was safe with Grace that she simply didn't realise the implications. Perhaps that worked in her favour.

'Good old Grace,' she said. 'I'm going to take her some flowers to thank her.'

She'd bought herself a couple of bunches of poppies which she whipped out of the vase she'd put them in and re-wrapped. She was as excited as a child on Christmas Eve, but that was Suzie. Depths of despair one moment, high as a bus load of old hippies the next. I watched her skip away down the drive and braced myself for the explosion. It never came. I suppose Grace had to put Tush down to accept the flowers, and that Suzie had pounced at that precise instant. That is what I think happened, and that Suzie was too overjoyed to realise her tactical brilliance. Suzie maintained that Grace had made no effort to keep Tush on that occasion, and was consequently all the more surprised when she did.

Nevertheless, score round one to Suzie. She was to lose a lot more before she got another score on the board.

Suzie worked for herself and kept her own hours. Sometimes the hours were painfully long and the rewards pathetically small. In the time we'd known her she'd gone from making fitted terry-towelling sheets to a line of T-shirts. Any success was hard won. She allowed no compromise with quality in either the cloth, make-up or printing, and was ruthless with suppliers who didn't share her commitment. A running state of war existed between them, with suppliers delivering late, filling orders incorrectly and Suzie withholding payment. On top of all this, she did her own marketing and selling. But doing everything herself gave her flexibility, so for the next two days Suzie celebrated Tush's return by confining herself to jobs she could do at home. Tush never left her side. It was easy to believe that the initial skirmish had never taken place.

I didn't see Grace again until Suzie had once more hit the road. Grace was posting letters in her own inimitable style. She simply stood by the side of the road, walked out in front of the first car that happened along, and handed the driver her mail with instructions to post it. Again, no one ever refused her. Probably they were grateful to get off so lightly.

'Good afternoon, Mrs Beaulieu,' I called to her. 'Anything we can do for you?'

'Bit late aren't you?' she replied, caustically, and set off on her regular afternoon walk.

I saw her again on her return.

'That Mrs Thing,' she said. 'Hasn't she aged!'

This was a running joke between Mary and me. The Mrs Thing Grace referred to was Rose Elcott, another ninety-year-old widow who lived opposite us. Whereas Grace was rich but never society, Rose was the epitome of society but no longer rich. They were opposite ends of the spectrum, the snob and the *bon viveur*, and had known each other for probably forty years. When they passed each other on their walks, they'd unfailingly greet each other with unbending formality.

'Good afternoon, Mrs Beaulieu. I trust you're keeping well,' Rose would say.

'Good afternoon, Mrs Elcott,' Grace would reply. 'I am indeed, and I trust you are as well.'

Then each in turn would come to us at the first opportunity with the news that the other was on her last legs. Unfortunately in this instance, Grace was right and Rose was wrong. Mary and I kept an eye out for Rose and we'd suggested to her nieces that the time had come for her to go into care. Rose's deterioration put a spring into Grace's step. She seemed to draw strength from it. The straw hat she always wore on her outings seemed set jauntier than ever, but that just may have been because she held her head higher. She'd won the longevity stakes and outlasted them all. Although I can never assert that the two events were related, that night Grace repossessed Tush.

When Suzie went to see her Grace flatly denied that she had Tush, and refused to admit Suzie into her house. Suzie pleaded with her, but to no avail. She even pointed out that the front of Grace's dress was covered in tufts of Tush-coloured cat fur. Tush was moulting at the time.

'No Suzannah, you're wrong,' Grace replied. 'It isn't cat fur it's flour. I've been baking.'

The scale of the lie was outrageous. Grace had never learned to cook anything but the most basic meals. She'd never had to. As the saying went, the only thing she'd ever learned to make was a reservation. But there was nothing Suzie could do about it except come to us for sympathy. Grace had slammed the door in her face.

Tush was absent from home for the next two days while Suzie became more and more desperate. She went to see Grace almost on the hour every hour, and Grace even had the audacity to greet her at the door with Tush in her arms. Each time she'd give Suzie the belly-button argument before slamming the door. Of course, I got co-opted to try and so did Mary, but neither of us fared any better. Finally we tracked down some of Grace's nephews and appealed to them for help. They found it very hard to take Suzie seriously and were reluctant to make the trek up from the other side of Sydney. I must say, it did sound like a storm in a teacup, and I can understand why they chose to do nothing.

About this time poor old Rose Elcott was moved into a nursing home. Mary thought it would be a good ploy if we all went to visit Rose and invited Grace to come with us. She thought that in the spirit of friendship and over afternoon tea at the Cafe Ibiza later, we could persuade Grace to surrender Tush. It seemed the ideal opportunity so we went ahead. I can recall us standing around Rose's bed when Rose leaned forward conspiratorially, checked to see that no staff were about and asked us the question that had obviously been troubling her.

'Just between you and me, my dears,' she said, 'have I been put away?'

Mrs Beaulieu had the good grace to allow Suzie and me to bumble a suitably positive response, but afterwards in the cafe she couldn't leave it alone. Her victory was confirmed, and she puffed herself up like a rooster with a new batch of hens. She even strutted like one.

'Ha!' she cackled. 'Has she been put away? Ha! Never let anyone do that to me.'

When we raised the question of Tush we did so half-heartedly. She was flush with her victory and brazenly defiant. Yes, she had a cat, but no, it was certainly not Tush. Tush had a white belly button, she insisted. Later that day Suzie informed us that she was going to try the relatives once more and if that failed, the police. Suzie took no pleasure in calling in the heavy artillery. Throughout it all, she hadn't lost her affection for Grace and I'm certain Grace knew this and exploited it.

This time the nephews were more obliging. I suppose they were in their sixties, younger than me but hardly the image of a nephew. At first they were rather reluctant to join the battle. I think they managed to procrastinate through three cups of tea. Again understandable. It's natural for kin to side with their own and, besides, Grace was a wealthy woman and due to fall off the perch. There was little wisdom in upsetting her while she still had time to alter her will. But they listened patiently to Suzie while she related chapter and verse of the struggle to date, and then confronted Grace. I don't know what they said but they returned an hour or so later carrying Tush.

'It's all settled,' they said.

'We've had a heart to heart with Grace and sorted things out,' they said.

'You won't have any more problems,' they said and left thoroughly convinced of their negotiating skills. But all negotiations are dependent on each party keeping their side of the bargain, and Grace had no intention of keeping hers. Suzie enjoyed Tush's company for three days before she disappeared once more.

Understandably, the nephews were reluctant to repeat their long trek north. They rang Grace and negotiated by phone, but she persisted in her belief that the cat in her arms was hers and not Suzie's. Once again she tendered the belly-button fabrication as evidence. When she wanted to be, Grace could be very convincing and it wasn't long before the nephews were on the phone to Suzie suggesting that she might be the one who was confused. Poor Suzie. The pendulum of her emotions swung back and forth between rage and abject depression. Her latest on and off love affair had finally foundered and now people were trying to take her cat away from her. I don't know what she said to the police or how hysterical she was, but they came to our place before going to hers. To say they were skeptical is to understate the case. The mistake they made was to reveal their skepticism to Suzie. She gave them the works. Tears and fury, demanded their resignations and to speak to their superior. The constables were both young, one a man the other a woman, and to their credit they managed to calm Suzie down. But they wouldn't let her accompany them when they confronted Grace.

According to the policewoman, Grace turned on all her charm and flirted outrageously with her colleague and, although the gap between their ages was closer to seventy years than sixty, the young policeman was flattered by her attentions. It certainly interfered with his judgement. He returned empty handed and also suggested to Suzie that she might be the one confused. Mrs Beaulieu had showed them the cat and it did not have a white belly button.

In hindsight it seems ridiculous but Suzie actually talked about suicide. We'd tried reasoning with the young constables, but they'd handed down their judgement and were prepared to stick by it. Mary and I were both worried about Suzie and sat with her until two in the morning. Lord only knows what would have happened if the two constables hadn't returned the following day.

Apparently Mrs Beaulieu was known to the police. The two constables had discovered this on their return to the main station at Mona Vale. Over the past few years, Grace had rung them to complain about neighbours who had upset her. One lot were a lovely family who owned a pharmacy business. Grace had noted the scum and froth on the ocean after a storm and accused them of causing it by dumping shampoo and perfume into the drains. On another occasion she'd rung about a neighbour who suffered terribly from insomnia and would turn his lights on at all hours of the night. Grace had called the police and accused him of dealing in drugs. The police thought she was just dotty, but I think she was just lonely and drawing attention to herself. As I say, everyone tended to underestimate her.

Suzie could have been rude to the two embarrassed officers but instead was totally forgiving. She knew how intelligent Grace was and how persuasive she could be. This time she accompanied them to see Grace, and Grace finally released the cat. Though massively outgunned, however, she didn't buckle under. She was defiant to the last, insisting that Tush was her cat. As they left they told Suzie to call them straight away if there was any further trouble.

Things might have been resolved from a human point of view but nobody had resolved anything with Tush. She liked Grace, and in the long hours when Suzie was out selling, she took herself off to visit her friend. Grace didn't always put her out again at night so she could return home and Suzie was obliged to ring the police. They came four more times in all, probably regretting their kind offer every step of the way. The amazing thing is, throughout this period, Suzie and Grace began to patch up their relationship. Occasionally Suzie drove her down to the shops or picked her up. She made cakes for her, and Mary and I would hear them laughing as they took tea in the garden and Grace told more of her ribald tales. Tush was the one subject they never mentioned until the police threatened Grace with court action. While their relationship struggled to recover its full bloom, Suzie struck a truce with Grace and it lasted pretty well up until the day Grace died.

The deal was typical of Suzie's generosity and concern for others. She told Grace that she could have Tush during the daytime while she was away, but had to surrender her every night. That way they could both share the little darling's company and affection. Grace's response was typical of her, and even while she was confined to her chair and in the thrall of serious doses of morphine, her position never wavered.

'This is not your cat, Suzannah,' she insisted. 'This is my cat. Your cat has a white belly button and mine does not. See? No white belly button. However, as you appear to have misplaced your cat, you may share mine.'

Suzie accepted the deal.

Grace died at home as she always said she would, with Tush asleep in her arms. Suzie, Mary and I were the only locals to attend her funeral which I found rather sad. But most of those who knew her had already died and those who hadn't didn't like her. Sad but true, she was not well liked, but then she hardly deserved to be. We were invited along to the reading of the will. Suzie was discreetly informed by the solicitors that she was named in it. Was Suzie excited? Of course she was! We sat there as this relative and that relative were handed parcels of shares or cash until millions were disposed of, and we were in awe that there could possibly be more. We leaned forward on the edges of our seats when Suzie's name was read out.

'And to my good friend Suzannah . . .' read the solicitor. He paused and looked at her over his glasses. I think by this stage everyone was looking at Suzie and you could have heard a pin drop. 'And to my good friend Suzannah,' he repeated, 'I leave . . . my beloved cat . . . Tush.'

The battle of the bonsai cat was over, but Grace Beaulieu never surrendered.

Dead Pussy

'Forgive me, Father, for I have sinned.'

Jerry and Jago stopped hauling up the mainsail to laugh and make me feel worse than I already felt. Hell of an entrance, though. That was the only thing I felt good about.

'You look like shit,' said Sandy who had the helm.

'Like puke,' said Jerry.

'Like a dog's arse in action,' said Jago.

I couldn't understand it. I'd drunk megalitres less than they had yet they were up, good-natured, smiling and functioning. I'd once been shooting a commercial with these guys out west near Bourke. For three nights in a row they'd tried to drink the town dry, never got to bed before four in the morning, but were up each day at five to shoot the dawn. No apparent ill effects. Even when the sun was hot enough to melt granite, they kept on filming. I didn't know whether to feel proud of them or ashamed. Maybe they got their rest in the breaks between shots. You spend a lot of time just sitting around when you're shooting commercials, and that was when we discovered our common interest in ocean sailing. Sandy was my art director, Jerry a cinematographer, and Jago – short for Jacobson – was a film electrician.

'Shoulda had the cold Cold,' said Jago. 'All of us did.'

The cold Cold doesn't bear thinking about but the guys swear it works. They knock back a bottle of Carlton Cold the instant they get up. The Cold isn't just cold, but one degree short of being frozen solid. They skull it as fast as they can. The beer sits on the belly until the belly wakes up to the horrible thing happening to it. Then it rebels. And rebels so enthusiastically that it also gets rid of all the stale beer and undigested pizza left over from the night before. The guys take great pride in the distance they can get before gravity comes into effect. It's outrageous, disgusting and inexcusable and, according to the guys, works every time. Given the way I felt and the way they looked, the evidence was overwhelmingly in their favour.

I turned off the motor to escape the fumes. I looked east and doubled over in pain. The sun had just cleared the horizon and glowed like a nuclear explosion, which was reprised a billion times in the sluggish sea. Every glint seared my eyeballs. I could feel a gentle breeze fill the sails and our *Oceanic* begin to surge. Overhead the sky was pale blue and cloudless. Our decision to wait a couple of days before setting out on our maiden voyage had paid off handsomely. The storms had gone, the skies had cleared and the forecast ten to fifteen knot winds suited my hang-over right down to the ground.

The *Oceanic* had been pretty run down and neglected when we'd bought her, but it was amazing what four guys, a couple of set builders, and a mountain of beer can achieve. We could have doubled our money easily if we'd put her back on the market. Being more a willing helper than a tradesman, I'd scored the job of scraping the hull and anti-fouling it. Let me tell you, it was a work of art by the time

I'd finished. I was more proud of the job I'd done than of any of my award-winning commercials. We'd sunk money into new sails, new radio, satnav, depth finders, the motor and safety gear. We might carry on like cowboys but that's just bullshit. We're as serious as anyone when it comes to the business of sailing.

North Head fell away behind us as we set course north-east for Lord Howe Island. The guys had left me at the helm while they went below to find something they could fry for breakfast. They claimed the fat absorbed the alcohol still in their blood. Who was going to argue? I threw a lure out and gave it about fifty metres of line. You never know what's out there unless you ask, and we were all suckers for yellowfin tuna sashimi.

'Keep an eye out for logs and branches,' said Sandy. He stuck his head up the stairwell to pass on this advice. 'Storm's washed heaps of shit into the water.'

I slapped on a centimetre-thick coating of Blockout, put on my American, wrap-around, Polaroid sunglasses, and pulled my Stussi cap as far down over my forehead as it would go. Where's the *Vogue* photographer when you need one? The smell of frying bacon wafted up on deck. Surprisingly, it smelled all right to me, in fact, it smelled fantastic. It had taken me a while but I'd finally realised why I was the only one with a hang-over. I was the only one who'd been to bed. All the talk of cold Colds was bullshit. The others had still been drinking when I'd come up top.

'Get this into ya.' Jerry stuck his head up and waved a hand holding two leaking fried eggs and a dozen rashers of bacon sandwiched between two doorstep-sized slices of white bread. 'Salt, pepper, worcestershire sauce and chilli.'

'Ta.' Jerry's famous hang-over cure, for once without the anchovies. This was the trade-off for taking the first watch. The others were going to grab some sleep as soon as they'd had breakfast. I took a good look around. There were a couple of yachts north of us, way to seaward and one skirting Long Reef. There were three or four game boats heading out to the shelf and another one just clearing the heads. A container ship had passed by heading south about five miles out, probably making for Botany Bay. Overhead, an Air New Zealand Boeing and a Garuda Airbus jockeyed with a Cessna fitted with long-range fuel tanks to see which would be first in after curfew. Other than that we had the sea to ourselves. I got stuck into the sandwich. No gourmet meal ever tasted better, and the fat seemed to soak up the alcohol just as the guys had said it would. At this point I would've liked to have just sat back and watched the telltales to make sure the sails were set optimally, but I figured we were still too close in to be casual. It wasn't only flotsam that worried me. One day we'd come across four Italians in a three-point-five metre aluminium dinghy, bottom bouncing for morwong about eight miles out. We were almost onto them before we spotted them, even though the seas were slight. We could've cut them in half.

I guess it was the birds that attracted my attention. They were swooping as if working a school of fish, but not going through with their dives. They kept pulling out at the last instant and wheeling around as if confused. I fancy myself as a bit of a fisherman as well as a sailor, and never say no to a chance of a hook-up. I changed course to run my lure as close as I could to whatever it was that had interested the birds. The glare didn't make things easy, but every now and then I saw something floating on the water, and an occasional splash. Interesting. But the more I watched, the less whatever it was behaved like any fish I'd ever seen. So what was exciting the birds? I closed to fifty metres, thirty, twenty, then eased away to get a good look. I got a good look all right and forgot all about fishing.

'Coming about!' I yelled. 'Get up here and give me a hand.'

I turned away from the breeze and waited for the guys to come up top.

'What's up?' they yelled.

'I want to do a circle and a slow pass where those birds are.'

'What did you drop?'

'Nothing.'

'Then what's up?'

'You'll see.'

We turned and crept gently up into the breeze.

'See that thing in the water?'

'Yeah . . .' Jago was standing at the bow squinting into the sun.

'Yeah . . . well I want you to dive in and get it.'

'What is it?'

'Your chance to be a hero to millions.'

'Eh?'

I watched, waited for the penny to drop.

'Bloody hell,' said Jago. He turned and looked at me in absolute amazement. Our sails hung limp and the cat was making more headway towards us than us to it. In fact, it seemed to be heading straight towards me.

'I don't believe it,' said Jerry. 'Cop a load of this.'

'Where'd he come from?' asked Sandy.

Jago grabbed a towel and held it over the side. The cat snatched hold and sank its claws in to the hilt. Jago slowly began to lift it out of the water.

'Miaowwwww . . .'

Sandy lay alongside Jago, reached though the rail and grabbed the cat by the scruff of its neck and hauled it aboard. It collapsed sodden and exhausted onto the deck.

'Bloody hell,' said Jerry. 'How the hell did he get out here?'

Good question. What was a black cat doing swimming in the ocean all by itself seven miles out to sea? Jago ducked below to get another dry towel.

'Bloody Duncan Armstrong,' said Sandy.

'Who's he?' asked Jerry.

'You know. Got us a gold medal at Seoul.'

'Better rinse Duncan off with fresh water before you dry him,' I said.

Jago was unsure. 'Seems a waste of fresh water.'

'It's either that or a beer shampoo.' That settled it. Water can be wasted but never beer. I steered and Sandy re-set the sails while Jago and Jerry fussed over the cat.

'Miaowwww . . .' it pleaded when Jago gave it another soaking. It fought but settled down once Jago started to towel it dry.

'What are we going to do with it?' he asked.

'Two choices,' I said. 'Return to the marina or take it with us.'

'I don't want to go back,' said Jago, and Jerry agreed.

'Can't have it,' said Sandy. 'Out of the question.'

'Why?' I asked. I should have seen it coming but I never do. That, the blokes tell me, is one of my most endearing features.

'Bad combination,' said Sandy. 'Four blokes on a boat and only one pussy between us.'

'Where's Dunk gunna piss?' asked Jago. Dunk was now the cat's name though Felix would have been more appropriate. It was black except for a white puff under its neck and another on its tummy.

'Where is he?' I asked.

'Curled up on Sandy's bunk. Both of them are fast asleep.'

We sat and contemplated the problem.

'We need some Kitty Litter,' said Jerry. 'I know, we could chuck the veges out of the box and put some newspaper in the bottom.'

'Good idea,' I said. 'Even better if we had some newspaper.' We stared at the sea and waited for another idea.

'Muesli,' said Jago.

'What?' I couldn't see the connection.

'Muesli. Nobody eats the bloody stuff, anyway. Let him piss in that.'

'No way,' I said. 'I eat muesli.'

'Fair go,' said Jago. 'Bloody stuff tastes so crook you wouldn't know if a cat had crapped in it or not.'

'I'd know.'

Jago turned away morosely.

'It's a good idea, though,' said Jerry. 'What can we use instead of muesli?'

'I might have the answer,' I said getting into the mood. 'Porridge.'

'Porridge?'

'Yeah. Wife packed some porridge. Good idea if you think about it. Great if we run into rough weather. Easy to cook, warming and gives you a sugar hit. I brought some in a biscuit tin.'

'Perfect,' said Jago. 'I'd rather pee in it myself than eat it.'

'What do we do when we run out of porridge?' asked Jerry.

'No problems,' said Jago who was now unstoppable. 'Weet-bix. We'll just crush up some Weet-bix.'

'Brilliant,' I said. I had to laugh.

Dunk got up with Sandy and hung around the galley until he gave it some milk and the end of an eye fillet. Jago introduced it to its make-shift Kitty Litter. A great cheer went up when Dunk hopped into the box and squatted. Normally cats get narrow-eyed and squinty when people watch them going about their business, but Dunk didn't seem to mind his audience at all. He dug a little hole and covered it up afterwards.

'Bloody bewdy!' said Jago, and spoke for all of us.

Sandy took over the helm and Jerry brought up the beer, four cans in polystyrene holders. Our noon ration. Dunk jumped onto my lap as I took my first sip.

'Just come to say thanks,' said Sandy. 'He slept on my bed, smooched around Jago, just about rubbed the hairs off Jerry's legs, and now it's your turn.'

I tickled Dunk under the chin and he immediately began purring. 'I'm the one who saved you,' I said. 'But for me you'd be a dead pussy.'

'That's what I told him,' said Jago.

'Me too,' said Jerry.

'Yeah, but he believed me,' said Sandy. 'Whose bunk did he choose to sleep on?'

'What I want to know,' I said, addressing the cat, 'is how the hell you ended up in the water? Where did you come from? How did you get there?'

'Maybe he was swimming over from New Zealand,' said Sandy. 'You know, like Lassie. Maybe his folks left him behind when they moved from Auckland to Bondi, and he just wanted to join them.'

'Long swim,' I said.

'Not for our our Dunk,' said Jago. 'Maybe he's just practising to be the first cat to swim around the world.'

'No,' I said, pissed off that the others were playing silly buggers when we had a real live mystery on our hands. We might never know the truth but at least we should be able to think up a plausible fiction. 'I want to know what Dunk was doing swimming seven miles off the coast of Sydney.'

'Maybe he fell off a boat,' said Sandy who, being my art director, picked up on the signals and knew I was serious.

'Too obvious,' I said, 'and unlikely. Cats are supposed to be sure-footed. In a rough sea, just maybe, but in these conditions, no way.'

'Maybe he was pushed,' said Jago.

'Yeah, but who'd throw a live cat overboard seven miles out to sea?'

'Maybe somebody wanted to get rid of him,' persisted Jago. 'Maybe he shat on the carpet and pissed in the pot plants. Maybe he clawed the curtains and ate the budgie.'

'Cats that piss in porridge don't piss in pot plants,' I said. 'This cat is well behaved.' Sandy and Jerry were lost in thought. I could almost hear their brains ticking over. They were beginning to realise the potential.

'What other boats did you see?' asked Jerry.

'At least two yachts left harbour ahead of us. One appeared to be sailing up the coast towards Pittwater, the other out to sea. They were the nearest though probably not the only ones. There were some game boats heading out to the shelf or down to the Peaks. Three or four of them would have gone out ahead of us. I think there were a couple of blokes bottom fishing, and a container ship heading south towards Botany. He probably passed across our bows. What else? Oh yeah, the airport had opened and a couple of international planes and a Cessna were lining up to land. That's all I saw but not necessarily all there was.'

'Interesting,' said Sandy. 'I think you can discount anything you didn't see. I'm not sure that cats can stay afloat for long, not even our Dunk.'

'I reckon,' said Jago thoughtfully, 'the bloke that comes up with the best reason for Dunk being where he was ought be given first crack at the best looking sheila on Lord Howe Island.'

'What's second prize?' snorted Jerry, but everyone ignored him. All four of us could spin a yarn and the challenge had been issued. What the hell was Dunk doing out there? We all looked at him at once.

But Dunk was as inscrutable as the Sphinx.

Sandy was younger than me and an eastern suburbs boy, a product of private schools and despairing parents. They were distraught when he turned down university, then elated when he breezed into Randwick Tech's graphic arts school. He was considerably less experienced than I and even naive about the business of advertising, but he brought to the partnership a refreshing disrespect for convention, an extraordinary natural flair for art direction, and a delicate touch that smacked of genius. He manoeuvred his way into being the first to tell his tale.

'Take a good look at Dunk,' he said. 'He look like a good ratter to you?'

'Reckon he'd give it a good go,' said Jago.

'Oh no! Don't tell me,' said Jerry. 'He chased a rat but didn't realise it was a water rat until he'd chased it all the way out to sea.'

We had to laugh.

'Give us a break,' said Sandy evenly. 'I'm serious. I reckon ratting's what got him into trouble.'

The game had begun. Bums shifted and legs found more comfortable positions as we settled back to hear Sandy's tale. It was a perfect evening with thousands of stars appearing by the minute in the blackening sky. The winds which had freshened during the afternoon had swung south and begun to ease. Jerry had managed to cook the whole eye fillet in the oven and served it rare enough for Jago to go looking for a pulse. Mashed potatoes and a mixed packet of frozen peas and beans helped fill the plate. Sandy had taken the helm and we'd all gone up top to join him.

'Strangely enough,' said Sandy, 'Dunk is Dunk's real name. Watch. Here Dunk! C'mon . . . come here. Puss, puss, puss . . .'

Dunk's head swivelled around. He got up off my lap, stretched and as casually as you like, ambled over to Sandy.

'See?' said Sandy triumphantly.

Jago turned to me and burst out laughing. Dunk hadn't moved a muscle until Sandy had called puss, puss, puss. But why spoil a good story with the facts?

'Last night Dunk was a happy cat. He had a happy home just up from Fairy Bower in the shadow of North Head, and his days held no mystery for him. He had to front up every morning and evening to be fed, miaow a bit, rub up against a couple of legs, and occasionally sleep on someone's lap. But the rest of the time was his to do as he pleased. So he wandered out through the cat-flap and decided to check the boundaries of his territory. He had a growing urge to bite something's head off – a rat, lizard, mouse, stray cow, whatever – and to make sure that ginger tom from across the street hadn't been sniffing around the cute little Siamese next door. You might remember it was a still and sultry evening, hot and humid, the sort of calm you get between storms. Dunk knew there was another storm coming and just wanted to kill something before he went back to sleep for another day or two.

'He wandered down the side fence, weaved through the agapanthas and snuck under the hydrangeas. Nothing. Not a lizard. No beetles. He crept over towards the gums, lay on his belly in the long grass and watched. Nothing. He reckoned he was a cert for a greengrocer, a black prince or at the very least a pisser, but there wasn't a cicada to be seen. The air was simply too oppressive and every living thing had ducked for cover except Dunk. This did not please him. He wanted to kill, and the longer he went without killing the more determined he became. He reached the edge of his territory, paused to spray the fence as a warning to the ginger tom, and leaped up onto the corner post.

'He gazed out over enemy territory, eyes wide, trying to spot movement. Nothing. He didn't like it. Maybe there was an owl around, maybe a cat-killing Powerful Owl. The thought sent a shiver down his spine and he dived for cover. Dunk feared Powerful Owls more than dogs. Dogs were stupid. If they were smart they'd have learned to climb trees. Besides, they always announced their intentions. They couldn't help themselves.

'"Gunna get ya!" they'd bark. "Gunna rip ya ugly head off! Gunna rip ya chicken-shit heart out." Those arrogant German shepherds were the worst.

'Dunk would leap up a tree and sit on a branch just out of their reach.

'"Bastard!" they'd growl. "You bastard!" they'd whine.

'Dunk would just sit there and laugh at them. Give them his most condescending, pitying look and drive them absolutely bananas. Sometimes they even frothed at the mouth. Dunk would roll over on the branch and pretend to slip, just to get them going. It never failed. It always amused Dunk that such humourless dogs could be so much fun.

'But Powerful Owls were a different story. They didn't announce their presence and they didn't make any sound. They swooped in like silent angels of death, grabbed their prey in their talons and disappeared into the night. Dunk had seen a young possum snatched that way one night and decided it wasn't the way he wanted to go. He glanced up at the sky. There wasn't even a glimmer of a moon so there'd be no fleeting moon shadow to warn him if an owl was on the prowl. Dunk shivered again and moved deeper into the undergrowth of North Head National Park.

'He was in disputed territory. A scruffy tabby had laid claim to it and spent a week spraying everything that didn't move. Dunk was wary of him because he only had one eye. But what really freaked Dunk were his claws. They were so long they didn't retract properly and Dunk reckoned he sharpened them on the sandstone blocks some of the older houses rested on. Lately a couple of ferals had moved in and they weren't to be taken lightly, either. Talk about dirty fighters!

'Dunk exercised the greatest caution as he made his way towards the culvert. There was always something at the culvert and that something was usually rats. Dunk liked rats best of all the animals he killed, better than rosellas and probably as good as a kookaburra – if he ever got the chance to find out just how good a kookaburra was. They certainly looked good. Dunk wanted to get one, just one, in his claws. See if it laughed then! Ha! Dunk stopped, sniffed, looked around. Nothing. No ferals up wind, but that didn't mean there were no ferals on the prowl. Dunk reckoned he'd give a feral a good go but also knew neither of them would look good the morning after. He wondered if that was how the scruffy tabby lost his eye.

'He carried on through the razor grass and scrub, past the old hollowed out log where he'd nailed the little swamp snake. Snakes were good fun, too, while they were little anyway. He reached the clearing where he once killed and ate a pigeon, and had feathers tickling his throat for weeks afterwards. He hated that. He listened to the night noises. Crickets and frogs. Dunk liked frogs. They were great fun to play with. The bloody things could jump miles. The trick, he discovered, was to tense up before he took his paw off them, and see if he could catch them in mid-air. He was good at that and was always disappointed when the frog had had enough.

'He felt the wind pick up, lift the top of the gums and shake the daylights out of them. Soon the gusts would build up and bring lightning and rain. Dunk wanted to kill something before that happened. He slipped stealthily down into the gully. Another gust hit the treetops, deflected off the opposite bank and rippled down through the undergrowth towards him. Time was definitely running out. He stopped, frozen in his tracks. He'd seen rats before but never one this big. It was a monster. The kind that frequented his dreams but he never expected to actually see. He checked the ears to make sure it wasn't a buck rabbit. No mistake. This rat was the king of the culvert. He'd seen its tracks before, sniffed its droppings, but never guessed that it would be so big. So absolutely gigantic! Its arse was as big as the north end of a south bound mule. He sank down onto his belly and let a ripple of excitement play through his fur. He could just imagine leaving its carcase by the fence post where the tabby was bound to find it. Let him try to top that! Then he'd bring the cute little Siamese down to check it out. She'd probably prop and cop right there.

'The rat sat up on its haunches, instantly alert. Its whiskers twitched as it sniffed the breeze. But it could only detect scents from up-wind. Dunk, the great rat hunter, was down wind. He eased forward, insinuating his way between the strands of lantana, moving silently and always in shadow. Kid's stuff. The real test would come when he had the rat cornered. The bloody thing was damn near as big as he was. He focussed all his attention on his quarry, became oblivious to the wind and all other living creatures on the planet. As he approached a thinly grassed patch of ground beneath the gums, he worked his way slightly uphill to keep tree trunks between him and his target. The rat was feeding again, but nervously. It suspected something was up but didn't know what. But that was life to the rat and he didn't know any other way. He was at once hunter and quarry, and only the quick-witted survived.

'Dunk crept through the clearing. If the rat was going to spot him and escape, this was his chance. Every nerve end sang with tension and it took the most teeth-grinding exercise of will to stop his tail from twitching. He didn't crawl so much as flow from one blade of grass to another. He couldn't believe his luck when the rat turned its back on him. This was the moment! His back legs tensed. One good leap and he'd have the monster by the neck, have his teeth sunk in right up to the gums, his claws sunk in right up to the pads, ripping, tearing, disembowelling. He could almost taste its blood, see the scarlet fountains. He poised, braced, leaped ... and suddenly he was flying, flying, way over the rat which bolted as if someone had fired a gun.

'The searing pain in his back should have told him. But it wasn't until another blasting gust of wind caught him, and caused feathers to touch his paws that he realised the mortal peril he was in. He sensed the hooked beak above him, plunging, reaching, trying for the killer blow. But the owl had misjudged its attack or been caught unawares by the speed of Dunk's leap at the rat. The owl's talons had grabbed him more by the haunches than the middle of his back. The error gave Dunk a fighting chance. He pivotted and fought back, his front claws raking at the owl's head. It reared in surprise, turned sideways into the wind and was immediately swept away in a wild gust.

'North Head fell away behind them. The owl tried desperately to turn into the wind and make headway, but Dunk created too much drag. It went into a dive to gather speed but that brought its head within reach of Dunk's flailing claws. It pulled up, wings out like air brakes, and paid the penalty. The storm which had been building up now roared in from the Blue Mountains, turbulent and boisterous, disturbed by its broken run over mountain, ridge and valley. It hurled itself upon Sydney, seeking out the weakness in trees, toppling them, snapping off branches, wiping out powerlines. A sudden gust sent the owl spiralling out to sea. It went with the wind and tried to adjust its hold on Dunk. But Dunk was awake to it. As soon as he felt one set of talons relax, he tried to squirm free. The owl still held on but its hold was less secure.

'Waves skipped past them, angry and foaming, close enough for salty flecks to sting Dunk's eyes. But that was nothing compared to the pain in his back. The owl must have felt the bite of the sea as well because it struggled for altitude, but every metre it gained took it another twenty out to sea. Dunk sensed the owl was tiring and doubled his efforts. He squirmed and wriggled and lashed out with his claws. He miaowed, he hissed, he growled. Yes! He was sure, the owl was tiring. The waves loomed up yet again and the owl seemed powerless to do anything about it. Dunk sensed victory. He killed birds, birds did not kill him. The same thought may have occurred to the owl for it suddenly unloaded him without warning, and wheeled away into the blackness.

'For a brief moment Dunk felt elated. He'd escaped! Beaten the odds! He was just beginning to realise that he was falling when he found himself swimming, swimming, swimming for his life. His eyes stung and his fur felt leaden. His struggle with the owl had exhausted him. He dog-paddled furiously but had no idea which way to go. He could feel himself weakening and the sea getting stronger when his paws touched something. Land? Hope flared briefly. But whatever he'd touched was having as rough a time as he was. It rose up on waves and tumbled into troughs. But it floated, and it floated with him riding on top of it. He clung to it desperately, miaowed in fright, vomited seawater. But he was floating where before he was sinking and that was a definite improvement. He hung on through the long turbulent night, till at last the winds eased and the seas subsided. But his joy was short lived. The foam cushion, which had blown off a cabin cruiser and been washed out to sea, finally succumbed to the infiltrating water. Dunk's raft sank.

'Dunk was almost resigned to his fate when he spotted the yacht, couldn't believe his good fortune when it turned towards him, couldn't bear the disappointment when it veered away. But it turned back towards him again, and this time Dunk was determined not to let it get away. It trailed something soft in the water and he sunk every one of his claws in up to the hilt. He wasn't going to let the yacht escape like he'd let that monster rat escape. He felt himself being lifted up and deposited on something solid. Heard friendly voices, felt a comforting hand. But how could he be comforted? That rat had really been something to boast about but instead he'd let it get away. He just knew he'd never see another like it. What made matters worse was the fact that he'd also missed out on the owl. He was certain the tide of the battle had turned and that he was getting the upper hand just as the owl had dropped him. Bloody typical! He tried to visualise the awe in the cute little Siamese's face when he presented her with a Powerful Owl. She'd have kittens, and all of them would be his.

'"Miaowwwww," he said in bitter disappointment. Winced as he was hit with a bucket of fresh water. As if he wasn't suffering enough.'

'Powerful Owl, eh?' said Jago once the applause had died down. 'Nice story, but a Powerful Owl . . . ?'

'Friends of mine up at Avalon had their pet cat snatched by a Powerful Owl that came over from West Head.'

'You're kidding.'

'Nope. Take my word for it or look it up like I did. They're also known as the Eagle Owl. They eat ringtail possums, gliders and small brushies, so a cat's a snack. They have a wing span up to sixty-five centimetres, and the lifting capacity of a Huey helicopter. Some naturalists reckon each adult eats in excess of three hundred possums a year. Anything else you want to know?'

'How about that?' I said to Dunk who was still sitting comfortably on Sandy's lap. He flinched as I reached over and stroked him.

'Careful,' said Sandy. 'His back's still sore.'

'No cat,' said Jago as we tucked into lunch on the following day, 'has ever been in deeper shit than Dunk.'

Jerry began to laugh. There was always an expectation of the outrageous whenever Jago told a tale. He'd left school at the end of year eleven and walked straight into an apprenticeship as an electrician. He'd still be stringing wires on lamp posts if his job hadn't taken him up to the northern beaches one day when the 'Home and Away' crew were filming an episode. He saw a truck with Electrician written on the side and figured he'd found a more exciting way to play with wires. It helped that he had the ideal personality for a film crew and an inexhaustible capacity for beer. He'd become so popular and sought after, he'd formed his own company. But none of his brushes with the famous and almost famous had worn off any of his rough edges. He lived life closer to the bone than the rest of us, and it never failed to show.

'I've been up to my neck in it,' Jago went on, 'but Dunk's been all the way up the creek to the source. Being left seven miles out to sea waiting for the gulls to peck his eyes out, or a passing white pointer to turn him into mincemeat was nothing compared to what he's been through. All because this randy little bugger has the sex drive of an adolescent dolphin.'

'I didn't know dolphins were sex maniacs?'

'Well, Sandy, you can take my word for it or look it up like I did.'

Jerry snorted and sprayed beer over his plate.

'Dolphins are among the randiest creatures on earth. They're at it all day every day, which is why they always have that bloody stupid grin on their faces. They're not particularly discriminating, either. With dolphins it's a case of wham, bam, thank you Ma'am . . . oops! sorry Sir!, when they leap before they look.'

'You're not suggesting our Dunk is a switch-hitter are you?' asked Jerry when he'd stopped laughing.

'No way. Dunk is rigidly hetero. You know that cute little Siamese you mentioned, well she's into her third litter of little Dunks. Twelve kittens she's had so far and every one has been black with white pubes. Those two ferals you talked about. Both females. You made out like Dunk was scared of them. Bullshit. They're both pregnant and think he's the cat's whiskers. That one-eyed tabby? Pregnant. Tabbies are female and Dunk's not one to let a tabby pass him by. In his time Dunk's even had it off with Fifi, a prissy little French poodle that lives up the street, at least a dozen possums and a koala. Dunk has paid a call on every female cat from Harbord to Balgowlah. Just take a drive through Manly. Every second cat you see is black and white and that's all Dunk's doing. And the truth is, Dunk would be back home right now blowing into the cute little Siamese's ear if he hadn't got carried away by his own publicity, if he hadn't got over-ambitious, and if the zoo's Sumatran tiger hadn't had cubs.'

'Oh give us a break,' interrupted Sandy. 'You're not going to tell us that Dunk had it off with a Sumatran tiger?'

'Nah . . .' said Jago, 'but it put ideas in his head. Seeing those cubs on TV got him wondering what it would be like to have a horizontal dance with a real wildcat. Having it off with a feral was one thing, but bonking a dinky-di wildcat was sex on the cutting edge as far as our Dunk was concerned, and about as unsafe as sex could get. He didn't expect to come away from such an encounter unscathed. But he figured it would make him a legend.'

'So what did he do?' asked Jerry. 'Bonk a lion?'

'Nah . . . a North American bobcat.'

'A bobcat?' Jago had sucked us all in. We went up together as if appealing for a catch behind.

'Yeah, he was doing his rounds up Fairlight way to see if any hot new sex kittens had landed into his territory, when he saw a crowd of humans gathered around a building site at the top of the hill. He saw a crane lower a cage off the back of a truck and, being of a curious nature, decided to investigate. He wandered up behind some kids and took a peek between their legs. He froze, went weak at the knees and collapsed jelly-like onto the ground. If it was possible for cats to go ga-ga, Dunk would have gone ga-ga. The kids laughed. They thought he'd had the fright of his life, but they couldn't have been further from the truth. Dunk had been bowled over, blown away, gob-smacked by the sexiest looking she-cat he'd ever seen. Fourteen kilos of sheer animal magnetism. He didn't know that what he was looking at was a North American bobcat, but knew instantly she was the wildcat of his dreams. It was pure, unadulterated lust that had caused Dunk's knees to buckle. He could feel his bits rising to the challenge.

'Apparently a local company had begun importing bobcat diggers from Topeka, and they were doing a demonstration of their capabilities on a site next to their showroom. Some PR whizz kid thought it would be a great idea to bring out a real bobcat from America as a publicity stunt, to show that the Topeka Bobcat wasn't just another Jap techno toy. Dunk didn't give a shit about earth movers, but he was dead keen on seeing if he could make the earth move for the bobcat. The closest he'd ever got to rumpy-pumping anything that size was a boxer bitch sleeping off her dinner – or so Dunk thought. He was lucky to escape with his crown jewels intact.

'It was almost time for the saucer to hit the floor so, reluctantly, Dunk dragged himself away and headed for home. But he couldn't get the bobcat out of his mind. He thought about her over dinner and during the statutory ten minute grovel on his human's lap. The more he thought about her, the more obsessed he became. Sure she was a big mother, bigger by far than any feral he'd ever seen, wild and savage, unforgiving and murderous, but she was also absolutely gorgeous. A genuine redhead with kinky black markings. Dunk really wanted to know what black bobcat kittens with white pubes would look like. He simply couldn't get the thought out of his mind. Besides, he had a soft spot for that building site. That was one of his happy hunting grounds. That was where he'd met up with the Persian with the sultry accent who'd taught him the Persian position, and other things he'd never ever dreamed possible. He was really cut up when she darted under a bus. No, the problem was the bobcat's sheer size and savagery. Get too close to the wrong end and he knew beyond doubt what would happen. He wouldn't have her, she'd have him. For dinner.

'He decided that Cheyenne – which was the bobcat's name – was an opportunity he could not let pass despite the risks involved. He thought about her all the following day and that night decided to take the plunge. After all, he hadn't had any complaints before, not from any cats anyway. And, at the end of the day, what was Cheyenne but just a very large cat?

'He avoided Manly beach front because people walked their dogs there and didn't always keep them on a leash. Dunk wasn't scared of dogs, but didn't want to waste his energy climbing up trees. All going well, he figured he'd need every bit of energy he had. He did the roofs down to the ferry wharf, did a death-defying dash across the intersection, then took the fence line to the top of the hill at Fairlight. He passed by the corner where his Persian princess was turned into pizza, paused briefly out of respect for her, and also to get himself into the right frame of mind. He couldn't think of her without thinking dirty.

'He got his first shock when he reached the building site. Maybe the business with the boxer had misled him, but he'd imagined the bobcat would be chained to a kennel or cage on the building site, sort of like a guard dog. In this politically correct day, Dunk failed to see why there couldn't also be guard cats. That made as much sense as anything else. But not only was the lovely Cheyenne not chained to a kennel, she wasn't even on the site. Dunk was devastated until he spotted humans staring into the window of the showroom next door. He sauntered over, rose on his hind legs with his front paws against the glass and peered inside. His blood froze once more. There, not two metres away was Cheyenne, left to roam freely around the showroom at night. She was even more awesome than he remembered, but more than that, she was eyeballing him with an interest that had little to do with sexual appetite and a helluva lot to do with hunger. Dunk didn't hear the spectators laughing at the sight of him pressed up against the window, every strand of fur rigid with apprehension. He couldn't take his eyes off her. She was magnificent. Short, stocky, powerful and without a tail to hide the more interesting bits. His own bits which had shrunken in fright rose to take a peek of their own. Dunk threw her his best, most roguish, I'm-here-to-look-after-you-babe smile. Cheyenne curled her top lip back in contempt and snarled ferociously. Even the humans pulled away from the window. Dunk's bits went back into hiding. Cheyenne had teeth like a full set of chef's knives, and looked like she knew how to use them. But it didn't matter. Dunk, the great feline finurgler and pussy pirate, had fallen head over heels in love.

'He had a number of problems, not least of which was how to get into the showroom. But Dunk figured there had to be fresh air coming in from somewhere because he'd never heard of a wildcat being house trained. That big cat was going to do what all cats do and not give a damn where she did it. And being such a big mother, there was bound to be quite a lot that she didn't give a damn about. Dunk hunted around and found a side window which opened outwards and upwards, about three metres off the ground. As luck would have it, the window was next to a down pipe. Dunk had watched possums climb up down pipes and figured if a dumb marsupial could do it, so could he. The scrape of claws on galvanised iron set his teeth on edge, but he managed to inch his way upwards. He reached the window and hauled himself stealthily up onto the sill. He didn't dare breathe in case Cheyenne heard him. He peeped over the edge and found his love preoccupied with a tiny baby one of the humans was holding. Dunk just knew she was trying to figure out a way to get through the glass and eat the baby. He often wore a similar look himself when he was hunting and saw something tasty that would fit nicely inside his stomach.

'Holy Mehitabel, he thought. How could he possibly jig-a-jig with a cat that thought nothing of eating human babies? It was time for a change of heart, but his heart was no longer his to change. Instead, his darting eyes took in the layout of the showroom. Topeka's local architects had decided that the showroom's ceiling made the place look pokey and had it removed. This exposed the rafters that braced the walls and helped support the roof. They crisscrossed from one side wall to the other and interconnected with diagonal braces. Dunk was overjoyed. It was almost as if the architects had foreseen his needs. He figured he'd creep out along the rafters until he was in position above and slightly behind his true love, then drop like a de-winged cupid. The absence of tail gave him a target he could not miss. He reckoned he'd be onto her and into the powerstrokes before she even realised it was her lucky day. Typically, Dunk had not worked out an escape route. It hadn't occurred to him that he'd need one. In his conceit he believed that once Cheyenne had sampled his wares she'd be begging him for more. Just like all the other cats had done. He conveniently overlooked the fact that Cheyenne was not just another cat.

'Dunk was almost into position when one of the humans noticed him and pointed. He had no choice but to launch himself before Cheyenne reacted. His aim was perfect, but without the preliminaries it was more a case of break and enter than sneaky seduction. Cheyenne gasped in outrage.

Nothing much had shocked her in her life before, and she'd never for an instant imagined she'd ever be shocked so rudely. It took her all of a millionth of a nano-second to gather her wits, launch herself into the air, and buck like a bronco with a prickle up its bum. Dunk was stunned by the sheer ferocity of her reaction, but never missed a stroke. He hung on and went for it as if all his lives depended upon it, which of course they did. She rolled over, spat, hissed, snarled, threw herself against the walls. She bolted under the desk and slammed into the bucket of the ridiculous machine that had stolen the name of her species. Dunk dug his claws in and kept pumping. Some of the humans on the other side of the glass were crying with laughter, others shrieking in horror, but neither camp showed the slightest intention of leaving until they'd seen what happened when Dunk finally let go. Dunk was having the ride of his life, but it was beginning to dawn on him that the ride was coming to an end. He had an awful, shrinking feeling that his latest conquest would not be begging him for more.

'He winced as she smashed his face into the edge of the bobcat's shovel, flattened himself flatter than a Persian pizza as Cheyenne bolted between the wheels. He experienced the final, exquisite moment of ecstasy instants before his latest conquest leaped into the air, executed a perfect double inverted somersault, went into a steep dive and pulled off the classic parachutist's roll on landing. Dunk had never experienced so many contradictory g-forces at one time, nor any as powerful. He didn't know which way to turn, where to hold on hardest, or where it would all end. But end it did with the parachutist's roll, and Dunk found himself shaken free and staring into the eyes of a very pissed off bobcat. And the jaws of a very messy death.

'"You are going to die!" hissed the bobcat, or words to that effect because she spoke a native American language which Dunk couldn't understand. Nevertheless, there was no mistaking her meaning.

'The humans outside gasped in horror. Someone suggested calling a vet. Somebody smarter suggested a bucket and a mop. They looked on in morbid fascination, like ancient Romans watching Christians take on the lions. On the whole, the Christians probably had a better chance of survival. This thought must have occurred to Dunk because he took off like a rocket. He screamed around the showroom with a furious Cheyenne snapping centimetres from his tail. He threw in a couple of his legendary Scandinavian flick U-turns, which gained him a valuable half a metre as the larger cat lost traction and skidded on the vinyl tile floor. The trouble was the turns sapped his strength and he couldn't keep doing Scandinavian flick U-turns all night. On the other side of the window his cheer squad was in full cry. Around and around the showroom he raced with the larger cat gradually making up lost ground. Dunk had to face the fact that he'd surrender all nine of his lives simultaneously unless he came up with an idea pretty quickly. As he completed a circuit he noticed a door to a back room left ajar. He threw in a Scandinavian flick U-turn and bolted for the gap. He had no idea what was on the other side of the door, hoped that maybe it would slam behind him. Had he known he was running into the toilet he might have had second thoughts. But he didn't and he hadn't and it was too late to slam the door because Cheyenne was already halfway through. Dunk dived for the only possible sanctuary, and thanked Mehitabel that the last person in there had left the toilet seat up.

'Cheyenne hit the cistern with the force of a small truck. The top of the toilet seat shattered, the porcelain top of the cistern popped and the flushing mechanism engaged. Poor Dunk. He'd just hit the bowl as the water hit him and his own momentum helped carry him away. He screeched in fright. He'd pulled off some tight turns before but none tighter than the S-bends he was suddenly negotiating. His back legs were still heading downwards as his head was propelled up, out and down. Down, down, down he plunged, along the foulest water chute imaginable, gasping for air and immediately wishing he hadn't. Suddenly he was flying through space. Saved! he thought. Then had his hopes dashed as he splashed down into a large underground tunnel, with a deep, fast-flowing canal in the middle of it. Dunk didn't know where he was or what a sewer was. But he knew enough to know this – he was in deep, deep shit.

'Dunk had dropped into the main sewer that ran down from Fairlight to the sewage treatment works at North Head. All he knew was that he was going downhill in a hurry and that humans had a funny way of burying their do-doos. Luckily for him, stormwater drains tapped illegally into the sewer all along the way, discharging the detritus of civilisation. Big Mac wrappers, Popper packs, annual reports, condoms, real estate brochures and literary reviews. Dunk had no idea what he was clinging to on his helter-skelter race through black space, but it was a four litre Lindemans riesling wine cask. He was doing fine until he hit the grille that stopped wine casks proceeding any further into the sewage plant. Dunk hurtled forward from the cask, felt the tips of his whiskers brush the sides of two steel uprights, either of which could have split his skull and ended his career, then tumbled once more through space and splashed down into yet another subterranean canal. This one was bigger and faster flowing and there were no wine casks to hang onto. Dunk panicked.

'Fortunately for Dunk, he wasn't the only one panicking. Just down stream from him and closing rapidly were a bunch of humans about to throw the rule book out of the window. They probably would have if they'd had a window, but they didn't because they were also deep underground. They were the people who treated the sewage and sorted out the oils, sludge and heavy metals. Their problem was a big problem. All the storms had flooded the stormwater drains, which in turn had flooded the sewers to the point where the separation tanks could no longer cope. Any thoughts about treatment or separation processes had become entirely irrelevant. Instead, they allowed the flow to run straight out into the pipes leading to the deep water outfall, two kilometres off the coast. But even that wasn't discharging the build-up fast enough. The foreman had little choice. He could open the flood gates and cop the blame when big brown blind mullet floated up onto the peninsula beaches, or allow the waters to back up. The latter course of action would've given people sitting on their loos a few reasons to complain as well. Just as Dunk was about to be drowned in shit hundreds of metres below the surface of the ocean, the foreman ordered the old outfall re-opened.

'Dunk felt the sudden surge but had no idea what it signified. He had only one thought in his head which was "Keep it above water".

'"Bloody hell!" said one of the workers. "What was that?"

'"What was what?" asked his mate.

'"That thing that just went whizzing past. Looked like a live cat!"

'"It's the gases down here," said his mate. "They get to you after a while."

'Dunk had one chance to grab a lungfull of air and took it. Then down he went, surfing the face of the flood, propelled by five hundred thousand emptying toilets. He closed his eyes. He hit the ocean about seven metres below the surface, raced past a couple of blue gropers, startled a kingfish, scattered a school of trevally and put the fear of marauding tuna into a school of chopper tailor. Dunk was oblivious to all this. He was propelled through the water like a poorly designed torpedo, tumbling, twisting, helplessly out of control. But the maelstrom weakened the further he went out to sea. He felt himself floating upwards and with the last breath in his lungs, kicked out for the stars.

'The ebb tide and off-shore breeze did the rest. Dunk had got out of the poo only to find himself all at sea, his hope and strength fading. When he saw the yacht coming towards him he never thought for a second that it would stop to pick him up. There was no way just one ocean could have washed away the disgusting traces of where he'd been. But the humans in the yacht did stop and pick him up. And if that wasn't enough to blow Dunk right out of the water, one of the humans even let him sleep on his bunk!'

Dunk had curled up on my lap while Jago had told his tale and I found myself wishing that he hadn't. He didn't jump down even when I was jiggling about laughing. And I couldn't put him down because that would mean that I went along with Jago's story.

'It isn't possible to flush a cat down a toilet,' said Sandy.

'How do you know if you haven't tried it?' said Jago. 'Mate of mine's a plumber. You wouldn't believe what he's found stuck in pipes.'

'I don't care whether a cat can be flushed down the toilet or not,' I said. 'I don't believe for a second that our Dunk, as randy as you say he is, could ever make it with a bobcat. They're too big, too fast, too strong. Dunk would've been dead meat in two seconds.'

'You underestimate Dunk,' said Jago. 'As far as he's concerned, where there's a willy there's a way. Shit! What's that!'

The lure I'd put out a day and half earlier had decided to do its job. Jerry grabbed the line and skull-dragged in a fifteen kilo yellowfin. Sandy whooped and Jago joined him. Fresh sashimi! The fish had only just hit the deck when Dunk lunged. Never mind the thrashing fins or the flailing hooks, Dunk went straight for the throat and sank his teeth in.

'Bloody hell!' yelled Sandy, trying to pull the cat off the fish. 'Bastard wants it all to himself! Wants to eat the whole fish!'

'No way,' said Jago triumphantly. 'He wants to screw it!'

The tuna was about the size of a bobcat. We all looked at Dunk with new respect.

Sometime during the night the wind swung around to the north-east and intensified into the kind of constant twenty to thirty knot breeze sailboarders dream about. Unfortunately, we were not on sailboards. It took us right on the nose and set us off on a starboard beat well east of the rhum line. Some sailors revel in these conditions, enjoy the pounding of the hull, the sting of the spray and the pervading dampness which makes biscuits soft and sugar hard. We accept head winds as part of sailing, set sails and plot courses with skill, talk up our expertise and wish all the time that the wind would swing behind us. This kind of sailing is plain uncomfortable.

Fortunately for us, Dunk turned out to be a good sailor and not at all discomforted by the heaving and tossing. He curled up on Sandy's bunk and only left it to 'add lumps to the porridge'. He'd impressed us with his appetite. Jago had thrown him the tuna head as a joke and nearly lost a hand when he'd tried to take it back off him. Dunk chewed his way through the whole thing, eyes, cheeks, skull and tiny brain. He made such a clean job of it, Jago also gave him the fins. No cat ever had prouder adoptive parents.

'Pity he's a septic,' said Jerry.

Ours ears pricked up. We'd gathered together in the cockpit after dinner to keep Sandy company and watch the stars appear, and this was clearly the opening gambit of Jerry's story. I was hoping he'd come up with something because I hadn't, and I was beginning to realise the handicap of being one of the last cabs off the rank. I was running out of options.

'What do you mean?' I asked.

'Well, anyone with any brain at all can see that Dunk is quite clearly an American cat.'

'Bullshit,' said Jago amiably.

'Fair dinkum,' said Jerry. 'Just listen to his miaow. Got that plaintive, southern states drawl. Trouble with you guys is you've got no ear for accents.'

'Miaoooooowww,' said Dunk, announcing his presence on deck with a sense of timing Bob Hope would envy.

'What did I tell you?' crowed Jerry triumphantly. 'Dead set rebel yell! Haul your ass over here, little fella.' Dunk responded to Jerry's attempt at a southern accent, hauled ass as requested and leaped up onto Jerry's lap. 'Dunk could never fall off a yacht because he was born on one and has probably done more sailing than the four of us put together. He's a professional sailor, an itinerant globe-trotter and hasn't set foot on shore for quarantine reasons since he left Fort Lauderdale, Florida, five years ago on a fifty foot ketch.'

'Like the one moored out in front of the marina?' I asked.

'Like the one that *was* moored out in front of the marina,' said Jerry. 'If you'd drunk fewer beers you might've noticed she left before us.'

'I never saw a cat on her,' said Jago.

'Did you look for a cat?'

'No.'

'Maybe you should've.' Jerry's powers of observation were legendary and were one reason why he was such a great cinematographer. Most people only see what they expect to see, but Jerry saw everything. If he said there was a cat aboard the Yankee ketch then there was a cat aboard. We'd learned never to argue detail with him. If someone inadvertently moved a prop between shots while we were shooting a commercial, he'd always pick it even if it had only been moved a centimetre. Some people said he was pedantic but we all knew he was a perfectionist gifted with an uncanny eye.

'Dunk,' said Jerry reflectively, 'was very nearly another victim of the Medellin cartel.'

Once more bums squeaked on perches as we eased down and made ourselves comfortable for one of Jerry's epics. Jerry would've made a rotten rally driver because he always chose the longest, most indirect way of getting from one place to another. We were looking at possible reasons why Dunk was dog-paddling seven miles off North Head. Of course, Jerry would begin his story with the Medellin cartel. Sandy had already begun laughing.

'Let me tell you right from the start that this isn't a story about Dunk. Dunk was an innocent bystander, a victim who happened to be in the wrong place at the wrong time. The fact that in the end he achieved more than anyone else was able to is immaterial. But while this is not Dunk's story, it does explain why we found him seven miles out to sea.

'If this story is about anyone or anything it would have to be Burgess. Burgess was the drug squad's most outstanding recruit ever. He was born with a nose for hard drugs and a taste for low life. Some of the other cops reckoned he could sniff out a gram of coke through thirty centimetres of concrete. He was no less able with heroin, hash, grass, ecstasy and amphetamines. It was common knowledge that Burgess was also a user which was a helluva incentive for him, and whenever he detected a stash the other cops had to beat him to it, often beat him away with their truncheons, or the evidence would disappear up his nose or down his throat.

'Given his extraordinary success rate and the number of arrests that could be directly attributed to him, you might think Burgess was a candidate for promotion. But, in truth, that was never a possibility. Even the New South Wales Police Force frowns on junkies being promoted to senior rank, particularly those that fart in front of ladies, urinate in public places and defecate on people's shoes. Mind you, Burgess was a Bassett hound, which makes that kind of behaviour marginally more acceptable.

'Burgess's handler was Detective Sergeant Geoffrey Belcher. He would have made Detective Inspector easily but for the fact that he shared many of Burgess's bad habits. Not the lavatorial ones, but he did feel more at home among the low life and dregs around Kings Cross, and liked to party all night, ease down with the not always legal relaxant of his choice, and get horny round about four am. The owner of the Dateless and Desperate bar they frequented always kept a bitsa bitch out back for Burgess, and a blousy blonde out front for DS Belcher. Some people might think their relationship with the bar owner smacked of corruption, but DS Belcher liked to think of it as symbiotic. The bar owner stuck them with their nickname which was immediately adopted in the streets and in the force. Mutt and Geoff, he christened them, and the arguments raged over which one of them was the mutt. If someone wanted to pick a fight with DS Belcher – and plenty did – all they had to do was call Mutt Geoff. Geoff could work out the rest.

'The truth was, if they weren't so good at their job, and if the drug squad wasn't so dependent on them to make their charge sheets look good, both would have been kicked off the force long ago. As it was, they spent half their time on unpaid leave drying out, sobering up or recovering from nasty little infections of their nether regions. And there were the other days when their triple short blacks were ineffectual against the excesses of the previous night, and they simply didn't show. Neither Mutt nor Geoff could face the day without a hit of poisonously strong black coffee sweetened by a sizeable percentage of the Queensland sugar-cane harvest. Burgess flatly refused to move until his best mate put a bowl of coffee in front of him. Some mornings he'd need the hit so bad that he'd get stuck into it before it had a chance to cool, scald his tongue and yelp with every lick. Geoff would try to take the bowl off him but that only made matters worse. Burgess would peel back his scalded lips and struggle up into attack position. A hung-over, slobbering Bassett in attack position was silly enough to make a cat laugh out loud, but Geoff never doubted Burgess' intentions. They never actually got into a fight because Geoff was smart enough to give him his bowl back. Now while many people sweat on their morning caffeine infusion, Burgess' dependent personality meant that he sweated more than most. He became addicted, completely and desperately addicted. Geoff wasn't aware of the extent of his partner's addiction until he totally disgraced him in an arrival bay of Sydney International Airport.

'Customs had received a tip that a passenger aboard an Aerolineas Argentina flight had a substantial amount of pure cocaine in his possession. Given that there were eleven Colombians on the flight, the tip was about as obvious as the Fine Cotton ring-in. As the passengers filed off the flight, who were waiting to meet them but Mutt and Geoff. The passengers were asked to leave all their hand baggage in a line in the middle of the hall and stand against the walls. Burgess found nothing of interest in the first fourteen bags but almost swallowed the fifteenth bag whole. It took Geoff and three Customs officers five minutes to haul him off it, while another two officers escorted the distraught owner of the bag away for a quiet chat. They'd already called the paddy wagon and were filling in the charge sheets when a downcast Geoff confirmed that what the Senior Executive Sales Director of the Colombia Coffee Agency was trying to tell them was, in fact, the truth. The once pristine and now tattered Louis Vuitton cabin bag did not contain drugs but samples of the latest Colombian coffee crop.

'Both Mutt and Geoff were suspended while Geoff helped Mutt go cold turkey on his addiction to premium grade, uncut, unground, prize Colombian coffee beans. The end result of their humiliation was that they were forbidden to ever set foot or paw in the passenger terminal again, and were relegated to checking baggage before it was placed on carousels. It was cold and draughty and the cafeteria only served Nescafé. Burgess caught a head cold that refused to respond to treatment and couldn't smell hash even when baggage handlers smoked it in front of him. Geoff just shrugged despondently when the force assigned them to freight. Oddly enough, the facilities were better and so was the coffee. Burgess' head cold cleared up and his nose stopped running. On their second day on duty, Burgess made a hero of himself and Geoff by sniffing out fifteen kilos of heroin hidden in a container of blue cheese. Everyone would have patted Burgess and made a fuss of him if he hadn't swallowed a couple of kilos of gorgonzola while everybody was concentrating on the bags of white powder, and begun a series of gas emissions that resulted in the airconditioning being turned up to full blast, and every door and window opened wide. All to no avail. Burgess lost more friends than he made.

'But reputations were restored, senior officers appeased and charges laid, and nobody asked or expected more of the dynamic duo than that. Mutt and Geoff were welcomed back to the Dateless and Desperate bar in the Cross, rather ruefully as it turned out because the owner was depending on that particular shipment of Thailand's finest and had pre-sold the bulk of it to his regulars. Still, Burgess wasn't to know. When, three weeks later, Burgess sniffed fifty kilos of Colombian snort in a container filled with books, Detective

Inspector Chivers of the drug squad decided to mount an operation to see if they could follow the trail back to the Mr Big. Given the levels of corruption within the force which went far beyond symbiosis, Geoff thought they had about as much chance of trapping Mr Big as he had of making Commissioner, and Burgess had of making the Commissioner's wife's standard poodle. All three were impossible dreams. But DI Chivers – known throughout the force as Fig Jam – wasn't to be deterred. He had his eyes on promotion. Fig Jam didn't know the other officers called him Fig Jam, and would have been pissed off if he'd found out. He'd overheard cops referring to him as FJ and associated the initials with a much loved old model Holden. He took it as a compliment. Fig Jam was in fact an acronym for "Fuck I'm good, just ask me".

'They followed the container to a warehouse in Ultimo that was leased by a company which imported novelty and specialty books from the US, the kind that offer authentic Italian pasta and antipasto dishes all written, photographed and printed in Muncie, Indiana. Fig Jam discreetly checked on the owner who turned out to be married with two kids and living in a rather ordinary, triple-fronted, brick veneer in Dee Why. On the surface at least, he did not appear to be a Mr Big or even a Mr Moderately Big. Fig Jam checked out the carrier and that was exactly what he turned out to be – a carrier hired for the job – but who, rather curiously, added that he'd been slipped a few bucks to ensure that the container was delivered as close to the end of the work day as possible.

'They watched fruitlessly for a week then decided to take the book importer into their confidence and elicit his help. The book importer was shocked, stunned, but even more than that he was amazed. He'd helped unload the container himself and there'd been no trace of drugs or anything other than the books he'd ordered. Fig Jam turned as white as the powder they were chasing. He turned even whiter when they discovered that more than half of the consignment of books had already been dispatched to retailers. As the importer explained, the books were so specialised and expensive he sold them in small numbers to book shops all over Australia. The cops had been watching for a large movement of product and hadn't thought about checking the mail or the small bundles whisked away by a constant stream of couriers. Fig Jam turned positively bloodless when he asked the importer about his security system. Yes, the place was alarmed, he said, but he'd turned it off for the sake of the neighbours after it had gone off late at night, and nothing had subsequently been found missing. Had it gone off in the last week, Fig Jam asked and was unsurprised to discover it had gone off the evening the container had arrived.

'Mutt and Geoff were called in to check the premises and the cartons of books that remained. They found nothing. They asked to check the container but by then it had already been returned to a shipping agent. Had somebody followed the container? Yes! They set off for the shipper's yard in Balmain with sirens blaring before they remembered they were on an undercover mission. The container had already gone out, hired by two very particular New Zealanders who joked that they were shipping possum skins for Davy Crockett hats back to the shaky isles. The cops roared around to the Kiwis' premises in Randwick, again only remembering at the last moment to turn off their lights and sirens.

'Fig Jam sent Mutt and Geoff in posing as man and dog, to check out the yard. Since neither was in uniform this was not especially difficult. The fact that it was slamming down with rain and neither had a raincoat might conceivably have aroused suspicions. But Burgess did his duty and wandered into the yard, located the container and cocked his leg on it which was their agreed signal. He then went into a hunch to begin a movement of a more substantial kind, another signal which this time meant "Paydirt baby!". Geoff was about to stroll in on the pretext of regathering Burgess when he heard a man call out.

'"Oh shut! Look et thet! Puss off, ya mongrel!" The man glanced up and got a good look at Geoff, but that couldn't be helped. "Gut thet mongrel outta heya und puss off!"

'DS Geoff Belcher did as asked. He'd heard all he wanted to hear. The man with the fractured vowels was undoubtedly Kiwi, and it was equally clear that the container had been used as a Trojan horse to get the cocaine out of the book importer's warehouse. He reported back to Fig Jam who was sufficiently relieved to congratulate Geoff and pat his partner. Burgess peed on FJ's shiny black shoes for a laugh, and went off to get a coffee.

'That night, specially trained officers surreptitiously entered the yard and the container and found nothing. Neither cocaine nor Kiwis nor possum skins. The birds had flown. They did find a false panel in the container, cruder than they expected, but good enough to get by if no one was looking for it. Meanwhile, other specially trained officers in a Ford panel van, a beige Commodore and a poverty pack Camry played tag with a couple of Kiwis. Mutt and Geoff were promptly dismissed as being surplus to requirements. This was a huge mistake though you'd have had to be clairvoyant to know it. Man and dog did what they always did when they were off duty. They headed for the grot and sleaze of the Cross where they could unwind and make themselves at home.

'Fig Jam followed the two Kiwis to an apartment in Kingsford, waited until they went out once more, assigned three cars to tail them, and searched their pad. He found a couple of kilos of talcum powder, more dishwashing powder than they could use in a year, drawers full of resealable plastic pouch bags, but nothing suspicious. He took photos, gathered fingerprints and went off to rejoin his team who were watching the two Kiwis eat a large snapper each at Doyles on the edge of Watsons Bay. The cops got takeaway hamburgers and spilled beetroot down their shirts, sat and watched the rain and lightning. Nobody complained because this was what they were paid to do. Fig Jam wanted to search the boot of the white Commodore the two Kiwis drove to make sure the coke was inside. But the boot was locked and his fellow officers warned against forcing it open in case they alerted their quarry. At eleven the Kiwis drove to a pub in Bondi. They enjoyed a couple of beers while the cops drank the kind of legal coke that comes in a bottle. Nobody complained because they could sense that this time they were going to make the arrest.

'As the night wore on the two Kiwis got more nervous and agitated. They kept checking their watches. When they got back into the Commodore the cops' scrotums tightened. This was it. This was what they'd been waiting for. Delivery time. Pay day.

'The Kiwis were nervous and it showed in the way they drove. When they swerved suddenly and hightailed it up a one-way street, Fig Jam thought they'd twigged to them. But no. They were just checking to see if they were being followed. Wisely, the Ford immediately behind them drove straight on while the other cars doubled around the block and renewed contact. They followed the car around Moore Park twice, followed it down Crown Street, down to Elizabeth Street, up to Cleveland Street and back to Crown Street. They were either very cautious or killing time. Around three am, just as Mutt and Geoff were beginning to feel numb enough to contemplate the bitsa bitch and the blousy blonde, the Kiwis turned their Commodore towards Kings Cross.

'For once, the owner of the Dateless and Desperate bar hadn't seemed all that pleased to see his favourite customers. He'd hit them with free drinks to bring forward the moment when both man and dog plunged forward pissed out of their brains and dead to the world, but Mutt and Geoff had their own practised speed of drinking and couldn't be coaxed into hurrying. After all, there was the blonde and the bitsa to consider. The owner tried walking the blonde and the bitsa past their noses to give them a sniff of what they fancied, and entice them into taking an earlier run over the target. But neither Mutt nor Geoff needed to look at a watch to know there was still an hour to go before four am, and four am was when the cock crowed.

'The Kiwis' Commodore drove past the door of the Dateless and Desperate Bar three times, before stopping just long enough on the opposite side of the road for a passenger to get out. He melted into a doorway and stood watching the bar entrance. The Commodore drove away, chucked a U-turn unexpectedly and came roaring back. It passed the poverty pack Camry which nobody ever looks at, the Ford panel van and the beige Commodore. Nevertheless, the Kiwi in the doorway couldn't help take note. The Kiwi Commodore lapped the block and ghosted up outside the bar once more. It sat with its engine running. Five minutes passed. Ten. A patrol car cruised by with two bored young cops inside wondering if they'd get a chance to pick up the great looking prostitute in wet white tights down on William Street. They never gave the Kiwi Commodore a glance. Across the road the sentry signalled to the driver and headlights dimmed. Fig Jam watched from the beige Commodore parked up behind a street sweeping machine whose driver had knocked off for a joint. The poverty pack Camry sat on a corner up the street where the crew tried to explain to the two young cops in the patrol car that they weren't parking illegally, were undercover cops, were in the middle of an operation, and that if the two on patrol didn't get their arses out of Kings Cross immediately, their balls would be taken and used as ping-pong balls down at the officers club. The young cops were not convinced. The Ford panel van blocked a narrow laneway a hundred metres up the road, its occupants glued to their radio while junkies scratched their initials in the panels with their syringes. They figured the laneway was their territory, their concession to getting drugs off the street. They didn't appreciate the company.

'Inside the Dateless and Desperate, the owner was beginning to despair. DS Belcher was okay as far as cops went, but no cop in his right mind would turn a blind eye to fifty kilos of pure Colombian white gold. Two suitcases full of high denomination US and Australian dollars sat out back under guard, waiting to be exchanged for a white Commodore. Even though Mutt and Geoff would never lay eyes on the coke, much less get a sniff of it, he knew Geoff was smart enough even when pissed to know something was going down. The owner couldn't risk having them around.

Just as Kiwi passenger joined Kiwi driver outside the bar, the owner had an idea. He slipped a hundred dollar note to the thug he'd hired as bouncer for the night. For a hundred dollars, the thug should have guessed all was not as simple as it appeared.

'"Hi guys," the bouncer said to Mutt and Geoff. He reached down and patted Burgess on his befuddled head. "How are you, Geoff?" he asked the dog.

'Outside, Fig Jam's scrotum had tightened so much it was strangling him. Nobody really understood him when he said a good arrest was better than sex but, by God!, it was! He wanted to call his men in but knew this was the moment when maximum patience was called for. He had to find out who was receiving.

'"This one's mine," he said, and opened the car door. One of the Kiwis turned to look the instant the interior light went on.

'"Oh shit!" said Fig Jam and went to close the door.

'"Just keep going, Sir!" hissed his driver who couldn't believe how anyone as stupid as his boss could get into the police force in the first place, let alone get promoted. "Just keep going!"

'Fig Jam got out of the car, staggered across the pavement and puked into the closed doorway of a restaurant. Anyone looking would have thought he was just another drunk, and that's what the watching Kiwis thought. His driver knew better. His boss always puked when he stuffed up and promotion was on the line. Fig Jam staggered towards the Dateless and Desperate. The Kiwis watched contemptuously as he entered. Later Fig Jam would claim it was all a big act, but if it was it was worthy of an Oscar. Fig Jam was halfway through the door when Geoff and the

141

bouncer hit him full in the chest. He flew backwards through the air and crunched onto the pavement. He felt his head hit a car door and something piss on his shoes. He opened his eyes and looked around in confusion. Only one thing on earth pissed on his shoes.

'"Mutt!" he screamed. "And Geoff!"

'"Sir!" Geoff snapped back, responding to training and giving the bouncer a free shot at his unprotected chin.

'"Shut!" screamed a Kiwi. "Thet bloke! Thet dog! They were et the yard!"

'"Stop them!" screamed Fig Jam. "Stop! You're under arrest," he yelled hopefully. But the Commodore's motor was already screaming and its tyres smoking. The noise must have woken the driver of the street cleaner because he reversed without looking and cleaned the nose of the beige Commodore right up to the windscreen. The poverty pack Camry T-boned the two cops in the patrol car and went nowhere. The Ford panel van surged out of the laneway but it was immediately apparent to its occupants that they weren't going to get far with syringes stuck in their tyres.

'The Kiwis screamed off towards Rushcutters Bay, turned left and shot down New South Head Road. They were passed by a bunch of kids doing time trials in a ported, twin-rotor Mazda and took the next street left.

'"Where are we going?" yelled the driver.

'"I was hoping you knew," he yelled back.

'They stopped when they ran out of road, their headlights highlighting the hulls of the assembled yachts.

'"Bewdy," they said together.

'They were fortunate in that the owner of the big, beautiful, ocean-going ketch conveniently moored outside the marina, was at that moment whispering into the ear of a handsome woman he'd picked up at the Marble Bar in the Hilton. She'd chosen her place over his. The Kiwis threw as much of the precious white powder as they could into a dinghy, opened the car windows, drove the Commodore into the water, and rowed out. Being New Zealanders and holders of the Americas Cup, yachts held no fear for them despite the fact that neither had set foot on one before. They started the motor and crept away from the marina. They motored down harbour with lights out, past the restaurant that had fed them and towards the Heads, grateful that the storm had eased and that the moon had gone home early for the night. Neither of them had noticed that they had a passenger.

'"Jew know how tuh sail thus thung?" one of the Kiwis asked.

'"Nah. Jew?"

'"Nah. Whut'll we do when we run out uv guess?"

'"Learn tuh sail, I spose."

'Dunk overheard this exchange and knew he was in serious trouble.

'Dunk had ducked for cover the instant he heard the strangers come aboard. If the yacht's owner had wanted an animal to protect his ketch while he was out, Dunk figured he would have got a dog. Dunk was neither a guard dog nor a guard cat. He was hell bent on safeguarding his remaining seven lives. (He'd lost one rounding the Horn and another in a tropical cyclone off Fiji.) As soon as he'd heard footsteps on the deck, he'd ducked for cover on the top bunk of the crews' quarters. He thought he'd made a serious tactical error when the two intruders began to throw plastic bags full of white stuff onto the bunks from the doorway. He ducked, dived, side-stepped and blessed the fact that human beings couldn't see in the dark.

'He lay motionless among the little packets as the yacht eased away down harbour, ears up like radar dishes as he tried to work out what was happening, whether they'd feed him, or whether they'd toss him overboard. He lay motionless, past Watsons Bay, past Lady Jane until he felt the roll of the ocean swells on the hull and immediately got bored. Ocean swells meant endless days and weeks of boredom intermingled with bouts of acute discomfort. He looked around for something to amuse himself and didn't have to look far. He whacked one of the plastic packets with a paw. It was kind of heavy but soft like a fat rat's bum. He leaped on a packet, seized it between his front paws and tossed it into the air. It hit the ceiling and plunged back towards the bunk. But Dunk had played this game before and anticipated well. He leaped before the little packet had begun its descent and caught it just as it hit the bunk. This, he decided, was fun. He didn't realise that sharp claws and plastic bags were not an ideal combination, nor that plastic bags were not designed to be tossed about like a dead rat. Sooner or later something had to give.

'Up top, the Kiwis had decided to head for home. Australia was just too hot for them. They figured that so long as they headed east they had to hit New Zealand sooner or later or, failing that, Chile. A quick check of the galley by Bic lighter had revealed ample supplies of tinned and dried food, a couple of weeks' supply of beer, scotch, gin, vodka and a couple of Hunter reds. They began to feel good about being on a yacht, saw it as a bit of an adventure and even a holiday. They were about to congratulate each other on their good fortune when Dunk's imitation play rat bust its guts. Dunk sneezed.

'"Jew hear thet?"

'Both men stiffened as they digested the implications. The crazy thing was, neither of them had bothered to search the yacht to make sure no one else was aboard. When no one had challenged them, they'd assumed it was deserted. Now they knew differently. They were still too close to shore to turn on their lights, and neither liked the idea of going down into the bowels of the yacht alone. They didn't know who or what they might find down there.

'"Efta you," said one Kiwi.

'"No. Efta you," said the other.

'They crept down the ladder into the galley, armed themselves with a bottle of claret each which they held by the neck like a club. Neither was a sailor and neither realised the foolishness of abandoning watch so close in on a busy shoreline. Neither of them considered for an instant that there might be anyone else on the water apart from themselves. If either of them had even noticed the blacker than black shape off the port bow or caught a glimpse of the container ship's lights, it hadn't registered. The two men stole along the corridor between the cabins, bottles and Bic lighters at the ready.

'Dunk sat on the top bunk dazed, wondering if what had happened was his first original thought. If it was, he wanted another. He couldn't believe the light show and firework spectacular he'd seen as the transmitters and receptors in his brain had gone into overload and fused. He was curious to know what had caused all the excitement and suspected it was the white stuff that coated the top bunk. He sniffed to check it out. Whammo! Dunk sneezed himself off his paws.

'The two Kiwis froze. They'd been about to investigate the main cabin but there was no doubt where the sneeze had come from. They crept along to the crews' cabin and took up position either side of the door frame. The two men tensed and listened through the partially opened door. They were in no mood to take prisoners. They heard rustling and shuffling and knew somebody was messing with their stash of coke. That explained the sneeze. Someone was helping himself to freebies! They kicked the door wide open and leaped in swinging. One Kiwi swung too early and smashed the bottom off his bottle against the top of the door frame. He went through with his swing anyway, sending a shower of claret and glass across the ceiling and walls, and perforating another three bags of Colombia's finest. Foolishly he continued stabbing while his mate bludgeoned. Coke flew everywhere, including straight up his nose. He couldn't help himself. He sneezed, whereupon his mate immediately identified the whereabouts of what he imagined to be his target. He broke his club over his partner's head.

'"Gotcha!" he shouted, and wondered why his mate didn't share his glee.

'By this time Dunk was on deck and trying to climb the mast. As the men had burst in, he'd burst out. In the darkness they'd had no chance of seeing the blurry black and white comet that sped between them, nostrils like jet intakes, eyes like spinning helicopter rotors. Dunk was halfway up the mast before he realised it was aluminium and that cats can't climb aluminium. He looked around desperately to see where he'd land if he fell, when he was catapulted into space. Poor Dunk. He thought he was having another white powder inspired trip and vowed to keep his nose clean henceforth. But Dunk was just experiencing the inverted pendulum effect that occurs when container ships run over fifty foot ketches and you happen to be halfway up the mast at the time.

'The ketch went down like the first cold beer on a hot day, the container ship went on to Wollongong, and Dunk began teaching himself to dog-paddle, unaware that he was now on the Medellin Cartel's hit list. He just wanted to go back to Fort Lauderdale, Florida, and give up the life of a sea dog. When he saw us coming out through the Heads he thought that was where we were heading and thumbed a lift. So you see, there's no mystery to why we found Dunk swimming seven miles out from Sydney. He was just trying to hitch a ride home.'

I had to laugh at Jerry's effrontery. In fact we were all laughing, had been throughout the conclusion to his story. I ducked below for four more beers, figuring Jerry had earned his for his storytelling and the rest of us for our patience. When I got back on top nobody was laughing any more. They were all looking at me, even Dunk.

'Well,' said Sandy. 'You're last cab off the rank. You started this, you better finish it. How *did* Dunk get out there?'

How indeed.

I kept them waiting until lunch on the following day. By this stage they were all getting a touch impatient because Lord Howe Island was not only in sight but rapidly assuming form and substance. The outer reef showed like frilly lace around a bonnet. They were worried about who'd be first in line for a crack at the best looking sheila, but I was more concerned about my story. They hadn't left me a lot of room to move.

'Jerry's story has the most credibility so far,' I said to set the ball rolling.

'Whadya mean?' Jago was first to rise to the bait, and he had Sandy's full support.

'Well figure it out,' I said. 'Is this a competition for the best story or the most plausible reason for Dunk being where he was? If it's best story, then Jago gets my nod so far. Don't get me wrong, I liked the Powerful Owl and loved Burgess the bassett, but the idea of Dunk rogering fourteen kilos of bobcat and being flushed out through the North Head sewage treatment plant has my vote, and deserves yours as well. But I understood the competition to be about finding the most imaginative *plausible* reason for Dunk's being where he was and so far, only Jerry qualifies.'

'Bullshit!' said Jago.

'Where are the talon marks from the Powerful Owl? Where are the scars from Dunk's brush with the bobcat? I can't believe the bobcat wouldn't get some shots in for his corner. Besides, Dunk wasn't the least bit whiffy when we dragged him aboard and, by your own admission, it would take more than one ocean to wash the gunge from North Head's cloaca maximus off him. So, brilliant as your stories were, you disqualified yourselves. Only Jerry's story holds up. Dunk is not required to bear scars in Jerry's story so there is no issue with their absence. None of us here are prepared to argue that the American ketch was still on its mooring, and we do know that there was a container ship that passed ahead of us that could have rammed a yacht and been none the wiser. We have no evidence to discredit his story. Other than this.'

'Other than what?' asked Jerry defensively.

'Well, it's derisory to suggest Dunk is an American cat when quite patently he is a Kiwi cat. Listen to those fractured vowels when he miaows.' I turned to Dunk who had just come up on top and sat blinking in the glare of the sun. 'Come here cet und sut on my lep.' Dunk, God bless him, didn't hesitate. I knew Dunk was just looking for a lap to sit on, and also knew that the first person who spoke to him would be the likely provider. So it proved.

To their credit the guys scoffed, put aside their arguments and picked up the original spirit of the game. I guess they were beginning to realise that my opening argument was just a gambit, a preamble to predispose them my way. I couldn't compete with a toilet-travelling, bobcat-fighting, feline swordsman, powerful owls or hard-drinking, drug-addicted, coffee-sucking bassetts. My mind just doesn't work that way. I like to use known facts in the construction of my stories in the way that Jerry used the container ship, but make them more central to the plot. To my mind, the weakness in Jerry's story was that it wasn't really about Dunk at all, and the only relevance came as a tack on at the end. There again, perhaps I'm being unfair to Sandy who used the storm as a central element, and Jago who worked in the sewage treatment plant at North Head. Sandy fetched us beers while I tried to figure my way out of the hole I'd dug for myself. I realised I'd have to employ some of their shaggy dog tactics to compete.

'Dunk's downfall,' I began, 'was the result of his gluttony. That is the deadly sin that nearly caused him to rack his cue. When he went for the tuna he wasn't trying to bonk it, he was intending to eat it. Head, flesh, fins, bones and tail. I fed him about half a kilo of mince this morning, saw Jerry slip him a fried egg, Jago half of his bacon and a slice of buttered toast, and Sandy gave him a hunk of cheese. Since then he's helped us all eat our lunch, and added so much fruit to the muesli one of you kind fellows put in his dirt tray that I had to throw it overboard before we started shipping water over the gunwales. Sure he may be as horny as a hormonally turbo-charged dolphin, and guilty of sloth in the extreme, but it's the sin of gluttony that will ultimately write his ticket, dim his lights and cash his chips. Dunk is a greedy pig, that is his problem, and that's what landed him up to his neck in briny.'

'I also gave him half an Uncle Toby's Muesli Bar,' said Sandy guiltily.

'No shit,' said Jago in awe. 'He ate half my Mars Bar.'

Dunk yawned and stretched like the spoilt little moggy he was.

'Dunk was once the treasured pet of a Maori family that lived in Mangere, a southern suburb of Auckland. They were kind to him and generous. Maoris love food and seem to enjoy cooking and eating more than most other mortals. Dunk's family was no exception and their love of food extended to their pet. When they caught crayfish, Dunk feasted on feelers, legs and whatever was left stuck fast to the carapace. When they caught fish and gathered shellfish and sea urchins, Dunk enjoyed the sort of meals the Japanese pay fortunes for. When they roasted a pig, Dunk gorged on flesh, monstered the bones, and splintered crackling until his legs collapsed under the weight. But Dunk's great love was the backyard hangi, when the family dug a pit, fire heated river stones, and left the food to steam slowly in the pit beneath soaked sugar sacks and a mound of saturated soil. Sometimes they left the food steaming for six hours or more, which was okay for the family and friends who sang, played guitars and drank lots of beer to pass the time. But it wasn't okay for Dunk who didn't sing, play guitar or drink beer. He was driven mad by the tantalising odours leaking up through the soil and the knowledge of what lay beneath. He could feel the heat on the pads of his paws as he crossed the hallowed ground, nose vacuuming up wisps of steaming chicken, pork, snapper, kumara, cabbage and potato. Yes, Dunk would even eat cabbage if it was cooked in a hangi. Dunk would even eat the river stones given half a chance.

'Dunk would probably still be living happily with the Maori family, growing fatter by the second, if he hadn't done the unthinkable. Dunk succumbed to temptation. An hour before the scheduled meal time, while the family sang, played guitar, drank beer and entertained an elder of the Arawa tribe, Dunk did the unforgivable and dug up the hangi. He'd never had first crack at the goodies before and didn't waste the opportunity. He tore flesh off the breasts of chickens, ripped into the meaty haunches of pig, stole the cheeks and eyes out of the grandfather snapper, and licked the sweet juices off the veges. It was like a sauna in the pit and Dunk was forced to give up before he'd totally gorged himself. This is what saved his life. One more mouthful and he never would have been able to claw his way out.

'When the first shout went up he knew he was in big trouble. He just managed to duck the spade which was thrown at him with enough force to separate head from torso. He wasn't so lucky with the beer bottle that clipped him over the ear. Dunk leaped for his life, scrambled up the earth wall and ran. Modern Maoris don't sit around sharpening spears any more, but they're still pretty handy with teatree stakes. There was a bundle nearby, gathered and shaped to support the young tomato plants. They were thrown with astounding accuracy. Dunk leaped like a startled hare, ducked, swerved and still copped one dead amidships which sent him sprawling. A house brick substituting for a *mere* war club flattened his whiskers. If the

Maori wielding it had sunk just one less beer it would probably have flattened his brains. There was a hole in the paling fence which Dunk used when he was teasing dogs, and he went for it. A river stone travelling at Mach 2 helped him through it. Unfortunately, the enemy in the shape of a bull terrier and a really stupid cocker spaniel had come to make enquiries as to the source of the disturbance, and were waiting on the other side. They could hardly believe their luck when the cat that had tormented them and teased them into sticking their snouts through the hole in the fence appeared magically before them. They remembered all the times Dunk had wiped their noses with his scimitar claws while they tried desperately to withdraw their heads. The bull terrier sank its teeth into Dunk's neck while the spaniel grabbed a back leg. They took off in opposite directions almost as if they'd planned the tactic. Dunk's eyes bulged and his tongue lolled out of his mouth. He desperately needed a suck of oxygen but his diaphragm couldn't rise to the occasion. He knew he was a goner, gone in the most humiliating way of all, in the jaws of stupid dogs.

'Dunk's salvation came from the most unlikely source. The Maoris still hadn't forgiven Dunk and hadn't given up the chase. A tomato stake launched from the paling palisade caught the bull terrier right under the tail, completely burying its point. They say that once bull terriers sink their jaws into something, nothing short of death can force them apart. But whoever said that had never considered the impact of a stake up the date. The bull terrier's jaw dropped, its eyes boggled, it stood motionless for two-point-seven seconds while it absorbed the full shock of the assault, then bolted. Its one objective was to run as far away from its fractured freckle as possible. The spaniel chased after it, not knowing why or even wondering. Spaniels are incapable of thinking for themselves and always do what others do.

'When a garden trowel buried itself up to the handle right by his nose, Dunk remembered that he still had lives left to save and the opportunity to save them. He jinked left, left, right, left, right, swerved around a neighbour's Hill's hoist, ducked between two garbage bins, and took the first road south. He ran and ran till night fell and he managed to slip beneath a cyclone fence, and find sanctuary in a strange box with coloured lights and shutters. The pilot of an Air New Zealand Boeing approaching Auckland International Airport reported an anomaly in one of the t-vasis landing lights, which cautioned pilots if they were approaching too high, too low or off course. Dunk was that anomaly, and the anomaly had fallen into deep and troubled sleep. Dunk was now an orphan, a waif and a stray. More importantly, he hadn't a clue where his next meal was coming from.

'When day dawned, Dunk found himself in the biggest backyard he'd ever seen, but it didn't take him long to realise he'd snuck into the roost of the big, noisy, mechanical birds. He'd never paused to consider if they were edible, but he did now. He waited, crouched low, until a Fokker fluttered in, watched it race down the strip of black and creep slowly to its nesting place. He could hardly believe his eyes when human beings disgorged from its bottom. The birds ate human beings! How could he catch, kill and monster a bird that ate human beings? Dunk's depression sank lower than bubble gum stuck to a pavement. But the more he thought about those digested human beings the more his spirits rallied. Digested or not, those human beings were still walking and talking and he knew enough about humans to know that if they walked and talked they also ate. Where there was food for humans there was food for cats.

'Dunk stalked around the perimeter fence towards the terminal buildings. Ride-on mowers were hopeless near fences and he used the longer grass for cover. He started wondering again when he saw a second bunch of humans willingly sacrifice themselves to the appetite of another big mechanical bird. Slowly it dawned on him that the mechanical birds might be flying versions of cars. Dunk knew all about cars. They'd flattened some of his best friends and the matey Dalmatian pup that liked to play with him. He watched a car-thing drag a trailer towards the mechanical bird and begin to load something into its stomach. Dunk sniffed the air and cautiously crawled forward. He detected the unmistakable aroma of steak mignonettes, with baby boiled potatoes and peas, covered in a rich, dark gravy. And, yes, chicken breasts with white sauce and cauli. His stomach began rumbling louder than the auxiliary jet that powered the aircraft's internal systems.

'Luck was on his side. He leaped unnoticed aboard a passing baggage trailer and hitched a ride out to the aircraft. After that it was the easiest trick in the world to transfer to the food trailer just as it was lifted into the bowels of the plane. It was a tight fit and a less voracious cat would have balked at the challenge. But Dunk managed to squeeze himself onto one of the food trays before the container clunked into its berth. Dunk had never been quite so uncomfortable. He had to make room for himself and there was only one way to do that. He tucked into the mignonettes and chicken breasts as if it was the first meal of his life and threatened to be the last. But take-off scared the shit out of him.

'His plaintive cries for help as the plane buffeted through wind pockets saved his goose from being cooked along with the trays of beef and chicken he hadn't been able to reach. The flight attendant who rescued him was stunned and momentarily amused when his head appeared, then stunned and unamused when she caught a whiff of Dunk's terrible indiscretion. It hadn't occurred to the catering crew to put a scratch tray in among the food trays and probably never would have. Dunk was hauled out unceremoniously and passed through to the engineer on the flight deck, which was the only place on the 747 where they could hope to keep his presence a secret. The engineer couldn't stop laughing when he heard about the disaster on the food trolley, but stopped soon enough when he realised it was also his lunch on the line. He felt even less like laughing when he drew the short straw, which meant he'd have to taste test a meal from the trays immediately above and below Dunk's, to see whether the stench had contaminated them. He was a bad choice. His favourite food was hot meat pies, which in both taste and consistency were not a million miles away from Dunk's do-doos. He passed both as fit for human consumption.

'It says something about airline food that only one passenger complained that his lunch tasted and smelled of cat shit. The Chief Steward laughed it off and plied the passenger with enough cordon bleu cognac to buy his incoherence. Meanwhile, Dunk ingratiated himself into the affections of the crew. They decided to call him Muldoon after a late Prime Minister who had seemed to enjoy airline food as much as Dunk obviously had. When the 747 touched down in Hawaii, a carton of Kitty Litter was brought aboard by the new crew who took to Dunk as enthusiastically as the departing one. Eight hours later Dunk landed in Los Angeles and was featured on local TV. He was not, however, allowed to leave the plane. Being a celebrity, Dunk was given the freedom of the plane for the return flight to Hawaii, and subsequently on to Auckland. He was re-united with his original crew on the final leg and greeted them like long-lost friends, even though they knew something he didn't. The RSPCA was waiting to take charge of him the instant he landed in Auckland, and his chances of being adopted ahead of all the cute abandoned kittens were slightly less than being whisked away by a flying saucer to a distant planet, where cats were given an endless array of Chihuahuas to torment. Dunk was headed for nowhere but death row.

'It would be nice to think that Dunk had a sixth sense about these things, but he didn't. He spent the last hours of the return journey on the lap of an eighty-year-old granny, who occupied herself for the entire trip knitting little woollen squares to be made up into blankets and sent to the homeless and destitute in far-flung corners of the earth. She gave Dunk her supper and even unwrapped her little Belgian airline chocolate for him. Dunk liked her so much he snuck into her bag of knitting when she went to the toilet. The ground crew were on full cat alert as the passengers disembarked to make sure Dunk didn't escape. They helped carry bags for the little old lady who was last off the plane. One of the flight attendants carried her bag of knitting as far as Customs. Then the ground crew began their search for Dunk in earnest. The 747 was grounded for eleven hours while they searched through every nook and cranny, inside the wings, the undercarriage assembly, the garbage and waste tanks. Finally, it loaded up with disgruntled, delayed passengers and took off for Australia.

'The eighty-year-old granny didn't look like a dope fiend so Customs didn't bother to search her. Because of this they failed to find either Dunk or the block of hash she was bringing in for her favourite grandson. Dunk waited until her grandson had escorted her to his car in the carpark before making his dash for freedom. Dunk, who'd been raised on fresh seafood and hangis, had discovered another gastronomic experience and was infatuated by it. He'd discovered a passion for airline food and couldn't imagine why nobody had yet had the idea of putting it in cans for cat food. Nothing could be more appropriate.

'Over the next few months Dunk became something of a legend, popping up unexpectedly on both national and international flights. The RSPCA grew tired of sending cat catchers and vans to greet incoming flights because Dunk grew expert at finding ways to elude them. Besides, he was now famous, and Air New Zealand pretended to adopt him as a mascot when, in truth, management couldn't wait to get shot of the little bugger. Every aircraft was made to carry a bag of Kitty Litter just in case. But Air New Zealand had never had so much publicity since one of their flights had had the misfortune to plough into Mt Erebus, and this time all the publicity was good. Passenger numbers soared as customers chose to fly Air New Zealand in the hope that Dunk would grace them with his presence. More passengers meant more profits and management had no choice but to sit back and grit their teeth. Health inspectors were encouraged to make meaningless but high-sounding statements to the media, and look the other way. Their job was made easier when Dunk found ways of sneaking aboard other than inside the food containers, and no longer disgraced himself on take-off. But within the airline industry Air New Zealand became the laughing stock, and the aircrews got sick of being called cat cockies, stewards of being hermaphrodites and female flight attendants of tasteless pussy jokes. Management decided that Muldoon – aka Dunk – had to go.

'When Dunk popped up on a flight to Fiji, the airline instructed the immediate quarantining of the aircraft on landing, and arranged with Customs to do everything short of body searching the passengers. The PR department cranked out a story of how Dunk had become attached to a flight attendant and been adopted by her, when really Dunk was destined at last for the RSPCA's furnaces. A photographer stood by to take warm and fuzzy photos. The flight attendant was chosen because cameras loved her, and because she was on her last warning following a series of indiscretions on late night flights five miles above the Pacific. The airline promised to wipe her slate clean if she played along. All the way back to Auckland the hostie kept picking Dunk up off passengers' laps and giving him a cuddle so that they could bond. She failed to appreciate the fundamental tenet of cat ownership – people don't own cats. People don't choose cats, cats choose people. They choose laps to rest upon on the basis of smell, body heat, level and type of padding, vibes of the host, and other factors that nobody has yet figured out. Though the hostie was well padded where it mattered, and generated a level of body heat Dunk had only previously encountered in back alleys with she-cats that were hot to trot, he had a problem with her vibes. He could tell the instant he laid eyes on her, before she even laid hands on him, that the hostie didn't like cats.

'Dunk hid. He chose a little Shirley Temple with long, curly, blonde hair, startling green eyes, a smile that could make iron men wilt, and a bag filled with soft, cuddly toys.

Dunk felt right at home among the stuffed rabbits, teddies, ridiculous button-eyed puppies and a shaggy rag doll that looked, as all favourite dolls do, like it had led the charge against the Iraqis in the Gulf war.

'The passengers moaned and groaned as every bag and camera case was opened and tediously searched. The official explanation was that they were looking for drugs, and that the search was an inconvenient but necessary step in the fight against that insidious corrupter of the nation's young. It took a particular bastard – known throughout the New Zealand Customs Service as "the bastard" – to demand that Shirley Temple open her bag and spill the contents out upon the bench. Tears flooded the little girl's eyes and angry pasengers rose as one to condemn the bastard. Their outrage and fury seemed justified when all they found was Dunk.

'The hostie pounced like a marauding shark and clutched her little slate-wiper to her breast. The PR team moved in and the photographer wondered whether he should do the black and whites first, or use his colour camera with the wedding veil taped over the lens and do the shots for the women's glossies. He dithered as all photographers do, little realising that he was about to lose his shot. Dunk was waking up fast. The little girl's bag was the softest, snuggest place he'd ever been, and the little swings from Shirley Temple's arm had rocked him blissfully like a hammock strung between two palm trees on a balmy tropical isle. Of course, he'd fallen asleep, but now that he was wide awake he wasn't falling for the drug search bullshit. He knew he was in trouble. He knew he wasn't being cuddled but held captive. He knew the vibes.

'The photographer crouched over to focus, the hostie smiled, pursed her lips and tilted her head forward as if to kiss Dunk, but really to accentuate the size and fullness of her breasts. The PR people recognised the manoeuvre and smiled at the hostie's professionalism. They failed to appreciate that it also brought her nose two millimetres within range of Dunk's scything claws. Dunk struck as the flash went off. In that blinding instant, Dunk scarred the hostie for life and bolted away between the bastard's legs. The hostie screamed, somebody laughed, others cheered. And when the Customs, PR and airport security forces took off after Dunk, passengers deliberately blocked their way to get revenge for the delay. Dunk saw his bolt hole and went for it, skidded and nearly lost his footing when the ground moved from under him, nearly got crushed as a suitcase narrowly missed toppling down on him, then leaped desperately for the opening. He got the shock of his life when the opening tried to spit him back out. Ahead of him, other bags rose to meet him and a set of golf clubs to trip him. His world had gone mad. Still he sprinted, ducking the obstacles and battling the ground that moved in the opposite direction to the one he wanted to go. He saw light at the end of the tunnel and went for it. At that moment word passed through to the baggage handlers to stop the conveyor belt and block the tunnel. They switched off. Dunk, who'd been putting everything into making speed down the chute, suddenly accelerated. No Formula One Grand Prix car ever left a grid faster. Dunk shot past the baggage handlers at such a rate no one was later able to swear that they actually saw him. Dunk hit the tarmac and bolted towards the first set of aircraft wheels he saw, spotted a likely hiding place and leaped into it. He crawled into its dimmest recess and crouched, waiting for the hydraulic lift that would transfer him into the body of the plane. Gradually his heartbeat slowed to something approaching normal and his fur coat lost its punk look. He peered around at the container he was in and failed to recognise anything. He smiled as cats rarely do in public but often do in private. He figured he'd discovered a new way of sneaking aboard. He slipped off to sleep nursing that happy thought.

'The sound of engines warming up should have alerted him, but he'd grown accustomed to the noise and slept right through it. The sound of hydraulics should have alerted him too, but that was a sound he associated with the beginning of another pleasurable journey and slept through that, too. It was the draught that woke him, as it slowly built from breeze to tropical cyclone. And the noise was different, it battered and buffeted him as much as the wind. His eyes shot open and the very first thing he saw filled him with terror. He saw the ground hurtling by beneath him instants before he parted company with it. Dunk shrank back into the recess, as far from the gaping hole and howling wind as he could. He saw the world as birds saw it, and understood immediately why kiwis didn't bother to fly. Flight had nothing to recommend it. Hydraulics whirred and dark shape rose to fill the hole and block out the light. Dunk prayed to whatever god looks after cats in distress. His ears popped and the temperature dropped. He crawled towards a panel that generated heat and pressed himself against it. At first the vibrations and the battering noise drove him back, but in the end he had to decide between the cold and the noise and chose the noise.

'The flight seemed interminable. Where it was warm it was uncomfortable. Where it was comfortable it was cold. Dunk found one spot that was softer than the rest and absorbed vibrations, so he retreated there when things finally started to warm up and settle down. It wasn't like being in a bag of knitting or a bag of soft toys, but cats take satisfaction in knowing they occupy the best of the available places. His ears started popping again but he'd learned how to solve that. As the comfort levels rose, Dunk gradually relaxed and with the relaxation came drowsiness. He was no longer cold, uncomfortable or frightened. He'd survived with all his remaining lives intact. Dunk the indefatigable aviator and mascot to a nation of air travellers finally fell asleep. He hadn't a clue that the pilot of the twin-engine Cessna with the long-range fuel tanks was on final approach to Sydney airport. The pilot lowered the undercarriage.

'Dunk had the weirdest sensation that he was falling, which sometimes happened to him in his dreams. There was the time he'd dreamed that he'd been chased up a tree by three rapacious Rottweilers, and was teasing them on a branch beyond their reach when the branch had snapped. He'd woken millimetres from their slavering jaws, leaped in fright and knocked a coffee clean out of the hands of the person whose lap he'd been sleeping on. Nevertheless, this time felt more realistic than usual. He opened one eye and saw the sun peeping over the horizon beneath him. Beneath him? He opened the other and realised instantly why everything was suddenly so quiet and peaceful. He and the plane had gone their own separate ways. To his credit he didn't panic. He realised he was falling and did what any cat in his position would do instinctively. He pointed his paws earthwards and relaxed.

'Dunk hit the ocean with a splash that attracted every gannet, tern, gull and sea eagle between Botany Bay and Palm Beach. He gave himself a saltwater enema that made colonic irrigation seem like a splash from an eye dropper in the Harbour Tunnel, and suffered an impact on his nether regions which was like . . . well . . . a kick in the balls. It brought a tear to his eyes. He splashed around in desperation because swimming had never been one of his sports, and he refused to engage in any activity to which stupid dogs had lent their generic name. He didn't so much dog-paddle as cat-flap, an action which is unlikely to attract a following on the basis that it doesn't work. Dunk was drowning when we chanced upon him. As we dragged him aboard, the pilot of the Cessna was being interviewed about a unidentified object which was observed falling from his aircraft by the pilot of the Garuda Airbus, whose place in the queue he'd jumped. Customs suspected drugs. Nobody suspected it was Dunk so nobody came looking for him.

'The problem for us is, all cats are forbidden from landing at Lord Howe Island and Dunk is forbidden from landing anywhere in Australia without first going through quarantine. Dunk isn't just ours for the trip. He's ours – or more accurately – the boat's for as long as he lives. We didn't just pick up a cat when we rescued him, we picked up a lifetime responsibility.'

'What a crock of shit!'

'What do you mean?' It had all sounded perfectly reasonable and plausible to me. Everyone had laughed in all the right places and they were hanging on every word right to the end. But Jago was up in arms.

'No cat can survive a fall from a plane. How high was the bloody thing? Had to be at least a thousand, fifteen hundred feet. No cat could survive that.'

'On the contrary,' I said, pleased for the opportunity to air some trivia I'd picked up. 'It's a proven fact that cats have a better chance of surviving a fall above the height of seven storeys than they do below it.'

'Bullshit!'

'No, Jago, it's true. Above seven stories cats have time to realise they're falling and relax. Below seven they're still panicking.'

'That's right,' said Sandy. 'I also remember reading that in the paper.'

'Still bullshit,' said Jago without conviction.

'No,' said Jerry buying into the debate. 'They're right, Jago, and you're wrong. But that doesn't explain how Dunk managed to wipe off two hundred and fifty knots of airspeed.'

They all looked at me triumphantly. I picked Dunk up off my lap and tossed him at Jago. Jago's eyes boggled and his arms flailed as he prepared to catch the flying cat, but that was nothing compared to what Dunk did. All four legs spread wide and pawed the air as he twisted his body so that his belly pointed downwards. His ears flared, his nostrils flared, his fur flared, every strand on end and tilted forward like air-brakes as he tried to wash off speed. Jago caught him on the full and cradled him in his arms.

'Jesus, what did you do that for?'

I guess you could say I had everybody's rapt attention, particularly Dunk's. I started to laugh, couldn't help myself.

'You bastard! Poor Dunk. What did you do that for?' Jago was outraged and refused to join in the laughter.

'Just making a point,' I said. 'Cats can be many things. When they want to be streamlined, like when they're leaping after a bird or escaping a dog, they can be as aerodynamic as the Concorde. But when they don't want to be aerodynamic they know how to go about it. How long do you reckon it would have taken Dunk to scrub off his forward momentum? Sure he would have fallen in an arc but I'll bet my left bollock, shortly to be employed upon the best looking sheila on Lord Howe Island, that Dunk was falling to all intents and purposes vertically when he hit the water.' I reached for Dunk. 'Would you like a replay?'

'Piss off!' said Jago. 'Even supposing you're right, that doesn't make your story the best.'

That began the debate, and the debate raged until we lined up the gap between the outer reef, and sailed into sheltered waters off Homestead Beach. There were still dark mutterings as we picked up a spare mooring and began packing away our sails. Jerry suggested an independent arbiter and I agreed immediately. Theoretically, however, this meant we'd each have to repeat our stories to some poor unsuspecting soul ashore. I don't think any one of us wanted that for a second. The competition had served its purpose by keeping our minds and imaginations out of the doldrums of boredom, and entertaining us in a way that television never could. It reaffirmed our mateship. Nobody really cared who won so long as nobody lost. So we settled on the solution that saved face all round because we had no intention of employing it.

We were about to lower our tender when we saw a large Avon inflatable motoring out to meet us. It never ceases to surprise me. Wherever we sail there are always fellow sailors keen to make our acquaintance, check out our rig, have a few drinks and shower us with kindness. This bloke was no exception, an enthusiastic sailor who'd made his home on the island.

'G'day,' he said, and introduced himself as Bill. He'd brought a dozen icy Vic Bitters with him so we took to him immediately. He'd hardly been on board a minute before Dunk stepped forward to be introduced.

'Chichester!' said Bill. 'You bastard.'

Chichester?

Bill and Dunk greeted each other like the old mates they were.

'Bugger sailed with me once,' said Bill. 'We were forty miles out from Sydney before he announced his presence.'

We were dumbstruck, to put it mildly. Dunk was called Chichester? Bill had sailed with him?

'Sit down,' said Jerry, 'there's one or two things we want to ask you.'

'Chichester,' said Bill, 'is the resident ratter at Cammeray Marina. That is, he's supposed to be resident ratter but he's more like the resident napper. He has a penchant for ocean-going yachts and it's his habit to sleep on board them. The yacht has not yet been built that's impenetrable as far as this cat's concerned. He's been to New Caledonia with a French family, Tahiti with the Greenpeace flotilla, New Zealand, Fiji, the Whitsundays and here more times than I can remember. Mostly he wakes up in time and skips ashore. A couple of times that I know of he's managed to jump overboard and swim ashore after the yacht's set sail. He was on my boat once when he jumped off at the Spit Bridge, and the crew of one boat that sailed here reckon he leaped overboard just off North Head. I guess you blokes are out of Cammeray?'

'No,' I said. 'Rose Bay.'

'We picked him up,' said Jerry. 'Hitching a ride about seven miles north east of North Head.'

'Maybe some bastard tossed him off their yacht,' said Jago.

'Nah,' said Bill. 'Nobody would do that to Chichester. No, he probably woke up a bit later than usual, didn't fancy a sail, saw land and jumped. Swims like a fish, you know. Where was he headed?'

'Towards shore,' I confirmed.

'See,' said Bill. 'There's a simple explanation for everything.'

Mushroom Omelette

The first glimpse of the Tenggarese wending their way up the hill towards us made me think I was back in Bali, that our travel agent had made a horrible mistake. It just goes to show what a lot of crap goes through your mind when it's vacant. In mitigation, we were heading towards the tail end of a four-hour hike that had begun at dawn, and the sun had subsequently sucked at least two litres of fluid out of our bodies. It bore down on us with tropical intensity, honed and amplified by the thin mountain air. It had no intention of letting up until it had sucked us dry. I braced myself for the maddeningly repetitious sound of the Tenggarese's gamelan music which swirled in endless percussive cycles, and is not recommended accompaniment to a dehydration headache. But their music failed to reach us.

'They've stopped,' said Steph, who is younger, fitter and clearly more observant than me.

Odd, I thought. We'd spent long enough on the slopes of Mt Bromo, on the eastern salient of Java, to know that nothing short of a nuclear detonation could stop the Tenggarese playing their music once they'd set their mind on it. I glanced heavenward for the mushroom cloud but the sweaty grey–blue sky was unblemished. We kept on down-hill towards them. Something was definitely up. The procession had halted, banners were in disarray, people edged backwards with their offerings of flowers and food piled high upon their heads. It occurred to me then that there might be a dozen really deadly snakes sunbathing on the trail, and that we might be wise to take a leaf out of our neighbours' book and back off as well. At the very least, I thought we should stop. I decided to share my thoughts with Steph.

'Crap,' she said. And laughed.

I stopped anyway, using the last suck on my bottle of mineral water as an excuse. Steph never faltered in her stride. The Tenggarese were heading up the mountain to a temple to offer tribute to whichever god was due to be favoured this particular day. They're like the Balinese that way. Hardly a week goes past without there being one religious procession or another. At first we were attracted by the music and used to race up and watch them. Then we used to follow along behind. Now I duck for cover with pillows over my head to blot out the sound. Like water torture, I told Steph. Like a thousand dripping taps. But Steph has greater tolerance than me and quite likes it. I caught up with her midway through the last bend before we reached the back-sliding procession. If there were a dozen deadly snakes I didn't want Steph charging in among them. When we saw the problem, Steph burst out laughing.

It only occurred to me then that we hadn't seen any cats in Java, and come to think of it, none in Bali either. If all Indonesian cats were like the one confronting the procession, there was a bloody good reason for their absence. It had the entire column bailed up. It crabbed sideways at them, back arched, front paw swiping the air, spitting fury. It looked like the moggy from hell, but even so, it was still only a common or garden cat. Black, scrawny and undersized. Yet nobody seemed terribly keen to deal with it. As we watched, one of the village men stepped forward. He was wearing sandals, a sarong and a turban-like head piece. His chest and arms were bare. He was big for an Indonesian and well-built. His shoulders were broad and his waist tiny. The morning sun defined and highlighted the muscles of his oiled and glistening torso, and I reckoned the cat had about two and a half seconds left to live. I figured Muscleman would wring its scrawny neck like church bells on Sunday. One of the village women sniggered nervously.

In hindsight, I guess he was too casual in his approach to the cat but, then again, why wouldn't he have been? It struck. It didn't shy away from the hands that reached to grab them, but attacked and tramlined them. Before Muscleman could withdraw, the moggy had sunk its teeth into the fleshy part of his right hand. He clouted the cat free with his left hand and jumped back. The entire procession jumped back with him, as if the move had been choreographed and rehearsed. It didn't do Muscleman any good. The cat went for his feet. He screamed, the cat yowled, and Steph nearly wet herself laughing. In fact, later she claimed she had and that she only got away with it because her sarong was already soaked with sweat. The cat let go but never took a backward step.

'Hold it, Steph,' I said. Steph does tend to rush in where angels fear to tread. She'd bent over and was clicking her fingers to attract kitty's attention. 'Cats get rabies, too.'

That stopped her. The cat turned and eyed us malevolently. Just as I was absolutely certain we were next on its menu, the son of the village headman stepped forward with a *parang*. Normally villagers don't carry *parangs* on religious processions. There is a vast difference between a *parang* and a ceremonial *keris* knife. The young man had either run back down to the village or borrowed it from one of the workers nearby. It was sharp and purposeful, ideal for beheading wayward moggies and making salami of snakes. He swung it threateningly, whirled it around the cat's ears, damn near trimming its whiskers in the process. But the fatal blow never came. Slowly the cat backed away until it was midway between them and us. This prompted me to whirl and twirl my Swiss Army knife in warning. Steph reckons she wet herself for the second time but, hell's bells, what was I supposed to do? Let him attack us instead? Anyway, the moggy decided he'd had enough fun and took off into the corn fields on the uphill side of the trail. I tried to put away my puny pen knife before the Tenggarese saw it, but I was too late. They howled with laughter. The headman's son gave me a friendly wave of his *parang* as if delivering chapter one in a lesson on how to deal with psycho cats.

'Why you not chop off cat's head?' I asked indignantly, running my finger across my throat and pointing at the *parang*.

'Ooohhhh nooooo,' they chorused and looked at me as if I'd farted. Somebody tapped out time and I was spared further embarrassment as their music erupted forth. They smiled indulgently at us as they marched by.

'Bastard,' I said to Steph once they were out of hearing. 'Why the hell didn't he just top that moggy?'

'Maybe they thought it was one of their demons in disguise. Maybe they're not supposed to kill anything on the way to their temple, and the demon was sent to test them. Maybe beheading black cats brings bad luck.'

I hated it when Steph got all philosophical on me. Truth was, she was no more interested in the demons of the ancient Majapahit Empire than I was, nor was she a dabbler in eastern religions or mysticism.

'Maybe they know who the cat belongs to,' I said. 'Maybe it belongs to somebody important and they didn't want to get into trouble.'

Steph looked at me in amazement.

'Sometimes you amaze me,' she said.

Hell, sometimes I amaze myself.

All was revealed over lunch. We'd rented a house on the edge of the village, with a dramatic view down a V-shaped ravine. Both sides were terraced and given over to the cultivation of vegetables. Even the sheerest slopes were stepped with gardens which teetered precariously on the edge of oblivion, and probably produced insufficient crops to justify either the risk or labour involved. Evidence of landslides was every-where, newly greened but still treacherous. The soil was rich, a deep, dark, virginal, volcanic carpet, courtesy of the still active Mt Bromo and Mt Semeru, and other once active craters of the Tenggar caldera. Anything grew in it. If you left a wooden chair outside it grew into a sofa, if you dropped a pack of toothpicks it grew into a forest. The locals grew corn, spinach, beets, cauliflower, onions, garlic, lettuce, carrots, sweet potato, tomatoes, eggplant, peas, beans, radish, turnips, fiery red chillies and a wonderland of herbs. The only thing they didn't grow was rice. The whole northern hillside was so verdant and fecund I expected Steph to have triplets every time I crawled into bed with her. We'd chosen our rented home for the view, the locale, its proximity to burping, chirping, smoking Mt Bromo, and because it had a toilet that flushed. I don't know exactly where it flushed to. I didn't ask and certainly didn't go looking. Why spoil paradise with technicalities?

Though our village was far cooler than any in the lowlands of Java, the midday sun was merciless. Everyone downed tools, ate, slept, chatted or snuck away to imitate the beast with two backs. Lunch was their main meal of the day and soon became ours. A lot of people are wary about Indonesian village food, but we never had any real trouble. The little eating places we frequented were kept spotlessly clean, and they only cooked with water that had been thoroughly boiled. Often the plates were old and worn and occasionally even chipped, but they were never dirty. Even so, we had our rules. No raw vegetables and definitely no chicken unless it was one step short of being cremated. One piece of *kampung* chicken that isn't cooked right through will bring you to your knees faster than the Second Coming. The only chicken we ate was skewered in little, thin satays and double cooked over naked flames. Otherwise we feasted royally, preferring to eat out. Many of the *rumah makan* made dishes in the Padung style, which are slightly more fiery than Dresden at the height of the bombing. They burned the skin off our throats, snapped our breath, and sweat converted the creases in our faces to canals. It took us a while to become accustomed to them, but then they became our lunchtime choice. In the evenings we wandered around the village and grazed on barbecued sweet corn, sweet potato and satays.

We would have forgotten the incident with the cat if every customer who came into the *rumah makan* hadn't made a point of mimicking me trying to slice the bloody thing's head off with my Swiss Army knife. Then they'd laugh like drains. Their lives are boring until fools like me come along and make them interesting. There was no malice in what they were doing, in fact, just the opposite. I don't know how the other diners heard about the incident because they weren't part of the procession. Though Tenggarese, our fellow diners were either Moslems or Christians, unlike those in the procession who had their own peculiar form of Hindu–Buddhism, overlaid with lashings of animism. I guess you can't keep a good joke down and the restaurant buzzed with talk of the cat that held the procession at bay, and the pen-knife-brandishing Aussie. We speak a little Bahasa and some of the village people speak a little English. Steph claims to have picked up a little Tenggarese, but if I ever got into trouble – stepped on a snake or something – I didn't fancy my chances of her Tenggarese getting me out of it. Nevertheless, we managed to make our questions understood.

'Why didn't the headman's son kill the cat?' we asked.

'Noooo killlll cattttt,' they chorused in reply. They strung out the syllables so we knew they were serious, and that what we proposed was not only out of the question but beyond contemplation.

'Cat has rabies,' I said. 'One bite kill you dead.'

This shut them up.

'Cat has rabies?' asked one of the diners nearest to us.

'Maybe,' I said. 'Rabies make cat crazy. Make cat bite people.'

'Cat bite me,' said another diner. 'I not dead.'

Somebody translated and the restaurant erupted into laughter.

'Why cat bite you?' I asked.

'Cat bite me because cat crazy. Belong to crazy man.'

'What crazy man?'

'Crazy Australian painter man.'

Crazy Australian painter man? We'd lived in our little village of Lempung for three months and nobody had mentioned that a fellow Australian lived nearby.

'He live in Tamansari.'

Tamansari was not a million miles away. In fact, as the crow flies it was no more than one kilometre. The trouble was, you needed to be a crow to get there from Lempung, or as sure-footed as a cat. It was hidden from us by the towering western wall of our valley, which peaked on a razorback ridge. By road it was at least a hundred kilometres away. Nevertheless, in all our hikes it had never occurred to us to go anywhere other than within our own valley. Once a week we made the night-time pilgrimage up to the crater-lip town of Ngadisari, and rode horseback across the Sea of Sand to watch the sunrise through the mists and smoke of Mt Bromo. Other than that, we'd hiked up our valley, or down and across it. We'd unconsciously isolated ourselves from the world beyond the ridges that enveloped and cradled us. We were staggered by our lack of enterprise.

'Is it possible to walk to Tamansari?' Steph asked the restaurant owner.

'Of course it is possible.'

'Possible for us?'

'Of course,' he answered brightly. 'If you know the way.'

It's highly likely that everyone in the village knew the way to Tamansari, but finding someone who'd admit it was something else entirely. All we got were sheepish grins which indicated to us that the going would be no Sunday stroll. How could it be? The valley walls towered over us unbroken and seemingly unassailable. We would probably never have met our fellow countryman if we hadn't stumbled across Muscleman.

'Aiiiiieeeee!' he yelped.

It was the following evening and dark as a murderer's thoughts. For once the mountain mists hadn't settled in to blot out the stars and they glowed in all their glory. I've read somewhere that there are three thousand stars visible to the naked eye, but that night I think you could have safely trebled that number. The Milky Way hovered like a low cloud only just beyond reach. I was looking for the Southern Cross when I tripped over something that turned out to be Muscleman. He was not happy. Being Hindu–Buddhist rather than Islamic, he had no qualms about accepting a soothing beer from us. We sat with him and chatted. He showed us his swollen, bandaged, cat-damaged foot and the angry craters in his right hand. The cat had done a good job, no doubt about it, but all the same I was beginning to suspect that Muscleman was a bit of a wimp. As usual, Steph was way ahead of me. She struck an instant rapport with him, and I found myself left on the fringe of conversation, almost but not entirely irrelevant to proceedings. It rang familiar, and then it dawned on me why. Steph had a similar relationship with her sister. Then it really dawned on me. Steph caught me checking the angle of Muscleman's wrists and winked. Oh dear.

'Maybe cat has rabies,' I said. I don't know why I said that. Steph frowned. It was a low blow out of nowhere, uncalled for, and unrelated to a conversation they were having about the use of aloes in the prevention of wrinkles. They'd moved on from the medicinal applications.

'Aiieeeee!' Muscleman whimpered and recoiled. He clutched his damaged foot. 'This cat kill my foot.'

'Maybe this cat kill more than your foot,' I said, though God only knows why. If looks could kill Steph would have committed murder.

'There, there . . .' said Steph. But 'there, there' doesn't have a lot of therapeutic value in the land of the Tenggarese. I relented. I have nothing against gays but precious wimps are an affront to my male pride.

'Maybe cat not have rabies,' I said and tried to sound really convincing.

'Aiieeeee!' said Muscleman. I don't think he was overly fond of the word rabies.

'Maybe cat not sick,' I said. 'Cat bite other men. Other men not sick.' But Muscleman could not be placated. The rabies word had struck and stuck. He'd glimpsed his mortality. He'd realised his beautiful body would one day go the way of all flesh.

'This cat kill my foot,' he moaned.

I sighed. Repetition can kill good lines. By this stage I was getting a bit weary of the trend in the conversation, and feeling a tad guilty. I had to do something.

'I know,' I said. 'You show us way to Tamansari. We ask Australian painter man if his cat is sick.' Muscleman looked at me as if I'd just accused him of having sex with a woman.

'This cat killll myyyy fooooot!' He pointed to his injuries and left me to guess the rest. I suppose I was a bit optimistic in thinking I could con him into guiding us over the ridge on one leg, but it was worth a try nonetheless. I gave up on Muscleman and started thinking about the delicious sweet corn barbecuing to perfection just metres away, and the tangy, smokey smells from the satay grills.

'Maybe your brother take us to Tamansari.'

You have to admire Steph. First the waves of sympathy, then the golden stiletto. And she rarely misses. Muscleman perked up immediately. His eyes brightened and filled with hope. I thought for a moment he was going to cuddle Steph, cling to her in a sisterly embrace.

'*Dik*!' he called, which is Bahasa for 'younger brother', and to my mind a thoroughly appropriate word for junior members of the family. Younger brother duly answered the call and stood before older brother to await instructions. That's one of the things I admire about Indonesia. The pecking order is well and truly established, and everyone knows their place and responsibilities. I recognised younger brother immediately as one of the boys who brought us our bottles of mineral water. He was handsome, shy, still as slim as bamboo and was totally in Steph's thrall. She always gave him a drink, some sweets and a few rupiah for his trouble. He was shy but sly, and hard to get rid of when Steph was in her bikini. Younger brother was definitely not destined to follow the same path as older brother. *Dik* listened to instructions and nodded.

'Tomorrow morning younger brother take you to Tamansari. He come at dawn.'

'Thank you,' said Steph. 'And thank you, *Dik*.' She reached out her hand and took his to seal the deal. Little Dick – as we took to calling him – shook Steph's hand and promptly forgot to let go. Talk about a love-sick pup. But we'd found our guide and the key to a new adventure. We'd meet our fellow countryman and perhaps even uncover one of the great secrets of the universe – what goes on inside the mind of cats.

'You tell him give me money,' said Muscleman sourly. 'For medicine. For rabies.'

Well, well. Big Dick was putting in a claim for compensation.

One of the things you must do in Indonesia is look after your feet. Every cut, scratch and blister must be attended to immediately and swabbed with disinfectant and anti-septic cream. Every precaution must be taken against athlete's foot, and anti-fungal cream applied at the slightest sign. This might sound a bit over the top, but it isn't. Everything flourishes in this climate, including bacteria and fungi. I've heard of people being evacuated home to Australia in wheelchairs because of athlete's foot. Or spending the entire flight with their hands scabbling in their pockets because of near-terminal jock itch. Indonesia is cruel to the cavalier.

That night Steph and I put away our sneakers and dragged out our hiking boots with the thickly ridged soles and ankle support. We wore them for an hour or two before going to bed to soften them up and make sure neither our feet nor our boots had changed between uses. We chose a lightweight backpack on an aluminium frame, set out maps, sunscreens, insect repellant, torches, first-aid kit, water bottles, boiled sweets, dried fruit and a good Aussie chardonnay. Well, you can't go visiting empty-handed.

We were up and ready by the time Little Dick knocked on our door. He seemed disappointed that Steph had dressed already. We chucked in an extra litre of water for our guide and set off in the cool morning air. Three months of hiking around the mountain had hardened and toned our muscles, and made us fitter than we'd ever been in our lives. Even so, Little Dick set a pace that soon had us puffing. I was prepared for a testing but short hike, a hard vertical climb before ducking through a cleft in the ridge that wasn't apparent until you were upon it. A kind of secret passage. As it turned out, there was a secret passage, but it was a good ten kilometres up the hill, and those ten kilometres were among the hardest and most dangerous we'd ever attempted. The ridge walls were almost vertical and the track never more than thirty centimetres wide. Sometimes we had to lean out from the cliff to negotiate overhangs. One slip and it would have been goodnight Dick. If that wasn't enough to inspire the adrenalin pumps into overdrive, the soil beneath our feet was clearly unstable. Time and time again the track detoured around landslides and washouts. Time and time again we were forced down onto our hands and knees, toes digging in for purchase, fingers jammed in crevices or clutching at vines or shrubs for support. The view must have been spectacular, but I promise you I never got the chance to look. No wonder nobody in the village was keen to admit they knew the way.

It took us around four hours to reach the hole in the wall. Little Dick called a halt. Steph's face was as red as sunset so I imagine my own was no better. We downed a litre bottle of mineral water between us while Little Dick slowly sipped on his. I began to worry about the trip back. I didn't want to be caught up on the ridge in fading light.

'Dick,' I said, 'is this the only way through to Tamansari?'

'Oooohhhh nooooo,' he said shyly. 'Other way much quicker. This safe way.'

Steph burst out laughing. Bloody hell! I'd kind of positioned myself as Edmund Hillary on the tail of his faithful guide Sherpa Tensing. It was a helluva blow to discover we'd only come the kindergarten route.

'How long to Tamansari, you little dick?' I asked.

Little Dick laughed. 'Not long.'

'How long not long?'

'Not long.'

'Maybe two hours,' Steph suggested helpfully.

'Maybe,' said Little Dick.

'Maybe three hours,' I said caustically.

'Nooooooo . . .' said Little Dick. 'Noooo threeeee hourrrrrssss.' He looked at me as if I'd just crawled out from under a rock. Silly me.

We stepped through the cleft into a valley three or four times the size of our own, and spread with a patchwork of gardens. The going was far easier and safer but we still had ten kilometres to cover. On the plus side, the views were mind snapping, although we had little time to take them in. Six hours either way left very little time for socialising and I had no desire to do the wall of death by torchlight. At least we were now on the shady side of the hill and had begun to lose our beetroot bloom. Workers in the fields hailed us with cheery good mornings as we passed, and teenage girls giggled and turned their faces away. I got the distinct impression that Little Dick had been here before.

'You dirty devil,' I said.

He didn't understand the words but understood the tone well enough, and flashed me his locker-room grin.

'You've got competition,' I said to Steph.

'So have you,' said Steph.

Now what was that supposed to mean?

'Hello, you must be lost. Sit down, have a drink.' The voice boomed from a face creased with smiles.

Little Dick had walked us right up to the gates of the Australian painter man's house. It was surrounded by musty pink walls tumbling with bougainvillea like you'd expect to find in Tuscany, but inside, the grounds and buildings were typically Balinese. There were mango trees, lime trees and apple trees. Lots of shady lawn and gardens scattered with hibiscus. There were buildings for sleeping, buildings for cooking, a large open one for living, and a small one for painting. Water from a stream which ran through the grounds had been diverted through filters and into a kidney shaped swimming pool. Two exquisite young women lay in the shade by the pool, naked but for the bottom halves of string bikinis.

'Eyes right,' said Steph, but I ignored her.

It turned out that the painter's name was Nicholas Johnson. Steph claimed she'd heard of him but then I'd expected her to. If his name was pretty ordinary, he was anything but. He was overweight and florid, with a mass of grey hair, not especially tall but with enormous presence. He wore a loosely tied sarong and, as I subsequently discovered, nothing else. He had a booming voice and mischief in his eyes, and a face that indicated an unquenchable thirst for life. I immediately felt I'd known him forever, and wished I'd known him longer. He told us to call him Johnson and monstered Steph with his mischievous eyes as we introduced ourselves. She didn't seem to mind a bit. For that matter, neither did I.

'What's it to be?' Johnson asked as we knocked back the beers he gave us. 'A chaser, a swim, food, or the opportunity to tell me how great my paintings are?'

'Swim,' I said. I was hot and sweaty and couldn't remember when a pool looked more inviting. He took Steph's hand and guided her to the pool.

'Meet my girls,' he said. 'The one with the big tits is Jo. The one with the really big tits is Marg.'

'Hi,' said Jo who looked about twenty.

'Hi,' said Marg who looked about a month older.

Johnson untied his sarong, let it fall to his feet, strode stark bollocky naked towards the pool and dived in.

Steph and I looked at each other, shrugged, laughed and stripped. If Little Dick hadn't gone off with the servants to their quarters I think he would have freaked.

'Know what your prick reminds me of?' boomed Johnson as we surfaced.

'No,' I answered innocently.

'My own,' said Johnson. 'Only smaller!' He roared with laughter. So did Steph, Jo and Marg. And so did I. Well why not? It wasn't true, anyway. Well, not in my opinion.

That was the way the conversation went. Nothing was sacred but nothing was rude or crude, either. Johnson just ignored conventions. We wrapped sarongs around our waists while Johnson regaled us with stories and the servants prepared lunch for us. We drank riesling as cold and fresh as snow. I'd totally forgotten the reason for our visit when I spotted the cat from hell drinking from the pool.

'Ahhh . . .' I said. 'Your cat! That's one of the reasons we've come.'

Johnson started laughing.

'Here Button,' he called. He scooped it up, flipped it on its back and rubbed its stomach as if his intention was to collapse all of its ribs. The cat purred its evil heart out.

'Great cat,' he said. 'Wonderful!'

'Vicious cat,' I said. 'Dangerous.'

'Dangerous?' said Johnson. He threw Button at me. I had no choice but to catch the beast and hope I survived.

The cat gazed up at me, padded its front paws gently on my bare chest and purred in contentment.

'Not dangerous,' I said. 'Not even vicious.'

'I must admit there have been occasions when his conduct has been less than exemplary.' Johnson laughed.

'I tell you what,' I said. 'He gave a bloody good impression of a rabid tiger with toothache a couple of days ago.' I told him how he held the village procession at bay, tramlined Muscleman's arms and killed his foot. 'Why do you think he did that?' I asked.

'Who knows what goes on inside the mind of a cat?' he said. I could recall thinking something similar myself.

'Is he schizophrenic?' I asked.

'Aren't we all?' said Johnson.

'Muscleman wants compensation.'

'Then give him fifty dollars,' said Johnson. 'Give him a hundred. Who cares?' He started to laugh and I couldn't help joining in. A hundred dollars seemed so trivial even when I realised he was giving away my money. The whole cat business seemed so trivial. I could hardly believe I'd even thought to bring it up. The servants came in with a swag of tasty little treats then surprised us with a mushroom omelette.

'Specialty of the house,' boomed Johnson. 'You've got to have some.' He began to dish it out, and Jo and Marg got stuck into it even before Johnson had finished serving himself. I didn't know what the hurry was because we'd already had plenty to eat, and there was a lot of omelette left over. It tasted fine, but I'd have to say as the specialty of the house it was pretty disappointing. Other dishes we'd had were far better. It took me a while to realise the mushrooms in the omelette weren't ordinary mushrooms and why the dish was special. But by then it was far too late.

A long time ago I'd experimented with LSD and eaten mushroom omelettes up at Noosa, but I'd never had anything like Johnson's mushrooms. For the next twelve hours, all bets were off and all conventions cancelled. Stars collided, whole worlds vanished. The universe and everything in it altered, changed form, substance and meaning. Nymphs and satyrs danced and ran riot, chased each other around the garden and recklessly indulged their appetites. Colours were reinvented, brighter, wilder, more vivid and pyrotechnic. I also know that we were all gloriously happy and that nothing that happened mattered. I remember waking up in the dark and relieving myself on the lawn, aware that reality was knocking on the door but I was still not completely aware of who or where I was.

When morning came I found Steph fast asleep alongside me, and no sign of Johnson, Jo or Marg. I came across them later in another sleeping house, dead to the world and bound together as tightly as a ball of mating eels. My throat felt full of sand and tasted like carrion. I desperately needed a drink and some fruit. I wandered through the main house and stopped to re-examine Johnson's paintings. I was standing staring at them when Steph ghosted up beside me.

'Christ,' she said.

'Christ,' I answered. I think we were both referring to the aftermath of the mushroom omelette, not the paintings. But the funny thing was, we could have been. Under the influence of the fungi they'd seemed magical and mystical, vibrant, alive, fluorescent and overwhelmingly audacious, laden with meaning and cosmic insight. Now they just seemed unremarkable. The sort of paintings usually described as 'interesting' when nobody can quite determine whether they're good or bad. Steph took my hand and squeezed it. She led me back outside, plucked an apple from a tree and tempted me with it. Well, we could have been in the Garden of Eden. We were both still naked. The new day's sun glistened on every leaf and blade of grass. The hibiscus dazzled. We made a silent pact not to dwell upon or discuss the previous night, probably the wisest thing we ever did.

We ambled over to the building where all the cooking was done, found a fridge stacked with bottles of mineral water and shared one. We swam, lay in the shade and dozed. Johnson woke us up by giving Steph a big, fat kiss square on the lips. I thought this was outrageous until he did the same to me.

'Good morning!' he boomed. He rubbed his enormous belly and looked around him with obvious satisfaction. I couldn't believe how sparkly he was. Steph and I both felt as though we'd been hit by a runaway bus. 'Welcome back to reality,' he said. 'Or have we just left it?'

'This feels like reality to me,' I said.

'You think so?'

'Unreal,' I said after due consideration, 'would probably describe last night.'

Johnson laughed and sat down on the lawn beside us. 'Reality,' he said, 'is good wine, good food and a good woman – or man, whichever the case may be. We make our own realities by accepting what we're prepared to accept, or by not accepting what we're meant to accept. You make your reality, I make mine. Last night you wanted to buy all my paintings, this morning you want your money back. No, no!' He waved aside our feeble protestations. 'The paintings you saw are crap. They sell, but they're crap. The question is, which is the reality? The paintings you loved, that opened your eyes, that made your scrotum shrivel up into a tiny tight ball and made bells ring inside your head? Are they reality, or are the ones you rejected reality?'

'Perhaps reality isn't a constant,' I muttered.

'Excellent!' roared Johnson. 'Come, I'll show you the only decent paintings I ever did.' He took Steph's hand and led us upstairs to an attic room. The one exterior wall was all glass and faced south through the shady branches of a giant fig. There was no furniture in the room save for a solitary wooden chair, chunkily built and low to the ground, rather like a chair made for a fat child. There was no prize for guessing who the fat child was, or what the room was. It was a shrine. There were three paintings, one on each wall, and none bore the slightest resemblance to the riotous abstracts downstairs. They were magnificent, pale and delicately coloured, and superbly drafted. If I'd had to pick an influence I would have pointed immediately to the French impressionists.

The larger painting showed two naked women upon a woven palm mat in the garden, surrounded by a picnic of tropical fruits. All the fruit was sliced open and glistened wetly. The two women were touching each other. The effect was simultaneously erotic and innocent, calming and disturbing. I couldn't drag my eyes away or bring myself to utter a word.

The second showed a much younger Johnson sitting naked on a bed. Behind him a young woman slept on obliviously, her face and body turned away from him. Early morning light cast a golden haze through the folds of a mosquito net, which had been pulled back at each end of the bed and framed the figure of Johnson. The image had such lightness, delicacy and sensitivity I was in awe of the hand that had created it. I could almost see the dust motes in the air, feel the warmth of the morning sun, smell the aftermath of their lovemaking.

The third was of the same young woman peering at us through hibiscus blooms. The overwhelming impression was of light, pure and golden and ephemeral. The subject merged with her surroundings so that I was only ever certain of the presence of her eyes and the tumble of her blonde hair. Yet the painting had a transparency that had me wondering whether I was looking at a portrait or a memory.

'My late wife,' he said in a voice both soft and gentle and all the more surprising because of it. Neither Steph nor I acknowledged his words. We felt privileged and privy to something immensely personal and private. 'She adored it here, swore she'd live here forever. We created our own reality, a world without hunger, hate, envy, sorrow or regret. We created our own heaven on earth, painting, laughing, loving. One night after a mushroom omelette she thought she could fly. She couldn't of course. That was reality.'

I don't know when Johnson left us standing there or how long we stared at the paintings. I don't know if I'd ever been more moved in my life. I recall Steph sobbing quietly but didn't offer a comforting arm because it seemed so pointless. The man still grieved and grieved through the paintings we'd seen downstairs. There was anger in them, despair, frustration, pain and above all the fury of failure. His wife had gone and the gift had gone with her because he couldn't face life without her. His reality had gone, too, but the search for it continued.

We heard Johnson's booming laughter as we wandered downstairs. The girls were up and sharing a joke over a breakfast of papaya and lime, melon, mangoes, sliced apple and mangosteens. They drank from coffee cups as big as soup bowls. We sat and helped ourselves to some. I noticed Steph's eyes were still moist, but if Johnson did he gave no indication.

'Anyone for omelette?' he asked mischievously. The two girls shrieked. 'There's plenty left.'

'No, I think we'll give the omelette a miss,' I said. I sliced a mango open for Steph, crisscrossed it and folded it out. Juice dripped over her breasts but she didn't seem to notice. 'I guess after breakfast we'd better have a swim and then start heading back to Lempung.'

'Never to return?'

I looked up at Johnson, surprised by his comment. He had a curious expression on his face, guarded and perhaps even a shade desperate. 'Depends,' I said, 'on whether you promise to go easy on the mushrooms.'

Johnson roared, reached down and grabbed me in a bear hug.

'It also depends on your bloody, psychotic cat. If I give Muscleman compensation I'll have half the village beating down my door every time your stupid moggy yawns.'

'I'll tell him to behave himself,' said Johnson. 'Oh shit.'

We turned as one and followed Johnson's gaze. One of the servants had scraped the remains of the omelette into the cat's bowl. I had the feeling this wasn't the first time Button had tucked into magic mushroom omelette for breakfast. The reason for the cat's name became apparent.

'Oh shit!' echoed Steph. It was broad daylight but the cat's eyes were as big as car tyres. Suddenly the unfortunate animal leaped into the air hissing and spitting, clawing desperately at unseen demons.

'Oh shit,' said Johnson again and started laughing helplessly.

'Well,' I said. 'At least I can tell Muscleman he ain't got rabies.'

We visited Johnson on two more occasions. He was always delighted to see us and an entertaining and generous host. He wasn't the least bit offended when we declined the house specialty, and insisted Button did as well. Jo and Marg moved on and another exquisite young lady moved in. God only knows where he dug them up from. But nothing was as it had first appeared. Johnson lived life to the full, but his life was emptier than a crushed beer can. He was a man with a past, but no present or future. In the end we couldn't handle the sadness.

The V.12 E-type Cat

Gavin liked to say he was born with an innate sense of timing. Others said he was just a tin-bum. They claimed he was so tinny that if he ever sat in a puddle he'd rust. What Gavin accepted as good judgement his work mates called sheer bloody luck, and they seethed as time and time again he left them looking foolish. Gavin was a currency dealer and made and lost millions on the shift of a few points. He'd take a position against prevailing sentiment, look a total bunny by lunchtime, and be the hero and the envy of every other dealer by dinner. His colleagues loathed and envied him for his luck, but his bosses loved him. They didn't mind the enormous commissions they paid him, because the more money he made the more money the bank made. The bank's only concern was that one day a competitor would offer him a percentage they couldn't match. Then the man who made the whole top floor look good would be gone, and that would not look good at all.

Gavin and his wife Sharon were yuppies. They were also dinkies, with a double income and no kids. Sharon was a gynaecologist in an exclusive clinic that only treated private patients with expensive ailments. Mind you, the way the clinic charged a simple case of thrush was worth a month-long holiday in Tuscany. Gavin and Sharon had everything any yuppie could want. They had the best house with the best view in one of the best streets in Vaucluse. They had a gardener, cleaners, laundry lady, ironing lady, a chef, waiter and bottle washer whenever they entertained, and a rent-a-butler when they wanted to impress. They had Pentium chip PCs, laptops, CD-ROMs, digital TV and VCR. They had tame interior designers who sold them good taste, swimming pool, spa and plunge pool, and a four-car garage. She drove a Mercedes 500 convertible, he a sleek black brute of a Porsche 911 Turbo. The only things they didn't have were children, pets, tropical fish or anything that required time, effort or affection.

Yet Gavin was still not satisfied. There was something missing from his life, something he'd dreamed of owning ever since he was a teenager and which he'd somehow inexplicably failed to acquire – a big, Coventry cat. What Gavin decided he wanted more than anything in the world was a manual, British racing green, V.12 E-type, drophead coupé Jaguar, with bone Connolly leather upholstery, and wire wheels. He mentioned this deficiency in his life to Sharon.

'Then get one,' she said, appalled that Gavin hadn't already done so. She couldn't understand how anyone could allow a delay to occur between desire and the satisfying of that desire, when it was all simply a matter of money and money didn't matter at all. Money only matters when you don't have any. Gavin and Sharon had lots. Gavin was also hated and envied by his stockbroker friends and acquaintances who liked a punt. He sold up all his holdings a month before the crash of October '87, reinvested and got out before the slump of '94. He shifted his money overseas and invested heavily on the New York stock exchange. That wasn't a bad move either. The truth was, Sharon was quite right. Money wasn't a problem. Gavin could afford as many E-type Jags as he liked.

He cruised the dealerships and studied the papers, took cars for test drives and stopped alongside shops with big windows so that he could see himself in the reflection. But as hard as he tried and as hard as he looked he couldn't find quite the right car. Colour wasn't a problem and neither was upholstery because both could be changed. The problem was no car quite matched his expectations or standards. He didn't just want any V.12 E-type, he wanted the best V.12 E-type in the country.

He was considering building one up from scratch using new spare parts when he came across the car he was looking for in the *Herald* classifieds. 'Jaguar V.12 E-type,' said the advertisement. 'Winner Concours d'Elegance five consecutive years.' Gavin read on, hardly believing what he was reading. 'British racing green, bone Connolly leather and trim, wire wheels. Manual transmission.' His hands shook as he jotted down the phone number, dumbstruck that someone else shared his dream. It never occurred to him that half of Australia's male population also shared the dream but, unlike him, lacked the excess of disposable income needed to indulge it.

The seller was the most miserable person Gavin had ever seen. Gavin thought he was on the verge of tears.

'The engine has been blueprinted,' said Misery Guts. 'The tolerances are perfect.'

Gavin had no cause to doubt him because the big cat purred.

'Fourteen coats of paint,' said Misery Guts. 'All rubbed down by hand, and three coats of clear. I flew a man out from Italy to buff it.'

Gavin had no reason to doubt him because the big cat glowed.

'The Connolly hides were perfectly matched for colour and grain,' said Misery Guts. 'I flew a man out from England to fit them. Twice,' he added.

Gavin had no reason to doubt him because the big cat's interior was as clean and pristine as a bridal gown.

'Enough,' said Gavin, and handed Misery Guts one hundred and fifty thousand dollars in cash. 'It's exactly what I'm looking for.'

'I thought you'd say that,' said Misery Guts miserably. 'I've already made out the papers.'

'I'll leave the hood down,' said Gavin. 'I'll send somebody to pick up the hard top.'

'Very wise,' said Misery Guts. 'Mehitabel prefers it when the top's down.'

'Mehitabel?' said Gavin. 'You called this beautiful car Mehitabel?'

'Of course not,' said Misery Guts. 'Mehitabel is the cat.'

'Cat?'

'Goes with the car.'

'What do you mean?'

'Floor well, passenger side. She's on her best behaviour. She normally sleeps on the passenger seat.'

Gavin looked and there, sure enough, was a black and white cat. He hadn't noticed her before because she blended in with the black leather foot pad sewn into the bone carpet.

She matched so beautifully she looked like she belonged. And according to the vendor, she did.

'No way,' said Gavin. 'We don't have pets. My wife loathes cats.'

'Mine, too,' said Misery Guts. 'It came down to an ultimatum. The cat goes or she goes. That's the only reason I'm selling.'

'Why don't you just toss the thing out?' said Gavin.

'Don't recommend that.' Misery Guts rolled up his sleeves to show Gavin his arms. 'Only ever tried that once.'

'My God!' said Gavin. Angry parallel scars ran down both arms and it was clear that at least two fingers had been re-attached surgically. 'Have you tried the RSPCA?'

'Yes,' said Misery Guts. 'They sent two men. Both of them sued.'

'What about starving her out?'

'Ripped the upholstery to shreds.'

'No!' said Gavin, aghast. 'Not the Connolly hides!'

'Told you I flew the man out twice.'

They stood in silence and contemplated the sacrilege. Connolly hides weren't just animal hides but hides from barbed wire and thorn free enclosures. Nothing was allowed to mar their perfection. The smell and feel of the leather was intrinsic to the appeal of Jaguars, and dear to the heart of every owner. The cat must have realised that.

'Locking her out?' asked Gavin.

'Chewed a hole in the soft top.'

'Hard top?'

'Scratched it down to bare metal.'

'Oh dear,' said Gavin.

'Best leave a bowl of food and milk nearby,' said Misery Guts. 'And a scratch tray.'

'Oh dear,' said Gavin.

'And don't forget to leave the passenger window open.'

'Oh dear,' said Gavin as if he was caught in a loop. Never in all his imaginings had he envisaged sharing his treasure with a cat. Neither had it ever entered his mind that a cat would enter his life. 'How . . . ?'

'Came with the car,' said Misery Guts. 'No choice, really.'

'Does she . . . ?'

'Only if you lock her in. Otherwise she's scrupulously clean.'

'Oh,' said Gavin as he prepared to drive away. 'What about the car alarm?'

'Don't need one,' said Misery Guts. 'You've got Mehitabel.'

Mehitabel leaped up onto the passenger seat alongside Gavin, sat up like a Dalmatian dog on a fire truck and began to purr. Her purring harmonised perfectly with the idling V.12.

'Take my advice,' called Misery Guts as Gavin let out the clutch and gently ran out of the the garage. 'Avoid busy streets.'

Gavin rarely ignored advice but gathered it and tossed it in with all the other random pieces of information he collected. He always argued that nothing was significant in itself, but collectively pointed to the tidal movement of sentiment, the waxing and waning of opportune times to buy and sell. Everything indicated something, and he believed this gathering of information was crucial to his sense of timing. After he sold all his shares in September '87, everyone had asked him how he knew the crash was coming. 'Everything pointed to it,' he'd replied, though he was hard pressed to produce a single piece of evidence. He'd simply followed the tidal drift.

So Gavin listened to Misery Guts' advice and duly took it on board even though he hadn't a clue what it meant. Avoid busy streets? Why? When you drive a head-turner, you go where the heads are so that you can watch them turn and read the admiration and envy in the eyes. That was the whole point. Gavin decided to test the advice by driving through Double Bay. It was barely eleven o'clock and Double Bay was always crowded on a Saturday morning. Traffic had slowed to a crawl when Gavin gently eased his immaculate, priapic, phallic symbol along the busy street. Heads spun around, drawn to gaze with lust and awe upon the magnificent machine as surely as society hangers-on are drawn to free champagne. Sunlight sparkled on the wire wheels, bounced off the chrome and flickered seductively along the flowing lines. Gavin glowed. He basked in the glory.

Then somebody spotted the cat and started laughing. Others spotted it and pointed it out, ridiculing it, the owner and the car. Gavin had never known such humiliation. He shrank back into his seat, pulled the peak of his bone-coloured leather cap as low over his face as he could to hide its embarrassed glow. But in an E-type there is nowhere to run and nowhere to hide. Gavin had no choice but to bear the humiliation and wish the stupid cat would meta-morphose into something more acceptable, like a Louis Vuitton valise, a willowy blonde starlet, or even a spotty Dalmatian dog. Anything would have been more acceptable than a cat. Mehitabel sat upright, head up and nose in the air, impervious to the scorn. Gavin tried to shove her into the foot well and had his antelope driving glove shredded in warning. He vowed there and then that Mehitabel had to go.

Sharon took a look at the E-type, decided it had a certain cachet and matched at least three of her outfits. She was never particularly impressed with Gavin's new toys, but was more impressed than usual. She was not, however, in the least bit impressed by Mehitabel.

'Get rid of it,' she said, appalled that Gavin hadn't already done so. She couldn't understand why people didn't get rid of things they didn't like the moment they decided they didn't like them, especially when you could always go and buy something you did like, provided that it was suitably expensive and had appeared at least once in *Vogue*, *Tattler* or *Vanity Fair*. Her dislike blossomed into full-blooded loathing when she allowed Gavin to take her for a drive. Mehitabel took exception to being displaced from her favourite seat. She sat on the ledge behind and between the two seats, fixed Sharon with her penetrating green eyes, and growled continually. Sharon insisted Gavin stop so that she could summon a limo on her mobile to take her home. Mehitabel managed to snag Sharon's pantyhose as she got out.

'I advise you to get rid of that thing,' she said. 'Either it goes or I go.'

Gavin took her advice on board. The cat had to go. The only question was how? He was driving through Bondi Junction when he saw the bikies. He pulled over. There were eight of them, unwashed, unkempt and tougher than trading in futures.

'How much to get rid of this cat?' asked Gavin.

'Mate,' said a bikie whose mouth was lost behind a thatch of matted bristles, 'we do cats for nuffin.' He looked contemptuously at the pussy car, the pussy driver, and the pussy pussy in the passenger seat. 'But for you, fifty bucks.'

Gavin handed over a crisp fifty dollar note.

'Go for it,' he said.

The bikie was really tough. He was a legend in the Desperados. He'd once got stabbed in a gang fight and lost a couple of fingers and his left ear. He'd gathered up his amputated bits, shoved his moll's padded bra into the gaping wound in his stomach, and had ridden to the hospital where they patched him up without anaesthetic. Anaesthetic, he believed, was for wimps and poseurs who drove poofy cars. Mehitabel was not impressed by his credentials. She only bothered to extend one claw and neatly opened the big blue vein on the bikie's wrist. The wound didn't bleed, it gushed. It was a toss-up whether it needed stitches or Red Adair to cap it. The bikie screamed for only the second time in his life. The first time was when the midwife slapped his bottom, but he'd fixed her up later. Gavin reeled back. Blood was spewing onto his lovely duco, and threatened to splash onto his lovely Connolly leather. He couldn't allow that. Everyone knew how hard it was to get blood stains out of Connolly leather, and some people claimed you never could. He dropped the clutch.

The E-type had the acceleration of an F.15 fighter plane but Harley-Davidsons aren't exactly slouches either, particularly in the hands of bikies who believe they've been set up. Mehitabel sat as calm as a saucer of milk while eight Desperados, one with a plug of chewing gum stuck in his punctured wrist, gave chase. She leant into the corners as Gavin gunned the Jag as hard as it had ever been gunned, braced herself for late braking, rocked back against the seat rest under acceleration. Gavin had the distinct impression that Mehitabel had been through all this before. He finally managed to give the Desperados the slip just south of Newcastle.

'Didn't you hear me?' said Sharon when he got home. 'Weren't you listening? Did you think I was joking? That cat goes or I go!'

At that precise moment Gavin didn't give a damn which of them went.

There was an upside to Mehitabel's presence. Gavin never had to lock the car, hide his valise, his Armani jacket or his CDs. Mehitabel was better than any guard dog and also had surprise on her side. Besides, a car thief might wrap a length of pipe around a guard dog's ears, but who'd do that to a cat? The thief would never live it down. Around the eastern suburbs, Mehitabel achieved a certain splendid notoriety. Wherever Gavin parked, children would rush over to see the only guard cat in Sydney. Mehitabel tolerated the kids so long as they didn't reach into the car or put their sticky fingers on the duco. And Gavin tolerated Mehitabel. But every time he ventured beyond the eastern suburbs, she attracted scorn and ridicule. It began to get to him.

He took a position in French francs against all the indicators, got laughed at as they began to wobble and openly ridiculed when they dropped. This time there was no end of trading recovery, no overnight miracle, and nothing to suggest that the franc would do anything other than continue its downward spiral. To the man in the street, the shift of a few points meant nothing and had little effect on the price of brie. But Gavin's untimely plunge cost the bank millions. His bosses took it on the chin because they knew that nobody was infallible, that everyone was entitled to one mistake, and generously gave Gavin twenty-four hours to rectify it or find another job. Who would hire him after such a juvenile blunder? Strangely enough, the stock market took a fifty-three point dip on the same day. He hadn't anticipated that either.

Gavin was not a stupid man and soon realised where the fault lay. It lay in lack of concentration. He'd been worrying about the cat when he should have been gathering information. He'd lost touch with the tides. There was only one thing he could do, so he did it. He went to the pub and dipped his toe back in the water. He sat and sipped soda, lime and bitters while colleagues told him what a mug he was, what indicators he'd missed, where the currency market was heading, who'd made killings and in which currency, and what trade figures were due out. Gavin absorbed it all, went back to work and put the bank's shirt into more French francs. That night the franc staged the sort of recovery that turns dealers grey overnight, makes the top floor seem prescient and reinstates prodigal sons. Gavin had learned his lesson.

The following Saturday, he took Mehitabel on what he expected to be a one-way trip into the country. One-way for Mehitabel, that is. He fitted the hard top on before he left and gave Mehitabel two bowls of milk laced with King Island cream. Mehitabel lapped them up. He drove up into the Blue Mountains and down into the Megalong Valley. He found a nice shady spot just off the road and parked. He opened the passenger door and settled down to wait. Mehitabel eyed him suspiciously then curled up on the passenger seat and slept. Gavin read the *Financial Review* from cover to cover and the *Herald* business section. He was in no hurry.

Mehitabel woke four hours later, yawned, stretched and got up to go for a pee. She was halfway out the door when she realised where she was. She turned and looked at Gavin. His nose was buried in the *Herald* and he appeared to be ignoring her. Mehitabel remembered the cute trick with the bikies. Something was up, but what?

Gavin held his breath, silently beseeching Mehitabel to take the extra step so that he could slam the door behind her, fire up the big V.12 and leave her choking on his dust. Mehitabel settled back down on the seat, this time facing Gavin and fixing him with her hard emerald eyes.

'Look,' said Gavin placatingly. 'I know you need a leak and you know you need a leak.'

Mehitabel looked suitably unimpressed.

'Tell you what,' said Gavin, 'we'll both get out of the car. We'll both have a pee, okay?' Gavin got out and unzipped. He pointed Percy at an unfortunate gum that had done absolutely nothing to deserve such cavalier treatment, and let fly. He knew the sound of his water splashing on the tree trunk would unsettle Mehitabel, and it did. The cat was bursting from its earlier excesses. She stepped out of the car warily, keeping Gavin in her line of sight through the opened doors. Gavin watched her over his shoulder, tensed to make a dash for the car the instant Mehitabel was committed to doing her business. He was zipping up his fly when Mehitabel disappeared below the passenger door sill.

'See? You had nothing to worry about,' said Gavin. 'I'm your mate. Mates can trust each other.' He maintained the cheery deceit while he crept closer and closer to the driver's door. It concerned him that he couldn't see the cat, but he also knew that cats don't appreciate an audience when they do their biz. He'd almost reached the car when Mehitabel reappeared with something in her mouth. She dropped it on the passenger seat, then calmly wandered off to the privacy of some nearby scrub. Gavin stared at the seat in horror. There on his Connolly leather was a hissing, cursing snake – no! not a snake because whatever it was had legs. It had legs, legs had feet, feet had claws! Feral claws and Connolly leather was not a combination calculated to bring Gavin joy. Apparently it brought the beast no pleasure either, because it opened its jaws threateningly and flashed its ridiculous blue tongue. Gavin had heard of blue-tongue lizards before, but had never actually seen one. He didn't know if they were poisonous or not, and decided that a wise man would not put himself in a position to find out. He was almost grateful when a relieved Mehitabel calmly wandered back, plucked the blue-tongue from its privileged perch and released it into the grass. The Connolly leather was mercifully unmarked.

To Gavin's absolute astonishment he began to laugh. He wasn't in the habit of laughing and wondered if he was having some kind of breakdown. But it didn't take long for him to realise that he was still in charge of his faculties, and that what had occurred was actually funny and justified the strange sounds he was making. Long dormant emotions stirred within him. His feelings towards the cat tilted suspiciously towards admiration. He reached over and scruffed Mehitabel's ears. She turned her motor on and began to purr.

'Well,' said Gavin. 'If I must have a cat, I'm lucky I've got a cat like you.' Luck was something Gavin understood. Luck was another word for good timing. The more he thought about Mehitabel, the luckier he felt. He was lucky to have a cat that was not only smart but also shared his passion for V.12 E-type Jaguars and Connolly leather.

'You and I make a good team,' he said to her, and found he liked talking to her. He found he liked having someone – or at least some animate thing – to talk to that didn't envy and hate him for his success, or ask anything of him. During the long drive home he told her all about his coup with the French francs and she listened attentively the whole time. What's more, she even purred. Sharon never listened to anything he had to say, nor did she ever purr.

Things came to a head when Sharon scraped her Mercedes against a pillar in the clinic carpark. Normally that would be enough for her to trade it in on another car, but she liked her Mercedes and decided to have it repaired. She assumed she'd be able to drive Gavin's Porsche in the meantime, while he drove his new toy. But she hadn't counted on the weather. A slow moving depression settled on the coast of New South Wales, and brought with it dark brooding clouds and near constant rain. Understandably, Gavin didn't allow the E-type out in the rain. Accidents happened in the rain, and upholstery and carpets got wet. He couldn't bear to see carpets muddied or his Connolly seats watermarked. So he told Sharon to hire a car, hopped into his Porsche and raced off to buy a hundred million US dollars worth of Indonesian Rupiah. Sharon was not impressed.

Sharon was not impressed when she discovered there were no Mercedes 500s, BMW 750s or Porsche turbos to hire. She was offered a Lexus, which is a fine automobile but not quite fine enough for Sharon. She rang the limo companies but none could supply a car immediately, nor one that could wait at her beck and call. She rang Jaguar and told them she was thinking of quitting her Mercedes and wondered if they could let her have an XJR for a few days. Sort of an extended test drive. They assured her she could, once it stopped raining. Jaguar weren't stupid either. They knew the figures on accidents in the wet. Sharon stamped her foot. She was running late for an important engagement, an assignation in a suite at the Regent with the clinic's best-looking male doctor. The clinic frowned on its staff engaging in affairs with patients because of the potential to lose business. Instead, they encouraged the staff to engage in affairs among themselves, which they did unselfishly at every available opportunity. Sharon only had one option left and decided to take it.

She ignored Mehitabel when she reared up, arched her back and spat, because Mehitabel always did that to her. But normally Sharon had Gavin to protect her. Her bottom had no sooner touched Connolly leather when Mehitabel struck. The amazing thing is that Sharon managed to get out of the car and away before her blood had a chance to drip onto the precious hide. She rose from the seat like an SAM missile. Once again, Mehitabel had gone for the wrist, and done so with characteristic accuracy. The upshot was that Sharon got her chauffeur driven ride, but it was to the clinic not to the hotel, and in an ambulance not a limo.

'That cat has to go,' screamed Sharon. 'It has to go or I go!'

'You tried to take the Jaguar out in the rain?' said Gavin, shaking his head in disbelief.

'You're not listening to me,' insisted Sharon. 'That cat goes or I go, and it goes tonight!'

'You tried to take the Jaguar out in the rain?'

'Make up your mind!' shrieked Sharon. 'It's me or the cat!'

'You tried to take the Jaguar out in the rain? Out in the *rain*?'

The clinic's best-looking male doctor picked Sharon up in his Bentley convertible half an hour later. She returned the following day for her things. Coincidentally, the clinic's best-looking male doctor was between wives, and Sharon was perfectly credentialled – once her divorce was finalised – to restore him to his dinky status. Gavin was lucky enough to have a pre-nuptial agreement in place, which made him even more disliked by his colleagues who'd undergone divorces without one.

Gavin stood in his four-car garage, which was now occupied by only two cars, and saw the potential for at least one other. Not just any other, but a real head-turner that first came to his notice when Stirling Moss drove one to victory in a stage of the Monte Carlo Rally. There weren't many gull-wing Mercedes in Australia, but Gavin knew there were a couple. He told Mehitabel all about his dream gull-wing. The metallic, hand buffed, silver body. The midnight blue reindeer hide interior. The blueprinted engine. Mehitabel hung on his every word.

The Ghost of Mrs Beedle

The house didn't look haunted. It would never have been used in a Hammer horror movie and the makers of *Count Dracula*, *Frankenstein* or *Buffy the Vampire Slayer* would not have given it a second glance. It had high, steeply pitched roofs enclosing an attic which, as everyone knows, is a prerequisite for a haunted house. It had a cockerel weather-vane on its highest point. It also had dormer windows from which ghostly apparitions could peer on stormy nights, and allow mere mortals a fleeting, heart-stopping glimpse of them, courtesy of a flash of lightning. But for all that, the house didn't look a bit haunted. It looked very nice instead, exactly the sort of house a rising middle-class family would aspire to. Besides, Strathfield was a long way from Transylvania.

The Brenders didn't find out the house was haunted until after they'd moved in. It was one of the first things their neighbour, Mrs Whybin, told them along with which nights to put out the rubbish bins, and which days the paper and bottles were collected. Colin Brender did not believe in ghosts, horoscopes, tarot reading, the afterlife, or any kind of psychic phenomena.

'The only weird thing about ghosts and horoscopes,' he said, 'are the people who believe in them.'

His wife Adrienne wasn't so sure. She believed there was 'something to it' but had no idea what the something was. Her response to Mrs Whybin was, 'Are they benevolent?' What she meant was, 'Are we in danger?' Mrs Whybin assured her that, to the best of her knowledge, the ghosts had never harmed anyone who'd lived in the house. Adrienne drew comfort from that.

Their eldest daughter, Bliss, thought it was a hoot. She was her father's daughter, sixteen years old, and claimed *Nightmare on Elm Street* was a giggle, Stephen King a wimp, and the *Addams Family* an absolute howl. She liked the idea of having a Thing, and looked forward – so she said – to meeting it.

The youngest daughter, Ellie, took after her mother. Being only eleven years old she had not yet become a cynic, nor did she have enough experience to have any secure foundation upon which to form an opinion. When Mrs Whybin said there were ghosts, she was inclined to take her at her word. Mrs Whybin was an adult and her mother had told her that adults didn't tell lies. That in itself disproved the theory, but Ellie even lacked the experience to realise that. She'd always been a serious child and naturally took the whole thing very seriously. Her father cursed Mrs Whybin when Ellie began having nightmares, and jumping or screaming every time a curtain moved in the wind. In desperation her father let the family cat, Minky, sleep on her bed for protection. Just how Minky was supposed to protect her was a mystery, but the cat moved in and the nightmares moved out. Colin Brender began to suspect the whole thing was a devious plot to let Minky sleep with Ellie. It was what Ellie had always wanted.

There were two ghosts, the last spectral remains of one Nathaniel Beedle and his unfortunate wife, Emily. According to Mrs Whybin, he was a drunkard, a womaniser and a bully. He'd been dispatched to the colonies just prior to the demise of Queen Victoria by his family, who could no longer tolerate his excesses or the scandals attached to them. He brought considerable wealth with him, his downtrodden wife, and a determination to tame the wild continent and bend it to his will. It must have come as something of a shock to discover that he wasn't the only drunkard, womaniser and bully in the new land, and his excesses not at all uncommon. It must have stunned him when the fledgling colony failed to buckle under the force of his will or cower at his feet. His lack of progress led to frustrations which he all too often vented upon his hapless wife. One night, after he'd returned from a week-long bout of boozing and whoring, he beat her unconscious. When she came to, she stole into his bedroom while he was sleeping off the effects of the alcohol, and proceeded to murder him.

She was weak and woosy which explains why she made such a hash of it. Her first attempt to plunge the kitchen knife into his evil heart was blocked by his ribs. No doubt it stung a bit all the same, because Nathaniel woke up. If he hadn't consumed so much rum he probably would have managed to defend himself and survive. Naturally he fought back and his poor wife had no choice but to try to stab whatever she could. Given that he was – to say the least – a moving target, that it was pitch black, and that she was light-headed and wobbly on her feet, murdering him was no piece of cake. Nathaniel actually suffered no fatal injury but succumbed to the sum total of all his wounds and the concomitant loss of blood. In the melee, the about-to-be widowed Mrs Beedle hacked into arms, legs, chest and abdomen, and hacked off fingers, toes, an ear, a bit of his nose and sundry other pieces of flesh amounting in all to just under a kilo. The room was splattered with blood and so was Mrs Beedle. Even though Emily recalled the events of that terrible night bravely and accurately, and despite the fact that witnesses came from far and wide to testify to the rages of the deceased, and the inhuman treatment he meted out to his poor wife, the court was nevertheless aghast at the apparent savagery of her response. The truth was, she'd put the fear of God into every man in New South Wales, so they hanged her before she could put ideas into the heads of other downtrodden women.

Mrs Whybin could only recall one previous occupier of the house admitting to seeing the ghost of Nathaniel Beedle, and he affirmed that the old rogue did appear deficient in a number of vital areas. Others simply reported trails of blood appearing and disappearing from time to time, and leaving no stain behind. Emily Beedle had been sighted more frequently, three or four times that Mrs Whybin could remember, crying pitifully, with her head hanging limp at an impossible angle.

'Rubbish!' said Colin Brender dismissively.

'You can't be sure of that,' said his wife defensively.

'What a hoot!' said Bliss, who promised faithfully never to tell Ellie, but did shortly afterwards to get even after being ratted on for snogging with her boyfriend while both parents were out. Nightmares followed despite the reassuring presence of Minky, and Bliss was grounded for an additional fortnight.

'All because of a drunk and an old cow with a knife,' said Bliss indignantly to her friends.

As time went by they all forgot about the ghosts and the ghostly bloodstains, even Ellie who had maintained a constant and fearful vigil. She went about her school work and her elder sister put her consuming fascination with boys to one side as she prepared for her final exams. Their father carried on doing what he was good at, which was running his restaurant. His formula for success was very simple.

'Never confuse commerce with art,' he instructed his chefs. 'The day a building contractor can come in here and polish off everything on his plate is the day we go out of business.'

He kept the food simple and kept it coming, dressed up just enough to be thought fancy and a bit special. The *Sydney Morning Herald* ignored his establishment entirely, but the local papers raved about it in exchange for not infrequent blow-outs on the house. Colin Brender called it his PR budget, and money well spent. Everyone knew that if you wanted to eat there you had to book early, though Colin always kept a table free in case any of his regulars should ring at short notice. It was a formula made workable by honest value, hard work and a refreshing lack of imagination.

Colin worked the back door as well as he worked the front. He dealt in large amounts of 'black' money, and what delivery dockets and invoices said didn't always tally exactly with what was delivered. It was a game they all played and profited by, united as they were against the common enemy, the tax man. The only discontent arose when Colin refused deliveries that failed to meet his requirements. Everything had to be fresh and top quality. He liked to say the only things aged in his establishment were the wines.

Minky was the one who reminded them of the presence of ghosts. He would be sleeping on the sofa when all of a sudden he'd leap into the air, and tear off into the nearest bedroom to hide under the bed. At first the family didn't know quite what to make of it. Then occasionally they'd hear a bit of a fuss and find Minky at the foot of the stairs, staring at something descending that only he could see. He'd hiss and snarl and back away, every strand of fur standing on end.

Little Ellie would run to her mother in fear, together they'd seek the protection of their father and husband, and even Bliss forgot to sneer. Something was definitely spooking the cat, but what? It would be nice to think that the faithful family cat was trying to alert them to something other-worldly and sinister, and perhaps that was his intention. But the trouble was, Minky was not the brightest cat in the world. This aberrant behaviour was only part of an overall pattern of aberrant behaviour. Kept inside most of the time so that he wouldn't attack birds, Minky attacked flies, mosquitoes and moths with an enthusiasm bordering on the suicidal. He was like a cross between an Acapulco cliff diver and a World Cup goalie, a gold medal gymnast and a loose cannon. He launched himself off sofas, sideboards and window ledges. He leaped vertically off carpets and on at least two occasions his enthusiasm had sent him flying through space from the top of the stairs. His quest for all creatures small had sent him climbing up curtains and, during his hour-long toilet break in the garden, sent him climbing up lamp posts. While Minky was a skilled climber, he was an abject failure as a descender. The Brenders had been forced to call the fire brigade twice to effect a rescue. They promised not to come on a third occasion. The fireman in charge suggested they get a dog and send him up after the cat.

The end result was that while Minky may have panicked when seeing the ghosts, the family tended to dismiss his warnings. Minky simply didn't carry enough credibility. They didn't trust him enough to take too much notice. But he did succeed in raising the issue of the resident ghosts. Ellie had a couple more bad dreams. Adrienne worried as all mothers do. Bliss had a couple more spooky stories to tell her friends. And her father just scoffed. Things settled down until one night Adrienne woke up and thought she heard a window open, doors squeak and footsteps on the stairs. She woke Colin who thought he heard something, too. They both thought the ghosts of Nathaniel and Emily Beedle were abroad, and were totally unprepared when their bedroom light came on, and the real horror burst through their bedroom door.

The leaden weight crashed into the side of Colin's head, not hard enough to knock him unconscious but certainly hard enough to quell any thought of resistance. If he'd had the time to think about it, he might eventually have guessed that he'd been hit with a bar from a set of handweights, thoughtfully wrapped in a towel so that it stunned without breaking bone. Adrienne tried to scream but her scream was cut off by a hand over her mouth, and a wicked looking knife held in front of her face. She wanted to scream again when she heard her daughters scream and heard their screams also cut off. Adrienne honestly thought she was going to die from fright.

'Get up! Get up!'

She felt herself being dragged to her feet and tried to cling to the bedcover. She was wearing her baby doll pyjamas which were embarrassingly see-through, and she worried more about this than about the knife at her throat. Eyes glared at her from ragged holes in a black balaclava. The hand holding the knife reached around and ripped the bedcover from her grasp, and another arm came up under hers and squashed her breasts. She immediately felt violated, felt herself being lifted and knew beyond doubt that she was going to be raped. Adrienne whimpered. She feared rape more than anything, even more than death. Her fear of being raped while Colin was working late at his restaurant had resulted in a rape button being fixed to the wall next to her side of the bed. Colin had refused to install a burglar alarm system because he claimed they were no more reliable than car alarms, and went off every time the wind blew. He thought they were a blight on suburbia and showed a lack of consideration for neighbours. But Adrienne had insisted on a rape alarm, and her fear of imminent rape made her think of the button, but the opportunity to use it was long gone. She glanced despairingly towards it as she was dragged out of the bedroom and down the stairs. She vomited in fright, forcing the hand over her mouth to release its hold. The man cursed, wiped his hand on her panties, then gagged her by tying a cloth over her mouth and knotting it behind her head.

Colin allowed the man holding him to gag him, and frog-march him down the stairs with his arm bent painfully up behind his back. He didn't resist. He hadn't managed much of a look at his assailant, saw only that he was big and burly, and wore a grey balaclava. His brain had slowly started to function. He knew exactly what the men wanted and the businessman in him began to work out ways to deny them. They wanted his cash, his black money, and the rich Friday night takings. He supposed they'd knock him around but wouldn't harm his family beyond giving them the fright of their sheltered lives. At least that was what he hoped. He was figuring the odds when there was a piercing shriek and he nearly fell. He'd stood on Minky as she was fleeing the mayhem.

'Uddy cat!' he managed to mumble through the gag. The intruder marching him down actually laughed.

They took him and Adrienne into the lounge, pulled the curtains closed and switched on the light. His grey-masked captor spun Colin around and threw him into an armchair. He stared up at the two intruders, one of whom was holding his wife around the shoulders and breasts. Her top had ridden up exposing her thighs and panties, and it suddenly dawned on him that their assailants mightn't just be satisfied with robbery. Years of living together had made him blind to the flimsiness of Adrienne's night apparel, but now he saw her as any other man would. She may as well have been naked. He wanted to leap to her defence, but what could he do against two men armed with a knife and a metal cosh? What could he do against four?

The other two men carried Bliss and Ellie gagged into the lounge room. Colin felt sick and for the first time really frightened. Only then did he begin to fully appreciate the seriousness of the situation. What if they violated his girls? One of them threw Ellie onto the sofa, but the other held onto Bliss. He watched in disbelief as Bliss' assailant lowered her feet to the ground and cuffed her viciously to stop her struggling. He reacted instinctively and leaped to his feet. But grey-face pushed him back effortlessly into the chair and laughed.

Bliss was wearing knickers and an INXS T-shirt. She looked terribly young and even more vulnerable than Adrienne. She was sobbing uncontrollably. Colin's throat dried and his heart pounded. The horrifying, terrifying thing was his helplessness, the fact that the intruders had absolute power over them. Absolute power to take whatever they wanted, do whatever they wanted. And there wasn't a bloody thing he could do about it. Ellie was sobbing hysterically on the sofa, lying on her belly with her head buried in a pillow, too scared to even look. He wanted to go to her but knew he couldn't go anywhere.

'Orright shithead, tell us where ya money is.' Grey-face was clearly the ring leader.

'Innnnaaasayyy.'

Grey-face made no attempt to untie the gag, but simply pulled it down so that it hung loosely around Colin's throat.

'It's in the safe.' Colin thought his voice sounded strange and distant, foreign even to himself.

'Then get it for us, shithead!'

Grey-face accompanied Colin to the heavy metal safe in his study. It was fire-proof, bomb-proof and would take hours to cut open with acetylene, but there was no defence against intruders with knives held at the throats of wife and daughters. Colin spun the combination and turned the key. His captor kicked him aside before he could reach in. He needn't have bothered. There was no gun or weapon inside, just the Friday night takings and Adrienne's more valuable jewellery. Grey-face ignored the jewellery and grabbed the bag of cash, cheques and credit card receipts. He marched Colin back to the lounge. His wife and daughters were the same as before, except that Adrienne seemed closer to fainting.

'Okay, prick, now where's the rest?'

'What do you mean?'

'Where's the rest, prick!' Yelling now, leaning right into Colin's face. Peppering him with spit.

'You've got it all.'

'Ah shit!' The intruder slammed his fist into the side of Colin's face, grabbed him and forced him to look at his wife. His accomplice ripped away the front of her pyjama top. Adrienne's knees buckled, but her assailant forced her to stand upright and display her nakedness.

'No!' cried Colin. Grey-face again shoved him back into the armchair and stood over him ready to bend his cosh over his head. It was at this precise moment that Minky caught sight of one of the ghosts. He shot out from beneath the sofa, executed a perfect aerial pirouette, and dashed away upstairs. At any other time it would have been comical.

'Bloody hero, that cat,' said one of the men. 'Oughta have a dog.'

Colin had ridiculed the idea of ghosts, but would have gladly sacrificed a month's takings to have Mr and Mrs Beedle glide into the room right then.

'Okay, shithead, what's it to be?' Grey-face glanced meaningfully towards Adrienne. 'Her or the money?'

'No! No ... no ... please! Don't touch her. I'll show you.' Colin led his captor into the kitchen, stood on a chair and removed a flour tin from the cupboard. He pulled out a wad of notes wrapped in plastic. Adrienne's slush fund, the untraceable money she used to buy clothes for herself and the two girls, and pay tradesmen who came to fix things. He watched as grey-face counted it.

'Two thousand four hundred and fifty dollars. You're jerkin' us around. We can jerk people around, too, prick!

Startin' with your pretty wife. Now where's the rest of it!' He hauled Colin up by the collar of his pyjamas.

'Okay, okay!' Colin was beaten as he knew all along he would be. So why had he held out? He thought of his wife and daughters, near naked and in the hands of thugs who probably raped as casually as they swilled beer. What had he hoped to achieve? Some act of defiance? 'It's downstairs,' he said. 'In the basement. You leave my wife and kids alone. I'll show you where it is.'

'You'll show me where it is wevver we leave your little pussies alone or not!' Grey-face laughed.

Colin led the way downstairs, through the basement and through the little service trap door that led to the foundations beneath the house. He lifted down a steel box hidden on top of a beam between two pillars.

'First place I woulda looked,' said the intruder scornfully. 'Get outta here.'

Colin led the way back up to the lounge. He stopped stricken in the doorway. Bliss' T-shirt was pulled up around her shoulders. He'd never seen his daughter's breasts before, didn't want to now, didn't want anybody to see them. Certainly didn't want to see her captor playing with them. Just as his muscles tensed to spring and rip the thug apart with his bare hands, Grey-face wrenched him backwards.

'Open the bloody box, shithead.'

Colin did as he was asked, did it as fast as he could, anything, *anything* to placate his captors. Grey-face whistled when he saw the stack of grey–blue notes.

'Got it,' he said triumphantly. 'Tie the prick up!'

The man standing over Ellie leaped to obey his leader, grabbed Colin and tied his hands and feet together.

218

'Now,' said Grey-face, 'this is for not tellin' us where the money was the first time we asked ya.' His mates sniggered as he began to unzip his fly. Adrienne struggled desperately but in vain. Bliss cowered and whimpered. The helplessness, the sheer helplessness overwhelmed Colin, and he was blinded by tears of rage and frustration. There was nothing he could do! Nothing anybody could do! Nothing! Dear God! And he had to bear witness. He closed his eyes and silently beseeched the ghosts to appear. Surely Mrs Beedle could not stand by and allow Adrienne to be treated as badly as Nathaniel had treated her.

Grey-face jumped a mile when the silence shattered, when the rules changed, when everything changed. His mates turned to him, poised, alert, on their toes, surprise and shock on their faces. Colin's mouth dropped open. It was hard to say who was stunned the most.

The rape alarm had exploded into life. It whooped, it rang and a crescendoing siren hit a pitch physically painful to the human ear.

'Shit! Let's get outta here!' Grey-face grabbed the cash and the intruders bolted. Adrienne collapsed sobbing onto the carpet the moment her means of support legged it, Ellie buried her head further beneath the cushions to escape the terrifying noise, and Bliss ran screaming to her mother, to cling tightly to her and exorcise the fears of what might have happened.

'Untie me!' screamed Colin, but nobody could hear him above the din. 'Untie me! Somebody!'

Eventually somebody did.

'So what set off the rape alarm?' asked the detective.

Colin shrugged helplessly. He'd asked himself the same question a hundred times and didn't like the answer he kept coming up with. Could a hand reach back from beyond the grave, to give others the protection denied her in her tragic life? No, said his brain. Then what? it asked. Then who? And what had spooked Minky?

'Detective, if I told you what I think happened you'd lock me away.'

'Try me.'

'Where's my wife?'

'Your wife and daughters are being comforted and counselled. Our people are good at that so don't worry about them for the moment.'

'My wife can back me up.'

'I'm sure she'll be glad to.'

'So can Mrs Whybin next door.'

'Great. Corroboration, we like that. Now, who set off the rape alarm?'

'Detective,' said Colin feeling utterly foolish, 'do you believe in ghosts?'

Upstairs in the master bedroom, Minky stuck his head out from under the bed, eyes burning, his body rigid, legs like tensioned springs. The stupid moth was spiralling back into range, looking for somewhere to settle. Minky tensed, shivered with excitement, then launched himself at the wall.

He missed the moth by millimetres and almost hit the rape button for a second time. That would have been fun.

Village Chicken

'*Eka, deka, tuna . . .*' counted Beth conscientiously.

I hadn't wanted to come to Sri Lanka. It seems to me that the Third World is full of people who'd give anything to leave it. Why, then, would anyone want to reverse the trend? I can honestly say that I'd never once in my life woken up and said, 'Sri Lanka! Now there's the place for a holiday.' My only knowledge of Sri Lanka came from watching their national cricket team. The most remarkable thing about them was that they all had names longer than the picket fences surrounding the ovals they played on.

'*Haya, hata, ata . . .*'

'Beth,' I said patiently, 'they speak English here. At least anyone you need to talk to does.' But Beth wouldn't be deterred. Beth is one of those people who pride themselves on 'absorbing the local culture' wherever they go. You'd think the way tourism has developed that locals the world over would have learned to avoid people like Beth by now, but I saw no evidence of it.

'*Namaya, dahaya!*' said Beth triumphantly.

Whoop-de-do! She'd counted all the way to ten.

'Lomotil, Imodium, Maloprim and Fansidar.' I had my own mantra, one I considered far more likely to be gainfully employed than Beth's.

'That's enough,' snapped Beth.

She was trying to put a brave face on things to overcome the inauspicious beginning to our stopover holiday. Our travel agent had booked us into a Browns Beach hotel and pre-paid. Not a good move as things had turned out. They had our money and we had a room that was so damp I was tempted to wear my face mask and snorkel to bed. The bed linen stuck to our skin like a wet T-shirt. The furniture needed shaving daily to keep down the fungal growth. The carpet needed a good mow, and the bathroom was the perfect place to grow mushrooms. The grout between the tiles was as black as jet. We'd tried opening the doors onto our pocket handkerchief-sized balcony to air the room, and nearly got blasted back into the corridor. Our room faced into the teeth of a howling gale. Welcome to Sri Lanka.

'Third World,' I remember saying. 'What the hell did you expect?'

We'd agreed at about two am to move to another hotel and forget about the money we'd pre-paid. We'd already had an argument with the manager at reception, in front of his staff, his wife, his children, his mother, his mother-in-law, three cousins, two aunts and many curious bystanders. Now we were packing our bags. The lost money was like an open wound and if Beth hadn't started her Sinhala language lessons again I think I could have left it alone to heal. But she didn't leave the lessons alone.

'*Aaibowan*,' she said, which is the way one Sinhalese greets another. 'Hello' is what they say when they greet people like us, and they expect us to say 'hello' back. It had worked that way right through the airport as we pushed past two and a half thousand touts, all of whom knew where we could get cheap rubies, a nice, clean girl, and a better hotel than the one we were heading for. 'Hello' worked perfectly all the way through to check-in and up to our room. The bell-hop who'd carried our bags had even said 'Hello' when he meant 'Goodbye'. Alas, 'Hello' was not good enough for Beth so I had to suffer the '*Aaibowans*'.

'Cholera,' I said beginning my other mantra. 'Malaria, typhoid, hepatitis, dysentery.'

'That's enough!'

Tit for tat, I thought, and added, 'Tetracycline and metronidazole.'

We still weren't talking as we marched past reception and into our hire car. I'd asked for a large car with driver and had actually used the word 'limo'. What we got was a small Nissan. I guess it qualified as a limo because it was black and had tinted windows.

'Where are we going, please?' asked the driver in perfect though accented English.

'You tell him,' I said to Beth. 'You speak the lingo.'

Beth just glared out the window.

Actually, the driver's question was a lot trickier than it seemed. I hadn't thought beyond quitting what we had come to regard as the worst hotel and greatest clip joint in the whole of Asia. I hadn't a clue where to go.

'Take us to the best hotel on the coast.'

'But sir, but madam, we are already there.'

I groaned. Beth glared. I noticed the driver glancing over towards reception and began to understand his predicament. Our driver could not afford to lose favour with our hotel. A small performance was called for. I wound down my window so that my voice would carry to the audience at reception and said, 'In that case, my man, take us to the second best hotel in Negombo.'

The driver shook his head with a great deal of resignation, shrugged his shoulders helplessly and engaged gear. A born thespian.

'Take us to the Sea Lion,' said Beth.

'My God, you've mastered Sinhala already!' I said in mock amazement, but I could see the joke had worn perilously thin.

'Sea Lion all booked,' said the driver. 'Tour group from Germany arrive last night.'

'Take us there, anyway,' commanded Beth.

'What do you know about this place?' I asked.

'A woman in the deli told me about it just before we left. It was too late to change our booking.'

I didn't groan, roll my eyes or say anything.

'It's new. Built by one of these huge Asian resort chains. She said it's five star, modern, full of marble, and every group of rooms has its own swimming pool. She said it's the only civilised place to stay.'

'Except that it's full up,' I said. 'With krauts.'

'Hotels always have vacancies,' she said, but didn't elaborate.

Our driver waited patiently while we were told what we already knew.

'So very sorry. The hotel is fully booked.' The duty manager smiled apologetically.

'We're not moving,' said Beth. 'We're going to sit here with our bags until you find us a room.'

'But we are fully occupied,' said the duty manager. His eyes had widened and his facade was beginning to crumble.

He obviously wasn't accustomed to dealing with guests who didn't know how to take no for an answer. I could've given him the tip. Beth didn't get in this sort of mood very often, but when she did it was best to give in and give in both quickly and graciously.

Beth placed our suitcases in the middle of the hallway where they would cause the most disruption and calmly sat on them. She stroked the cats that cruised up to her to investigate the source of the disturbance. I was feeling sufficiently embarrassed by her conduct to leave her to handle the crisis. I wandered through to the bar and dining area. The lady in the deli was right. The place was beautiful. And civilised. Marble columns, marble floors, tables spaced widely apart and elegantly set, and open on two sides to a glistening tropical tapestry of palms, blossoms and swimming pools. This was my kind of place. I wondered if it was an appropriate time to drag out my schoolboy German and pretend that we were misplaced members of the tour group. I wandered back to reception where the duty manager was engaged in heavy conversation with our driver all to no avail. Beth stayed put. Frostily immobile, as determined as any woman you have ever seen. I thought I might join her.

There were aspects to this place that really appealed to me. The whole hotel was surrounded by a two metre-high wall with broken glass on top. And there was an armed guard and boomgate across the only entrance. I liked that, liked it very much. It shut the Third World out completely. If only it could have shut the cats out as well. I don't know why there were so many cats or why a hotel so obviously upmarket tolerated them. I thought it must be some Buddhist thing. They wandered casually among the tables as if they owned the joint and draped themselves elegantly on the steps. I figured if we could come to a satisfactory arrangement with the management I'd gladly put up with the cats. This was no small concession on my part. Cats and I don't get on.

'The manager has asked me to politely inform you that the hotel is deeply regretful but they have no accommodation available.'

'Really? Tell him to try harder.' Beth gave the driver a look that could've shrivelled granite.

'But Madam, but Sir . . .'

The driver turned to the manager and shrugged hopelessly. I sat down on the cases alongside Beth and smiled my most entrenched smile. We waited and watched while they exchanged some more rather excited Sinhala.

'The manager requests that you wait a moment.' The driver addressed this comment to Beth. He didn't even spare me a glance. I could see that he was trying desperately to keep the admiration out of his voice. Beth wore her little, tight-lipped smile of triumph.

The duty manager put us in a new block of rooms which had not quite been completed. He pointed out that it was still in the process of being painted, and that we would need to vacate our room from nine in the morning until four in the afternoon. He made it sound as off-putting as he could and was flabbergasted that we found the proposal totally to our satisfaction. The way we saw it, we'd be out all day every day sightseeing and absorbing the local culture. If not, they had an excellent bar, an endless variety of swimming pools, and the wonderful marble-pillared, cat-infested, open dining area. I could see myself happily doing a swimming pool version of a pub crawl, vigorously pursued by colourfully attired boys and girls with trays of exotic drinks. I doubted very much that we'd ever set eyes on the painters.

I changed into shorts and a Hawaiian shirt and wandered back to the reception to brief our driver and work out an itinerary. He seemed disappointed to see me. He wanted the organ grinder not the monkey, however I managed to buy his interest very cheaply, disguising the bribe as a fee for his earlier negotiations on our behalf. Beth was waiting for me in the dining room which was almost deserted.

'Where are the Germans?' I asked.

'Ordered onto their tour buses at seven this morning. They're not due back until seven tonight. The place is ours, well almost. Apparently there are some Brits and French also wandering around avoiding each other.'

Paradise! And all credit to Beth. This was my idea of a holiday. If only I could convince Beth not to venture beyond the glass-topped walls. Our table was the only one occupied and there were at least twenty waiters and waitresses waiting for a call to action. I turned, raised a desultory hand, and set off a Le Mans start of waiters with menus, wine lists, and jugs of water which we had been assured were absolutely pure. Like I say, paradise. But there is a serpent in every paradise and the one in ours sat purring upon Beth's lap. It was a sort of tortoiseshell, quite pretty I suppose but still a cat, and God only knows what nasties it was carrying.

'You'll get ringworm,' I said.

'Hotels like this,' said Beth smugly, 'do not allow ringworm.'

Lunch was delicious if you like prawn and mango salad, goat's cheese on toasted mignons of French bread, elegant tomato and basil pasta, and a fruity little Sancerre. Beth, however, was disappointed and said so. The only culture she was absorbing was European. There wasn't a Sri Lankan dish to be found. Where were the curries, sambals, chutneys, chilli, coconut and yoghurt dishes? Where were the lip-stinging samousas? The only vaguely Sri Lankan dish I could find was a thing called a hopper and that was on the breakfast menu.

'Never mind,' I said to Beth, 'it seems you can have Sri Lankan grasshoppers for breakfast.'

Beth was not amused. She wanted her curries. She did not want my facetious jokes. She called the waiter over and demanded to know when she could have a good, traditional, Sri Lankan curry. The waiter brought us another menu for the Sri Lankan buffet which took place around the two pools nearest to the dining room. It made mouth-watering reading but soon turned sour. Sri Lankan nights were every Thursday. We were scheduled to leave Thursday morning. Beth began to get that look again. She demanded to see the duty manager.

'Yes, Madam, may I be of service?'

I had to admire the bloke and his professionalism. His smile seemed awfully genuine. However, he held his hands behind his back so I couldn't tell if they were shaking or if he was reaching for a concealed weapon.

'We did not come to Sri Lanka to eat second-rate European hotel food.' Beth has this wonderful technique for setting the agenda in the bluntest possible fashion, thereby putting her adversaries immediately on the defensive.

'Sri Lanka has a wonderful cuisine, Madam,' said the duty manager quite indignantly. 'Unfortunately, the guests of this hotel have not yet come to that realisation. They demand

European food and as their hosts we are obliged to provide it.'

'Except on Thursday nights.'

'Except on Thursday nights, indeed, Madam.'

'We leave on Thursday morning and so would like to realise our appreciation of Sri Lanka's wonderful cuisine some time before then.'

'I am afraid that is not possible, Madam. We cannot do that.'

'Oh, I would have thought that as our hosts you had an obligation.'

The duty manager flinched, as he realised he'd sown the seeds of his own defeat. To his credit he held his smile.

'I will speak to the chef,' he said.

'Do that, and you will come straight back and let us know what he says, won't you?'

'Of course, Madam, my pleasure.'

The duty manager wheeled away and strode off towards the kitchen. I think if he'd had a concealed weapon he would have used it. I couldn't help smiling. This was supposed to be the stress-free, feet up and relax part of our holiday, before we did battle with the jewellery makers and wholesalers in Amsterdam. Since when has the Third World been free of stress?

'More wine, dear?' I asked, and re-filled her glass before she had a chance to reply. The wine waiter was looking terribly chagrined. He'd been waiting for Beth to finish her glass before doing the honours. Doubtless he was concerned about the effect my intervention might have on the size of the tip.

'That manager,' said Beth, 'I bet he's the product of one of those Swiss hotel colleges. You know, where they take warm human beings and turn them into snotty little permanent-press robots.' She reached down and picked up her adopted tortoiseshell moggy and slipped it a leftover prawn. 'They're taught not to sweat, you know. Nor smell of anything. I sometimes think the colleges coat them in a fine, impermeable plastic spray.'

'I'm sure you're right, dear.' To be honest, I like graduates from Swiss hotel colleges. They're my kind of hotel people. Efficient, courteous and arrogant in an immaculately civilised way. They understand the servant–guest relationship perfectly, and don't try to be your friend or feel any obligation to enlighten you with their conversation. They are there to serve and serve they do. I quite liked the duty manager for exhibiting these traits. His only discernible failing was his slowness in realising that in dealing with Beth, resistance was not only useless but counterproductive. I watched him walk back to our table, eyes bright and mouth full of teeth, and wondered if he'd learned anything during his absence.

'Madam, I am pleased to inform you that I am in a position to comply with your wishes.'

Very good. The walk seemed to have cleared his brain.

'However . . .'

Uh oh.

'. . . the chef requires forty-eight hours' notice to prepare an authentic Sri Lankan curry.'

'He may have it,' said Beth with a smile totally devoid of any warmth. 'Wednesday dinner, it is. Our last dinner in Sri Lanka. You can make us a meal to remember you by.'

I shivered unexpectedly. Somebody walked over my grave. Call it a premonition or just put it down to having witnessed Beth in action throughout our married life. Her choice of words struck me as odd and rather unfortunate.

'What will it be?' asked the duty manager smoothly. 'Seafood, lamb, chicken . . .'

'Chicken,' said Beth. 'Better not risk seafood before a long flight.'

'Very wise, Madam,' said the duty manager.

Somebody walked over my grave again and I still couldn't figure out why.

Sri Lanka is very green and very hot. Our mini limo was almost airconditioned. That is, it was airconditioned but the airconditioner was in sore need of re-gassing. All the same, we might have got by in moderate discomfort if Beth hadn't insisted on stopping the car all the time to 'absorb the local culture'. We stopped so Beth could absorb the fact that farmers still ploughed paddy fields with wooden ploughs yoked up to water buffalos, and followed behind them crotch-deep in a soup of shit and mud. Beth insisted on wandering out along the paddy walls to take a photo and slip the farmers a couple of rupees each in the cause of fostering Australian–Sri Lankan relations.

We stopped further up in the hills when we came across women winnowing rice. Beth took more photos and did a bit more fostering. Little children came up to have their photos taken at one rupee a pop, also in the cause of good relations. We stopped so Beth could buy rambutans and mangosteens. Stopped so Beth could buy some 'eschtrees' with little carved elephants on them, even though neither of us smoked. Stopped again so she could wander through a rubber plantation.

'*Mee mokadda*?' she'd ask. 'What's that?'

'*Hari honday*,' the driver would answer and pull over resignedly. *Hari honday*, I learned, was Sinhala for 'okay'. I thought the driver was on my side until I realised he just hated stopping at places where he didn't get a cut.

He took us to gem factories and was bitterly disappointed when he realised that we knew our stuff. Beth put the glass to her eye and gave the salesmen hell. Cut was always a problem in that the gems were cut artlessly by kids with manual wheels which they pedalled. The facets were uneven, but Beth found other reasons to humiliate the salesmen. Colour, clarity and cost.

'Don't waste my time,' she said. 'Bring me your best. I'm only interested in your best.'

And they brought their best, but of course their best was never good enough. As we'd suspected, any premium gems were sold directly to the State Gem Corporation and what we were looking at were fodder for gullible tourists. Beth criticised them mercilessly, all this from the same kind, generous woman who'd spent all morning fostering relations.

In desperation, our driver took us to tea rooms where he was also on a percentage. We expected to find suspicious samousas and fiery curries. Not so, we were offered strong tea the colour of the Ganges in flood and massively sugared, and sandwiches made from grey coloured bread with mystery fillings. I made do with a beer which was the most expensive thing on the menu and almost cold. Oh the joys of travel in the Third World. My stomach rumbled. Apart from the odd rambutan and mangosteen, we hadn't had a thing to eat since the egg hoppers Beth insisted we had for breakfast. If you've ever had an egg fried in the middle of a small pancake you've had an egg hopper. Not something you'd wait in a queue for. At that point I'd have given anything to be safely back among the cats, with a plate of cold pasta and mango salad.

'What do you say?' I said to Beth. 'Fancy a nice swim in the pool, followed by a fluffy duck?' Fluffy ducks were her favourite cocktails.

'After the elephant orphanage.'

The elephant orphanage was at least another insufferably hot hour away at a place called Kegalle.

'*Hari honday*,' said the driver miserably. The heat was also getting to him.

'What are you doing?' Beth shrieked. 'It's well after four!'

'Hello,' said the three painters in excellent English. They flashed white teeth in broad smiles as if they were really happy to see us. Unfortunately, we weren't quite so happy to see them. We'd stayed longer than we'd wanted to at the elephant orphanage so that the painters would be gone by the time we got back. We'd oohhed and aaahhhed at the little baby elephants, by far the smallest I'd ever seen, all the while making sure their mothers and fathers didn't tread on us and turn us into egg hoppers. We'd endured trial by elephant fart, not something to be taken lightly. I don't know whether to blame the foul odours on the heat, the humidity or whatever it was they fed the elephants, but it seemed nothing could disperse them. They hung in the torpid air, an invisible, odorous and no doubt volatile presence which could have laid waste the entire surrounding rainforest if anyone had been foolish enough to try to light a smoke. We'd put up with a lot so that we'd come home to a room to ourselves. To chuck off sweaty clothing, shower and lay naked on the bed, with cold air from the airconditioner rustling through our pubes. We did not come home to be smiled at by idiot painters.

'Fetch the duty manager!' ordered Beth, and I duly trotted off. I have to say that he didn't look all that pleased to see me. I don't think the Swiss college that trained him would regard him as the pinnacle of their achievement.

'Can I help you, Sir?' he asked bluntly. Where had his manners gone, I wondered, where was his finesse? Was I the one who'd been rude to him or demanding? No, I was not! *Hari honday*, if he wanted to be discourteous I considered it my bounden duty to be unreasonable.

'Look here,' I said, 'it's bad enough that you have the audacity to put us into a room that is unfinished, and submit us to the indignity and inconvenience of sharing it with tradesmen . . .' I paused for effect there. The duty manager's jaw had dropped open and his eyes fair boggled. 'May I also point out that we only agreed to take the room following your absolute assurance that all tradesmen would be gone by four in the afternoon, and that we would have the room entirely to ourselves thereafter. May I also remind you that you are charging us full tariff. Now Sir, if you wouldn't mind, could you please tell me what time it is and what those intruders are doing in our room?' I'd worked myself into a state of high dudgeon, and had even begun to believe my version of events.

The duty manager looked up at the clock above reception and turned back to me searching for adequate words. There were none, of course, not now that we had an audience of people who wanted to send faxes, pay accounts and cash travellers cheques, all of whom were horrified that the hotel would put anybody into an unfinished room and expect them to share it with tradesmen. If the duty manager had hoped for sympathy he was out of luck. All he got was hostility. I turned to my audience and went for the stake through the heart.

'I'm sorry to inconvenience you all,' I said apologetically. 'Perhaps I should wait until you've all been attended to.'

'Not at all!'

'*Nein*!'

'*Non*!'

I turned back to the manager and smiled thinly. God and the cash paying customers were all on my side. Let that teach the little squib for ignoring his training. In Switzerland people were sent to gaol for less.

'My apologies,' said the duty manager. He smiled obsequiously at all and sundry. 'Please accompany me, Sir, and we shall attend to the matter immediately.'

'So you bloody well should,' said an English voice behind me.

Tuesday night was English night. We sat in the warmth of a Sri Lankan evening eating over-cooked roast beef, roast pork, baked potatoes and Yorkshire pudding, with an equally bemused assortment of Germans and thoroughly bewildered French. Only the English and the staff really got into the spirit of things. Oh, and the cats. People at other tables indulged their cats in much the same way Beth indulged her tortoiseshell.

The only light relief came from a young couple from Melbourne who were celebrating their adoption of a Sinhalese baby boy. They showed us a photo of the tiny fella.

'Have you given him a name?' asked Beth.

'Yes. According to the papers they gave us his name is Aravinda,' said the proud new father, 'but we've decided to call him Harry because that's what all the Sri Lankans call him.'

'Harry?' Beth was clearly puzzled.

'Yes,' said the bright-eyed, new mother, 'they come up, tickle his little chest and call him Harry something.'

'*Hari honday?*' I asked.

'Yes!' they cried excitedly. 'That's it!'

'A very popular name here,' I said, and looked them straight in the eye.

The following morning I had the job of informing our driver that we'd absorbed enough Sri Lankan culture and that we didn't want to see him again until it was time to take us to the airport. He demanded a fee for lost business, insisting that we'd booked him for the duration of our stay. I suggested a compromise and when he didn't agree, threatened him with Beth. He agreed. We both knew he'd spend the rest of the day driving someone else around, anyway.

Beth and I decided we'd occupy the day swimming two full lengths of every pool in the resort, which multiplied by twenty came as near as dammit to two kilometres. Along the way we determined to maintain a healthy level of fluffy duck and ice-cold beer in our respective glasses. This was the paradise I'd hoped for. Forget sightseeing and playing gastronomic Russian roulette with food and water along the way. Forget the touts and all the kids with their hands out, forget the beggars and the poverty, the open drains, the rat holes of houses, and elephant farts. This was all I wanted from the Third World – absolute luxury made possible by cheap labour. We decided to forgo lunch in favour of a light snack at the poolside. After all, we had an authentic Sri Lankan chicken curry to prepare ourselves for.

The tortoiseshell cat accompanied us on our epic swim until just after our snack, when it was whisked away by one of the beautiful sari-clad young ladies who fetched us our drinks. I approved of this. It was bad enough that the cats had the run of the main building. It was nice to know there were some places they weren't allowed.

At four o'clock we retired to our room, showered, lay naked on the bed, got silly, and had to shower all over again. All in all, the ideal preparation for an authentic Sri Lankan chicken curry. The sun had managed to penetrate the gallons of sunscreen we'd sloshed on each other just sufficiently to give us both a healthy glow. Beth wore one of her little, black summery numbers that showed off all her back and nearly all of her front. I'm sure she uses double-sided sticky tape to keep it up. Then it was off to dinner and the only part of the local culture I was interested in absorbing.

Let me tell you, we were the envy of the dining room when the parade of twelve waitresses brought the various dishes and side dishes to our table. The duty manager himself came to wish us *bon appetit* and explain the various dishes.

'True Sri Lankan curries consist of many dishes,' he said, 'and they are best eaten using the fingers of the right hand.'

He then proceeded to tell us how to ball up a piece of rice, mix in the various flavours and the selected piece of chicken, then, with the fingers slightly cupped, push the rice ball into our mouths with the thumb. He made it sound so easy. We were both drooling as he introduced us to each of the dishes.

There was yoghurt and curd, or buffalo yoghurt, if the curries were too fiery. *Pol sambol*, a red-hot grated coconut chilli dish if they were too bland. There were four vegetable dishes including *thali* from south India and *kool*, a speciality from Jaffna. There was fish as well. A small bowl of prawns in a coconut curry and *ambul thiyul*, a sour fish pickle made from tuna. There were tiny string hoppers for dipping into sauces, some *naan*, and more chutneys than you could poke a stick at. In the middle of it all, fragrant and inviting, sat our chicken curry. The duty manager had done us proud and neither Beth nor I hesitated to tell him so.

'The pleasure is entirely mine,' he assured us. He wore a smile as wide as piano keys as he made his way over to join the array of waiters lined up along the back wall, beaming at all the other tables along the way. He seemed pleased that at least two of his guests had the wisdom to indulge in Sri Lanka's wonderful cuisine. Our insistence had become his statement, and a magnificent statement at that. As I said, we were the envy of the dining room. The duty manager and the staff weren't the only ones watching us tuck in.

Perhaps it was the variety of dishes that distracted me. I was almost ready to surrender and play with my last serve of chicken curry when I had the first intimations that all was not what it seemed. I looked up at the duty manager who met my eye, smiled his Swiss-trained smile of superiority, and turned away to return to reception. I could swear there was a jauntiness in his walk that hadn't been evident before. I couldn't help but recall Beth's last words and my disquiet when she'd ordered our curry. If my suspicions were well founded, the duty manager certainly had given us a meal to remember him by.

I must tell you, I've always taken pride in my prowess with the carving knife. I know how to carve meat, know exactly where the bones are, and I'm particularly adept with poultry. What I saw worried me. I gave Beth's plate a quick once-over and stirred the leftovers in the bowl at the centre of the table, looking for evidence that would put an end to my suspicions. But there was no wishbone, no telltale breastbone, no wing bone and no drumstick. Oh, there were bones all right, but they were more like bones from my childhood, like those left on the plate down on my uncle's farm near Cooma after the men had been hunting. The implications sickened me but I dared not show a thing. If they sickened me, what would they do to Beth?

We toyed with the caramel-tasting pudding they brought us, and shared a mango. Beth was unusually quiet as we finished our tea. I hoped it was just because she'd over-eaten.

'That chicken taste all right to you?' she asked suddenly.

'Terrific,' I said. 'Why, didn't you like it?'

'I liked it,' she said. 'Who wouldn't? It just didn't taste like chicken, not like any chicken I've ever had before.'

'You're lucky if you could taste anything through the curry.'

'It had a different taste,' she said. 'I recognised it but I just can't put my finger on it.'

'Don't worry about it,' I said, more in hope than anything else.

'Rabbit!'

'Wha . . . ?' I rolled over and found Beth sitting bolt upright in bed. The red numbers on the bedside clock said 2.22.

'Rabbit!' she repeated.

'What are you talking about?'

'That taste I couldn't recognise. It's rabbit.'

'Don't be silly,' I said. 'I was practically raised on rabbit so I'd know. Besides, I don't think there are any rabbits in Sri

Lanka.' I'd accused Beth of being silly, but that wasn't the smartest thing I'd ever said, either. 'Go back to sleep.'

One look at Beth and I could tell she hadn't slept much, if at all. She packed our bags like an automaton. When we made our way down to reception we found our driver engaged in animated chat with the duty manager and having a good old laugh. Perhaps they were discussing the Tamil terrorist who'd just blown himself up in Colombo before he'd reached his intended target, but somehow I doubt it. It might have been my imagination but I thought our driver looked up some-what guiltily as we entered, as if he'd been talking about us. I settled the bill while Beth wandered through to the dining area to say a fond farewell to the tortoiseshell cat.

'Thank you for choosing to stay with us,' said the duty manager.

'Thank you for finding us accommodation at such short notice,' I said. 'And,' I added, 'thank you for the excellent curry.'

'Always our pleasure, Sir.'

'The chicken . . . it tasted a little unusual.' I gave him my best polite but resolute stare, the one I normally reserve for account queries.

'Village chicken,' he said. 'They have a stronger taste which makes them ideal for currying.'

'Unusual bones, too,' I added. 'Does that make them ideal for soup?'

The duty manager flinched, he definitely flinched. I was about to give him a piece of advice he'd never receive at any Swiss college when Beth returned.

'I can't find him anywhere,' she said. 'He's not in the dining room or on the steps by the pool. Come to think of it, I haven't seen him since lunchtime yesterday.'

'Perhaps he's found new guests who are more generous with the handouts,' I said, but I could see that Beth was clearly worried. Oh dear, and we had thirteen hours in a plane ahead of us. I couldn't bear the thought of the truth coming out on the way to Amsterdam, but I could see that she was heading inexorably towards sharing my awful suspicions.

Oh God! How much can those airline paper bags stand?

Must Like Cats

Melanie promised her mother faithfully that she wouldn't stay away longer than a year. Even more bindingly, she made the same promise to her cat, Cooper, a cream Birman that lay around the various rooms of their house like a bundle of fleece astray on a shearing-shed floor. Cooper shared Melanie's bed and her whispered secrets, and had been told from the time he was a kitten to prepare himself for the day when she would up and leave him.

All her life Melanie had harboured just one ambition – to go overseas to London just as her mother had in the mid-sixties. Her mother had spent four years in London, lived the glory days of Carnaby Street and the Kings Road, the Beatles and the Stones, and furnished the flat she and her girlfriends shared with pop-art posters and Victoriana picked up for a song from Austins of Peckham. She claimed she could not just remember every day but every magic moment, and had filled Melanie's ears with tales of her exploits almost from the instant she was born.

Melanie was raised believing that London was Camelot. She was fiercely determined that one day she, too, would enter its magic, mystical realm. She believed London would welcome her with open arms and embrace her as it had embraced her mother thirty years earlier. Embrace the true believer, the loyal subject of the Queen, the colonial daughter returning to the fold. It all seemed so certain seen from her mother-coloured perspective, far away in the northern Sydney suburb of Pymble.

Perhaps she'd have seen things more clearly if she'd spread her wings a little before she left home. Spent more time with boys who weren't quite so Cliff Richard in their conduct towards her. Perhaps if she'd read less of Brontë and Thomas Hardy and more of *Rolling Stone* magazine. Perhaps if she'd gone to a public school instead of Pymble Ladies College. Perhaps if she'd saved less assiduously both her money and her virtue. Perhaps if she'd spent less time inside the idealised world of her imaginings and more time in the world outside her door, then, she might have been more prepared.

Nobody ever landed at Heathrow with greater hopes and aspirations, nor viewed the rain and sleet-washed tarmac with more optimism. Not even the endless chain of moving walkways nor the interminable queue at Immigration dampened her spirits. She was determined to ride blithely over the inconveniences and indignities, attributing them all to the unavoidable travails of travel. Yet she was disconcerted by all the foreign, non-Anglo-Saxon faces she saw and the confusion of languages and accents, none of which had rated a mention in her mother's stories. She also expected to pass unhindered through the gate for British passport holders and visitors from the EEC. She was momentarily stunned when she was sent to the back of the aliens queue, and realised her Australian citizenship ranked her behind such unlikely, unfriendly nations as France and Germany.

More disquiet followed when the Pakistani-born Customs inspector decided to open her suitcases and examine their contents. No man had ever rifled through her underwear before, and she blushed when he found her anti-rape spray, a precaution her mother insisted she kept in her handbag and the airline insisted she didn't. The Customs inspector wasn't sure if it was an illegal import, and engaged in a lengthy conversation with his colleagues before letting it through.

But these were minor adjustments, inconveniences that would be forgotten the moment the great doors opened and she passed through to Camelot. She expected smiling faces, a panorama of peaches and cream lightly filtered and back-lit so that everyone and everything glowed with light halation. She didn't expect to be met by a wall of faces representing every nation and creed on earth, all of which ignored her completely. She stopped dead in the walkway. A slight gasp escaped her lips. She recognised nothing and no one recognised her. She would have stood there indefinitely if a Kuwaiti woman hadn't rammed her heel with her trolley and shooed her onwards. No one recognised her. There wasn't a sign of her girlfriend who'd left Sydney six months earlier and had been primed to meet her, take her home and share her lodgings.

Melanie only had two suitcases and her cabin bag on the trolley, but it seemed that everybody in the milling throng was determined to stumble over them and curse her for her lack of consideration. But what could she do but stand and wait to be found? There'd been no contingency plan, no arrangements for delay, no fallback. She waited twenty minutes, half an hour and was on the verge of tears when she heard her name called.

'Melanie!'

'Janice!' Melanie threw her arms around her rescuer and hugged her like long lost buddies do. Janice reciprocated. It took Melanie a moment or two before she recognised the sweet smell of alcohol on her girlfriend's breath.

'We've been waiting ages,' said Janice. 'Why didn't you look in the bar?'

It was only then that Melanie noticed that Janice was not alone.

'Like you to meet Tony,' she said, rolling her eyes the way she used to do at school when they saw a boy they thought was dishy.

'Hi. Nice to meet you,' said Melanie, trying hard to mean it. She hadn't expected to share Janice and struggled to absorb the ramifications.

'Pleasure I'm sure,' said Tony. He put his arm around Janice so that his wrist rested comfortably on her shoulder, and his hand flopped casually millimetres above her breasts. Melanie couldn't help notice the familiarity, and dismay welled up inside her. This wasn't how it was supposed to be. They were supposed to share a flat as her mother and her girlfriends had, and have adventures together. While she and Janice had never been the closest of friends, they were old school mates and old school mates were supposed to stick together.

'C'mon,' said Tony. 'Let's get you home. It's not exactly a palace but we'll fit you in somewhere.'

Melanie managed a smile but had no idea how. Coming on top of everything else the *we* knocked the stuffing out of her. Janice flashed her a smile and giggled nervously. She and

Tony were living together. And *they* were going to try to fit her in. Temporarily. She'd thought she'd be Janice's jolly flatmate but instead had become a gooseberry with a short shelf-life. Where did that leave her when the welcome wore off?

Besides all alone.

Melanie lay huddled on the single mattress jammed between the dining table and the wall, and pulled her blankets tightly around her. The seeping cold still found a way in. It was the beginning of the most exciting time of her life and yet she couldn't find a single reason to get out of bed. Tony and Janice had both left for work and she was relieved to see them go even though it meant she'd be alone. She had a lot to think about and come to terms with.

This wasn't at all how it was supposed to be.

The flat was tiny, no bigger than the cabana by their pool back in Pymble. It had a kitchen the size of a cupboard which Tony and Janice referred to as 'the galley', a single bedroom which took a double bed, wardrobe and dressing table and barely left room for people, and a tiny living room which was dining room, lounge and now bedroom to Melanie. The toilet and bathroom occupied a single room at the rear of the house, on the landing between the first and second floor of the three-storey house. A total of eight people from three flats shared both toilet and bathroom. Melanie was warned not to leave her toothbrush or toothpaste down there.

Melanie spent much of her first night in the bathroom to get away from the noises Tony and Janice were making in the bedroom. Melanie had never made love nor heard anyone make love before, and was mortally embarrassed. The thin walls and ill-fitting door screened nothing. She couldn't believe her girlfriend could carry on the way she had, or indeed that anyone else could for that matter. She was driven back to her bed by the cold and the pounding on the door by other tenants needing to excuse themselves.

This wasn't the way it was supposed to be.

Melanie added a few tears to the general soaking Great Britain was receiving, courtesy of a low which reached from the Russian steppes to the mid-North Atlantic. The long-range weather forecast was for rain, followed by more rain, with occasional storms in between. She was puzzled by the smell in the air and tried hard to remember where she'd encountered it before. Then it came to her. A camping holiday in Merimbula with her parents when it had rained for five days straight. What she smelled was damp and this time she knew there'd be no blazing summer sun to mop it up.

Melanie wished desperately she'd come in summer with Janice as she'd intended, before her brother's wedding pushed her plans onto the back burner. She'd had no choice. There was no way she could have left home before her brother's wedding. If she'd come then, Janice wouldn't be living with Tony, Melanie wouldn't be lying on an old mattress in a dingy, smelly, poky apology for a flat, and she wouldn't be in the mess she now found herself in. She knew she'd have to move out, sooner rather than later, but move where? With whom? The latter question was easy to answer. With no one, because there was no one. When she moved she'd move alone, set up home alone, then begin the serious business of meeting people, making friends, and having the best time of her life.

The way things were supposed to be.

The determination to act was enough to harden her resolve and get her out of bed long enough to make a cup of tea. She propped herself up in the corner with her blankets pulled up over her shoulders, one hand braving the elements to hold her steaming mug, and set about making new plans. She decided to get a flat of her own or at least a bedsit, whatever she could afford. Tony had told her they were lucky to get their little flat in Putney and that it took their combined wages to pay the rent. If that was so, Putney was out of the question. Melanie smiled for the first time that day. She'd dismissed Putney without seeing any more of it than the four walls of the flat. Perhaps there were other parts with gardens, trees, flowers, pets and maybe even a view. After all, how much could anyone charge for a bedsit, even one with a view? The scalding tea reached down into her extremities reactivating dormant tissue, and up into her brain where it re-heated her dreams. She remembered her mother telling her how on really cold days they'd go and stand around in Sainsburys or centrally heated department stores until they'd warmed up. Melanie decided to follow in her mother's footsteps, and racked her brain trying to remember which of her two suitcases carried her raincoat. There simply wasn't enough room in the flat to open both at the same time.

The rain was so different from the rain she was used to. It didn't fire into her, driven by a raging southerly or gusting westerly. Nor did it pelt down in blinding sheets that flooded roads and storm drains in minutes, and flattened crops. The drops that fell were tiny and apparently aimless, and seemed to waft about her without purpose. Yet, despite the protective cover of her umbrella, they saturated her raincoat, seeped through the neck and sat heavy like a dead man's hand upon her chest. She walked down Wadham Road and turned left into Putney Bridge Road. She knew from her street map that the Thames was nearby and ran parallel to the road. She felt a little buzz of excitement knowing it was so close and turned right into Deodar Road in the hope that she could catch a glimpse of it. After all, the river Thames had featured so much in history, her mother's stories and her dreams.

The Underground rattled overhead, drawing her attention to a flight of stone steps that led up onto the railway bridge walkway. The invitation was irresistible. Up she went and across, braving wind and rain until she stood as near as possible to the centre of the great river. She stared mesmerised at the swollen waters as they swirled around the bridge supports in a mad and pointless dirty brown rush towards Wandsworth. There was nothing the least bit inspiring about it. The Thames ran like a giant open drain, washing away the detritus of one of the world's largest and arguably dirtiest cities, yet Melanie saw it as a moment she would remember for the rest of her life.

'Don't jump, love. He isn't worth it. None of them are.'

Melanie turned with a start and met her first London bobby. He was West Indian, smiling but wary, and spoke just like Dennis Waterman from 'Minder'. He knew – though she obviously didn't – that a person had to be crazy to stand in the middle of Putney railway bridge on a wintry November day with the rain persisting down. Crazy enough to jump.

'Pardon me, what did you say?'

'Oh, Australian are you?' The policeman made this sound like a perfect explanation for her behaviour. 'I wouldn't stand out here too long, if I were you. You'll catch your death.'

'I'm just going,' said Melanie. 'Nice to meet you,' she added for want of something better to say.

'My pleasure entirely,' said the policeman who stood motionless until he'd seen her safely back across the bridge. He returned her wave as she began her descent of the stone steps, and spoke into his radio. Another tragedy averted.

Sainsburys was as warm and welcoming as her mother had said it would be, and she took her time examining the produce on the shelves. There were tinned and packaged goods from Belgium, France, Germany, Italy and Holland, bottles of wine with familiar names from Australia, lamb from New Zealand and bacon from Denmark. There were onions from Spain and all kinds of fruit from warmer latitudes. The butter was French or Danish, and all the continental countries seemed to be represented on the cheese shelves. What, she wondered, could she buy that was British? Chocolates? No, they were Swiss. After perusing the merchandise for half an hour while her hands and feet thawed, she bought a packet of Polo mints just as her mother had done.

She wandered back out into Putney High Street pondering her next move. Shop signs and windows were already glowing brightly and cars had their side lights on. High noon on a winter's day in London. She watched a double-decker bus lope past, promising herself a ride on one at the first opportunity, when her eye caught a sign that seemed to beckon to her. 'Putney Bridge Realty' it said, and added in tasteful script, 'Specialists in Rental Accommodation'. It drew her across the road.

'He's not in,' said a bored, uninterested voice in response to the bell that tinkled when Melanie pushed the door open.

'Beg your pardon?'

'He's gone to lunch.'

Melanie had no idea where the voice was coming from until a chubby, rather elderly woman rolled her chair out from behind a partition on the other side of the counter.

'It's his lunchtime, you see.'

'Oh,' said Melanie.

'Don't let the cat out!'

Melanie slammed the door shut behind her just as a tabby made its bid for freedom. She reached down and picked it up. It eyed her suspiciously and didn't respond at all favourably to her endearments. Cats don't like wet people.

'I'm sorry,' she said.

'Nothin' to be sorry about,' said the woman. She stood, reached over the counter and took the tabby from Melanie. 'Who's a naughty girl, then?' she soothed. She turned her attention back to Melanie. 'Can I take a message or something, or would you rather come back later? I'm his mum, see, his regular is off sick, like.'

'I just wanted to make enquiries about a bedsit somewhere nearby,' said Melanie. 'Something with a garden and a bit of a view perhaps.'

'Something with a garden and a bit of a view. Don't think so, love. You're not from around here are you?'

'Sydney,' said Melanie. 'Australia,' she added, just in case.

'Thought so. I'll tell him you came in and he can put his thinking cap on. Something to suit a nice young lady from Sydney, Australia. Yes, I'm sure he can manage that.'

'Thanks very much,' said Melanie. 'I'll call back tomorrow.'

'You do that,' said the agent's mum, and promptly forgot all about her.

That night Tony and Janice took her to their favourite pub and then on for a typical English meal at the local Indian.

When Melanie told them how she'd already begun her search for accommodation they were both mightily impressed.

'You don't muck around, do you?' said Tony admiringly. Her get-up-and-go meant she'd soon be got up and gone and they'd have their little flat to themselves, and wouldn't have to try to be quiet while they engaged in their nightly rumpy-pumpy. Her presence so close in the room next door had unnerved them. They thought it was very mature and sporting of her when she nicked off to the loo.

If Janice felt any guilt at all about letting Melanie down she kept it well hidden. She made Tony order another bottle of wine. Why not? They had something to celebrate. She had dreaded Melanie's arrival, regretted all the promises she'd made to her and the lies she'd been obliged to tell in her letters. But mostly she'd worried about what would happen if they'd got stuck with Melanie, Little Miss Pure and Innocent, the school Goody-Two-Shoes. She was sure her relationship with Tony couldn't handle the strain. Tony could have any girl he wanted, he'd told her that often enough. Yet Melanie had surprised her with a maturity and independence she just hadn't expected. Janice knew she could soon come to an arrangement with her over exactly what was communicated in letters back home to Pymble. She knew this new Melanie would understand.

Mr Higgins the Real Estate Agent, Harold not Henry as he insisted on pointing out, was accomplished in covering up for his mother's discrepancies, and soon had Melanie chasing around Putney and the fringes of Wandsworth and Richmond. Melanie always set off with high hopes and always returned with them dashed. She was convinced there wasn't a dry room in all of England, nor one that admitted sufficient daylight through its window to make switching on the light unnecessary. She couldn't understand how anyone could exist with a single small gas ring on the hearth or, in the more expensive bedsits which had partitioned off kitchens, cook on a single-element Baby Belling cooker. All week and Saturday morning she walked the rain-swept streets to no avail. Tony and Janice were beginning to revise their earlier opinion of her. They were beginning to wonder if she was trying hard enough.

'Your expectations are too high,' they told her. 'You can't expect to live here like you did back in Sydney.' They began to make her feel unwelcome, as if she was the one who'd broken promises, as if she was the one who'd gone back on her word.

Tears came close at night-time when she couldn't sleep for the noise of Tony and Janice's lovemaking, but she steeled herself and promised herself that this was all a bad dream. Things had to get better. She'd make them get better. Janice wasn't going to spoil things for her. Once she'd found a place to live she'd soon sort things out, and make them the way they were supposed to be. She snuggled down, head under the pillow, ignoring the cold and her bitterness and cherishing her dreams. They lit the darkness and chased away the cold. Her dreams were her reason for being in England. They were her reason to live. Janice, she decided, was a poor choice as a flatmate anyway. Even at school there'd been rumours about her lack of morals. Melanie decided she'd get along fine without her. She'd find someone else, someone who knew better and who could share her dreams.

The constant drizzle gave way to intermittent showers, but the wind had picked up and with it came a biting cold and occasional flurries of sleet. Melanie was hard pressed to see where she was better off. She still trudged the streets searching for a dry, light and airy bedsit, one with something approaching a real kitchen and with a loo that wasn't more than one flight of stairs away. Not a lot to ask, she thought, but disappointment piled upon disappointment and she could tell that Harold Higgins, specialist in rental accommodation, was ready to give up on her.

She'd begun to look further afield, straying west into the wider, quieter streets of suburban Richmond where the houses were bigger and newer and not so decrepit. She saw gardens lying fallow, stunted rose bushes bracing themselves for the snow that had to come, orderly grey–brown patches with nicely trimmed edges where they abutted lawn, and found in them the promise of spring. The promise of re-birth, of a new beginning. Ahhhhh . . . ! She lived, breathed, slept with the promise of a new beginning.

She slipped into an antique shop on Upper Richmond Road to escape a sudden cloudburst, and occupied herself by examining the heavy, often ugly furniture from Queen Victoria's reign. Why, she wondered, hadn't her mother chosen to get interested in Georgian furniture instead? The beaded lampshades and brocaded and tassled chaise longues and sofas were all too Aubrey Beardsley for her taste, while the Georgian pieces spoke of a timeless elegance. The price differential seemed to confirm her observations.

'Can I help you at all?'

Melanie turned to the shopkeeper, ready to throw her usual 'Just looking thanks', and met a smiling face with the classic peaches-and-cream complexion she'd expected everyone in Britain to have, and eyes that invited conversation.

'My mother came to London in the sixties,' she said tentatively, 'and developed a passion for Victoriana.' She smiled. The shop was warm and for the first time in ages she felt she was with someone of her own kind. 'I can't understand the attraction.'

The shopkeeper smiled. 'And how long have you been here?' she asked.

'About twelve days,' Melanie confessed sheepishly. 'I'm still looking for somewhere to live.'

The shopkeeper invited Melanie to take off her raincoat and sit down. She made her a cup of tea and listened sympathetically while Melanie told her all about her fruitless search for a bedsit.

'I think you're barking up the wrong tree,' said the shopkeeper. 'You don't want a bedsit, you want to move in with a nice family. Lodge with them. Find someone with a spare room to let and grab it. I know a woman who is separated. She has two lodgers. They help with the cooking and washing up and babysit her kids. One big happy family but they each have their own life. That sort of thing would be perfect for you. There'd always be someone there when you came home.'

Melanie wasn't aware of her mouth dropping open as she listened. Why hadn't she thought of lodging before? Perhaps it wasn't what her mother had done, but it was the ideal solution for someone in her situation. Her mind was awash with possibilities. She'd give anything to be part of a real home among decent people.

'Well?' asked the shopkeeper. 'What do you think?'

Melanie wanted to hug her, to kiss her, to thank her in a way that expressed her true feelings, but also knew that the British didn't go in for that sort of thing.

'I think you're a genius,' said Melanie. 'You're absolutely one hundred percent right. I don't know how to thank you.'

The shopkeeper laughed. 'You've said enough. Here.' She passed Melanie a thin tabloid newspaper, the *Richmond Recorder*. 'You might find what you're looking for in here, in the classifieds. It's a bit of a parish pump but I find it quite useful.'

'Thank you,' gushed Melanie. 'I'll let you know how I get on.'

'Good luck!' The shopkeeper saw Melanie out of her shop and shook her head in disbelief. How could anyone be so naive in this day and age, she wondered? And also wondered what it was in Australian women that made them travel halfway around the world when so often they were barely fit to cross the street.

Melanie went straight home, had a hot bath, and sat down at the tiny dining room table. She opened the *Richmond Recorder* and began by looking under L for Lodgings and found what she was looking for under R for Rooms to Let. There were three ads that seemed promising, two on the Putney side of Richmond, one of which stood out from the page like a beacon on a storm-swept sea. It beckoned to Melanie, seemed specially written for her, singled her out and called to her.

'Room to Let,' it said. 'Older woman seeks lodger/ companion. Share duties. Own bathroom/toilet. Suit young, single woman. *Must like cats*.'

Must like cats! Melanie adored cats and missed Cooper, her Birman, almost as much as she missed her mother. She circled the ad and underlined the phone number. The rent was less than half what she was prepared to pay for a bedsit. She tossed up whether or not to once more brave the wind and rain and phone from the public call box on the corner.

But the street lights were already glowing brightly in the gathering gloom, and there was no guarantee that the phone wouldn't have been vandalised after Chelsea soccer team's home defeat. She decided to wait until the next day and phone from Putney High Street.

She imagined a kindly Miss Marple figure, a lover of cats and grower of roses, someone like her granny who she could shop for, clean house and care for. Someone who would care for her in return and listen attentively as she recounted her adventures. Melanie pictured three cats, thought she might even adopt one of them as her own for the duration of her stay.

When Janice and Tony came home and asked why she was so happy she simply said she thought she had her accommodation problem solved. She didn't want to say too much for fear of putting the mockers on. Instead, she kept her hopes to herself, saved them up to examine and re-examine once she'd climbed into bed, in the hope that they would lull her into blissful sleep before the lovemaking began.

This is more like it, she thought. This is how it was meant to be. She felt the excited tingle of old.

A pale, bleak sun greeted Melanie as she stepped out of the tiny flat in Wadham Road and began the walk to Putney High Street. She saw its appearance as a good omen. It hung low on the horizon as if lacking the strength to break through the yellow–brown haze that engulfed it and climb to its noonday heights. Nevertheless, its wan light seemed to signal the new beginning she longed for.

Her hands shook as she dropped the coins into the slot and lifted the receiver. The phone rang, and rang, and rang.

She hung up, disbelieving. Not once had she considered the possibility that the dear, sweet lady who shared her passion for cats might not be waiting on the other end of the phone for her call. She stood momentarily at a loss. Obviously she'd have to ring back and keep ringing back until the phone was answered. She wandered into a cafe and ordered a pot of tea, shaken by another unwelcome prospect. What if the room was already let? What if someone else had already grabbed her place? She bit her lip and worried and sipped her tea until the large hand on her watch completed a full revolution. She rang again. No one was home.

The sun had found some clouds to slip in and out of, but Melanie decided to take advantage of the milder temperature to explore the Thames. She walked across the road bridge and stepped down onto a tow path that ran along the northern bank. The trees looked forlorn without their foliage but nevertheless everything around her had a shine to it, a clean sparkle courtesy of past rains. It was not what Melanie had come to regard as beautiful but was not entirely unattractive. She tried to imagine what it would be like in spring, when flowers were in bloom and leaves covered the trees, and squirrels came looking for a handout. That would be beautiful, she decided. She checked her watch. Time to call.

'Hello?' enquired a voice almost immediately. It wasn't the sort of voice Melanie expected to hear. It didn't sound old or in the least bit delicate. Though obviously a woman's voice it was flat and somehow masculine.

'Hello?'

'Oh,' said Melanie. 'Hello. I'm calling about the advertisement in the *Richmond Recorder*.'

'Oh yes?'

'I believe you have a room to let.'

'Yes. You does like cats, don't you?'

'Yes,' said Melanie. 'Oh yes I do.'

'That's important,' said the voice matter-of-factly.

'Can I come and see the room?'

'Four o'clock would suit me,' said the voice. 'How does that suit you?'

'Fine,' said Melanie.

'Australian, are you?'

'Yes.'

'All alone?'

'Yes,' said Melanie once more. 'I've only been here two weeks.'

'Good,' said the voice. 'We likes Australians. We've had them before. Four o'clock then. Number forty-three, it is.'

'Four o'clock,' agreed Melanie. The phone clicked in her ear. She replaced the handset and wondered how on earth she'd fill in the next four hours. She cursed herself for not speaking up and suggesting an earlier time. Like right away. She wandered back to the flat to make herself toast spread with a little of her precious Vegemite, and tried to put form to the voice. Her previous image of a gentle, smiling Miss Marple didn't seem to fit. Nor could she conjure up any image of an older woman to match the voice she'd heard. But she didn't allow it to distract her. She had too much riding on the accommodation proving entirely to her satisfaction. There was also the matter of the cats. She was looking forward to having a cat to cuddle, a constant purring presence watching her every move.

The bus dropped her off on Upper Richmond Road and she turned down the street which led eventually to Balaclava

Road. Melanie had been in the vicinity before but now looked around her with proprietary interest. This would be her bus stop. This would be the way she walked to the bus and walked home. She viewed the wider than normal street with approval. Even though it was quite dark the street lights were adequate. Houses were set back from the road behind little fences and hedges, with lawn and garden in between. Dogs barked and house martins swooped after insects in the spill from the street lights. It had a decidedly more Pymble feel about it.

She turned left into Balaclava Road and began counting off the houses. It didn't take long to work out that number forty-three was mid-way along the street and that it would take a lot less than ten minutes to reach it. She decided to walk past and double back, and get a better feel for her new neighbourhood in the process. She glanced up at number forty-three as she walked by and thought she saw somebody momentarily peeping through the curtains. They certainly swayed and closed, but was it simply the effect of a breeze? She kept walking, turned at the end of the street, retraced her steps and rang the doorbell at precisely four o'clock.

The woman who opened the door was not what she expected. She was no Miss Marple and nor was she old. Early forties, Melanie guessed, and close to six foot with a post-war sense of dress. A heavy, hand-knitted grey sweater hung loosely over massive shoulders and breasts, and fell to hip length over a heavy grey worsted skirt. She wore no make-up but had made some attempt to drag her hair into a semblance of order. No, she wasn't at all what Melanie had pictured. She'd pictured Miss Marple but what she got was more like Kathy Bates on steroids.

'Come in, girlie,' she said. 'We've been expecting you.' She took Melanie's arm and almost dragged her inside.

That was the first intimation Melanie had that something was seriously awry. The second came hard on its heels. She was almost battered to the floor by an overpowering smell of cat ordure and the pungent tang of urine. It didn't take her long to establish the source. Cats rushed to investigate the newcomer. Melanie had never seen so many cats in her life. They poured down the staircase like water over rapids. They lined up across the hall in ranks, heads high sniffing the air.

'Come into the light, girlie, so's we can take a look at you.'

'No I . . .'

'Don't be silly girl, you can't stand out here all night.'

Melanie didn't want to stand anywhere. She wanted to run. She wanted to run as far away from the foul smelling house as she could, fill her lungs with untainted air and breathe again. She wanted to get away from the big woman who held her arm in a grip that threatened to bruise and led her firmly into the drawing room.

'Not been here long, you say?'

'No,' said Melanie, hardly listening. It was brighter in the drawing room and what she saw left her nigh lost for words. Cats covered every chair, the seat, arms and back. They covered the piano and even lined up nose to tail along the mantelpiece. And they all watched her, tails flicking, whiskers twitching, noses investigating.

'No time to make friends, then?'

'No,' said Melanie. She was stunned. The landlady was carrying on as if having cats draped everywhere, fouling everything, was quite normal. She appeared oblivious to their presence and, unbelievably, oblivious to the smell.

'Told anyone where you were going?'

'No,' said Melanie and instantly regretted it.

'Good,' said the big woman. 'Single woman living alone can't be too careful. We doesn't want to be preyed upon, does we my lovelies? No we does not. That's why I always say I'm older than I am. We doesn't want the wrong people getting ideas.'

Melanie tried to pull her arm away from the landlady's grasp but got nowhere. The big woman seemed unaware that she was holding onto her.

'I has my rules,' she said. 'No bringing men friends home.'

Melanie couldn't conceive of wanting to bring anyone home to such a foul place.

'No staying out after ten at night. I shuts the door at ten and it stays shut. I knows that and my lovelies know that. Out after ten, it's out all night as far as I'm concerned.'

'Ouch!' said Melanie. 'That cat bit me! He bit me!'

The landlady reached down and grabbed hold of the offending cat.

'Now, now Mr Puddlepuss. Who's a naughty boy, then?' she spoke to the cat in a little girly voice. 'Who's got no manners? Who's going to miss out on dinner if he's not very careful?' She put the cat down on the piano, shooing another cat off to make space.

Melanie rubbed the back of her ankle where the cat had bitten her. Her handbag slipped off her shoulder and she had to grab it quickly before it hit the floor. At least the landlady had let go of her arm.

'Come and I'll show you upstairs.'

'No . . . no . . . it's not necessary,' stammered Melanie. 'I'm afraid it isn't suitable. Not suitable at all.' She began to back towards the door. She was beginning to feel scared, really scared without knowing exactly what it was she was really scared of. 'I'm sorry.'

'Don't be silly,' said the landlady. 'You can't come all this way and not even see your room, can she my lovelies? That doesn't make sense, does it? No, it does not.' The hand reached out once more and clasped hold of Melanie's arm.

'No really,' said Melanie. Her voice shook and she'd lost control of the pitch. She warbled more than spoke.

The cats followed them as they set off upstairs. Those waiting in line began to miaow and others picked up the call. There were more cats upstairs, some lying in wait on the landing and in the hallway, others scratching behind doors. The cat wailing intensified. The light was poor, but as they passed beneath the naked bulb on the landing Melanie caught a good look at the landlady's face. The smile was still on the lips but her eyes were cold and hard and more terrifying than anything Melanie had ever seen before. She had to stifle a cry.

'That naughty Mr Puddlepuss hasn't bitten you again, has he? He'll get what for if he keeps that up, my word he will.'

'Please . . . you're hurting my arm.'

'Am I? Sorry.' But the landlady didn't let go.

'This here is your bedroom.'

But for the cat piss which patterned the carpet and assaulted the senses, the room was by far the best Melanie had been offered. It was the best room in the house, right at the front with large windows that faced south. It had an enormous double bed with reproduction black and brass bedends inset with porcelain. But Melanie was beyond inspecting, beyond admiring, and beyond even looking. She felt trapped and in mortal danger, and the big woman still had hold of her arm. Cats milled around her legs, miaowing, sniffing, rubbing, sniffing, sniffing . . .

'I want to go!' said Melanie, fighting back her panic. 'It's not at all what I want. Sorry. Just let me go!'

'But we hasn't seen the bathroom yet, has we? How many places offers you your own bathroom? Come along!'

'No, please! Please!'

'Don't be silly, girlie. You has to visit the bathroom. Everyone has to visit the bathroom.' She snorted as if she'd just told a very witty joke.

'No! I don't want to visit the bathroom!'

'But you have to, girlie.' She opened a door on the landing and pushed Melanie through. 'That's why you're here.'

Melanie felt the hand let go of her arm and spun around to make a dash for the front door, away from this woman who was clearly insane. But she was too late. The bathroom door slammed shut behind her. Even more ominously, she heard the key turn in the lock.

'We'll be back in a moment girlie, won't we my lovelies?'

Melanie stood frozen in shock listening to the footsteps retreating down the stairs. What was going on? What was going on? This couldn't be happening to her! Couldn't be happening! She rushed over to the window to pull back the curtains. Perhaps she thought she could break the glass and call for help. She ripped the curtains apart and screamed, gave voice to her fears with a scream that came from her very soul. The window had been bricked up.

She looked around her in desperation. There had to be another way out. But there wasn't. Just a toilet, well scrubbed and glistening. And a bath, also well scrubbed. And a solid wooden bench like an old laundry scrubbing bench. It was also well scrubbed. The tiles on the floor were spotless and sloped to a large drain hole in the middle. But there were no towels, no soap, no toothbrush holder and certainly no means of escape.

She heard the footsteps coming back up the stairs and stifled a scream. She thought about hiding behind the door and jumping the landlady as she came in, but knew instantly that she had no chance against the woman's bulk and strength. The key turned in the lock. Melanie backed as far away from the door as she could, backed hard up against the wall opposite.

The door opened and the landlady stood there. She'd changed and put on a long black leather apron. Her sleeves were rolled up. The smile was gone and she looked at Melanie with eyes that were as cold and lifeless as a dead fish's.

'Now, now, girlie. Don't go making a fuss. My lovelies has to be fed and that's all there is to it.' She stepped into the bathroom and closed the door behind her. She put the key in the lock, turned it and slipped it back into the pocket of her apron.

'No! No!' screamed Melanie. 'Don't hurt me! Don't hurt me!'

'Hurt you, girlie? If you just stop being silly you'll hardly feel a thing.' She pulled a long butcher's knife from a scabbard hanging from the belt around her apron. She placed it on the wooden bench. She reached a hand behind her and produced a cleaver. Reached again and produced a small saw.

Melanie screamed. And screamed. Her screaming was the only thing that stopped her from fainting.

'Don't be silly, girlie. My lovelies has to be fed. I've told you.' She picked the butcher's knife up off the bench and took a step towards Melanie, her eyes unblinking, her gaze never wavering.

Somewhere in the midst of all the panic, cells in Melanie's brain made frantic connection. Her hand grabbed inside her bag.

'Don't be silly gir . . . aahhhhh!'

Melanie pressed the button on top of her anti-rape spray and never let up. The landlady reeled backwards, her eyes on fire. The butcher's knife clattered to the floor.

'Aaghhhhh!' screamed the landlady. 'Oooohhhhh . . . !'

Melanie reached for the key in the apron pouch and immediately felt a massive hand grab hold of her arm.

'No!' she screamed. But there was nothing she could do. The landlady pulled hard on her arm and threw her up against the bench. Melanie saw the cleaver, grabbed it, raised it and brought it crashing down upon the landlady's head. She felt the hand let go, pulled her arm free and unlocked the bathroom door. She had to battle past cats clawing to get in. She trod on them, tripped over them, and ran on top of them as she dashed frantically down the stairs. Unearthly screams and cries came from above. Curses and shrieks mingled with the screeching cries of the cats. They spurred her on. She hit the front door running. Locked. But the key was still in the lock. She twisted. Nothing. Wrong way. 'Oh God,' she sobbed. 'Oh God! Somebody help me! Help me!'

Twist, twist, the other way. Click. Push! No, pull! The door opened and she forced her way outside. She never heard the door close behind her as she raced down the path. Never heard the gate close behind her as she raced out onto the road. Never heard the squeal of brakes or the thump of metal on human flesh as she was hurled upwards . . . into oblivion.

It wasn't until ten o'clock that night that Tony and Janice decided to report Melanie missing. They gave the police a description and told them about Melanie looking for somewhere to live in the Putney–Richmond area. It took no time at all for the police to make the connection with the unidentified white female knocked down by a car in Balaclava Road. The police had canvassed the houses in the street but no one had seen the girl before, knew why she was there, nor why she had run blindly out in front of a car. Only number forty-three had failed to respond to their knock. The police rushed Tony and Janice to the hospital to make an identification, and decided to carry on with their enquiries. Number forty-three was their priority.

The morning newspapers and television were full of the horror. There were stories of bones beneath floorboards, pictures of missing girls, though, of course, they didn't show any pictures of the landlady or, at least, what was left of her. She'd said her lovelies had to be fed, and they had fed. Only the menu had changed.

As for Melanie, she spent a week longer in hospital than she had in the little flat in Putney. Qantas flew her home as soon as the doctors gave her permission to fly. She arrived in a wheelchair with an arm and a leg encased in plaster, her ribs strapped, and dirty yellow and blue bruising that no amount of make-up could hide.

Nevertheless, Pymble never felt so good.

Genetic Memory

It's hard to know whether Granny Brunsden stayed alive to look after her cat Min, or whether Min kept plodding on to look after Granny Brunsden. Neither would ever climb apple trees again, that was for sure. Granny was ninety not out, but nobody would bet her on batting right through to her century. Min was eighteen, old for a tabby and it showed in the way she measured Granny's lap for a good ten minutes before attempting the jump up. More often than not, the old lady would reach down and spare Min the agony of once more pushing her arthritic limbs to their very limit, but there were always the times when Granny forgot and fell asleep before Min had gained her favoured position. These were the times Min dreaded, but she could no more creep away into some sunny little spot to sleep than die. She couldn't leave her mistress to fend for herself.

The ladies from Meals on Wheels always brought scraps for the cat when they delivered Gran's lunch and dinner. They soon learned to match the scraps with Granny Brunsden's lunch or Min wouldn't touch them. The two old girls always ate like sparrows, and left more than they took.

Gran liked chicken best and that suited Min right down to the ground.

Everyone waited for the pair to die. They knew that when one of them went, the other would follow close behind.

Gran had lived all her married life in the little workingman's cottage in Birchgrove, a relic of Victorian times altered only to accept the wonder of piped gas and electricity, and to accommodate an inside toilet, a shower, electric cooker and fridge. She'd raised five children there, lost one in the Vietnam War, and her husband to a heart attack that struck without warning. Her sons kept her home in good repair but could not prevent its age from showing. The house had a run down, worn out, ineffable weariness about it as if it, too, was waiting for the old lady to die so that it could be demolished to make way for a new house built of younger timbers. Gran didn't keep her home as neat and clean as she should, but her failing sight made her blind to its disorder. She refused help. There were only three things left she felt capable of doing and would surrender none of them. She could look after herself, look after Min, and look after her home. She still put her bin out herself on rubbish nights, and lit a fire in the hearth when the long winter shadows crept down her narrow street, dragging the dark and cold of night behind them.

Min would warm the armchair as the old lady set and lit the fire, move onto the arm when Gran was ready to sit down, and take up station on her lap the moment Gran had made herself comfortable. They ate their dinner there, in the glow of the flames and the portable telly, but the TV pictures seemed ever more irrelevant to them, and more and more the flickering dance of the flames won their attention. It was hard to believe that seven people had once vied for space around the hearth for there barely seemed room for two. Gran's home was never her castle, more her cave, only three metres at its widest, single storey with tiny rooms hanging off a narrow corridor. Railway carriage homes they called them, and it was easy to see the similarity.

Gran's two greatest pleasures in life were sitting in front of the fire, and sunning herself out on her tiny verandah in her twisted seagrass chair where the wind couldn't reach her. Then her husband came back to her and her lost soldier-boy son, brothers and sisters and times long gone. They were all so young and gay, and full of life and hope. The old lady could forget her lunch or why she'd tottered along to the corner shop, but nature provided beautiful compensation. Old memories resurfaced, scrubbed up, polished and shining like new pennies. As her eyelids grew heavy and drooped, yesterday glowed brightly in infinite detail and never seemed more distant than the day just gone.

It was the flames that drew forth the deepest memories. Gran stared at them, the unhurried way they licked around the split grey gum, warming and comforting, turning blue when oils ignited, occasionally crackling and shooting a spark into the guard. The flames reflected in her glasses and in Min's eyes. She could see them shining back at her whenever she looked up at the framed photo of her husband above the mantelpiece. The sun made her think of her children and their growing up, but the flames made her think of her youth, her own childhood, her first memories of her own dear mother. Sometimes the flames took her back to her childish dreams, when her head swum with princesses and princes, when Snow White and Cinderella were real and could so easily have been her.

She glanced up at her husband once more, saw the reflected light in Min's eyes dim until her companion dropped off to sleep, felt her own eyes blur as the flames worked their spell, dragging her back into her memories with sweet siren song. Back she went, past the time when her family was still together, beyond the timorous little girl perched on the stiff, formal knee of the gentle man who was her father, past the soap and lavender smells of her mother, back, back in time and imagination. Min lay heavy on her lap, whiskers twitching, paws flexing at images only she could see. They disappeared, each into their own world. Their dreams were their comfort and refuge, coming at their bidding but not of their choosing. Dormant, distant cells activated at random to give up their knowledge, garnered through experience and learning, through fleeting images and snatches of conversation, gained first hand and passed on through successive generations, imprinted in the genetic memory, a gift from their forebears.

Night stole in upon a hostile world, hustled in before its time by towering banks of dark roiling clouds. In the plains below, a small group of hominids increased their pace, whimpering anxiously as they went. Night was the time of killing, the time of eating and the strange, two-legged creatures knew the plains were no place to be. Not when night fell. Not at the killing time. Around them the air exploded in deafening, blinding flashes that made the coarse hair covering their bodies go rigid, and made them cry out in fear. Fear. The calling card of prey to predator, the unmistakeable scent, the summons to a kill. Fear. Come hyena, come leopard, come sabre-toothed tiger. It is the killing time and we are here to be killed.

The big male stopped and sniffed the air, his little band gathering in close around him. Mothers clutched juveniles to their breasts, all wide-eyed with fear. The wind brought the smell of rain, cold and heavy, of lightning strike, of danger. The leader scanned the cliff walls. Experience had taught him the necessity for shelter. They had to find shelter or die. Shelter from the rain, protection from their enemies. Sanctuary, a place they could defend and rest in until dawn. He reached down and scraped his finger through a dung heap, and sniffed it. His primitive brain associated the smell with the gigantic animals that grazed the plains. Mastodons. No threat to them, not like the packs of hyenas which whipped themselves into a frenzy before ripping limbs from body. He had once watched from the safety of high rocks when a marauding pack of hyenas had attacked a band of animals he had no name for, which were similar though larger than himself. Aeons later, fossil remains would identify these larger hominids as *Australopithecus robustus*. He'd watched in awe as the band defended itself, clubbing and beating off their attackers. They lost a female and a juvenile, and that seemed to satisfy the hyenas who broke off the attack to feed. He'd howled and barked threats at the hyenas, sharing the partial victory with his distant relatives. But even in that brief moment of triumph he was aware that he and his kind would never prevail even partially. His species, *Homo erectus*, simply lacked the strength.

A young female cried out and his band whimpered in fear. The wind carried sound as well as smells, and what they heard chilled them to the bone. The big cat had called to them, the big cat with the fearsome teeth that fed upon their kind. Once more the leader scanned the cliff wall, looking for fissures, for caves, aware of the potential danger within them, and the certainty of death without. Their enemy had announced its presence and intention, yet the big male had no choice but to lead his terrified band in the direction of the threat. Behind them the wind began to laugh. The leader started to run and his band ran with him, surrounding him, fearful of falling behind, fearful of running too far ahead, staying close, seeking his protection.

The big cat knew the territory well. It stalked through the rocks, flitting from shadow to shadow, watching its prey approach, anticipating its every move. The time of killing was drawing nigh, and after the killing came the feasting. The sabre-toothed tiger felt the rumble in its stomach and snarled. She stiffened. The wind carried the demented laugh of hyenas. Had they caught the scent of the creatures scurrying towards her? Night closed in and her pupils widened. She scanned the plains, picked up distant movement, erratic but determined. Her competition. She snarled in threat and warning, loudly enough for the sound to carry to her prey. It was time to kill or be killed, to eat or be eaten. The killing time had come.

The big male ran harder. Already some of his band were struggling to keep up. The cliff ahead of them had dulled to a dark, threatening presence, but he'd seen what he needed to see and struck out instinctively towards it. The hyenas drew closer behind them, their carrion breath urging the weary band on. The big male knew that if they could reach shelter, reach the cave and the protection of its stone sides, they could defend the opening. Lightning slashed the air around them, briefly lit the opening to the cave. He stumbled and almost fell, bashed his shins painfully against fallen rocks and realised how close they were to sanctuary. Behind him juveniles screamed in fear as their mothers stumbled. They began to climb, furiously but blindly, driven by fear and the fiendish howling. A tree exploded in front of them in a shattering flash of light, showering the ground with burning branches and embers. Shock waves of thunder battered them to their knees. His little band shrunk back from the flames, encircled, trapped, screaming and clutching each other in fear. It was the sort of delay that ordinarily proved fatal, but the big male was about to make a discovery so monumental, so absolutely staggering, it would ensure the survival of his species, while the bigger, stronger *robustus* would go the way of the dinosaur. Incredibly, the big male was about to use his brain.

He snarled and bared his teeth as the hyenas caught up with them, watched helplessly as they danced around in triumph and laughed in anticipation of the feast. He jumped to his feet and pretended to charge. Smoke filled his eyes and stung his nostrils. His frightened band clung off every part of his body. They were beaten, caught in the open and defenceless, yet he gradually became aware of a strange thing taking place. His enemy had seen them fall, had them defenceless yet had not begun to attack. They howled and laughed and circled and circled, but none dared attack. Something was different. Something had changed. His primitive brain wasn't up to much but it slowly dawned on him what the difference was. Fire. The big male had never been a great fan of fire and noticed that the hyenas shared his prejudice. He summoned his courage, picked up a burning branch and hurled it with all his strength at the attackers. He hooted and barked when he saw them scatter. He hurled another branch and another, each time achieving the same result. He jumped up and down in glee. Something truly astonishing was happening though his brain lacked the ability to define precisely what. The young males watched their leader and became emboldened. They copied him. Hominid see, hominid do. They charged at the hyenas with firebrands in their hands, eyes wide, lips curled back over enormous grinding teeth. They didn't understand cause and effect, but they understood aggression and territorial defence. They hurled abuse when they saw the hyenas scatter and retreat.

The big male was unsure what to do next. Thought was altogether far too fresh a novelty to sustain. He knew they were safe within the circle of fire, but instinct insisted they find sanctuary. Yet how could they leave the circle of fire and survive? He watched the young males with their burning branches, and picked up a burning branch himself. His band gathered around him. A second thought occurred to him on this momentous day. Why leave the fire when they could take it with them? He raised his firebrand and the young males did likewise. Together they moved onwards and upwards, carrying the spitting flames with them, yelling threats at their frustrated attackers. The hyenas backed off and gave up as the climb steepened. One young male threw down his burning branch in triumph. The big male snarled at him, abused him until he'd regathered it. He could barely comprehend what was so important about keeping the burning branch but he understood this – it was the killing time and they hadn't been killed. It was the time of darkness and yet they could see. Whatever importance was, fire was it. The big male led his little band to the opening of the cave and hesitated, filled with dread and foreboding. He sniffed the air and walls within. The whimpering began almost immediately. They could smell their death, cruel, relentless and merciless. Up above them the big cat had watched their progress with keen interest. Providence had delivered her prey to the very door of her lair.

The sabre-toothed tiger ruled the cliffs. There was no place she didn't know. No pathway, no burrow, no fissure, no cave. The cliffs were her domain and she ruled ruthlessly. Any creature that trespassed upon her territory paid the ultimate price, bird, reptile or mammal. She was especially fond of the two-legged beasts, particularly the smaller variety, and their remains littered the floor of her cave. She growled softly, back in her throat, a low rumbling that seemed capable of penetrating rock. It penetrated the cave where the little band of *Homo erectus* clutched tightly to one another, and squeezed as close to their bundle of firebrands as they could go without singeing. They whimpered and keened, unwilling to enter deeper into the cave yet, equally, unwilling to return into the open.

The sabre-toothed tiger slipped between two rocks and down a cleft that led to a bottle-neck shaft which opened into a cave. Her cave. Her nostrils quivered at the unfamiliar burning smell wafting through the crevice yet she didn't hesitate. It was the killing time. Her time. And nature had made her the most efficient killing machine the world had ever known. She crept silently through the inner cave, eyes wide like starscopes amplifying the available light so that every rock and pit could be easily negotiated. She paused, forced to blink and clear her eyes. That had never happened to her before.

The sounds of death carried up to the cave from the plains. Leopards and hyenas moved in on the horned grazers and browsers, separating the weak and the young, isolating the stragglers and nature's failures, their pathetic cries soon lost in the cacophony of the victorious and the squabbling over the spoils. The little band of hominids shrunk back in their cave grateful for its protection, relieved they were no longer exposed and vulnerable upon the plains.

The sabre-toothed tiger paused once more to blink away the film of water that covered her eyes. She wanted to cough, to purge her throat and nostrils of the vile fumes but knew better. It was the killing time, time to kill and time to eat, and she knew better than to risk scattering her prey. She dropped onto her haunches. There they were silhouetted against the night and . . . and . . . huddled around fire! The big cat was momentarily confused. She knew about fire and knew to avoid it, but fire had never interfered in a kill before. She stared coldly at the unlikely combination. Food and fire. Food and fear. Her brain struggled with the implications but couldn't reach beyond what survival demanded and experience insisted. It was the killing time and there was food to be killed. Nothing else mattered. She half rose and edged slowly forward, her keen eyes selecting a young female for her prey. Already she could hear its shrill cry, sense the snap of the neck, taste the blood, feel the young bones crush beneath her jaws. Her whiskers twitched.

The big male looked down at his family and felt his eyelids grow heavy. The juveniles were already asleep on their mothers' breasts and their mothers not far behind them. He stared into the dying flames and wondered what it was about them he was supposed to remember. Whatever it was had dimmed with the fire. He shifted branches around, lay one on top of the other to see what would happen, to see if he could revive and prolong it. The flames made him feel good, warm and sleepy. That was something else he'd just discovered. He stared into the fire and tried as hard as he could to think about it.

The sabre-toothed tiger was desperate to cough. The big male was playing with the fire and the fire was sending more smoke snaking through the cave. She pushed her discomfort out of her mind and allowed her instincts to take over. Her tail twitched and fur prickled. She crept closer, closer. The muscles in her powerful legs tensed, her paws felt for traction. Everything was in its place. Everything was right for the kill. She roared as she leaped, one bound, two, her eyes fixed on the young female and her whole being geared for the strike. The screams of her prey filled her ears, filled the cave, bounced and echoed off the hard stone walls. Her eyes narrowed, her tongue retracted, her jaws extended. The magical, glorious, pandemonious moment of kill had finally come. The big male jumped to his feet, arms swinging. Fire arced towards her. Fire and fear. She shrieked, thrust out her forelegs to check her momentum. Too late! Too late! The fire met her whiskers, met her nose, reached for her eyes, crackling, snapping, searing. She tried to leap backwards but something was holding her back . . . holding her back . . .

'Min! Min! My goodness me!' Gran held her precious companion tightly in her arms. The grey gum crackled, sending sparks into the guard. Oils flared. 'My goodness me, Min, whatever were you dreaming about?'

Min looked around, confused. She'd once been young and strong, and hunted and killed. But before then, before then . . . way before then . . . The dream had slipped away and she couldn't quite bring it back. But it had been something grand, she was certain.

Something really grand.

Psychic Cat is Never Wrong

Morris and Fiona had lived in Hollywood for seven years before they decided to do what coaches filled with visitors did every day. They pulled off Wilshire Boulevard to look in on some of California's oldest inhabitants. Thinking back, neither of them could figure out what prompted them to stop because neither had the slightest interest in palaeontology, nor could either date the Pleistocene Epoch within ten million years. They stopped on a whim, because one or other of them had read something about the Devil's Cauldron tar pits coughing up another mammoth carcass, or because it was a nice day, or because Fiona had a couple of days free between assignments and Morris needed something to take his mind off a once-in-a-lifetime real estate coup that looked like falling over. Each had reason to blame the other for stopping but blamed fate instead. They just wished fate had kept the hell out of it and let them keep on driving by as they always did.

They talked about Jesus Guerrero as they walked from the carpark to the museum, cursed his forty acres of oranges and his implacable opposition to selling his land so that Morris could offer the entire Morelos Valley to the Sentia

Chemical Company for the construction of a new high-tech chemical plant and infrastructure, which included a small town. The Sentia Chemical Company had long since learned that the best way to stop townspeople complaining about noxious odours and lethal chemical leaks was to own the town. Nobody complained about 245T when the rent was cheap. When Morris had taken his proposal to the State Government they'd greeted it with enthusiasm. State Senator William J. Johnston publicly threw his weight and influence behind it, and discreetly invested a bundle of money. The Morelos Valley Project had everything going for it that an elected representative of the people could ask for. It brought truck loads of capital into his district, created jobs, and pointed to solid achievement when re-election time fell due. Morelos Valley also had the triple advantages of being out of sight, unheard of and unloved by the entire population of California, with just one exception – Jesus Guerrero, a seventy-year-old Mexican immigrant who was determined to live out the rest of his life among his orange trees, and if possible die among them. Morris was happy to accommodate him with the latter, but for the fact that society tended to take an unkindly view of murder.

'Stubborn,' said Morris. 'Mule-headed stubborn.'

'Selfish,' he added, and he was in a position to know since this was also one of Morris' more dominant traits.

'Isn't there anything you can do?' asked Fiona.

'Not unless you've got some ideas. The Senator's talked to him, I've talked to him. I've offered to buy him another valley, build him another house, transplant all his bloody orange trees and put a million dollars in his pocket.'

'That's a lot of money.'

'That's what the Senator said, too.'

'What did Jesus say?'

'What he always says. No *chem-i-cale*! No here. No anywhere. *No chem-i-cale*!' Morris did a passable Hispanic accent, usually for jokes, but this time neither of them were laughing. 'You'd think that when his shed burned down he'd take the hint, but no. Senator's really pissed, says we've got two weeks to make Jesus change his mind or the project will go to Montana.'

They reached the museum which was a window into the Pleistocene Epoch. The curators had done an excellent job of recreating the events that led to mammoths, sabre-toothed tigers and wolves being swallowed by the bubbling tar. The displays showed a California of two million years ago and it didn't look like a particularly friendly place for a holiday. They brooded over the exhibits and stared unenthusiastically at the mummified remains.

'See that mother there?' said Morris, pointing to a well preserved mammoth. 'About as dead as the Morelos Valley Project. Maybe not quite as dead. At least it left a bag of bones behind to be remembered by.'

Fiona could think of nothing to say that could cheer him up. The project had eaten more than one hundred thousand of their precious dollars, and the twenty million dollars they'd been so confident of making had little hope of realisation. As they left the museum and crossed the bridge on the way to the tar pits, a hand-painted sign caught her attention. Later she couldn't explain how or why that particular sign had caught her eye. It was neither the biggest nor the brightest, and insignificant compared to the ones offering sabre-toothed T-shirts, mammoth baseball hats and the usual worthless clutter tourists like to waste money on. Fate again. Fate was having a big day at their expense.

'Look,' said Fiona. 'C'mon.' She dragged Morris towards the sign and the table it was propped up on. Morris needed something to lift his spirits and give him hope, and Fiona thought she'd found it. She didn't care if the hope proved false. It wasn't the sort of thing they took seriously anyway.

'Psychic Cat,' said the sign. 'One dollar.'

'Go on,' said Fiona. 'You could discover you've been worrying for nothing. Maybe the psychic cat has the answer.'

Morris was unconvinced. There were two boxes on the counter, each of them containing little scrolls bound with ribbon. Behind them sat the cat, and behind the cat stood a short man with a greying black beard, and greying black hair poking out from beneath a worn and matted Cossack hat. He had the look of a bag-man. He wore a heavy black overcoat despite the sun and mid-seventy degree temperature. The coat, like the beard and hair, was also greying with age. The man hid his eyes behind black-rimmed dark glasses and showed no interest in them at all. Morris automatically assumed the man was Russian.

'What's another dollar?' asked Fiona.

Morris fished a note out of his pocket and handed it to the cat who accepted it by rising up on its haunches and taking the dollar bill between its front paws. It passed the money on to the Russian who took it mechanically and stuffed it in the pocket of his overcoat. Fiona automatically assumed the man was Russian Orthodox and muttering a quiet prayer of thanks to his god. The cat tipped over a counter-balanced peg on a stick so that it plucked a scroll from the box. It took the scroll in its paws and offered it to Morris. Fiona could barely keep from laughing, it was all so absurd.

'What's it say?' she asked.

Morris untied the ribbon bow and unrolled the scroll. Fiona threw an arm around him so she could read it, too.

'Shoot!' said Morris. Fiona said nothing. She was stunned speechless. She read the scroll over and over.

'*Your fortune is made as you dance on the grave,*' it said. Then underneath, '*Psychic Cat is never wrong.*'

They turned as one to look at the cat and the Russian. It was asleep or at least heading in that direction, and its Russian owner was still showing no interest in them whatsoever.

'Pure chance,' said Morris. 'Could apply to anything. Most people get something when somebody dies, and the more they get the more likely they are to feel happy about it.'

'Even so,' said Fiona.

'Even so nothing,' said Morris. 'Jesus Guerrero is going to live to be a hundred. You buy one, see what you get. These things are only what you're prepared to read into them.'

Fiona got out her dollar. The cat sat up. The Russian's hand moved mechanically. The peg dipped. Fiona had her psychic message.

'*Your country will celebrate the fact that you lived,*' said the scroll.

'Well,' said Morris, 'looks like Psychic Cat dipped out on that one.'

Fiona didn't like his tone. She never expected to be famous but hadn't entirely abandoned hope that one day fame would find her, and she'd be on the movies or TV. She resented the way Morris was so quick to dismiss her chances. 'You never know,' she said primly. Fiona did costume for commercials, had dressed some well-known stars and one day hoped to costume a movie. Others had gone from commercials to movies to Oscars, so why not her? One day for one brief moment, as she ascended the steps to the stage for the handshake and the little golden boy, the country might celebrate the fact that she lived. She felt a tiny thrill of excitement. She could never completely discount psychic messages and horoscopes even though she knew they were nonsense.

'I'm glad you lived anyway,' said Morris. 'Let's go grab lunch somewhere and celebrate the fact. The next dead animal I see I want to be on a plate or in a bun.'

Two days later, Senator William J. Johnston delivered a stirring speech on the Federal Courthouse steps, reaffirming his commitment to the Morelos Valley Project and berating the intransigence of people with no vision of the future, or concern for others in a state that needed jobs. He never mentioned Jesus Guerrero by name, but within hours everyone in America who could slob out in front of a TV or read a newspaper knew who he was talking about. Minutes after making his speech, just as Fiona and Morris came up to join him to discuss a last-ditch attempt to make the old orchardist see reason, Jesus Guerrero stepped out of the crowd and opened fire.

'No *chem-i-cale*!' he screamed and fired the first shot. 'No in my valley. No anywhere. No *chem-i-cale*!' He squeezed off a second shot instants before his skull stopped a bullet fired by a security man, and exploded in a shower of crimson.

But the damage had been done. Fiona heard the first shot and tried to get away. She foolishly stepped in front of the Senator just as Jesus Guerrero's second shot zeroed in.

Photos showed the Senator with Fiona's blood splashed all over his chest. Fiona dropped in a heap at his feet.

When the first shot came, Morris spun around and immediately recognised the old man with the rifle. In the same second he realised where it was pointed and wished he hadn't torched the old man's shed. Morris had never really considered that he might die before he became very, very rich and very, very old. The nearness of death, the silliness and suddenness of it, paralysed him. When Fiona screamed and fell he almost thanked God that Jesus Guerrero was such a bad shot.

Security men raced the Senator away, medics raced to transport Fiona to the best doctors and facilities the State of California could provide, and TV and press reporters fought for the best shot of the assassin, and the extraordinary young woman who had courageously sacrificed herself to shield his intended victim.

The hospital also admitted Morris. He knew who Jesus had really pointed his rifle at, knew how close he'd come to oblivion, to ceasing to be. He'd stood on the steps staring at the bloody bundle called Fiona, unable to move, unable to help, staggered at how easily that bloody bundle could have been him. Even when they got him to hospital he was so deep in shock he couldn't open his mouth to speak, which was a blessing. He wasn't so deeply in shock that his survival instincts had shut down altogether. He knew that keeping his mouth shut was the smartest thing he could have done.

When he felt better he switched on the TV by his bed. Every channel was full of the story about the attempted assassination of the Senator, of how the unselfish bravery of a courageous young woman had prevented another JFK, another Robert Kennedy, another Martin Luther King. The TV told him that Fiona was in a critical condition and that a nation held its breath and prayed for her recovery.

'Shoot,' said Morris softly, which was the very first word he'd said since he'd stared into the barrel of Jesus Guerrero's rifle, and thought he saw his name on the bullet. 'Don't die, Fiona,' he whispered. 'What'll I do if you die?'

The doctors removed the splintered ribs, repaired the punctured lung and saved enough of Fiona's right breast for other surgeons to fill it full of silicone at a later date. Three weeks after knocking on death's door, NBC knocked on the door of her ward to do an interview. Fiona had escaped death but still looked like she hadn't. The make-up lady made her suitable for general viewing, and Fiona complimented her on her skill as one professional to another. She had a minor disagreement with the costume lady over the colour of her nightie but it was soon settled. They told her what questions they'd ask so that she wouldn't take too long considering her spontaneous answers. Morris sat on a chair in the corner and watched.

Fiona had been around films long enough to know what viewers want and performed brilliantly, combining stoicism with just the right suggestion of intolerable pain. She completely fooled the interviewer who twice asked her anxiously if she wanted to continue. She even fooled the doctors who twice insisted that the interview should stop. Each time Fiona was able to smile bravely and soldier on. There was hardly a dry eye in the room. Hell, there was hardly a dry eye in the whole country. The interviewer's voice even warbled uncertainly at the conclusion when he reached over and took Fiona's brave little hand and said, 'Fiona, your country celebrates the fact that you lived.'

Live and on playback, two hundred million people witnessed heroic Fiona's sudden collapse.

Fiona's doctors were ecstatic. Their concerns had been vindicated in front of two hundred million viewers. They whacked her full of sedatives and retired to a bar to celebrate. Morris screamed at the news crew and threatened to sue. They caught that on camera as well but studio executives spiked the footage. Morris sat and read *Real Estate Monitor* from cover to cover while he waited for Fiona to wake up.

'Oh God . . .' she said.

Morris brought her a glass of iced water from the bubbler.

'Psychic Cat,' she said. 'It knew! It knew! It warned us and we took no notice.'

'Bullshit,' said Morris unconvincingly. 'It's just a coincidence.'

'It knew!' Fiona began to get upset again. 'Psychic Cat is never wrong.'

Morris pressed the button that brought the nurse who brought more sedative. Morris thought this was easier than arguing and rationalised that it was probably better for Fiona in the long run.

The State of California became trustee for the estate of the late Jesus Guerrero, and had no hesitation in accepting an offer of one million dollars for the forty acres of oranges. His seven sons and three daughters, all of whom had been pressing their father to sell, each put in a claim for the full one million dollars, thereby guaranteeing that the legal profession would get their hands on at least half of it.

Senator William J. Johnston summoned Morris to his office and greeted him with open arms. 'Call me Billy,' he said, and pulled the stopper on a bottle of Tennessee's finest. The Sentia Chemical Company had already begun buying up farmlands downstream from the river that ran through Morelos Valley. They'd learned that farmers were less likely to complain about what the company did to the water in the river abutting their property when they no longer had a vested interest in it.

'What are you going to do with your twenty million dollars?' asked Billy the Senator.

'State could do with a new smelter,' said the newest rich kid on the block. 'Got my eye on this parcel of land I saw in the *Real Estate Monitor*.'

'Tell me about it, son,' said the Senator. 'I'm inclined to agree with you.'

They got on just fine. By the time Morris arrived at the hospital to visit Fiona he was already calculating how long it would take him to overhaul the Sultan of Brunei, and become the world's richest man. It seemed only fair and reasonable to him that the world's richest man should be American.

'Hi,' said Fiona.

'As a kite,' said Morris.

Fiona laughed.

'That's the stuff,' said Morris. 'Good to see you laugh. When you get back on your feet, baby, guess where you'll be standing.'

'Where?' said Fiona.

'In clover,' said Morris. 'In clover up to here.' He held his hand as high as an elephant's eye. Days didn't get any better than this.

'You've done the deal?' asked Fiona excitedly.

'Signed and sealed,' said Morris. 'The cheque's in the bank. We're rich.' He paused. Raised his paper cup of iced water. 'Thank you, Jesus Guerrero, you dumb ass, thank you for setting yourself up as target practice for security. Yee-haaa!'

Fiona shifted uncomfortably. It hadn't been long since she was a target herself. 'Don't dance on his grave, Morris,' she said. Realised what she'd said and screamed.

Morris pressed the button that brought the nurse who brought the sedative. When he got home he had another half bottle of Tennessee sedative himself.

'Psychic Cat is always right,' said Fiona. 'You can't deny it. You can't dismiss both as coincidences. One maybe, not both. Psychic Cat knew. It knew.'

'I admit it seems that way,' said Morris begrudgingly. He didn't like the idea of anything or anyone having control over his destiny except himself. They passed the turn-off to the Devil's Cauldron, kept the car pointing towards home.

'So you finally admit that that damn cat was right?'

'No,' said Morris evenly. 'I only admit that it seems that way. I bet we could go back there and get two more psychic messages that would have no bearing on our lives whatsoever.'

'You won't get me back there.'

'Figure it out, Fiona. A bag-man and a cat. They don't know anything special. They don't have psychic powers. They're just pulling a scam for a buck. If that cat had psychic powers don't you think somebody would be using it to make real estate killings or a fortune on the stock market? That cat would be worth squillions, and I tell you, it would cost more than a buck for a consultation.'

'*Your country will celebrate the fact that you lived*,' said Fiona. '*Your fortune will be made as you dance on the grave.* How do you explain that? You can't just shrug that off. You can't just pretend it didn't happen. I got shot to prove it! Can't you accept for one moment that there might just be something in this world you don't know about, that you can't just talk away? It happened, Morris, it happened! Psychic Cat knew it was going to happen.' Another thought occurred to her which made her mind go blank in terror. 'Or *made* it happen.'

'Give me a break,' said Morris.

Their homecoming was not as happy as it should have been.

There was one small problem with the smelter site on the banks of Lake Biltmore. His name was Ed Durrow, a lover and protector of wildfowl and wetlands. He vowed to stop the Lake Biltmore Smelter Project if it was the last thing he did.

'Better think of something,' said Senator Billy to Morris. 'See if you can get the bastard to take a pot shot at Fiona.'

Everybody remarked on the change that had come over Fiona since the shooting. She wasn't fun anymore. Instead she was broody and morose, took little or no interest in things going on around her, and even seemed to have abandoned her dream of costuming a movie. Everybody blamed the shooting, except Morris. He knew better. He knew where the blame really lay. He blamed the Psychic Cat.

'C'mon,' he said to her one day. 'Get dressed and get in the car. You and me are going for a ride.'

'Where?' asked Fiona.

'Surprise,' said Morris.

'Oh my God, no!' said Fiona as they turned off Wilshire. 'No!' she shrieked as they passed through the entrance to the Devil's Cauldron.

'You gotta do it,' said Morris. 'It's like falling off a horse. You gotta get back up on it right away.'

'Please,' begged Fiona as Morris dragged her from the carpark.

'No,' begged Fiona as Morris steered her through the museum.

'Don't do it,' pleaded Fiona as they crossed the little bridge towards the tar pits.

'Shoot!' said Morris. 'Where the hell is he?'

They walked along to the gap in the stalls where the Psychic Cat had been. But for a message chalked onto the paving there was no sign of either cat or Russian. It didn't matter. The message was enough for Fiona. 'Psychic Cat is never wrong,' it said.

Morris dragged Fiona across the pathway to a stall set up to sell Cokes, ordered two and sat Fiona down at one of the little tables.

'Cut it out. You're making a scene,' he said. 'You're embarrassing me,' he added.

'That message was for us,' said Fiona. 'Psychic Cat knew we'd come back.'

'Crap,' said Morris. 'That message was for everyone. That message just marked out his spot so nobody else muscled in and took it. You stay here, I'll go ask somebody where he is.' Morris walked across to the stall that sold genuine plastic reproduction sabre-teeth on imitation silver chains.

'Where's the Ruskie and the cat?' he asked.

'Who's asking?' asked the tooth man.

'Seeing as how I'm the only person here apart from yourself, it seems I am,' said Morris. He hated it when people dumber than himself tried to be clever.

'Who's you?' asked tooth man.

'A dissatisfied customer,' said Morris.

'Ha!' said tooth man. 'Join the club.'

'Where's the Ruskie and the cat?' repeated Morris.

'Cat got hit by a truck and killed. Ruskie just moved on. You know, another town another hussle. Give the suckers what they want.'

'That a fact?'

'Yeah. And he ain't Russian. He's Armenian.'

'How long has he been gone?'

'Two weeks, who cares? You want your fortune told, go down Chinatown and buy a cookie.'

'Thanks.'

'Hey, Mister. What about my time? Ain't ya gunna buy a tooth for my time?'

Morris gave him a dollar bill. Told him to keep the tooth. Twenty million dollars had not made Morris any more generous.

'Psychic Cat got hit by a truck and killed,' said Morris. 'Never saw it coming. I guess that proves my point. If he was psychic he'd have known about the truck and waited or gone another way.'

'Is that for real?'

'Yep.'

Relief is an amazing tonic. Colour slowly flooded back into Fiona's face. A smile crinkled the corner of her mouth. It felt good not to have that cat messing with her destiny. She was free once more to be herself, live her life. 'I guess that's that, then,' she said.

They went straight home. Fiona rang her agent to see if there was any work going.

Six months later, Fiona scored her first movie assignment, an epic set in the Pleistocene Epoch called *The Clan of the Sabre-Toothed Tiger*. The producer liked to boast it had a mammoth budget. Names like Sean Penn, Nicholas Cage, John Travolta were bandied around as lead male, names like Sandra Bullock, Demi Moore and Madonna as lead female. Fiona got the job costuming and a brief to show 'as much tit and ass as can fit on a screen, but in a Dior kinda way'. Fiona was over the moon, ecstatic and as certain as she had ever been that a little golden boy by the name of Oscar was headed her way. She did her research and watched all the old dinosaur classics, watched Raquel Welch strut her stuff in fluffy little furry numbers that could have been made from the pelt of half a stoat, saw Schwarzenegger strut his stuff in less. Yet it troubled her that the sets and costumes looked phony. She knew she'd never get her Oscar faking it. She needed to immerse herself in the period and knew just how to go about it.

'Morris,' she said, 'get dressed and get in the car. You and me are going for a ride.'

'Where?' said Morris.

'Surprise,' said Fiona.

'Shoot!' said Morris as they turned off Wilshire. 'Shoot!' he said again as they passed through the entrance to the Devil's Cauldron. 'What brings us here?' he asked as Fiona nosed their Mercedes convertible into a parking spot.

'Research for my movie,' said Fiona. 'Besides, I thought you needed cheering up.'

Morris told her all about his problems with Ed Durrow as they walked from the carpark to the museum.

'Stubborn,' said Morris. 'Mule-headed stubborn. And selfish,' he added. 'It's not as if we haven't tried to be reasonable. I offered him new land thirty miles east, offered to dam the river there to make new wetlands and even offered to populate it with wild birds. You know what he did? He laughed in my face. Laughed! Laughed in the Senator's face as well. Ought to be arrested for doing that, laughing in the face of a US Senator.'

'Isn't there anything you can do?' asked Fiona.

'We did arrange a small chemical spill in one of the feeder rivers through our friends over at Sentia, killed a few fish and birds, but he still didn't take the hint. Only got a month to make the old bastard see reason or the whole project will go to Indiana.'

They walked through the glass doors into the Pleistocene Epoch. Fiona took notes and sly photos while Morris brooded.

'Have to take a look at the tar pits,' said Fiona. 'See how far the tar spits. Have to make the costumes out of synthetics tar washes off easily.'

They walked out across the bridge. Fiona stopped dead in her tracks when she saw the sign.

'Psychic Cat,' it said. 'One dollar.'

'You told me it was dead,' she screamed.

'He told me it was dead,' said Morris. 'That guy selling teeth.'

'You told me the cat was dead,' said Morris.

'So what?' said the tooth man.

'So why did you lie?'

'Hell, did I know who you were? Coulda been IRS. These are cash businesses you're looking at. Not a lot of tax paid around here.'

'So where was he?'

'Who knows? He comes and he goes. Maybe gets together enough money to get drunk and gets drunk. Who cares? Why ask me? You want to know something, you ask him.'

'Don't do it,' said Fiona. 'Whatever he's going to tell us I don't want to know.'

'It's all crap,' said Morris grimly. 'And I'm going to prove it.' He walked up to the Psychic Cat and held out a dollar bill. The cat rose on its haunches, took the bill and passed it on to the Russian–Armenian. He took the money mechanically and stuffed it in his coat pocket, taking no interest at all in Morris.

'Thanks,' said Morris sarcastically as he took the scroll from between the cat's paws. He untied the ribbon, read the message and laughed out loud. 'Look at this,' he said. 'Read it and weep. I've a good mind to ask for my money back.'

Fiona took the scroll and read the message.

'*You will fall into the arms of a tall dark stranger and spend Eternity together*,' it said.

'Tall dark stranger?' said Fiona. 'Not *the* tall, dark stranger.'

'That's the one,' said Morris. The two of them fell about laughing. 'Now get the monkey off your back,' said Morris. 'Go spend a dollar.'

Fiona undid the ribbon and stared at her message.

'*You will find comfort in the company of old friends*,' it said.

'Not *the* old friends!' said Morris.

'Right on!' said Fiona.

'Psychic Cat has goofed this time,' said Morris. 'Goofed big time.'

'Goofed in spades,' said Fiona. 'Besides, I'm the one who's always wanted to meet the tall, dark stranger, not you.'

The Psychic Cat curled up on the table, eyes closed, waiting for its next customer. The Russian–Armenian paid them no attention at all.

Elroy Washington was a deprived black American, deprived of sleep and the amphetamines he needed to keep pointing his truck to LA. He was also an ex-college basketball player who could fly like Michael Jordan until a gimpy knee grounded him. Elroy saw the convertible Mercedes travelling east towards him and paid it no attention. Elroy was beyond paying attention to anything, but it was a pity he didn't get a better look at the Mercedes since it was the last thing he ever saw.

'Shoot,' said Morris, as the same thoughts that had flashed across his brain when Jesus Guerrero pointed his rifle at him made the return journey. He wondered briefly if the truck had his name on it. It had, not that he had time to dwell on the fact. The impact shot him out of his seat, into the air, through the truck windshield and into the arms of Elroy Washington. A fuel line ignited which sent a flame which penetrated the disintegrating tank of liquid propane the truck was carrying. Highway Patrol claimed they'd never seen an inferno to match it. Both corpses were rendered to ashes indistinguishable from one another.

In one of the freaky little happenings that make accident investigators' lives interesting, and give them something to talk about to strangers in bars, Fiona was thrown out of her seat, into the air and onto the tray of a passing truck also heading east. The truck got blown over onto its side when the propane went up, but by then it had done its job. Even so, Fiona was in no fit state to express any appreciation. When she woke up she found she was back in the same hospital room she'd occupied after the shooting. They broke the news about Morris to her as gently as they could. Said they were sorry to be the bearers of such grim tidings, and expressed the hope that at least she'd find some comfort in being in the company of old friends.

Their words rang a bell with Fiona.

They in turn rang the bell that brought the nurse who brought the sedatives.

Rover the Mouse

'Good morning, Denton. Would you like to see my erection?'

Denton smiled. Palmi always asked Denton if he wanted to see his erection and Denton always smiled when he asked.

'Like concrete and steel?'

'Yes,' said Palmi excitedly. 'Like concrete and steel.'

The two men sat down at a table set for four, Denton smothering his chair with his bulk. A dazzling shaft of morning sunlight found an uninterrupted path through the rafis and kentia palms outside the armour glass and bathed their table in a pool of light.

'It is a good morning, isn't it Denton?' Palmi's face was as bright and sunny as the morning. It always was except when he freaked.

'The best,' said Denton. He glanced around the cafeteria to see if Bruise had come in to take the gloss off it. He hadn't yet, but he would. Just thinking about Bruise could spoil the morning, so Denton stopped thinking about him. 'Sleep well?' he asked Palmi.

'The best, Denton, the best! I saw them again.'

'The plans?'

'Yes, the plans. They are magnificent!' Palmi's face suddenly clouded over. 'And you, Denton, did you sleep well?'

'The best, Palmi, the best.' Denton watched his friend's face light up again. There was something extraordinarily touching about having someone care so deeply about his welfare. It didn't matter that his friend was certified. Palmi sat expectantly. Denton preferred to wait until the others had arrived and brought Bruise with them. He didn't like repeating his stories. They were never as good the second time around. But Palmi was like a hungry baby. You either fed him or he cried. Denton had to feed Palmi his story or Palmi would cry. Denton didn't want to do that to his friend, didn't want him to freak out, especially on such a beautiful morning.

'I dreamed I was back in Vietnam. Bruise was in charge of the patrol.' Denton watched Palmi's eyes light up with anticipation, saw his hand pick up the little plastic knife, the only kind they were allowed, and begin stabbing it against the laminex table top. Denton automatically adjusted the pace of his words to the rhythm of the stabbing. 'We knew the black pyjama brigade was out there in force, not the VCs but North Vietnamese Army regulars. Nobody wanted the job of tracking them down. You only ever found them by walking into one of their ambushes.' Denton heard a door open, saw Bruise walk in. Bruise was eating a Mars Bar for breakfast. Denton raised his voice so that Bruise couldn't help but overhear. Other inmates started wandering in, among them Julian and Joseph. Bruise glared at him. He didn't want to stop, didn't want to give Bruise the satisfaction, but had no choice. Palmi stopped stabbing.

'Good morning,' said Palmi. 'Would you like to see my erection?'

'Like concrete and steel, is it?' asked Joseph.

'Concrete and steel,' muttered Julian.

'Yes,' said Palmi exultantly. 'Like concrete and steel. Did you sleep well?'

'The best,' said Joseph.

'Best,' mumbled Julian.

'So did Denton,' said Palmi.

They all turned their attention to him, picked up their little plastic knives as he took his story back to the beginning, and set up a steady beat on the table top.

'I dreamed I was back in Vietnam. Bruise was in charge of the patrol, only our pal Brucie wasn't called Bruise then, he was called Brainless. We knew the black pyjama brigade was out there in force . . .' Denton slowly raised his eyes as he spoke until he made contact with Bruise's. Bruise scowled and mimed fitting electrodes to his scalp, then pointed his finger at him. With his other hand he mimed turning up the charge. Denton took no notice of Bruise's threats. He just fixed him with his unwavering, dead-eye look which Bruise hated more than anything. After all, Denton was certified, knew he was certified, knew why he was certified. He also knew that Bruise had been a psychiatric nurse long enough to know what his charges were capable of when they freaked. Bruise wouldn't be the first psychiatric nurse to be shredded. That was the threat psychiatric nurses lived with. That was the big stick Denton wielded. That was the only weapon he had.

'Brainless Brucie the bruise maker volunteered to take his platoon out to find the North Vietnamese. He was the only one to volunteer. Everyone thought he was mad. Everyone thought he should be certified.'

Bruise glowered but Denton's friends liked that bit. They always liked that bit. They thought Bruise should be certified. They didn't think they should be certified. They stabbed the laminex a little more forcefully. Denton told them how Bruise made him go point, made him go ahead of everyone else, volunteered him to make first contact with the North Vietnamese company, volunteered him to be first to put his foot on a mine, volunteered him to be first to kick the trip wires, volunteered him to be first to be killed, maimed, disembowelled.

Every time Denton said 'volunteered' his friends stabbed the table, like schoolboys clapping, like they were learning the beat of iambic pentameter. Bruise glowered.

'Bruise,' said Denton, 'always brought up the rear. He did that because he liked to minimise his personal risk factor. But he also did it because he liked looking at soldiers' bottoms.'

Crash went the little plastic knives. Bruise glowered.

'We began in single file but fanned out the further we went from camp. The platoon spread out through the rubber trees. There were good men either side of me, frightened but brave men, each of us watching out for the other. Except Bruise. He didn't watch out for anyone. We reached a clearing, encircled it, found no trace of the enemy. Walked on. It started raining. We couldn't hear anything but the sound of the rain on the rubber trees. We couldn't hear a thing. The rain fell heavier, began to steam in the heat so we couldn't see anything, either. We couldn't see more than fifty metres in any direction. We began to bunch up, stopped, turned to Bruise for direction. How could we spot an enemy we couldn't see? How could we hear an enemy we couldn't hear? It was madness to go on. Anyone who thought otherwise deserved to be certified. Bruise ordered us to go on.'

His friends liked that bit, too.

'We walked straight into an ambush. They opened up with machine-guns and grenade launchers. They hit the men on either side of me. Good men, brave men. I fired and rolled, fired and rolled, fired and rolled, trying to rejoin the main body of the platoon. I rolled into a ditch. One of my mates was already in it. He was a good man. A brave man. But now he was a dead man. Madness. I returned fire. I saw two more of my mates go down. And two more. I pulled back further. Then I saw Bruise. He had a ditch all to himself. He kept his head down and his weapon up, firing blindly. He didn't look where he was firing even though he knew his entire platoon had to be in front of him. He was firing through his own men. I saw two more men fall, shot not by the enemy in front but by the coward behind. By Bruise.'

Bruise smouldered. His lips twitched. He narrowed his eyes. He snapped a Picnic bar in two and stuffed one half in his mouth. Denton maintained his dead-eye look.

'They were good men. Brave men. Now they were dead men. Madness. I took a grenade, pulled out the pin, waited, then lobbed it into Bruise's personal ditch. He looked up when it hit him on the shoulder. He saw me. I lobbed another. He stared at me as if he couldn't believe what was happening, as if I'd do such a thing to him. He shit himself. A loud liquid fart then boom! The grenade exploded. Boom! Blew his guts out. Boom! Fragged him. Little bits of him flew everywhere.'

His friends stopped stabbing and started laughing. Tears rolled down their cheeks. They turned to look at Bruise, laughed even harder. They liked the idea of Bruise shitting himself and being blown to bits.

'I even got some of him on me. Little meaty bits and little bony bits. No brainy bits, though. I don't think there were any brainy bits. I scraped up the meaty bits of Brainless Brucie and wrapped them up in my hand-kerchief. When I got back to base I fed Bruise to my little friend. My little friend enjoyed eating Bruise. He was probably the only living thing in the whole of Vietnam who found anything to like about Bruise. He was the only living creature in the whole of Vietnam who would have liked to have seen more of him.' Denton paused, lowered his voice. 'Would you like to meet my little friend?' The men stopped laughing and stared at Denton, wondering what new surprise he had for them. Denton was their leader, he was their champion, he was the rock they clung to, he was their big stick, he was their only weapon against Bruise.

Denton leaned forward and made his friends do the same. He hunched his axe-handle shoulders. His friends hunched theirs. He reached into his shirt pocket, cupped his baseball mitt hand around something infinitely precious, drew it out and put his fist on the middle of the table. The men stared at the fist, waiting for the revelation. It was hesitant, slow in coming, but no less awe-inspiring for its timorous nature.

'What do you think?' asked Denton.

'The best!' whispered Palmi.

'The best,' agreed Joseph.

'The best,' mumbled Julian.

'His name's Rover,' said Denton. 'Our secret. Not a word.'

Rover the mouse withdrew into the sanctuary of Denton's hand as an orderly brought them their soggy, scrambled eggs. Denton transferred his little friend back to his pocket. Bruise strained to see what was going on but suspected that Denton was just setting him up to make a fool of him. Again.

'He is wonderful,' breathed Palmi. 'Thank you for showing him to us, Denton. After breakfast I will show you my erection.'

'Like concrete and steel,' mumbled Joseph.

'I'm sorry about the mice,' mumbled Julian.

They turned as one to look at him. Julian rarely said things. Denton led, Palmi enthused, Joseph agreed, Julian repeated things. That was their understanding except when Julian said things. Julian had the most brilliant mind the clinic had ever admitted. He'd been working on a protein that encased cancer cells, closed off their blood supply, and caused them to wither and die.

'Like a rubber band around your balls,' said Palmi.

Rumour had it that in a blinding moment of inspiration Julian had actually achieved his objective. He'd stayed sane long enough to turn to a colleague and say, 'I've done it!' Then his mind had got a little over-excited and shut down. He'd become violent when his mind wouldn't allow him to remember his blinding moment of brilliance.

'What mice?' asked Denton gently.

'All the dead mice. I know how to save them now, you know.' He began to weep. Joseph put his arm over Julian's shoulders. He didn't want Bruise to notice Julian's shoulders heaving or Bruise would come and take him away. Bruise always took people away by force. Bruise liked force.

'Would you like to see my erection?' asked Palmi.

'Concrete and steel,' said Denton.

'Concrete and steel,' agreed Joseph.

'After breakfast,' said Palmi, beaming more brightly than the morning sun. 'After breakfast I will show you all my erection.'

Alfredo 'Palmi' Palmisano was one of the smartest developers the clinic had ever admitted. He was caught by the recession which wasn't very smart of him at all. He went bankrupt on the front page of every newspaper in the country, penniless but for the mountain of money no one could prove that he had, and the mountains of money in trust accounts for his wife, children, and every second Palmisano in the telephone book.

Palmi's speciality was high rise. He had five new projects going when the banks lost their collective nerve and pulled the plug on him. None of the projects got off the ground – well not more than two storeys – and nearly put Palmi under it. He was trying to keep so many balls up in the air, his mind got confused and lost count. The many Palmisanos contributed generously towards his rehabilitation and recovery. They also settled out of court with the one loans officer Palmi had managed to get his hands on.

Bruise watched the four men pass by as they made their way to the creative therapy room. Nurse Clive was in charge of creative therapy. He clapped his hands as the four men trooped into his realm. He loved it when the patients showed enthusiasm. He believed passionately in the therapy of creativity. He felt elated, vindicated, worthy. He felt he'd made contact with lost souls who needed only to express their inner thoughts in clay, paint, coloured paper and glue, in order to find their pathway home. Nurse Clive was as wet as his clay.

'Relax,' said Denton. 'We've only come here so Palmi can show us his erection.'

'Oh,' said Nurse Clive.

'He's very proud of it,' said Denton.

'Give me a minute,' said Palmi. 'And no peeking.'

His friends dutifully closed their eyes as they always did.

'There!' said Palmi. 'Open up!'

'Like concrete and steel,' said Denton as he always did.

'Concrete and steel,' echoed Joseph admiringly.

'Concrete and steel,' repeated Julian, eyes wide with wonder. It always amazed Denton that Julian could look at Palmi's creation day after day as if he'd never seen it before.

'Shopping plaza down here. The red. The blue is the carpark.' Dwarfing everything else was Palmi's pride, a seventy-storey leaning tower of commerce, painstakingly constructed from decapitated redhead matches. He'd built it on a table fitted with castors so that it could be wheeled away to a place of safety when he wasn't working on it. Unfortunately, it didn't travel well, and what had begun as a minor shift from the vertical had progressed to the point where the laws of gravity would shortly be called into play.

'I think the top part could be a hotel,' said Palmi with sudden cunning. 'Denton, do we have any little friends who might like to live in a hotel?'

'I think our little friend is happy where he is,' said Denton. 'For the moment, at least,' he added compassionately when he saw his friend's face cloud over.

'Like concrete and steel,' said Joseph, anxious to move on to happier topics.

Everyone waited for the echo but instead Julian said, 'I had enough little friends for everyone. I had a little friend for you, too, Palmi. I'm very sorry.'

Palmi's face lit up once more. 'You had a little friend for me?'

'Yes. I had little friends for everyone.'

'Where is my little friend?' asked Palmi.

'I gave him cancer. He died.'

Clouds settled on Palmi's face, darkened and grew stormy. For a moment it looked as though the storm would pass on.

'You gave my little friend cancer?'

'Yes. He died. I'm sorry,' said Julian.

'That's enough,' said Denton.

'Enough,' said Joseph.

'You gave my little friend cancer? You gave him cancer?'

Nurse Clive rang the bell but wasn't fast enough. Denton tried to grab Palmi's arms but wasn't fast enough. Joseph tried to get Julian out of the way but wasn't fast enough. Palmi was quicker than all of them. He grabbed his seventy-storey tower of commerce and rammed the top eight floors down Julian's throat. He broke the shopping centre over Nurse Clive's head. He was well ahead on points before Bruise slammed him against the wall.

This was what Bruise was good at. This was what he had trained to do. Would still be doing in a neat helmet and bullet-proof vest if his enthusiasm for his job hadn't chosen to reveal itself in two ill-chosen moments of rank impetuosity. Twice, as a member of the police tactical response squad, he'd burst in on an armed offender, roughed him up and held a gun at his head, only to discover he'd burst into the wrong house. That was the trouble with terrace houses, their front doors were so close together. Anyone could have made the same mistake. But Bruise had made the same mistake twice when only once was permissible.

'Oohhhh!' gasped Palmi, as Bruise forearmed his head into the wall.

'Aghhhh!' screamed Palmi, as Bruise played knees-up with his balls.

Bruise tightened the armlock that had Palmi jammed hard up in a corner against the creative therapy walls, brought Palmi's arm so high up his back his shoulder was in danger of dislocation. Palmi started crying. It wasn't wise to express pain when Bruise was doing his job because it tended to make him more enthusiastic. Enthusiasm was not something he lacked.

'There's no need for that!'

Bruise held Palmi with one hand and turned to face Denton. He took note of the way Denton had set his feet, his slightly side-on stance. Denton was big, Denton was trained, but Denton was old enough to be his father. Denton was after a square-up but Denton was also on his last warning. Bruise could afford to be brave.

'What are you going to do, hero? Shove a grenade up my arse? Why aren't I shitting myself?' Bruise didn't like Denton, didn't like him at all, resented the fact that Denton had served in Vietnam. Bruise would have loved to have served in Vietnam. But the Army hadn't got around to calling up seven year olds.

'Leave him! Let me talk to him.' Denton could do nothing but talk. He also had Rover the mouse to consider. His little friend in his front pocket would be in the front line once punches started to be thrown. What if Bruise slammed him face first against the wall? What if they sedated him and hit him with electro convulsive therapy? Would Rover survive being zapped? What if he freaked out and fragged Bruise? What if he tore him apart? What if he shoved his hand down his throat, grabbed his arse and pulled him inside out? What would they do to him? Blood pounded in his temples. He knew what they'd do, knew he couldn't do anything, not if he wanted to go home. His hands itched. His friend was crying.

'Leave him, let me talk to him.'

'You want to talk to him, talk to him from there.'

Denton took a deep breath. Palmi was sobbing. Palmi was in pain. There was no sunlight in his face.

'Palmi listen. Do what Bruise says. Don't fight him. It's okay, Palmi, I've seen the plans. You listening? I've seen the plans.'

'Yes,' said Joseph. 'The plans.'

'Argh plans,' muttered Julian as Nurse Clive examined his bleeding throat.

'You've seen the plans?' Palmi's voice was barely a whisper and they had to strain to hear him. But the tears had stopped flowing and the clouds were beginning to lift.

'Yes, Palmi, I've seen the plans. They're the best!'

'The best!' said Joseph.

'Argh best,' mumbled Julian.

'My next erection,' said Palmi weakly.

Denton lay back on his bed as he was supposed to. They'd locked him in his room for the day and given him tablets to calm him down. They always made him swallow his medication in front of them and then looked under his tongue. They never looked between his upper lip and gums. Denton always acted out the effect of the drugs so they had no reason to ever suspect that his toilet swallowed as many drugs as he did. Denton always swallowed the tablets they gave him for his benefit. He only fudged on the ones they gave him for their own benefit.

He knew they'd look in on him through the spy hole in the door so he kept his knees up. That way they couldn't see his little friend playing on his chest. The mouse liked playing on his chest, liked slaloming around the buttons down the front of his shirt.

Denton tried to take stock of things. Perhaps it had been a mistake to show Rover to his friends. But they always did their best to share things. His little friend had brought him great comfort. He would have preferred a dog, a quick-witted border collie with big trusting eyes. Something to love and trust and be loved and trusted by in return. But all he had was Rover the mouse, and he only kept him by stealth.

He had ached for a pet, almost prayed for a pet, and one day his little friend had emerged from behind the skirting board at the rear corner of his bed. He thought of all the pieces of toast and Kraft cheddar slices he'd smuggled back for Rover, gradually enticing him further and further from his little mouse hole, and his joy when one day his little friend had sat boldly on the palm of his hand and begun to clean himself. The little creature's trust had got to Denton, the fact that the little mouse believed in him and trusted him not to crush him inside his massive hand. Denton believed he was getting better. He also believed that was the turning point.

Every evening he returned his little friend to his mouse hole where Denton was certain his pet had made a comfy little bed for himself from torn-up pieces of tissue. That way, Rover's reappearance every morning was a reaffirmation of his trust.

By the time they got him back to his room, Palmi had forgiven Julian and put the little incident out of his mind. He'd forgiven everyone including Bruise. He talked enthusiastically about the plans for his next erection. The clouds had lifted and the sun shone brightly. It didn't matter that one eye had closed over and the draining ache in his groin made him sick to the stomach. He put those matters out of his mind as well. All he wanted to do was talk to his friends about his plans for his next erection. It would be the best. The best! He felt the needle puncture the skin on his upper arm and smiled sadly. They were taking away the sun. They never understood. He felt the weight of dreamless sleep descend. There'd be no sunlight where he was going, no plans, no friends, no erections for the next three days. He felt briefly sad about that.

Joseph let them take him back to his room, agreed that it was best for everyone if he spent the rest of the day there, agreed to take the pills they gave him, agreed that it had all been a misunderstanding, apologised profusely even though he'd not actually done anything to apologise for. He burst into tears when they closed the door and left him. He didn't agree with what they were doing to him. He didn't agree with what they did to Palmi. He didn't agree that he belonged in the clinic. He wanted to be with his family, his sad, flawed family. He didn't want to be left alone, didn't want to go back to sleep, didn't want the pills. He wanted his friends! He wanted company. Why didn't they understand that he was frightened? Frightened of what had happened to him. Frightened of being alone.

'I'm sorry,' said Julian.

'That's okay,' said Nurse Clive as he tucked him in.

'I can save them, you know.'

'Save who?'

'The mice.'

'What mice?'

'The cancer mice.'

'Don't worry about it.'

'I can cure cancer.'

'Sure.'

'I know how.'

'So I believe.' Nurse Clive was getting impatient. He had a bruise on his head that needed attention. He helped himself to one of Julian's chocolates to make his head feel better. They all helped themselves to Julian's chocolates whenever they had a chance.

'I can save the mice.' Julian's voice became slow and distant.

'That's very nice of you.' Nurse Clive took comfort from the fact that the sedatives were cutting in. He helped himself to another of Julian's chocolates.

'Then we can all have a mouse.'

'Great,' said Nurse Clive, chewing on the caramel centre.

'Like Denton's,' said Julian.

'What?' said Nurse Clive, suddenly alert.

'What?' repeated Nurse Clive. 'Like what?' But he was talking to himself. Julian's exhausted brain had found sweet oblivion.

Denton dreamed he was back in Vietnam. He awoke, face sweaty, heart pounding, his friend Rover the mouse watching him anxiously from the sanctuary of his pocket. What would it be like for Rover, he wondered? Thump, thump, thump. Like trying to sleep through an earthquake. Gradually his heart slowed. He cupped his hand, lifted the tiny mouse and placed him in front of his mouse hole. Denton didn't like sleeping with Rover in his pocket. What if he rolled over?

He got up for a pee. He noticed his hands were still shaking. The stream wavered between the side of the bowl and the pool. Why had he started dreaming about Vietnam again? He'd gone twenty-five years without dreaming about Vietnam. He'd got over the shakes and the night sweats unlike some of his mates. It didn't seem fair. Repressed memories, the shrink said. Horrors shut away inside him, like a time bomb, ticking, ticking, ticking, just waiting for the moment to explode.

And hadn't they exploded! All for two hundred grams of pastrami, a loaf of wood-fired bread and an Evans and Tate dry white. To Denton, the shop was a deli that sold a bit of wine. To the young man with the mask and shotgun it was a liquor store with bulging cash register and poor security. He'd bashed the woman shopkeeper over the head with the barrel of his shotgun as she was slicing Denton's pastrami. He hadn't seen Denton because Denton had been bending over selecting his bottle of wine. The robber had jumped the counter. He must have heard Denton jump over after him because he'd swung around. The barrel had clubbed Denton over the eye. The Evans and Tate had clubbed the robber over the eye. Denton had thrown a punch, felt it land, grabbed the robber's mask and pulled. They'd fought over the screaming shopkeeper, fought for possession of the shotgun. It had discharged, turning the edam into jarlsberg, the olives into oil. The woman had screamed in fright. Denton had managed to rip the shotgun away and toss it over the counter. The robber had picked up the deli sandwich knife and attacked. Denton had let his training take over. He'd caught the robber's wrist, twisted his arm, turned him. Then he'd disarmed him by running the slicer neatly through the robber's wrist so that his severed hand collapsed onto the sliced pastrami. Perhaps he would have fed the rest of the robber through the slicer too if the woman's screams for help hadn't been answered.

They'd packed the robber's severed hand in party-ice and Denton in a straightjacket. His mind had kicked back to Vietnam and had become confused. When help arrived, he'd tried to feed them through the slicer, too. Denton was as strong as he was big. It had taken five men to hold him down. He often wondered if things would have turned out differently if the robber hadn't been Asian.

He'd only fought hand-to-hand against the Viet Cong once and that had been in the dark, underground in their dreaded tunnels. He'd dropped his torch and had to fight by feel. Knife fight at two paces ten metres underground. A big man out of his element, cramped for room, suffocating, scared shitless. He'd kept his life intact and shredded his enemy. But his arms still bore the scars. So, apparently, did his mind.

Bruise had been waiting for him when they checked him into the clinic. Bruise knocked the fight out of him. Bruise let him know what to expect when he stepped out of line. Let him know who he'd have to answer to whenever he freaked out. Bruise also stole the boxes of chocolates the deli sent Denton instead of flowers.

Denton shot to his feet ready to kill when they came for Rover. They'd looked through the spy hole. They thought he was sound asleep. They had the wit to withdraw when they saw he wasn't, when they saw the look in his eye, the set of his feet, and saw he was about to freak. They let him be. He had nowhere to go, nowhere to hide, and nowhere to conceal so much as the head of a pimple.

Let alone an entire mouse.

'I was the last one to make a dash for the chopper,' said Denton. 'Everyone else was either dead or dying. Bullets were flying everywhere, shredding trees, shredding people, shredding helicopters. I ducked low. The chopper was returning fire right over my head. It started to lift off. I ran doubled over, ran for my life through the hail of bullets. I jumped up, caught hold of the skids. The chopper dipped and accelerated. Plok, plok, plok. I could hear bullets punch holes in the chopper.'

Plink, plink, plink. The plastic knives stabbed into the laminex. Three faces watched intently.

'I reached up with one hand to the soldier in the doorway. Treetops tore at my legs, tried to tear my hands away from the skids. The Huey was overloaded and struggled for altitude. But it could make it. There was still room for one more, there was still room for me. I reached up so the soldier could grab my hand and haul me aboard. He ignored me. I grabbed his ankle. He kicked out. "Help me!" I screamed. He wouldn't even look at me. Now the slipstream was trying to tear me away. We were starting to climb but he wouldn't help me aboard. I could hear the blades grab big bites of air. Whump, whump, whump.'

Plink, plink, plink. Plastic on laminex.

'I looked up to see the face of the soldier who wouldn't lend a hand to help his mate. It was him.' Denton looked up and fixed Bruise with his dead-eye look. 'But he made a mistake, didn't he? He kicked out again, didn't he? And when that didn't work he took his hand off the airframe to push me away. Silly man. Did I tell you we used to call him Brainless? Well Brainless lived up to his name. Quick as a flash I grabbed hold of his hand and pulled him out of the chopper. He looked me straight in the eye as he flew past. You should have seen the look on his face. He couldn't believe what was happening, couldn't believe what I'd done. He dropped like a stone, flew like a brick. Straight into the blades of the chopper beneath us. Slash, slash, splash, splash. Like a frog in a blender.'

They loved that part, stopped stabbing and started laughing. They turned as one to look at Bruise and gloat. Bruise scowled, chewed on his peanut brittle. Palmi's left eye was still closed for repairs but he had no trouble seeing with the other.

'Like a frog in a blender,' Palmi echoed delightedly. 'Slash, slash, splash, splash. Did you keep some of him for your little friend?'

'There was nothing left to keep. Bruise turned into soup. Fell like a light shower over the Viet Cong. Red rain. Blood, flesh and bone, but no brain. The VC licked their lips to see what the red rain was and promptly threw up. Some of them even died. In the whole time Bruise was in Vietnam that was the only time he caused injury to the enemy.'

The men laughed harder. Bruise smouldered, narrowed his eyes.

'How is your little friend?' asked Joseph.

'Yes,' said Palmi. 'How is your little friend?'

'Elusive,' said Denton. 'They search my room when I'm not there. They search my clothes when I take them off. They think I don't know, but I do. They haven't mentioned our little friend to me because they don't want me to know that they're looking. That way I won't feel any need to hide him.'

The men laughed again, treasured their secret, their little triumph.

'Honestly, when you think how much our families must be paying to keep us here, you'd think they'd hire smarter people.'

'Yes!' said Palmi enthusiastically.

'Indeed,' agreed Joseph.

'My company pays,' said Julian. 'They want me to get better so that I can tell them how to cure cancer.'

Denton looked up, suddenly on guard. Two orderlies had come into the cafeteria and glanced quickly towards them. He saw Bruise nod.

'Oh Christ!' he said. He'd forgotten what day it was. There was no escape.

'Are you ready to come with us, Mr Mills?'

'Yes,' said Denton. He felt the tiny movement in his shirt pocket.

'Come along, then. With the progress you're making this should be the last time.'

'Thank you,' said Denton politely. 'Please allow me to farewell my friends.'

'Come along. There's no need for that. You'll see them again tomorrow.'

'Goodbye Palmi.' Denton stood and held his arms out to hug his friend. Palmi still hadn't caught on. He heard the sadness in his friend's voice and it spread to him. He rose, teary eyed.

'Get Rover,' hissed Denton.

'What?' said Palmi.

'Pocket!' hissed Denton desperately.

'He has something for you in his pocket,' said Joseph helpfully.

Circuits connected inside Palmi's brain.

'Chocolate?' said Palmi, and reached inside Denton's pocket.

'Come along,' said the orderly.

'Got it,' said Palmi proudly. And he had. He had Rover safely cupped in his hand. But the mouse panicked. This hand was not the hand that fed him. This hand was not the hand he trusted. So Rover did the only thing a mouse in his position could do. He bit.

'Yeoowwww!' said Palmi. His hand opened as he jerked back, ejecting Rover and firing him on a shallow trajectory straight towards the enemy.

The orderly was a trained psychiatric nurse. He'd been trained to expect the unexpected. But nowhere in his training had anyone prepared him for assault by mouse. It bounced off his face onto his shoulder and took off down his sleeve. He screamed. Joseph and Julian watched frozen in horror. Bruise pounced. His fist thudded into the table just as Rover landed upon it, missing by fractions. The mouse ran down the table leg, across the floor, ducked this way then that. Bruise lunged at it with his feet, Denton lunged at Bruise, but the orderly held him back.

'Don't blow it,' said the orderly who'd got over the shock of the mouse hurtling towards him. He got on well with Denton.

Bruise cornered the mouse, grabbed a chair to bash its brains out. But Julian got in first. Julian had quietly freaked. Julian was so quiet people sometimes forgot he was violent. He bent his chair over Bruise's head. Bruise dropped like someone had put a bullet through his brain.

'I can save them, you know,' said Julian proudly as the orderlies pinned his arms behind his back. 'I know how.'

'Where did the mouse go?' asked Denton as they prepared him for the ECT.

'Where do all mice go?' replied the orderly.

'Into mouse holes?' said Denton.

'Yeah, well it seems there's one under the servery. No one had noticed it until your mate escaped through it.'

'Good on him,' said Denton.

'I'm with you,' said the orderly. 'When you think about it, it's only logical that mice would have a hole in the cafeteria where all the food is.'

'What about Bruise?'

'He'll live.'

'What about Julian?'

'Three-day sleep. He has powerful friends. We have to get approval for his treatment. They've only just agreed to ECT.'

'We don't need electro convulsive therapy, you know,' said Denton. 'We don't need drug therapy. We don't need psychotropics and other anti-psychotics. And we don't need bouncer Bruise standing over us.'

'And you're going to tell me what you do need.' The orderly gently administered the anaesthetic that would put Denton under while they fired eighty joules through his brain.

'Pet therapy,' said Denton. 'Uncritical love. That's all we need.'

When Denton awoke his little friend was sitting on his chest watching him, waiting for him to wake up. He was still wearing the tunic they made him wear when they zapped him. It didn't have any pockets. Rover the mouse had nowhere to go. Denton cupped his friend in his hand and struggled to sit up. His brain felt emptied, his body wasted. He nursed Rover while he tried to get his thoughts together. In Vietnam they taught him to think like the enemy. He was having difficulty thinking like himself. The mouse fidgeted.

Denton thought about putting his friend back into his mouse hole, looked down and saw the crumbs. He dropped down on his knees and peered into the hole. He saw the rest of the bait. Rat Pak. Had Rover taken a nibble? Was he already dying? Had he just popped in to say goodbye? How could he tell? All he could do was make sure that Rover didn't eat any more and hope for the best. He dressed and put on a shirt with pockets.

'This is your home now,' he said to his little friend. 'Nowhere is safe.'

'Rat Pak,' said Denton. 'Everywhere.'

'Bastards,' said Palmi, trying to hold back his tears.

'Bastards,' agreed Joseph.

'What can we do?' asked Denton.

'Warfarin,' said Julian. They turned to look at him. He looked different. His three-day absence had changed him. The light was on and for once it seemed like someone was home. His eyes held steady. The desperation had gone. 'Warfarin,' he repeated. 'It's the active ingredient.'

'ECT,' said Denton. The others agreed. 'How do you feel, Julian?'

'The best, thank you Denton.'

'The best!' said Palmi triumphantly.

'The best,' agreed Joseph.

'Tell us about Warfarin,' said Denton.

'Anticoagulant,' said Julian. 'Thins the blood. Stops it clotting. Warfarin is the active ingredient in Rat Pak. Causes rodents to haemorrhage. They bleed to death.'

Later they would claim they all had the idea simultaneously.

Rover moved into Denton's pocket on a permanent basis. He lived there, ate there, slept there, did his little twinkies there. Denton padded his pocket with tissues for the sake of hygiene. Nowhere was safe. They found Rat Pak under the servery and everywhere where the skirting board was estranged from the floor.

'You'd think with the money they're paid to look after us, they'd put this stuff out of reach,' said Denton as they added to their stockpile. 'So no loony can find it and stick it in his mouth.'

'Bleeding loonies!' said Palmi.

That broke them up. They liked loony jokes. The joke, of course, was that nobody on staff suspected for a second that loonies were capable of doing what they were doing. They let Joseph doctor the chocs.

Joseph owned a chain of jewellery shops. His father had been a watchmaker and Joseph had taken things on from there. Up until he'd come home early with the flu and found his wife in bed with her tennis coach, he'd liked to keep his hand in by repairing the occasional watch. Perhaps if his son – who everyone knew was going to be a famous doctor – hadn't come home and confessed that he was HIV positive just minutes after Joseph had shown the tennis coach the door, Joseph wouldn't have tried to kill himself. Of course he'd freaked. He'd gone from successful businessman to failed husband, failed father, failed suicide, all in less than an hour.

Joseph was a wrist-slasher which is why they only ever gave them plastic knives and forks to eat with, and counted them afterwards before they let anyone out of the cafeteria. Joseph couldn't steal a knife because then they'd be searched. Even if the orderlies didn't find the knife they'd find Rover the mouse, and that would defeat the whole point of the exercise. So Joseph just bit the tip off one. The orderlies made everyone stand around while they tried to figure out what to do. The missing bit was small enough to swallow and, in the end, they decided that some loony had eaten it. That was a fair enough assumption. That was the sort of stupid thing guests of the clinic occasionally did.

Joseph honed the plastic chip on the sandstone wall when they were let out into the enclosed garden. They were supposed to be supervised, but they watched their supervisors more closely than any of their supervisors ever watched them. Joseph used the razor-sharp tip of the knife to doctor the chocs. He split the tops from the bottoms. He chose the strong, sickly ones with the overpowering flavours so they'd hide the taste of his additive. The mints, the strawberries and raspberries, cherry and marzipan. He ditched the mild ones and substituted them with more of the strong ones. Julian had no shortage of chocolates. His powerful friends in the drug company really wanted him to get well. Joseph heated a plastic spoon in a hot cup of tea, and used it to weld the pieces of chocolate together again. He was a watchmaker and he was good at his job. He pretended he was working on Rolex Oysters.

'What do you think?' he asked Denton when he'd put all the chocolates back into the box.

'Like concrete and steel,' said Denton.

'Like concrete and steel,' shouted Palmi enthusiastically.

'Good work,' said Julian, and even surprised himself.

'I want to apologise,' said Julian.

'I did wrong,' he said.

'I'd like you to have this box of chocolates as a token of my regret.'

They'd waited until Bruise was alone, when there were no other orderlies around. They didn't want Bruise sharing and knew he wouldn't if he didn't have to. Bruise eyed Julian suspiciously. He'd underestimated Julian before and still had eight stitches in his head to remind him. He looked over at Denton, Palmi and Joseph. They were deep in conversation. Bruise knew the rules about accepting things from inmates but chose to ignore them. Everyone ignored them. If they didn't, Julian would have been buried in chocolates. Bruise looked upon his impending transgression as an act of kindness, done in the best interests of the patient.

'Ta,' he said. Greed is so easy to rationalise. He stuffed the box under his uniform.

'I guess someone has to test the dosage,' said Denton. 'It can't be Julian because they'd stop giving him ECT and it seems to be doing him some good. It can't be Palmi because he's just freaked and they might send him away.'

'Then it's you or me,' said Joseph.

'You could throw a punch at a wall and miss,' said Denton. 'How are you going to hit Bruise? No. Rover is my mouse. Bruise is my responsibility.'

'No!' said Palmi.

'No,' echoed Julian.

'No,' said Joseph. 'You're on the way out of here, Denton, we can't let you blow it now. I'm the only one with a clean sheet and I've already doctored another two boxes of chocolates in case they're needed. I'm dispensable. I'll get him after breakfast tomorrow.'

Everyone reluctantly agreed.

Denton was first into the cafeteria. He sat waiting for his friends. The sun spilled in through the window, through the gap between the rafis and kentia palms. Not even the airconditioning could steal its warmth.

'Good morning, Denton,' said Palmi. 'It is a beautiful day, isn't it?'

'The best,' said Denton.

'Sleep well?'

'The best,' said Denton.

'And Rover?'

'Like a dog on a mat in front of a fire.'

Palmi clapped his hands at the image. 'Denton, after breakfast I'm going to start work on my new erection.'

'I thought Nurse Clive wouldn't let you make any more.'

'Out of cloth!' said Palmi excitedly. 'First I sew it, then I stuff it, then it stands up.'

'Brilliant,' said Denton. 'Like concrete and steel.'

'Concrete and steel! Yes!' said Palmi.

'Good morning,' said Joseph.

'Good morning,' said Julian.

'It is a good morning, isn't it?' said Palmi.

'The best,' said Joseph and Julian together.

'How are you going to do it?' asked Denton.

Joseph waited while the orderlies served them their poached eggs. They wobbled on the plates like tired tits.

'Have you ever seen pictures of Jews at the Wailing Wall?' asked Joseph. 'Have you ever seen the way they bob their heads?'

'No,' said Denton.

'Trust me,' said Joseph. 'It's our secret weapon. In Liverpool they call it a kiss.'

'You're kidding,' said Denton.

'I'm a practising Jew,' said Joseph. 'All my life, so I've had plenty of practice. His nose will bleed until Judgement Day.'

They all laughed but their laughter was nervous. Joseph wrung his hands to stop them from shaking. He wasn't normally a violent man. All he wanted to do was go home to his family. Bruise looked across at them.

'Wait,' said Denton. 'Look at his chin.'

'Look at his neck,' said Palmi.

Little white wads of tissue dotted the path left by his razor. Bruise had cut himself shaving and the nicks still bled.

'I think another dose is called for,' said Denton. 'I think I know how to administer it.'

'Another dose!' said Palmi.

'Yes!' said Julian.

'Thank God,' said Joseph.

On the way to creative therapy Denton tripped on a chair leg and accidentally bumped into Bruise.

'Watch it!' hissed Bruise and grabbed a handful of Denton's shirt. Bruise glowered.

'I'm sorry,' said Denton. 'It was an accident.'

'An accident,' echoed Palmi anxiously.

'An accident,' insisted Joseph and Julian.

'Accident, my arse!' said Bruise.

'Julian,' said Denton, 'we should make amends. Why don't you go get Bruise some more of your chocolates.'

'Good morning, Denton. Good morning, Palmi.' Joseph and Julian pulled out their chairs and sat. 'Look at his stitches!' hissed Joseph.

'His stitches,' hissed Julian.

Denton and Palmi turned to look at Bruise. The stitches on his head shone pink on a swollen black and blue background.

'Oh dear,' said Denton. 'They're not getting any better.'

'His arm's all bruised, too,' said Joseph. 'Where you bumped into him yesterday.'

'Excellent!' said Denton.

'Excellent!' said Palmi. Sunlight beamed from his face.

'Denton,' Joseph asked quietly. 'Is it time for me to pray?'

'No need for heroics,' said Denton. 'Another accidental bump should do the trick.'

'You or me?' asked Joseph.

'Me into you into him,' said Denton. 'Us loonies are always tripping over each other.'

They laughed.

'Where's Bruise?' Denton asked the orderly who liked him.

'Off sick with some kind of blood disorder.'

'No kidding.'

'No kidding. When Dr Chan tried to stop his nose bleed he found Bruise was really living up to his name. His whole body was covered in bruises.'

'How about that?'

'Seems we've seen the last of him. Can't do this sort of job if you're prone to bruising.'

'No, you're right there.'

'The clinic will compensate him, of course.'

'Of course.'

'It was your idea, wasn't it?'

'What idea?'

'You know very well what I'm talking about. How did you get him to swallow the stuff?'

'Who? What stuff?'

'The stuff the clinic denies it ever left lying around in the first place.'

Denton laughed.

'Anyway, you can tell your mates to stop looking. It's all been cleared away. For safety reasons.'

'I know someone who'd be glad to hear that.' Denton reached into his shirt pocket and laughed again. It sounded just like his laugh of old.